ABOUT THE AUTHOR

JUSTINA ROBSON has published nine novels, including the five-book Quantum Gravity series. The fifth book, *Down to the Bone*, was published in early 2011. She has been nominated for the Arthur C Clarke Award twice, the Philip K Dick Award three times, the British SF Association Award twice and the John W Campbell Award. Her first novel, *Silver Screen*, was published in 1999.

Heliotrope is her first collection.

HELIOTROPE

HELIOTROPE

stories by
JUSTINA ROBSON

T̴
p̴   Ticonderoga
publications

For the teachers, facilitators and students of Clarion West,
the writing workshop that first introduced me to short fiction.
Especially the crew of '96. Every time I write a short story
I think of all you guys.

Heliotrope by Justina Robson

Published by Ticonderoga Publications

Copyright © 2011 Justina Robson

Introduction copyright © 2011 Adam Roberts

All story introductions and afterwords copyright © 2011 Justina Robson

Cover design by Russell B. Farr

Designed and edited by Russell B. Farr
Typeset in Sabon and Fritz Quadrata

A Cataloging-in-Publications entry for this title is available from the National Library of Australia

ISBN   978–0–9807813–3–5 (hardcover)
          978–0–9807813–4–2 (trade paperback)
          978–0–9807813–5–9 (ebook)

Ticonderoga Publications
PO Box 29 Greenwood
Western Australia 6924

www.ticonderogapublications.com

10 9 8 7 6 5 4 3 2 1

ACKNOWLEDGEMENTS

I would like to thank Russell B. Farr first and foremost, for having the generous and kind thought of making this collection and for putting in so much work on my behalf with it. I am also humbly grateful to Adam Roberts for writing the introduction and giving my work such an insightful reading. Thanks also to the editors of the various presses and magazines who originally printed these stories: Andy Cox, Ian Whates, Gardner Dozois, Jonathan Strahan, Storm Constantine, Lou Anders, Peter Crowther, David Howe, Eric Brown, Jeremy Bloom, Alison Davies, Mick Sims, Len Maynard and Mike Ashley. And thanks to you too, the readers—of course!

CONTENTS

INTRODUCTION

ADAM ROBERTS

When Justina Robson started publishing novels she quickly acquired a reputation as a hard science fiction writer. I don't understand why. Don't get me wrong: she writes proper, unapologetic SF about spaceships, alien planets, computers and cyborgs she dishes out sense-of-wonder with the best of them. Her grasp of physics (and philosophy) cannot be faulted. She is as adept at handling AIs (as in her thumping debut novel, *Silver Screen*, 1999) as speculative neuroscience (*Mappa Mundi*, 2001) or interstellar space opera in which humanity shares the cosmos with gigantic human-upgrade machinic entities called "Forged" (the marvellous *Natural History*, 2005). Each of these novels provides all the pleasures of Hard SF, and does so with an unusually accomplished grasp of character, description and narrative.

Indeed, many of the stories in this collection play grace notes on Robson's novels: "Erie Lackawanna Song" fills you in on the mappa-mundi technology, for instance; "Cracklegrackle" and "The Adventurers' League" and both, well, Forged stories—and both are perfect examples of how well Robson handles the idiom of elegantly gnarled neo-gothic giganticism, and how effortlessly she achieves a kind of neo-Sublime. "Cracklegrackle" is one of the best things here, actually: an unflinching portrayal of the disconnect between father and daughter, is also one of the most moving stories Robson has written. But good Hard SF has always had a place for heart;

and whilst Robson's emotional intelligence is unusually nuanced and profound, it fits well in the larger traditions of of hard SF; and actual science, too.

So why do I find it hard to think of Robson as a Hard SF writer? It's two things, I think. One is that, although actual science is a set of disciplines of increasingly ornate complexity, most writers of Hard SF prefer to simplify: relatively uncomplicated characters, working their way through straightforward narratives in which unambiguous science is projected onto enormous scales of time and space. But Robson's imagination is drawn to complexity—to, for instance, formal and worldbuilding intricacy that may put off some more linear-minded fans of genre writing. Take, for example, *Living Next Door To The God of Love* (2005), a novel I suspect may be remembered as her masterpiece, although it divided reviewers and fans quite sharply. It is a sort of sequel to *Natural History*, although one of the things it does is to place in question many of the conventions of linear book-A-to-book-B sequelism. My point is that it is a fundamentally complex text; not a simple story wreathed with curlicues of complicated garnish, but a tale that understand its core themes—the relationship between reality and fantasy, the action of fall out of or into love—are complex all the way down. Robson braids alternate realities together with a lovely rococo sureness; narratives and characters slip from one nuclear orbit to another. If I'm making it sound forbidding, then I don't mean to; the novel steps nimbly and affectingly through its territory. But it does things very few novels do.

Robson's latest multi-volume work, the Quantum Gravity sequence—comprising: *Keeping It Real* (2006), *Selling Out* (2007), *Going Under* (2008), *Chasing the Dragon* (2009) and *Down to the Bone* (2011)—is a sort of expansion of many of the ideas found in *Living Next Door*: the crashing-together of different realities, the way radically different natures can coexist in one person. It takes the different realties generically (the dimensions correlate to "reality", to the worlds of SF, to Fantasy and to Horror) and it is rendered after a manner less likely to alienate the regular SF fan. They're fine novels: elegantly written, perceptive, incident filled, leavened with marvels and wonders. But their very accessibility means that they don't manage the beautiful embedded multiplicity of *Living Next Door*. At its core, I think both that novel and the

Quantum books are about falling in love, or more precisely about the way falling in love is mediation between reality and fantasy. This same dialectic ("reality", "fantasy") defines art as well, of course, something SF and Fantasy understand better, I think, than 'mainstream' literatures. And Robson organizes her writing about a dual apprehension of that. We fall in love with real people. That, in an important level, is what differentiates "love" from infatuations, childish crushes, ego projections and all the bag-and-baggage of emotional splurging of which we've all, of course, been guilty. But even *when* we fall in love with real people, fantasy has an integral part in the way we feel about them: they embody our fantasy, they are focuses for it. Fantasy, in the fullest sense, is the life of love.

And this is where the complexity comes from; because fantasy parses itself. Fantasy is life-enhancing, transcendent, playful and fun. But fantasy happens, ontological speaking, in the subjunctive mode: its idiom is "if . . ." This is a wonderful thing, because the conditional tense is all about *possibility*. But another of saying exactly that is that it construes *doubt*. That something might happen, with all the wondrous open-ended excitements that implies, is that something might not be.

This is my rather roundabout way of explaining why I've never seen Robson as a conventional Hard SF writer. By and large, Hard SF writers are drawn to Hard SF for the certainty: the unambiguousness of actual scientific laws and technological limits. Robson knows the science as well as any of them. But what she knows better than any of them—better, in fact, that any other novelist working today, is the *doubt*. The Ninja-Assassin protagonist of her story "The Girl Hero's Mirror Says She Is Not The One" knows what's I'm talking about.

> As she is washing her hands the Girl Hero feels an unpleasant feeling. It is like something scattering inside. She imagines that this is made from swarms of rats who have just noticed a terrible thing and are running, running, running for their lives. She often feels this. It is doubt.

T S Eliot, in an essay on *In Memoriam* (that monument of Victorian religious piety) argued that the faith in Tennyson's poem was limited and conventional stuff, but that what made Tennyson special was that *there was nothing about doubt he didn't know.*

Eliot considered doubt a much more important and ubiquitous business than faith. There's something similar at work in Robson's fiction. She understands that just as faith (belief, love, fantasy) is not a straightforward matter, neither is doubt.

I'm not suggesting that Robson's fiction is entirely a crooked house behind a crooked stile. On the contrary. She is perfectly well aware that (for instance) desire can run in dangerously straight lines: her accounts of the intensity of heterosexual female desire for the right sort of male: "The Bull Leapers" capture a female appreciation of, and appetite for, male sensual beauty. "Heliotrope", the collection's title story, goes straight to that place where artistic expression and desire combine to scorch the soul. But sexual desire is always tangled up with fantasy, and fantasy can be so opaque as to perfectly obscure hideous truths (I think that it what her disturbing contemporary Sea Siren fable, "Trésor", is about). "A Dream of Mars", original to this volume, reworks the Beauty and the Beast myth, turning beauty into a man hooked on solitude, and beast into a genetically engineered Martian beast. But the story moves us through the moment of climactic coming-together into the aftermath of desire, when the pinching restrictions of real-life encroach upon us. The beast is a fantasy creature condemned to live in real-life squalor. In a sense, any of our love-objects are the same thing.

The situation is not straightforward. Doubt can be terribly corrosive, psychologically speaking. "Cracklegrackle" literalises it as malign energy forces ("they live in the holes of the mind and eat the spirit"), to potent effect. But by the same token, without a touch of decent intersubjective obscurity, life would be a kind of hell. "Body of Evidence" is Robson's version of that scene in Annie Hall where Alvy and Annie's bland exchange of pleasantries is subtitled on-screen with that they are really thinking—except that Robson parses the conceit through its fearful and destructive potentials, rather than playing it for laughs. In "Heliotrope", the main character Elys becomes so absorbed in her artistic practice that it quite literally destroys her The story is a mercilessly bright-light, parched fable of artistic creation, its narrative of a shift from figurative painting to abstract (to, indeed a kind of Malevichian Suprematism) as a way of expressing the perils of complete absorption in the world of art. SF is probably more densely populated than other genres with people who, if only they could, would step *actually* into World of Warcraft and leave their real lives forever. Nor does Robson simplistically condemn that impulse. In "The Seventh Series" the fantasies offered by immersive computer games and the fantasies offered by the dream of real-life actualisation, via yoga, are deftly played off against one another.

Robson is at her best when writing novels and stories that juxtapose virtual realities and actual realities, mundane dimensions and fantastical dimensions, delusional states and rational thinking, worldly ordinariness and interplanetary wonders. She is evidently fascinated by the relationship between the worlds of the imagination and the world of reality. Of course, no writer worth his/her salt will be anything other than fascinated by that interaction. What differentiates Robson's particular interrogation of this larger dynamic is her grasp not only that the two states are not either-or, but that each is entirely present in each all the time.

This is best captured, I think, in "Legolas does the Dishes"— perhaps Robson's most fully accomplished short story, and a very major piece of writing. The narrator, Elizabeth, is an inmate of a mental institution (she poisoned her own mother) who gets it into her head that the new guy hired to wash dishes is actually Legolas from Tolkien's *Lord of the Rings*. Or to be more precise, she simultaneously knows that Legolas is a fictional character and the dish-washer is just some guy from Texas, *and* she knows that he is the actual Legolas from the actual realm of Middle Earth.

There is a print by M C Escher called "Three Worlds": a representation of a patch of lake. Reflected upon the surface of the water Escher has drawn the inverted reflection of trees and sky; floating on the surface itself are numerous leaves and lily pads; and also visible in the image is a carp, moving through the depths. "Legolas does the Dishes" reminds me of that image. Not that it has any carps in it (although there are leaves, and there is water); but because it has a similar clarity and beauty, because it evidences a comparable mastery of craft, and most of all because it manages the same extraordinary trick of superimposing three quite different worlds—the world of mundane "reality", the delusions of the schizophrenic and the realms of conscious fiction and art—in one space without tangling or confusing them. On the contrary, the story does is enable each of these three modes of being-in-the-world eloquently to illuminate one another. And in a broader sense, that wonderful poise and eloquence is what makes Robson so characteristic. It's what makes her much more than a writer of straightforward Hard SF.

There's no-one else writing who is quite as good at this as Justina Robson; something amply demonstrates by this generous, varied and altogether brilliant collection of short fiction. You should read her.

ADAM ROBERTS
FEBRUARY 2011

HELIOTROPE

HELIOTROPE

I first wrote this a long time ago when I was still trying to make the world in which it is set (the world of my Massively Unpublishable First Fantasy Epic) work. It does work just for this story, so at least all those millions of words weren't utterly wasted.

HELIOTROPE

The sign of the sun is a circle. Some think it is the space within that is held fast by the line. Some think it is the space without.

Elys arrived at the studio hot and out of breath even though it was still early. The sun had not risen high enough to do more than divide the streets into blue and white lozenges. At this time of day its softer tones would fall upon the face of her most recent subject and give it the gentled contours that the Lady in question would prefer to see. Elys shook her stiff arms out and blew her fringe up to cool herself. She could not remember a summer so hot in all the seventeen years she had been alive—years in which oil-paint did not run like water and in which the thick reed papers did not curl as soon as they were spread.

She stopped for a drink at the water barrel by the door and frowned at its brackish flavour. It was drawn from the bottom of the well and full of mud that would not settle out. She wiped her mouth on her sleeve and then remembered to glance nervously about and through the door again into the street.

There was no sign of Chelin's dog, although that was no guarantee of safety. Since the studio master next door had brought the mongrel home from the countryside the Art Market had become a gauntlet for apprentices arriving in the early, pre-customer hours of dawn. She had been foolish enough to forget this a week ago. The dog had launched itself at her from the cover of an alley entrance, silent with purpose and grey with dust, its small eyes white-ringed, and bitten her neatly on the ankle. She rubbed it.

The Lady was waiting for her in the smaller studio, reclining on the battered couch that Elys would paint in so differently—mending all its faults. Elys smiled as she took her position and threw back the cover on the panel to reveal the almost completed portrait. She took the tray of pastels from the slave who appeared at her elbow.

On her ankle the bite tingled faintly as she worked.

After the Lady had gone she went to the door and dawdled, looking at all the gaily coloured clothes against the cool whites and lavenders of the buildings. There was infinite variety of tone in the tanned skins around her; almost black beneath the shade of the market canopies they would emerge into the light red and glistening. She took up an apple and went to rest with the other apprentices in the shade of the courtyard where she leaned against the cool wall and closed her eyes, savouring the green flavour.

"Hey, did you hear?" Yban's voice made her open her eyes again, "Antian's up to the Palace in a week."

"For the commission of the statue?" she asked, "Who else?"

"Chelin and Melisa. They've all to make maquettes of their work and bring them along," he snorted, "good luck to them in this heat. Clay miniatures. Gods!"

"That doesn't leave much time," she said.

The Empress had decided she wanted a statue made of Jalaeka, the dancer who was currently the biggest draw of the Festival. Elys had seen him only from a distance. He was always the centre of a huge crowd or else cordoned off from the populace by guards and the exclusive surroundings of nobles.

There was a vast array of miniatures and portraits of him on sale, more in fact than of anyone else, including the Empress. It had become the fashion to paint him in profile facing a radiant sun because of a popular myth that he was an avatar of the Sun God. Looking at him Elys could see why, although not necessarily from the portraits, some of which were laughably inaccurate. Seeing them made her more eager to try herself.

Now she wondered how a maquette could be achieved in a week. Sketches must be made wherever they could be managed in public. She bit down into her apple, frowning, "Gethyn," she said, looking down at another of the senior apprentices, "you've been doing the copies of Jalaeka for the stall, where d'you get the sketches?"

"Oh, they're old," he said, mouth half-full, "taken by Antian a couple of years ago at the Arena before all the Sun God madness started getting a grip. Looks too young though, so I try and bring it in line with some that look more recent; a bit more angular, you know. Why, don't they look right?"

"I'm not sure any of them do."

"Yeah, it's hard painting someone you've never seen," he shrugged, "and you get so used to seeing copies that you start to copy your own mistakes too. But the customers don't care. After all, most of them have never seen him either. Any half-good-looking young man would do."

He had misunderstood her. She had been thinking of another reason why the pictures were wrong. It had recently begun to become clear to her that there was more to an accurate rendering of something than merely recording what met the eye. There was more to vision than sight. "But you couldn't use those sketches for the statue?"

"No. Anyway they're only head and shoulders studies."

"Could I see them?"

"In the folder under my desk," Gethyn shrugged, "You're not getting soft on him as well are you, Elys?" He grinned at her, "You and a thousand other people all slavering over him. I thought you were more individual."

"I *am*." She stared at him with hugely widened eyes, grinning to show she was well aware of the situation, and stuck her tongue out covered in half chewed apple.

Elys was certain that Antian's ability to capture a likeness was second to none. If he had seen the dancer then he would have made certain the sketches were as detailed as possible and there was something she wanted to check. In all the portraits she had seen there were variations; some copies had inky black hair whilst others both showed some degrees of chestnut in the darkness. One or two were virtually blonde in places. Everyone painted the eyes large and dark but some were brown and others blue. There'd be no colour in the sketches but she would be able to settle the other disputed matters of lipshape and nasal profile. She was shocked at the lack of consensus on the face. It seemed to exemplify the dissatisfaction she had begun to feel with other portraits—if the true essence of the person had been captured there would be no need for variations.

On the way to fetching the drawings however Antian came in from his private room and stopped her,

"A word with you, Elys, if you don't mind."

Elys followed the Master's short, be-smocked figure into the relative privacy of his study. She had been here only a few times before and was nervous now. Meetings with the Master were always serious. She sank down obediently into the chair he pointed at and glanced around at the drawings, tacked three thick on the walls, new over old.

"I won't make a meal of it," he said, "I think you've done enough on the Lady Vath-Arber's portrait."

"But . . .!"

"And I'm going to give it to Gethyn to finish," he said. He glanced away from her, his hand doodling with a piece of charcoal on his desk. She was devastated. Her palms began to sweat and her heart juddered, what had she done? She must have forgotten something or rendered it poorly and not seen.

"But what's wrong with it?" she couldn't help blurting at last.

The Master's eyes swept back to her face from a distant regard, "What? Nothing, nothing! No, I am not punishing you. The work is perfectly fine if a little over-ambitious, no. I want to move you to another task."

Elys sat rock steady. She was still irritated at being deprived of the right to finish her own drawing; it had been the first work she had done herself from the start and was to have been the initial part of her transition to independent status and a little studio of her own. Since the death of her parents it was all she had worked for. But something in the Master's unaccustomed hesitancy drew her attention. Had she not known better she would have thought him embarrassed.

"As you know this Jalaeka thing has come up," he paused, "and there'll be the fiercest competition you've ever seen to make the winning piece; not just because of the money for it and the revenue from copies and replicas," he sighed, "but the fame." He gazed around at his pictures as though they irritated him and searched around on his desk for something, "Anyhow," he snapped back to focus with a slap on the table top, "I can't go and do the drawings myself so I want you to go do them. I know you can draw."

"But, why can't you?" she asked, the implication of what she had just heard barely registering yet, "You draw better than I do, Master."

"I do. But I cannot see clearly enough any more," he said, looking directly at her, "Oh, I can see if it's quite close, even twenty feet off with enough accuracy, yes, look, I can even see the little frown lines on your face from here, but I can't see anything with a sharp edge beyond that. I used to, but not now, too old. I can still sculpt the thing, and I'd do the drawings too if I could, don't be thinking that I rate you that highly, but the fact is I'd be lucky to get within thirty paces and that just isn't good enough."

Elys was stunned but she didn't yet have to speak because the Master continued, "I have been considering the later works of the others and I am certain that they will mostly be attempting poses that stand or sit or recline but that is not for me. I want to make a sculpture that is about movement; are you listening, girl? I want you to make drawings of him as he walks and talks and runs and dances. Nothing still and no fragments either. Get the full body even if you only manage a few lines. Do you understand?" he was intent, leaning across his desk now, "I'm depending on you Elys. Will you do this for your old Master?"

"Of course I will," she said. All thought of the earlier portrait was forgotten. She must go and practice this instant, change the habitual ways of seeing from paint and colour to shadow and light, to the opportunities of charcoal and chalk. She must practice with life models in motion. She bent and rubbed at the little tingling patch on her ankle.

"It is my understanding that he will be attending the celebrations in the Arena tomorrow afternoon when the Games are over. You will have my usual place in the seats and then you must find a way to get to the front of the crowd when he dances. It won't be easy."

"I can do it," she muttered. It was only when she was back out in the studio proper, standing automatically with the others as they got up and began to pick up their tools, that she realised she hadn't thanked him. She could do it later. She collected some pieces of ruined paper and charcoal and went to sit in the street and draw. When she stood up her head was spinning and when she went indoors she couldn't see a thing for almost a minute until her eyes had adjusted from the glare.

"Been outside all this time? You idiot," it was Yban. "Come and have a drink. Not even a hat!" For once she felt she had to obey his chiding and sat down where all the apprentices were sprawled, resting on wetted cloths. From time to time they rolled over as the cloth became warm under them. Flies dodged and hovered but at this time of day it was more energy than it was worth to shoo them. Elys rubbed water on her arms and watched it make grey smears with the charcoal from her fingers.

"Haven't seen much of Chelin's mutt," she said as her slow thoughts worked around to it, "have you?"

"Didn't you hear?" Gethyn said, rolling over and shielding his eyes, "it died."

"What? When?"

"Oh more than a week ago now."

"Yeah," Resila got up on her elbows, covered in chalk dust and reached for the last of the fruit, "got the Sun Disease," she screwed her eyes up and winced, "horrid."

"Everyone's getting it," Gethyn grunted, "they say it's a spell that Jalaeka puts them under you know."

Resila scoffed but she sounded unconvinced, "Really? Who told you?"

"Chelin when I asked about her dog. She said that those nutcases, the Love Followers—they all claim he's an avatar of the Sun God and that when you come down with it it's 'cos he's chosen you to be a disciple."

"Horseshit!" she retorted and bit down into the plum. "Ugh!" she spat it out, "this one's bad. Hey, do you think that's like a sign or something?

"It's a sign you can't tell why everyone else left it," Gethyn said and dodged the slap she made towards him, smiling.

"Are many people dying of it?" Elys asked.

"Elys, where have you been?" Yban said. He was wearing the face that told her, as if she needed telling again, that she ought to lighten up, was too intense, too serious, too gullible. Elys made a noncommittal face, embarrassed at being ignorant. She was suddenly and unpleasantly aware of not fitting-in as they stared at her and rolled their eyes. She wished she had not said anything.

He continued, "They're dropping like flies. I don't know if it's all the same thing though. Antian says the water's bad in many places and that's making people sick."

Elys sighed and the conversation turned to work and money before it trickled to a halt. She didn't listen to it. She shut her eyes and tried to rest.

They lay and dozed until later in the afternoon when the searing edge had been taken from the heat. Elys had time to regret the omission of a hat, her nose was burned and her cheeks. As she got up she had a headache. Too much sun. She looked back over her morning's work and threw most of it away. Too careful. She had to learn to do it faster and make people look less poised. Even the walking studies had a static air to them.

"Fussy marks," Gethyn said, looking at them over her shoulder.

"I know, I know!" She swept the drawings together and scrunched them up. She would have to go further afield to find someone moving faster, to force her to loosen up. She had a servant bring her fresh paper and a folder and a tea for her headache. She could go to the Baths. Even though it was hot they'd be playing under the lime trees on the men's side, running and jumping for the leather ball. She gulped the tea down despite its scalding temperature and took off.

That night she slept fitfully in her attic room. Anxiety and restlessness made her kick her sheet away in her sleep. She woke often in the dry heat to stare through the skylight at the waning sliver of the moon and was up at dawn. She skipped breakfast again, stomach too full of butterflies to have room for food and hurried through the only cool air of the day to the studio. Once there she went over yesterday's work and collected her materials.

"Good luck," Yban called after her as she hurried out into the furnace of late morning. Gethyn glanced up from his painting and managed a flourish of his brush. She had thought it would be secret . . . now it seemed like they all knew. Gethyn must be jealous . . . but her thoughts evaporated as she hit the street. Through the thin soles of her sandals the stone burned.

At the Arena's gates she was grateful that Antian's pass let her through straight away. The place was crowded with men and women wearing very little. They were horribly sunburned and their faces and arms were painted all over with green and yellow circles. They were singing some kind of hymn that sounded to Elys like a dirge and were insisting they be let through to the front. They wanted to worship their Lord directly, at his feet. They carried water with them in skins and defied their thirst by sprinkling it on the ground where it evaporated and attracted flies. As the gatekeeper checked her credentials she saw him look at them and snarl. He muttered something about having had enough of the Senate and its tolerant policies, then glanced at her, "Sorry. You look tired out. Better get yourself a drink. Can't be too careful in this heat," and added, "not like those buggers."

"Who are they?" she asked as she passed on.

"Love Followers," he said with gleeful disgust, "think that that dancing whore is the Sun God. Gah!" he spat a lump of yellow phlegm directly to the side of his foot and squashed it into the dust, "Don't you pay no attention to 'em."

"I won't," she said, as glad to get out of his company as she was to be free of the singing, and made her way beneath the shade of the seating tiers to her row.

It was too hot to sit on her stone seat at first so she put her folder underneath her, which also served the double purpose of keeping it safe. There were a good many hats about but none obscured her view of the main area where the jugglers' yellow, red and blue clubs twirled and twisted like bizarre wingless birds in the still air. Later, as musicians and story-singers took the floor she dozed, giving in to the listlessness that the heat poured softly into her blood.

She woke, head jerking upright, to see the place being raked and cleared. An expectant hush descended until only whispers like the ghost of rain pattered around the arena. Elys got her folder, unpacked charcoal sticks.

She would make a few pages of distant studies first. Her eyes were nearly glued shut with dried tears and sleep. She rubbed them and looked around for her cup of water but someone must have taken it. Applause rippled, pierced with whistles as the red and black clad Dance Drummers appeared from the performers' entrance and took their measured places on the sand. There was a scuffle in the crowds gathered close to the perimeter fence and she saw the yellow and green pasted army moving to the front of those who were standing, propped against one another in the swelter.

Suddenly everyone but her was standing up and cheering. The slippery gleaming shapes of the Love Followers strained over the barriers. They were chanting. And a lone body sailed onto the grounds, not on it but over it, not touching it but dabbing towards it and flying above it, difficult to resolve and see as a human being for its extreme volatility and its grace which almost looked like lassitude even involved as it was with movements of extreme effort.

Jalaeka did not look as Elys had expected. She could see him as the crowds settled back down, silenced so they could spend all their remaining energy in looking. She had thought that the Masters' drawings and the different paintings in the art market were all wrong. But as she watched him she saw just the opposite. For all their myriad differences every last one of them was right.

In the midst of speeding movements, jumping and springing from his hands, somersaulting in the scalding vaults above the ground, there was a quality of stillness in him like the eye of a storm, as though it was the whole world that was spinning about and he was its axis. His hair reflected all colours as though it were liquid—she could not say if it were truly blonde or red or black although surely it was dark against the blue of the burning sky and darker than his slick, sheened skin which was the pure and blinding gold of the sun.

Her hand had not moved an inch. The charcoal felt like the dead, ashen stick it was, held in a bundle of dead sticks.

The drums regulated him, or they seemed to. His feet struck the sand in time with them, his hands touched the ground and held up the sky with them, his body twisted in impossible elasticity winding around the rhythm only to join it again. Her mouth was open. She could taste dust and the body odour of the people beside her. She didn't know when her hand started to move or how, she just never took her eyes off his tall figure as it shaped itself over and over into lonely, free-flying forms. He moved like a flock of birds, like water, like . . .like sunlight on water and he burned with the fire of the sun and made the watcher also burn. Elys' dress clung to her in damp, unpleasant stickiness.

She began to feel alive. Her arm followed her hand. She swept one sheet away and began on another, then another. Her shoulder followed her arm. She was making the marks with more and more of her, following him, watching him; now his chest, now his arms, now his long, muscular legs . . .she could feel their depth, their peculiar, elastic hardness. Her hand moved with the same feeling. She glanced down. She was drawing in sections. Arms, legs, torsos flowed into one another without joining. She flung that sheet away.

She drew his head. She drew the whip-wave of his hair and she drew his face which was all one with his effort, joyful in it. Her eyes began to sting. Her ankle itched fiercely. Elys ignored them both. She was drawing as she had never drawn. Her whole body was making the drawings in the shape of his body. She saw and what she saw became real on the page. Her muscles began to burn with a fierce fire.

Jalaeka slowed. Sweat was pouring off him. He wove a sensual snakedance through the shimmering heat on the arena floor and she ran out of papers. She had covered them all, front and back. She scrabbled around but there was nothing left and in the scuffle she lost her charcoal and saw it trodden to black dust by the eagerly stamping foot of the woman next to her.

When she recovered herself he was done. She was so disappointed she could have cried. She would have sold her soul to watch him on and on, for hours or for days, for months or years. The cooing delirium of the Love Followers seemed thoroughly comprehensible to her. And as he fell earthwards for the last time his face looked towards the crowd and he saw her.

That night she lay awake in her room watching the shimmer of heat lightning on her wall. Her eyes were wide open the way they had been when he had looked at her. Only a moment it had been. A second split from time. He had met her eyes as he became still and she had thought he was in her arms the look was so intense, so personal between them. His dark eyes had caused something in her to blossom into fire. She had felt herself possessed, or if not then longing to be possessed and a heat had poured into her that made the heat of the day seem like the cool of a mountain stream.

It burned her now. She lay in a sweat that was cooling, her sheets tangled in her legs. On her table the drawings lay untouched and, since that fatal moment, unseen. She had barely remembered to bring them home. Every time she closed her eyes he was all she could see. She prayed for dawn and the return of the sun.

Elys took all but one sheet of the drawings to Antian at first light. She had been about to take them all but suddenly the thought of being without some image of him had seemed too disturbing— she had almost felt afraid—and so she left one behind, letting it fall from her hand to slide over the floorboards as though it were an accident. Outside the sun was so brilliant she had to pull her hat down all the way over her face and stare at the ground as she crossed the city.

Seated in Antian's room she watched him pore slowly over her work and nursed unease and discomfort in her stomach. She flicked her foot up and down, feeling irritated. The Master said nothing. He placed one sheet aside and looked at the next. Elys sipped a cup of well-water. She had looked over the drawings herself before taking them in and was both pleased and sharply dissatisfied.

They were extremely good. They had the same qualities of sinuous movement and fragile stillness that he had and they accurately conveyed every twist of muscle, every fibre of tendon. They were possibly masterpieces. None of her careful lines in them. No studied care of mark and fatal lack of understanding. These drawings told a tale of something vibrantly alive and of divine grace and form. No, they didn't look like her work at all.

And worse than that they placed him foremost in her mind so that she could not see anything else and didn't want to. She wanted to ask if she could be a part of the sculpture project, if she could do a painting of her own, but she dare not disturb the Master. He was frowning, his face close to the page, breathing over her drawings with his lips pursed and whitened in concentration. He looked with the same care at all of them and then sat back in his chair with his fingertips pressed against their contemporaries on the other hand, staring through the triangular gap he had made.

"Can you use them?" she asked suddenly, "I could go and do more, there must be opportunities again soon . . ."

He waved her quiet with a look of impatience, "These will do. It's enough." For a while he hardly moved, his hands with their spatulate fingers loosening themselves to hang uselessly without something to shape. Then he stood up and pinned her drawings onto the wall over his. "I'd ask you to copy the backs for me but I don't think you could. I'll just have to keep turning them over." He backed away from them and wiped a few traces of charcoal dust off his fingers and onto his tunic.

"Well," she said, reluctant to let them go, "if you're sure."

His eyes snapped around to her, sharp for all their inaccuracy of vision, "Sure? Am I sure? You've got eyes in your head. You must know how good these are, I don't need to tell you. In fact," he quieted, "I think that you may consider your apprenticeship served out. There's nothing more you can learn from me . . . but . . ." He turned away from the drawings and leant against his desk, his left hand automatically falling on the handle of a brush and beginning to make quick little strokes in the air, "You'll forgive me if I am somewhat surprised by you, Elys. To be honest, before I saw these, I wouldn't have said you had such vision in you."

Elys was torn between pride and indignation. She smiled and knotted her hands together in her lap, but her voice betrayed her, "If you had been there! If you had seen him!" She sat forward, kicking her discarded glass and sending its precious contents spilling out over the dry stone floor where they sank almost instantly into the porous rock, "These drawings are nothing compared to the real thing! I want to go back. I should go back and do better . . ."

He cut her off with his raised hand, "No. These are enough. And you look tired." His voice was very calm, warning her that she was about to go too far. She bit down on the rest of what she wanted to say, the desperate urge to convey not only how pleased she was with what she had done but how very much more she had missed. "I think you have worked hard enough already."

Elys ducked her head and stared at her lap. He didn't know what he was saying. It was important to get this work right. Again she felt both shy and angry that her intensity was showing. Nobody liked it in a girl, even an artist. It was suspicious.

"And I have seen him before," he continued, ignoring her, "and I felt the same about my drawings then. They were and they were not like him. But I think yours may be closer. You have done me a great service. I can win the prize with these. I can help set you up in a little business eventually."

She had to fight not to say that the prize was not really going to be his, but hers. It was her vision he would have. But she wasn't concerned for the money. Her mind seemed to swim for a moment, as though dazzled by the offer.

"I'd like to do some portraits of him. Those others, out there," she gestured in the direction of the street, "they're not right. Not enough. I think I could do better. I'd do it and you could have the profit. I . . ."

"Elys," Antian said. He put the brush down and came across to her, bending to pick up her water glass, staying in a crouch to look at eye level into her face, "you look feverish. I hope you haven't drunk bad water. Why don't we go into the shade in the yard and talk it through with some better drink than this? I bought some spring water this morning, all the way from the valleys. I'm sure we can arrange something."

Elys couldn't meet his eyes. She felt as though he wasn't seeing her and was becoming disinclined to agree with anything he said. She had a feeling that he might try to stop her just as she was reaching something like a vocational drive to go on and dare more. Why did everyone try to stall her? She was certain she had the ability to go further than anyone. She could show the world what Jalaeka was really like in her painting, in her drawing. But she obeyed and they sat for a few hours looking out over the other apprentices' stoneworks and sipping clear, tasteless water from lidded vessels.

Elys stretched her legs out in front of her and took a long, indulgent draft of the precious water as he stood up and excused himself. She tipped her hat over her eyes and breathed the baking air for a few moments in the last peace she would allow herself to enjoy. Days and days of glorious work stretched out before her . . . she felt a little sick at the thought of it and her starving stomach finally caught her attention. She picked bread out of the apprentices' basket and ate until it stopped bothering her.

She worked all day on the Master's portrait and left only when it was too dark to do more. In her attic bedroom she prepared a large panel for her first study.

The timbers of the roof cracked in the absence of the sun. Above the scent of the rapidly drying clay and glue preparation on her panel Elys could smell the sharp grey odour of charcoal barbecues on the street and imagine in their white heat that there was a face, searching for her. The face in the flame of her oil lamp, in the fires he had stirred in her soul. She spent another sleepless night, staring into the shivering dark, listening to the faint thunder that whispered of rain but never brought it.

The next day went badly. She was tired, listless and weak yet she felt full of a peculiar energy that drove her up and out early. Faces in this warming dawn seemed suspicious to her. She walked in a rush through the stinking alleys and fly-filled back streets instead of the main thoroughfare. She wanted the hidden places and the shade where the sun couldn't see her.

That day's heat seemed no more than usual yet the paint ran and was difficult to handle. She shouted at the servants for putting too much oil in it. The volume of her own voice was oddly loud. It made her shrink and look around to see if everyone were looking at her. But they were busy.

There was not even the ghost of a breeze. By the time midday came Elys felt sick. The taste of the extra water she had sent out for did nothing to help her and now she was not sure of what she was doing. When she had first started out, safe with the confidence of her recent mastery, her colour and shade had been decisive and bold, following exactly the Master's well-known style. Now she felt doubt when she looked at the section of the panel she was working on and when she drew back to observe the whole it seemed to her that the colour balance was most strange as though the colours on her palette had changed whilst she was not looking. She put her brushes aside and decided to go early for her break, passing the outside stalls where all the pictures for sale were hung. Her head swam.

No sooner had she seen the first of the thousand portraits of Jalaeka than she felt a keen sense, almost like the flash of genius that had set her immobile hand drawing in the Arena, but this time tainted with the cold metal colours of dread—the sense that she must start her work now and forestall the inevitable result of that dark-eyed and longing look. Hadn't Yban and the others already told her that he was the Sun God? That he called out and they must follow who had heard his voice and seen his face? But she would not be like the delirious Love Followers with their crazy antics. She would transform this energy of his, make light into paint, into a picture, render it different, all its power altered by her channelling into a vision of power without the ability to destroy. This was her kind of talent. Seized by this idea she turned back into the studio and organised a drawing desk for sketching her portrait. No simple profile. She would give them all the glance of his eyes. She dashed the hat from her head where it seemed to be blocking her sight. The drawing would save her too, from the disease that he brought, from willing herself into the sun's power.

Elys began to draw him, full face, full body, seated as though just pausing in rest, watching the viewer in casual contemplation. Her ankle tingled a little, like pins and needles. She ignored it.

When Yban came to see her she sent him and the others away. For a split second part of her wanted to go and laugh with them in the yard and sharp inner pang of separation cut into her so she almost got up and went after them, but she glanced at her page and the impulse died.

"You're no fun any more," Yban complained. She didn't even hear what he said.

Afternoon deepened. Sweat marked her paper, dried, marked it again. A scratching sound began to distract her. She looked around in irritation. When she glanced back she was surprised to see that the drawing was done. It was well done too. The face captured her own and held it with its inanimate stare.

Quickly she rolled the drawing and put it under her arm, wanting to get out and get home before anyone spoke to her. She did not want to show them the drawing. They might want it. She felt weak. As she got up from the stool the leg that had been tingling gave way under her and she almost fell.

A peculiar sensation came over her that she would never see the room again. It was foolish but the foreboding only deepened with her scorn of it. She walked back through the main studio towards the yard, the drawing tucked under her arm. She almost wished now that one of her friends would see her and ask about it. She could show it to them and they would tell her that she was no disciple of his. They would tell her she was fine and so she would be. They could laugh together about her silly moods. But her wanting them only made her more shy and she didn't speak. She went home.

It took a long time for her to mix the paint she wanted to use as a sketching base. Her thoughts distracted her and she found herself being irritated by the noise of her knife swirling the gritty pigment, chalk and oil around on the tile she used. Tiny particles of colour broke under her pressure, turning the oil opaque, then smooth and thick with brown like dark cocoa being added to sugar syrup. She felt thirsty but she stayed under the brilliant shine beneath her skylight. Just looking towards the cool corner where her bought skin of spring water, her bread and fruit were sitting ready for her filled her mouth with peculiar saliva. It made her hungry but changed her mouth so that the imagined taste of food was bitter.

The paper was yellow under the white heat. Sweat was breaking out on her skin. She felt hot and feverish. Her leg went weak again as she stood to work with difficulty and she fell to her hands and knees in the light-well, a worshipper of the sun if ever she was anything, all her mind full of him.

I am not, she thought, I will not be that thing. I must get him out of me onto this panel. And a tiny part of her, the part that wanted her friends around her, was afraid.

All the rest of the day she laboured for vision. She would make no mark until she could see the whole of what she wanted in her mind's eye. It must be unique and perfect, the essence of what he was, something like a flash, but caught and stilled without destroying its movement. She held a brush in her hand and stared at the white purity of the ground, glanced at the fluid lines of the sketches, black on yellow. The sun began to go down and she still could not see it all—only one thing at a time, a hand or a foot, the face laughing at her with its inscrutable dark eyes that had lit her, lit her . . .

In the twilight she moved her aching legs and laid the brush back in its stand. The wintry purity of the panel stared back at her across the room, across her bed. She was fiercely thirsty and hot. Her head ached. She could feel her blood burning away. She must drink.

She watched the bright water pour over the lip of the skin's metal opening and heard it sound out in low splashing as it filled her cup. The water was like ghosts. A tiny droplet, bouncing out over the rim with its quenching vigour, landed on her arm. Elys froze. She did not know what was frightening her but it had to do with the water. Every muscle in her arms and back seized with alarming speed, locked her head and her hands in place so that she must stare at that droplet with its terrifying reflective clarity, its sweet, changing coolness on her skin, the wet trail it made as it ran over her and evaporated in the baking heat. Its path was icy.

She began to shake. Water went everywhere. She could not breathe. Her muscles were like iron. Her spine hurt. She felt it bending her backwards, away from the loathsome stuff. Her blood was already too much fire, too much sun. It wouldn't let her drink if it could. She opened her mouth to scream—

—and came-to lying where she had fallen a minute or two later. The boards around her were drying. The water was mostly all gone. It was difficult to imagine what had frightened her so badly. She felt a little foolish as she stoppered the skin and felt its contents slosh limply—there was only a cupful or two left. A deep tiredness was claiming her. She lay on her bed and let her body slump to nothing.

He came into her room towards dawn. He was clothed in the dancing clothes he had worn before—something light and floating that blew against him and outlined every contour with just the breeze of his going. He did not come through the door. He came through the skylight, drifting down like dust in the moon's quickwater stare, blocking it out with a golden gleam.

There was a beating, steady and loud in her ears. His drum. Her heart.

He touched down on her floor and began to dance to it, the rhythm of blood feeding the flame-weaving of his limbs as he started to teach her the meanings of fire. Elys watched him and he was clear as day, as real as her own hand in front of her. She dare not breathe and her heart grew quicker and made him shiver so that the first panel of silken stuff floated down on the heated currents of air, still shimmering with the movement of his golden skin that it had abandoned. She thought it might burn up to a crisp. It lay over her paints and began to bleach them.

Elys found herself chilled by a movement of air. He flung his head back and all his hair fanned out black against the light of the moon, the black of charcoal, as soft as soot but with the hardening brought on by the long embrace of flame. His coal eyes lit on hers and she was lifted with a thrill of racing blood to her fingertips, her lips, between her legs and over her breasts.

Shyness and a shock of the unknown made her try to shrink but the blood was more than she. Her throat was aching. One by one the silk coverings on him fled away. His eyes never let her go. Her heart leapt—he saw her, he wanted her, he wasn't disturbed by her awkward ways. All the coldwater light falling on him was transformed instantly to golden rivers of desert heat. That kind of water she could drink. She opened her mouth and stretched out her tongue towards him.

He fell on her when he was naked and his flesh was lighter than the silk, burning her where it touched but with a good burning that was like the taste of sugar, like the quench of water but better, bringing her skin up to his awake and. He pinned her down and his tongue, wet like the trail of the droplet, drew the lines of his body all over her from her neck to her feet.

His mouth closed around the healed bite mark on her ankle. He told her that the dogs were the best of his messengers, finding only the loveliest and the best. He told her that she would speak once with a dog's voice and then he would come for her one last time. He would take her in.

She felt she should be glad but instead she was afraid.

He placed his lips on hers, held her wrists with his gossamer iron hands and the smudge darkness of his hair brushed against her neck and over her breasts as he slid inside her. It didn't hurt her. She wanted it to go on, up and up into her stomach and through her neck like glowing metal, until it burst her mouth and made her burn as he did, taking all her insides out and making her into the same, plastic creature with a thin and supple perfect skin and the heat of a thousand fires in her glance.

He blew gently into her open mouth and fire licked her lungs and throat. She cried and her tears ran down towards her ears in tickling streams that dried to steam before they got there. He blew into her mouth and sealed it with his own; two circles.

She could see the water skin in the corner of her eye. She wondered if she could kill him by throwing it over him and felt his mouth smile against hers. She sighed and he drew her breath back into his mouth. He glowed brighter with it and seemed suddenly more solid. His skin began to burn her.

He pushed his long tongue into her mouth. It went down and down, deeper and deeper through her belly and met up with him so that he held her through the inside in a perfect circle. The sign of completion. Every colour in the world exploded into her body, making her a blazing rainbow, arched over and through him. She saw the blue of the cloudless sky.

He left her like a soft vapour, drawing slowly into the air in tendrils of smoke-twined golden dust where he coalesced again in the dying moon glow.

"Elys," he said and his smile was all she ever wanted to see with the way it touched her in her changed and molten heart, "call me." Those black ash eyes, deep as night.

When she woke in the morning she was soaked in sweat and desperately thirsty. As she moved to get to the water a peculiar sensation in her ankle made her reach down to touch it, smiling as she recalled the night, her smile fading as she touched the place.

It was completely numb. She could feel nothing, even when she scratched it with her fingernails.

Tears spilled unexpectedly. For some reason she was thinking of herself and her friends at the studio. She felt close to all of them with a pain like sentiment, like nostalgia. I won't leave you, she thought, I won't let you all go as easily as that, no. I'll get rid of him. She brushed the tears away and a rush of moisture came into her mouth. The thirst was not aided by it but she only had to reach out towards the water and a cold, bitter sense of fear began to clamp down on her chest. Her neck went rigid. She would not have water. Her body was telling her that it must purge itself of all watery things. Fire and water . . . she must not.

After a little she picked up her brush and began to draw on the panel. But as the day edged on from warm to hot, from hot to stifling, she became unable to sit still. She ground paint, she paced back and forth in the motionless room. There was no air in it to breathe that wasn't tainted by the heavy, chemical smell of turpentine, the acrid resins in the varnish, the thick, slumbrous, drinkable smell of the oil as it oozed and ran. On her tile she added chalk on chalk to absorb it. When it ran it made her neck ache.

She had to pace, to walk back and forth over her few feet of creaking floorboards. The movement made her approaches to her work swift and darting but she could see him taking shape now. He was coming out, through her arm, into the paint, onto the warm two dimensional trap of the panel. She could, if she hurried, get free of him. Then she would be able to drink that leathered water and sleep and live. At the same time she saw that all her efforts had started to produce the vision she wanted. A true sight, something really understood beyond its physical form, not as the eye sees but as the mind and the heart see, not perfectly mimicking the visual, but deeper in and deeper, shape becoming expressive, becoming pure. Her success made her want to shout and laugh, and cry. Now she knew she would be good enough to make it on her own and that she could start to see all the world this way and show it to everyone.

But through the skylight he watched her. His light was violent and hard in her eyes so that she couldn't see much else, so that everything was becoming the colour of light.

Elys struggled on. Her tongue was swollen in her mouth. She wanted to drink so badly she did not know how many more minutes she could prevent herself from going to the skin. All her thoughts flowed one into another. Maybe, if she didn't see the water, if he didn't see the water . . . if she fooled herself and him that there was no water, there was only an action of drinking. She could. She kept her eyes on his image in the paint as though she were sizing it up from the distance, checking its proportion and balance as she groped behind her for the skin.

She got it off the nail without making it sound out, got it to her bedcovers in the same mesmerised silence. There, beneath the blackout of her sheet and blanket, with movements that shook from weakness, she moved the skin until the stopper was near her mouth and until the pitiful bulge in its belly was silently poised to flow. She worked at the stopper with concentration as her abandoned brush dug her in the ribs. A giddiness rose in her skull. She knew that if she did not manage this then she would die. Yet she felt okay, like she had a summer cold and could throw it off after a day's rest. It was peculiar to feel such things side by side. In this moment the possibility of death seemed remote and ludicrous. Just don't think of . . .

Water

The stopper came out suddenly with the spasmodic jerk of her fingers and as the precious fluid spilled out over her it made a gurgling sound in running out of the hole. A cut throat, laughing.

Laughing at her as she doubles back in pain, her head coming free of the blankets and into the sunlight to blind her, eyes unable to close, neck arching as if she is an ostrich, but she isn't. Her neck won't. It won't do what his body can do. It can't take on those arches and curves, those circle-shapes. The sign of the sun is a circle. With the body it is made backwards so the head and the feet meet one another in the round.

The water pours over her.

She feels its cool, damp clutch spread through the fabric of her clothes. If she could tear them off her she would. Its touch is death. In steam it rises, making sun-covering clouds, the blasphemous vapours that will make her torment longer. And she cannot see anything but white. The white is the colour of the sun and the colour of the pain that the fire has let into her veins. Her muscles are struggling to become white. Her spine is fighting bone and sinew, tendon and cartilage—yes, the very stuff of an artist's life, the things that painting grounds are made of where the hot rendered glue is poured in a bubbling mess over the canvas or the board—she thinks, her last thoughts that can escape the fear. The water has made the fire in her burn brighter. It is terrified that the water will put it out. "I'm sorry!" she screams, pleading with him to let her go, to stop the terror that she cannot escape.

And now the fire claims her thoughts as well. She does not know who she is any longer, only that she must get away from the water on her, the water over her, the cooling poison of its touch and the cold power it lends to the air. She will crack, like cheap iron plunged in the smith's trough, like glass shattering. She will be nothing more than pieces and fragments struggling to find one another. Oh, she thinks, in her last moment. Why is it me? What did I do to get your attention? Did you dislike me for being intent too?

Something in her back gives way. Something in her head snaps and the white pain fills it. Elys shimmers for one moment, all her memories turning to ash even as she sees them for an instant, every one burned alive.

Antian and Yban make the heated trek through the streets slowly. They struggle through the walls of temperature that rise to meet them, so dry now that even the wet and fetid stink of the mess in the open sewers has been reduced to nothing more than desiccated motes of dust. With scarves drawn across their faces to protect them from this airborne plague they come to her door and step into a shade that is no relief from the eternal, beating rhythm of the heat. As the door opens an angry black whirl of flies rises in the stairwell and they move quickly through into the dark.

Together and silently they climb the circular ranks of wood to the highest room—a door you just step up to from the last stair because her building is cheap and the landing was a saving. The Master knocks. His hands are steady but tired. Every crack in them is filled with flaking grey paste and his nails are permanently black-lined. He has come to tell Elys that the work is done, the maquette of the sun has been made from the earth and the water, from clay, that human substance. He has followed her ideals and he has done the impossible. He is longing for her to answer.

But a silence, crisp and dead, falls on his ears.

Yban is remembering the little dog. He is remembering Elys as she was before she saw Jalaeka and his dancing and wishing he could hear her rare and halting laugh. He is thinking that the sign of the sun is a circle and of the shape of the tiny bite upon the white flesh of her ankle. He poured vinegar on it and bandaged it for her. Suppose vinegar were not enough?

Together the young and older man press their shoulders to the door and heave at its fragile handle. It is not locked. They spill together across the threshold, falling and barking their shins on the high doorstep with their own force. By the time they have picked themselves up they can see Elys.

She is sitting in front of her painting, a sack of chalk and a bag of white oxides next to her knee. She hardly moves but what she does is work. She stares with huge, wide eyes and her hand with a heavy brush moves across the board. Around her in a scatter are her remaining drawings, splattered with white. It is so hot in the attic that neither man can properly breathe. It is like sucking in the air that rises from the door of the firing oven.

As he moves towards her the Master is struck by this image and his own hands, still full of the memory of shaping cold earth. Elys' skin has a brittle look. She is being fired in this attic. Somehow, she is becoming a thing that abandons water, that will be so dry that it can never turn to clay again.

He has felt this possibility, has dreamt it in the few times he has rested from work. The shapes that his hands made were all curving and flowing with the slow drag of heat and as soon as he took them away from the statue they dried instantly and took the moisture from his skin with them so that now he does not bother to wash or clean away the clay because it will only suck him dry again.

She turns towards them both. Her face is stricken. With one hand she makes a pushing motion. Towards the door. She gestures to her picture. The brush jogs in her hand.

The drawings show the man in all his dancing flight. They fill the Master with a doubt that he has not completed his work successfully. He would speak, but Elys' silence forces him into complicity because it is her penultimate silence and not his to break. He gestures to Yban to shut the door as she glances round at it again and fear twitches in her cheek.

"The picture," she croaks. Her voice is hardly there, it is quiet, garbled. She tried again, clutching his arm, dropping the brush. Her grip is weak, "Can you see it? Can you see it? It is him, isn't it? He is there?"

Antian holds her shoulders, gets down on his knees beside her and stares.

He can see nothing but white. A heavy impasto of the most brilliant white, tainted only here and there by a trace of some bled-away colour. The paint is so thick that is has the texture of earth. Yet there is something about this white that has covered all colour, has blinded its witnesses to the form beneath. There is something about this white . . . and within the marks of it formed by her fingers and her grinding knife . . . there is a certain kind of completeness, sealed both within and without.

"Yes," he says, still not sure, not knowing why he must say yes to this strangest image, this no-image, this hidden thing.

Yban has reached the door. He pushes it closed with a weary swing of his young man's arm and it clatters to the frame. A slight breeze from the curve it cuts in the air follows and passes him as he turns towards the man and the girl crouched in the skylight's brilliant glare. He sees that she is smiling. It is at him, then, as the air touches her face, the smile goes beyond him. She turns her head into the light. Her mouth is wide, gaping and from it, through her swollen and parched-to-nothing throat a harsh, inhuman sound jerks out, a sound that to him is nothing more than the bark of a dog.

The next moments flow past like oil. He is recoiling from her in fear even as he feels sympathy too. The Master is trying to hold her but she is too strong for him, fighting the breeze that is gone now. Her barking goes on, grating into Yban's ears and she is convulsing. The panel is kicked away, the oxides spilt. The Master is calling her name but she is bent with fear and terror, her staring eyes struggle against the rest of her to look up into the skylight as though she sees something there. The Master tries to restrain her and she throws herself even harder. The white chalk sack explodes from a blow of her foot. In the dry, scorching air it plumes rapidly into huge white clouds and begins to fall all around them in a weak mockery of snow.

The Master cries out and Elys' stops making a noise.

Yban approaches them through the softly falling white powder.

The panel is face down on the floor a short way off, making a shadow clearly as the dust falls on it and not the boards. The Master is covered in chalk powder. His greyed head is white like an old man's where it bends over Elys and he looks at his hand where the flesh is marked beneath the grey clay. In his arms Elys' limbs all are arched as is her back. Everything about her is a curve. Her eyes are open, still looking. Her cheeks are stretched with her final expression, one which has remained on her face to contort it. The chalk powder is falling gently onto her open eyes, onto her nose and into her open mouth where her lips are reddened with something brilliant and wet and are stretched into a perfect O.

The sign of the sun is a circle. Some think it is the space within that is defined by the line. Some think it is the space without.

HELIOTROPE

One of my so-far unlived lives was as an illustrative artist, and what I most remember about my abortive early art career was the passion I had for my work. I felt like a burning soul. It was heavenly. It does feel like the kind of fire that can kill you. Better than fading away, say I, although my pixies are giving me a stern look like "when did you last burn out a gasket, Sparky?" And I have to return the same to them. It's true that at the time of writing this I'm in a doldrum, having finished a five book series and come to the end of one of those artistic torchlight parades that mark a Significant Project. Like the girl in the story I've gone as far as I could go and that was the end of that line. Luckily for me I didn't literally kill myself in the effort. I can hear the pixies muttering as I write.

BODY OF EVIDENCE

BODY OF EVIDENCE

This story caused me some trouble because while I had an idea I really wanted to write I couldn't find a scenario that fitted it and was usable in a short format. I wasn't able to develop it as fully as I would have liked, so what you have here is a story which could have used a little more evolution in hindsight. See what you think.

BODY OF EVIDENCE

Rachel opened the package at the breakfast table. The device was smaller than she'd thought. It looked just like a wireless ear speaker, the kind you could get free with most personal music players. A small chip in a staticfree wrapper completed the set. She put that into her phone and listened to the instructions.

"Thank you for agreeing to participate in the first public testing of Mind's Eye, the body language and energy reader . . ." blah blah blah it went on about legal requirements and things she had to thumbprint for—she did—and secrecy and the rest of it.

She made a second cup of coffee as she waited for it all to be over, putting her thumb on the screen at the right moments and authorising the little thing to not only read the 'truth' from the people she met that day, but also to pick up her reactions and transmit them back to the data centre where the trial was being assessed. Finally, and most satisfyingly after all that trivia, she was sent a hundred euros direct to her account in agreed payment for her participation with the promise of another thousand once she had completed her twelve hour trial run.

She put the device over her ear and ran the test and setup as she loaded the dishwasher and got ready for work. The device spoke with a woman's calm and assertive voice in a neutral tone, quietly but loud enough for her to hear clearly over mostly any ordinary noises. The battery worked. She agreed that until the trial period had passed she would not remove or switch off the device.

"In just a few moments, Mind's Eye will commence. Your normal experience and perception of your life will remain undisturbed so that you are able to continue with your day uninterrupted. Only you will know that you are now able to perceive the truth of every situation you encounter. Where matters are not as they seem Mind's Eye will speak to you and inform you of what's really going on! When you are ready to begin, enter the personal code on the outside of the box."

Of course, for the first hour there was really nothing much going on. Rachel was alone in her flat, doing boring things like tidying her bedroom, fixing her makeup and getting her lunch together, so nothing happened. It was only in the last five minutes that she thought she'd put the radio on and just check the weather before setting off. She hated carrying her umbrella, so if it wasn't going to rain, she wouldn't. Her handbag was small and compact. She hated being loaded down. Thank goodness the Mind's Eye was so tiny.

"You hate your job," said the pleasant woman in her ear.

Rachel straightened up too sharply from putting on her shoes, overbalanced and had to grab the wall for support. She wasn't entirely sure she'd heard it right. Why would it say something about her job when she was only trying to figure out if it might rain?

On the radio the weather girl was saying cheerily, ". . . a good chance of showers in the Sheffield area, with light winds and very overcast. And now, back to Mark with the traffic report."

"She would like to smack Mark," said the voice in Rachel's ear. "She does not like him."

Rachel turned off the radio. She pulled the device from her ear but then it beeped until, slowly, cautiously, she put it back. A glance at the clock confirmed it was time to go.

The morning continued in the same vein. On the bus, in the coffee shop, on the street Rachel overheard snippets of conversation, and where the Mind's Eye also observed and detected an anomaly it whispered its translation into her ear with the warm confidence of a surrogate deity.

" . . . so, don't you want to go out with me then, or what?"	Please validate me.
"It's not that, Bev. It's complicated."	No.
"Don't you like me?"	Please validate me. You bastard.
"Yeah. Lots."	You bore me.

" . . . and you shouldn't speak to your mother like that!"

I'm the boss here. Me. Me. Me.

"I'm not!"

I hate you.

"What size would you like that?"

"Grande . . . no, just a tall I think."

Venti.

"With whip?"

"Er . . . no. Just as it is."

Yes, and lots of it. Give me it all.

"Rachel! Have you got that document ready? I need it this morning."

I've forgotten about my meeting. I don't know if there is a document but if there is you must have it.

"Ehhhh . . . oh, sure. I'll bring it to your office."

What document?

It was at this stage that Rachel began to settle down and her heart stopped racing. What the device said was really not much different to what she had always thought people meant, in spite of what they said or did. In fact it was reassuring to have her suspicions confirmed. However, the more time went on, the more she became aware that everyone around her was a liar, and so was she. This hadn't mattered when it had all been ordinary conversation, the stuff that politely and efficiently glued the social world together, and the lies were only halftruths or fudges, so they weren't entirely dishonest. She expected as much, so it didn't disturb her to have the subtexts pointed up in clear, perfect prose though that did spoil the effect and leave her impatient and annoyed. By lunchtime the office was an ugly place of unremitting minor whinges and she was longing for the bloody plain spoken bitch in her ear to shut up and stop reminding her of it. Only the thought of her overdraft prevented her yanking the Mind's Eye off her head and shoving it into the bottom drawer of her desk.

As soon as she was able to she grabbed her coat and bag and headed for the park to eat her sandwich, hoping she would find a bench far enough away from people to be in relative peace. The very thought of going to her usual coffee shop filled her with panic. Outside it was drizzling, a fine, grey English sort of drizzle that kept people indoors with the lights on and the central heating up, so to her relief there were plenty of wet spaces to sit on and hardly any passers by.

She was just biting into the first half of ham salad on rye, trying to ignore the cold, seeping feeling of the bench through her thin coat, when the Mind's Eye said,

"You hate this place."

"Shut up! You're not meant to talk to me!" Rachel snarled, spilling lettuce and mayo on herself and then getting up to brush it off, making things worse.

An old man walking a Yorkshire terrier gave her an odd look and went onto the grass to avoid walking too close to her. She glared at him and sat back down. "As if I didn't already know. Think you're so smart. I knew all that stuff. Nobody needs you to tell them."

The device was silent. Rachel tore into the sandwich, chewing and swallowing with savagery. Why the hell was it talking to her? It was supposed to listen to others, not to her. Anyway, how did it know what she was thinking? Didn't it work off speech only or something? Surely this was a violation of her rights, not to mention false advertising. She shoved the last two bites into her mouth and dug into her bag for the paperwork and her phone, thinking she'd call the Mind's Eye people and give them a piece of her mind. Her hands were stupidly shaking and she fumbled the phone and dropped it. Her stomach protested as she leant forwards to pick it up off the soaking gravel.

After an age of turning wrinkling pages she found the number, dialled.

A familiar voice answered, startling her with its calm, precise neutrality. "Hello. You are through to the Mind's Eye answering service. As detailed in our contractual agreements no calls can be answered until the trial period of your test has concluded. If you would please call again at . . . nineteen thirty-one hours . . . we will be happy to speak with you then. Please hang up."

The same bloody woman! Was it some kind of torture? Or, fiendishly, some kind of psychological test that wasn't what they said it was but something completely different to lull you into a false sense of knowing so that you weren't able to do things that made the test invalid, or something? Rachel gripped the phone tightly. She wanted to call someone, but the thought of hearing that voice dissect their every word stayed her hands. She rolled up the paper notes, badly printed and cheap as they were, and rammed them into her bag. She'd read them, every damn word, once she got back to the warm. Beside her, the other half of the sandwich was getting wet. She put the lid on the box. She already had indigestion. She should eat more slowly. Chew. Chew thirty times, wasn't that it?

She was aware that she was thinking fast, so fast that she could pre-empt the device from its self-satisfied commentary by thinking of everything it could say before it could get a word in. It wasn't until some time later, when she realised someone was standing near her, not moving, that she realised she was sitting rigid, staring into space, and had been for a good while. She glanced at the person who was also very still. They did nothing, as if stalled out halfway on the kitty corner that saved a loop of path, bringing them almost to her bench. It was another young woman in business clothing, her neat hair dripping with water into her collar, almost but not quite hiding the dark sluglike shape of a Mind's Eye curled around her ear.

Into the sudden silence the device said, "You are afraid."

"Genius," Rachel muttered under her breath sarcastically although she felt a jolt of surprise. Fear was the feeling she was having, but left to herself she'd have classified it as something else, or probably not put it into words at all, just stuffed it down and ignored it and been vaguely anxious after. "Hey," she said aloud, before she could stop herself. "Hey! Hello."

The new woman turned, her eyes focusing slowly as if she had been a long way from her body and was disoriented on returning to it. She looked at Rachel, who was pointing at her ear.

"Snap," said Rachel, so glad to see anyone else who might be able to share or relieve even one second of the horrible experience.

Her new friend lit up and came over quickly in that odd springing jog that women have when they are crossing soggy ground in high heeled boots. "You have one too! Oh, I'm sorry. I was so caught up I didn't even see you . . ." she stopped at the bench as if Rachel owned it and when Rachel patted it, sat down.

"Should we be talking?" said the new woman quickly, making

no effort to stop. "I'm Sally. They are awful, aren't they? I thought they'd be fun, you know, but it's driving me mad." She had a big bag with her instead of Rachel's small one. The ragged ends of gossip magazines and dailies stuck out of it and prevented it from closing properly. She clutched this bag to her side as she spoke. "Can't even read without it harping on. Blab blab blab. Non stop."

Rachel nodded, beginning to feel despair creeping on her. "I wish I could take it off."

"Oh me too!" Sally nodded in an exaggerated way, one that Rachel could see was a habit.

Nod, nod, nod, she thought. Nice girls always agree, always glad to see, always smiling friendly, nice nice nice. Her face could feel that smile as if she were wearing it. She wore it a lot, all day long.

"She can't stand you," said the Mind's Eye in Rachel's ear. "She wishes she'd never set eyes on you. You remind her of herself."

Rachel froze for an instant, and saw the same tiny jerk of the shoulders higher, the hunted expression on the other woman's face that meant the slug thing was talking to her. "What did it say?" she demanded.

Sally looked at her with wide, disturbed eyes. She started to smile, stopped herself, tried again, failed and stuttered, "Said you think I'm an idiot." Then she smiled apologetically. "I was starting to wonder if . . ."

"No, that's right," Rachel said, frowning. "I did think that. I'm sorry." She glanced down at the magazines and then back up at the other woman's face. "I think things like that all the time but I never pay attention. I mean, it's not very pleasant. And my mother said if you can't say something nice then don't say anything at all."

Sally bit her lips together into a white line but she was nodding. Her hands tightened on the bag. "I know," she said and then, "What did it say about me?"

Rachel tried not to grimace, "That you hated me on sight because I remind you of you."

Sally sniffed, nodded and looked down at the path where muddy puddles were beginning to form. A few silent walkers passed by. Sally groped around in her huge bag and eventually found some tissues. She blew her nose. "I hate myself," she whispered. "It says that too. Does it say that to you? No?"

"No. It tells me I hate this place and my job," Rachel said, sorry to find she was comforted by the other's acute pain, and at the same time sorry for her.

Sally nodded and scrubbed at her nose with the tissue, firmly and too violently. Rachel could just see Sally's mother doing that to toddler Sally's small nose; a piece of care that was a warning not to make a fuss and not to ask for any more.

"At first I thought it was just . . . I don't know . . . just today," Rachel said. She wanted to give Sally something. "But then I started to realise I do hate it here. I'm not sure that anywhere else is better though. People everywhere are pretending things just like they do here," she touched her ear where the now silent device sat and then let her hand fall into her lap.

"And worse in places. Or they do worse, and don't lie. I don't know if that's better. I suppose it's honest. Do you know what happened this morning? I went in to work—I work with a law firm—and we were discussing this case and my colleague was talking about the details of it and all the time she was saying in my ear how much he despised the clients and thought they were stupid and they deserved to lose. And when I said something he was saying his point of view about it and she said he didn't value my opinions and even if I was right he'd rather get his own way because he didn't want me to be right. I kind of thought that before but . . ."

"But it never hurt like it does now?"

"Yes! Because she never stops. You can't not hear her saying those things. I got so mad, I started going through the papers that came with it, looking for ways I could sue the bastards who made it, you know? I thought there must be some wording that would give me grounds to make a formal complaint but halfway through I read . . ." she did another excavation of the bag, finally throwing the magazines onto the bench beside them so she could get some light into the huge expanse, and pulled out the familiar brochure, opened and folded and marked with a green highlighter pen. "This, look."

Rachel bent closer and read the tiny print.

"Mind's Eye works by reading the energy signals given off around it, from the wearer and from nearby others. It also scans and processes information from a range of well-recognised body language signals when others come within visual range of the camera. This information is relayed by radio frequency to a local base station where the AI controller interprets the data and returns the analysis to the headset. It is possible for Mind's Eye to make mistaken interpretations based on insufficient data. Therefore the manufacturers do not recommend that any decisions are taken based on information provided by Mind's Eye and its related products, nor that its statements are taken as fact rather than possible interpretation. When in doubt, always rely on your own judgement."

"Possible interpretation," Sally said. "D'you see?"

But Rachel was looking at the last sentence. "The weird thing is," she said, sitting up and staring across the grey park, "I actually feel like it agrees with me. Only I never wanted to know what it was that I already knew."

Sally paused, her sudden moment of confidence engendered by familiar work gone. "But it says my mother doesn't like me."

Rachel shivered and put her hand over Sally's hand on top of the bag. "Why are you still wearing it?" She didn't believe Sally needed cash. Her clothes were good, even the damned bag was one of those that Rachel would only ever see in the windows of couture shops, ugly or not.

"My credit card . . ." Sally began, distracted, staring off into space though this time Rachel was sure the machine wasn't saying anything. She half lifted one hand towards the earpiece but hesitated and it fell back. "I . . . d'you know my lunch hour is just about up and I have to go." She winced and was suddenly standing, turning, trying to stuff everything back into the bag and be off but she was hurrying so much she kept fumbling things. She turned and the last magazine slithered free and onto the bench. She was already two steps away by the time Rachel said loudly,

"No. Wait! Say what it just said!"

Sally turned half back. She was unwilling but against Rachel's sudden determination and her own misery that both drove her to stay and to go she hadn't the strength to win.

"Say it!"

"I . . . I want to go. I want to leave. I wish I hadn't met you. I wish I didn't have this thing on." By now she was turning this way, that way, looking for a direction but none of them drew her. She was fixed to the spot and increasingly desperate.

"How was that?" Rachel was almost gleeful. She felt possessed by sudden energy.

Sally cast about, "Awful," she said, nearly crying with her need to escape. She rolled her eyes and head at the same time as if the Mind's Eye had suddenly bit her. "No! You're wrong!"

Rachel thought she had gone too far. Awareness of what she was doing made her sit back down. "Yes, probably . . . I'm sorry. I'm sorry."

But a strange half smile appeared on Sally's face. "It was quiet," she said after a moment. "It didn't contradict me. I feel awful."

Rachel wanted to turn things. She also had other questions she must ask before she lost the chance. "Did you try to take it off?"

Slowly Sally began to inch back towards the bench, then she loosened up and came back and sat down, the bag on her lap, her bottom on the magazine. "I did, when my mother called. But it said I'd lose all my money and I thought I could at least last until the evening, it isn't so long. And then it'll be gone." As she finished there was a catch in her voice.

"It won't ever be gone," Rachel said.

Sally gave the wan smile of someone who can't laugh. "You said that at the same time it did." Her red eyes said quite clearly too that she knew Rachel didn't mean the device wouldn't be gone. She meant that their seeing and hearing would not be gone. They would not be able to stop the knowledge that they had already picked up with their ordinary human bodies from one another. At least, not for a while.

A few seconds or minutes passed.

"Now I know why drinkers drink," Rachel said. Sally just nodded.

"I did hear one nice thing," Sally said. "I think the trouble is I've been around some unhappy people. Or maybe, like you say, it's the day."

"It's not the day," said Sally, Rachel and the device all at the same time. Rachel found herself looking at the other woman's face and laughing, sharing a laugh at themselves and the instant. It didn't last long but she felt suddenly much better.

"I should probably look for another job," Rachel said, oddly lightened by the thought.

"I definitely should," Sally said.

They were interrupted by the jolly sound of a popsong coming from the enormous bag. Sally picked out her phone and looked at it, then decisively thumbed it off. "My mother," she said and sighed. She got up, picked up her magazine and looked around for a trashcan. "I should be going. Really this time. Lunch is really over."

"Me too," Rachel got up, stretched her stiff back and picked up her lunchbox.

"It was nice to meet you."

"You too."

They both waited, eyebrows raised, but there was nothing to hear. Then with a smile and a wave they parted and went their different ways along the path.

In the evening at the right time the Mind's Eye finally said. "That concludes today's test. Please remove the headset and return it in the box provided. Your payment will be authorised upon receipt."

Rachel packed it away and sat for a moment, rubbing the space it had occupied behind her ear. She almost missed it.

"But I won't forget," she said into the silence and for the first time in her life she didn't mind the silence, didn't want an answer, or a reply, or an affirmation or anything.

BODY OF EVIDENCE

What I would have done with it, given a second run, is flesh out the possibilities of revealing denied feelings across a much wider range. Here the focus is kept very narrow, while the idea itself really begs for much more exploration. At the time I wrote it I thought I had to do this to prevent narrative sprawl but I think now that a few sharply engineered moments of wit, disaster or embarrassment might have done the job and not spoiled any timings. This is one case where the pixies were foiled by the Should Imps—you know, the little voices in your head that say Stories Should Be Like This, Writing Should Go This Way, You Should . . . You Ought To . . . They'll All Laugh if You Don't . . . Hey ho, live and learn.

THE ADVENTURERS' LEAGUE

THE ADVENTURERS' LEAGUE

I wrote this for the anthology based on the feeling I get when reading older genre writing, especially by Verne of course. I don't say it is intended to match his style exactly, it is my response to his work rather.

THE ADVENTURERS' LEAGUE

Riba leant out of the window and looked up. His body was at an awkward twist because he dare not let go of the ledge. It was twelve floors down to the pavement. Just above him and to his right, outside the Newsdesk window, the summons' posts of the Avian Messenger Service jutted out of the brickwork. One of them was occupied by the sturdy form of an external maintenance Parrokeet who was testing the wirework for the new satellite dish the editor had just had installed. The other two were empty.

Riba pulled his head in and ran a hand through his hair reflexively. The posts and local environs were crusted with foul-smelling bird muck which had a habit of flaking loose. He lived in dread of inhaling the stuff, but he seemed to have escaped this once.

"Go stir up some trouble, Riba, you're spoiling the view." Slattery, who was supposed to be writing the minority sports column, had his feet up on his desk. A printed magazine was laid over his face as he leant back in his chair, arms behind his head.

"Something's going on," Riba told him, stuffing his hands into his pockets and leaning against the wall so that he could look out across the city towards Downing Street. "I can tell by the way everything's flying."

Slattery snorted. "Mmn, yes, maybe in some uncharted corner of the universe there still exists some angle on the day's big story that's not entirely shredded and bedded. The small pets of the world may be bursting to give you their reactions to the reactions on the reactions so far. I can see it now. Impossible Space Journey—a hamster speaks. *I was in my wheel, you know, just doing a few laps, when suddenly . . ."*

But Riba was already out of the door and moving out of the paper's network footprint. In a café a half a mile distant he sat down and opened his Abacand—a handheld device of infinite practical use. Using the money from his last major investigative assignment he pump-primed his account with DarkNet, the non-governmental AI communications service.

He drank his way through four espressos and oiled, smoothed and bribed his way through all but a handful of dollars in the next few hours. Finally, as lights began to come on across the city, he felt that lifting of the hairs on the back of his neck as an old contact from the Forged Uluru network came on line. Using the café's integral holographic units they projected their avatar into the empty chair opposite Riba's.

Forged people, whose bodies might be far distant or in a form not suitable for talking, in order to manifest themselves in the form of Original, or Unevolved human beings, used Avatars as a matter of course in order to communicate more effectively. Their appearance conventionally revealed much about the personality behind their design. This one took the form of an ancient Chinese man with a pot belly. He wore orange robes, had a shaved head, and smoked a meerschaum pipe that gave off a fierce blast of smoke every so often, like a the funnel of a tug-boat. Riba knew this avatar, even though he knew nothing about who it really was, and he was used to the fact that it never spoke. Instead it gave him an amused smile and sent his Abacand him the time and departure point of a trans-Atlantic flight. Then, with an extra-large puff of smoke, it did the genie-thing and vanished.

The notes included a brief description of a person. Riba had used this contact before, when it gained him access to a file that revealed the identities of a half a dozen businessmen involved in financing interplanetary piracy. Upon receiving this new instruction he immediately called in a couple of favours from other journalists to borrow enough money to buy a ticket and by the time Slattery was ploughing his way through the volleyball scores Riba was stepping aboard the helium airship Byzantium, bound for New York.

The Byzantium was a passenger craft ideally suited to extending journey time beyond the practical and into the realms of affluence.

No vehicle appealed less to Riba personally but, if it led him to definite information on the peculiar circumstances of Voyager Lonestar Isol's return to Earth space, then it was the best transport in the world. That this return was a matter that required serious investigation was beyond question.

The Voyager was an early type of Forged human being, an engineered mind in an engineered body which was suited for the long years, great speeds and incredible tedium of interstellar exploration. Her Manifest Photograph was currently showing on every newscast in the system. Riba flinched instinctively every time he saw it. Isol looked like fifty different kinds of assassin bug wedded to the toughest machinery money could buy. She was as inhuman as he could imagine, on the outside at least. On the way to catch his flight he did his best to forget it although it was the kind of thing that had a way of stamping itself on the mind.

Isol had returned only yesterday from a journey of over thirty years' duration. According to the official story she had followed a single, accurate trajectory out of the Sol system towards its near neighbour, Barnard's Star. All had been well. There were some nice photographs of nebulae, some pertinent observations on planets, black holes, the galactic hub and other such matters of importance to science. There were also many transmissions to and from the Forged Independence Party Headquarters.

Riba re-read these and their latest updates with the feeling that at last here was something he could get his teeth into. Isol was a political agitator and a radical of the out-there order. She wrote vehemently about the obsolescence of Old Monkey—the humans like Riba who were as nature had made them. It was Isol's view that the Forged should create an independent state beyond the legislative and economic grip of the present Solar Government so that they could pursue their own reproduction and evolution unhindered by "historical and unsympathetic" views of their destiny.

Riba viewed the looming prospect of a civil war with mixed feelings. For the last few years the Forged Independence movement had grown. Together with in increasing lawlessness out in the wider system it had built an ominous momentum with incident after incident of piracy and assault out on the frontiers of Solar space. The Unevolved fear of their stronger and faster gengineered cousins had grown and on Earth there were daily incidents of violence and misunderstanding between the two. The Forged resented their slavery. The Unevolved envied the Forged their power. But the Forged supplied the Unevolved settlements with essential resources from the wider system, and the Unevolved . . . well, sometimes it was difficult to see exactly how the Unevolved fit into the macroeconomics of it all, but you could safely say they still had the dollars to buy in. They were a big market and the Forged had a lot to sell.

That was the big story as it was being broadcast, but Riba was more interested in what the little newsnets and the independents had to say. Their reporters had rounded on the fact that, for anyone with an Abacand and a half decent recollection of secondary education, you could see that it was clearly impossible to return to Earth within three years when you'd been travelling away from it as fast as possible for thirty. Besides, General Machen, the commander in chief of all Solar military and police forces, had issued a statement that morning in Riba's very paper, warning against action until a thorough and full account of Isol's journey could be published. And that level of explanation meant there was something very bad going on.

By the time Riba took his seat upon the Byzantium's viewing deck and observed the tedious rituals of Buck's Fizz before cast-off and salutes to the captain, he was already planning an in-depth exposé. He would write carefully of what facts he might find and he would argue with meticulous daring for the case of allowing the Forged complete freedom to self-govern—an angle his editor and the paper's owner were also not averse to because they hoped it would mean that most of the Forged would disappear from Earth.

They were an hour into their flight and had just begun the low-altitude portion of the journey to allow a spot of whale-watching when Riba decided to take himself on a tour of the ship. But after a few minutes he was sure that he was being followed. He thought it might be his contact. He took a few turns that led him into the relative privacy of the luxurious upper deck accommodation corridor and waited. Thirty seconds later a man approached him and Riba's neck hair stood on end for a second time that day. Not a woman in a green coat holding a leather bag but a man with long blond hair bound back into a queue and dark glasses, his powerful form almost entirely covered by a grey trenchcoat with its collar turned up high.

"Regrettably your investigation must end for the time being," this young man said without preamble. He took Riba's hand and arm in the semblance of a casual conversational hold though it effectively prisoned Riba in a vice-like grip. "I have been sent to send you to your contact." He began to tow Riba along the corridor at a swift pace.

Riba struggled, at first without trying to appear in trouble, but then more violently. He didn't like changes and he really didn't care for the strength that so easily overpowered his own.

"Don't make this difficult," the man warned him in a low tone and Riba realised that he wasn't the only one who was nervous.

"You are interfering with the lawful free press!" Riba asserted loudly in the textbook style. He was ignored in the same vein and found himself hauled along the ramp towards the aft gliding decks where wind-hangers and the elegant lines of individual air-yachts were moored by rope to the smooth flanks of the Byzantium.

"Yes, yes," said the agent. "That's my job."

"Help! This man is robbing me!" Riba shouted, but the Byzantium's crew were busy at distant posts and the few passengers who were within earshot were of the kind who sank deeper in their seats or hurried away, afraid and embarrassed. Within moments both he and his captor were standing on the air deck, nothing in front of them except ten metres of beautifully finished hardwood landing strip and the blustery air over the ocean.

Riba scrabbled with his free hand in his pocket and signalled out with his Abacand, cuing emergency messages he'd had in place for just this awful moment. To his dismay a flat beep informed him that they were all blocked.

"It's nothing personal," said the agent, dragging him towards the edge of the launch pad. "And nothing permanent," he added as he anchored his own feet with miraculous traction and pushed Riba over the side. Riba thought he saw bare feet not boots in that instant, and that the soles of the feet were covered in suckers.

This impression was wiped from his mind by complete terror as Riba understood that he was falling more than a hundred metres towards the unbroken waters of the Atlantic. He heard screaming and felt a searing pain in his throat as the gigantic hull of the Byzantium passed over him. His limbs flailed. He thought of helpless mice he'd held by the tail at pet shows, of Slattery's high-pitched hamster saying *I bet you didn't ask the mice* . . .

Riba turned gently in the airstream and saw the sea rushing to meet him. As he marked the likely spot of his demise he saw something that almost made his heart stop prematurely.

Something was rising up through the water.

A great beast, pale and vast, more massive even than the largest whale—he couldn't make out its exact shape. There was a centre, solid and near-white, but then there were great reefs and rafts of less tangible matter, tentacles and sheets of flesh that ballooned and snaked about in the surface water. For miles they seemed to reach out, a billion arms . . . He thought he saw a single enormous eye staring up at him and at that instant tried hard to die.

He fell and beneath him the creature suddenly thrashed and convulsed, stirring up a mass of bubbles into a frothing whirlpool where the simple sea waves had been. There was then no more time for thought. Riba met the ocean—not the hard, unyielding density of solid water, but the soft foam of the creature's ferocious wake.

He felt himself falling still. To his astonishment the water accepted him in a gentle way. It drew him down unharmed into the cold of itself. Thoughts of the creature instantly made him kick and thrash. Riba stared wildly about him, seeing only dim greyness and the leisurely upward race of a trillion bubbles, feeling the pressure of endless water in his ears and against his lungs, just like the man's hand on his arm—hard and merciless. He was deafened to everything but the sound of his own panic.

Riba made the surface choking and coughing and saw the awful pale hulk of the creature again as the shield of bubbles dissipated around him. Huge arms and fingers of translucent jelly, pocked with pink-edged suckers the size of saucers, reached towards him through the water. He turned and began to swim, hopelessly, but the tentacles were everywhere, some breaking the surface and turning their tips towards him where he saw, with horror, the distinct shapes of primitive pigment patches—yet more eyes.

Something cold and powerful snaked around his legs and bound them tight. He opened his mouth but was pulled under. His last sensations were of cold water, cold strength in flesh that wasn't remotely like any flesh he knew. His last impression was of stealthy and nimble fingers making a thorough attempt to pick his pockets.

When he woke Riba found himself lying on solid ground. It was so unexpected that he gave a start and discovered that, all things considered, he didn't feel that bad. His skin was sore from salt water abrasion and he felt battered but he was able to move to hands and knees and then climb to his feet with almost ordinary ease. His solid ground turned out to be a long white sanded beach, fringed by tall palm trees which stretched up to the sky and out over the baby blue shallows of a small lagoon. Not four metres away from him he could see the rivulet of a fresh water stream cutting a shallow groove through wet sand to the sea. He moved towards this and bent down for a cautious handful. In moments he was on his hands and knees, drinking and splashing.

He impressed himself with his resourceful skills as he remembered to take off his clothing and rinse it out, spread it to dry on the sand, clean off the salt on his skin and then move quickly into some shade. The day was hot and the sand even hotter. A few flies came and gathered around his wet skin and then left him alone. It was only as he took a rest and began to notice more of his surroundings that it occurred to him to wonder where he was and how he had got there.

A search of his clothes proved what he already suspected—his Abacand was gone. Now he had cause to wish he had taken up the subdermal kind of machine, but he had never fancied a permanent link to the digital world until this moment. Its loss made him feel twice as naked and a thousand times more vulnerable.

The giant squid thing must have taken it before abandoning him here. Riba didn't like to think of it as a thing, but without a name or a clade to place it in he couldn't help thinking of it that way. Of him. Of her. Whatever.

Riba sat back and tried to think. What had the blond man promised? Ah yes, this was not personal and not forever. So he had some hope of returning to his old life after all, even if he was the subject of a peculiar kidnapping as it was beginning to seem.

Riba waited impatiently for his clothes to dry so that he could make a full inspection of what he guessed might be an island. He hoped that even without the Abacand he might remember some of the very clever survival skills he'd so often admired in documentaries and that maybe he would outfox his captors and figure out where they were holding him before they picked him up again. Even so, could the squid have carried him all the way from near Ireland to the Caribbean? Squid had prodigious powers of speed and agility in the water and it had been a mighty monster but, even with the potential of extra powers from engines and the like, it was no quick journey.

He set off on his reconnaissance at an eager pace which soon became more cautious. The sandy lagoon rim gave way to rocky headlands which required a lot of effort and patience to climb over. Soon he was very hungry and very tired. He took another drink from one of the many rivulets escaping to the sea and lay down in the shade beneath two palm trees for a rest.

When he woke it was late afternoon. He found a green stick and went digging for clams in the sand. Within an hour or so he had collected a reasonable plateful—enough for a paella—and he had also, pleased with his cunning, decided that if he couldn't get them out alive he would get them out roasted and hot after baking them in a fire.

There followed a most trying several hours. There was no dry wood. There was no dry tinder. Stupidly he had been travelling without a magnifying glass. After two hours of failed efforts at making fire he gave up and, one by one, began to fling the shellfish back into the sea. Halfheartedly he tried to crack one in his teeth but his teeth would have cracked first.

Riba wrote in his head, "Without his tools to help him Man loses the evolutionary arms race to a humble mussel." But it was hard to laugh.

A moment or two later he began to hear unmistakable sounds of the progress of something inside the woods that backed onto the sand. Too tired to feel very afraid just yet Riba turned to watch, thinking of pigs or deer.

To his complete surprise what emerged from between the palm trees was a man with white hair and a thick white beard. He wore a rather severe suit and a high white collar tied up with a white cravat. All the white things stood out clearly against the darkness of the forest and the indigo of the sky behind him. What interested Riba most about him however, was not his clothing, or his cane, with which he had parted the last fronds of green before emerging, but the fact that in his other hand he was holding what looked like a china plate with something on it.

The old man waved his stick at Riba in a friendly way. "Hello there," he called out. "You must be Arnau Riba. A tricky man to find it seems. Don't trouble yourself so much, dear fellow. Here, I've brought you a sandwich."

Riba would remember for the rest of his life the taste of that sandwich—it was cheese and pickle—and the way it felt to eat it, so salty and tangy and indescribably wholesome as he stood and studied the face of this peculiar stranger. The eyes beamed at him. The tweed suit—he did not know how to explain the mirage of colours in that lovely wool or how prickly and hot it seemed, or how it sat upon the cotton shirt beneath the thick beard or how the sandwich and the man both merged into a curious saving grace that was quite ridiculous to him in the same instant that it was perfect.

"Forgive me," said the man with another smile, "I have you at a disadvantage. I am Jules Verne, the Right Hand of Pelagic Bathysaur Island Iukina. At your service."

Riba stared at him, eyes bulging, cheeks bulging, chewing. He thought about asking the obvious questions—who, why, what— but took another bite instead. It seemed likely that answers would appear in time and they were less important right now than eating.

"Yes, Mr Riba," said Verne cordially, taking a deep, satisfied breath. "You are upon a living island afloat on the breast of the Atlantic. Me, in fact. And as such you are my guest. Welcome. I hope that you will forgive the delay in my locating you, but my eyes and ears, the flies, are easily diverted, and by the time they had told me of your whereabouts and I had made the journey, you were no longer at the location they remembered. A fly's memory, you know, is a strange and marvellous . . . ah—" Verne glanced down at the empty plate as Riba took the second half of the sandwich. Verne looked down, gently brushed off a few crumbs onto the sand. "I wonder if the crabs here will enjoy bread? No doubt they will. The water on this side is also very good of course, but many more refreshments are available a short journey away at the Club. I hope you feel able to manage a short walk?"

Riba, feeling the first hit of sugars arriving in his bloodstream had concluded, by the time that Verne began to speak of flies, that if the man were really a Hand—a physically human component of a greater human composite being—then he could be as dotty as he liked so long as there really were more sandwiches. Riba found it hard to believe in Forged like this one; that is, he had known intellectually that they existed, but he had never really thought about them in any practical fashion. He could not bring himself to quite believe that what he had stood on, sheltered on and been thwarted and restored by was a single being and not a volcanic atoll. But it made sense—there were no islands like this anywhere near the airship's course.

To the old man's question about walking he simply nodded. The old man smiled and turned, beating back stubborn bits of jungle with his walking stick as they retraced his steps. In less than two hundred metres Riba found himself standing on a hard dirt road. A small battery-powered car was parked there, looking neat and very red against the darkening green of the jungle. As the sun went down, and Riba sat feeling the roll of precision suspension carry him silently through the deep blue twilight, his surprise began to turn to curiosity.

His astonishment was completed when they rolled up towards the soft yellow lights of a large hut built on stilts. An expansive verandah ran all the way around it and the steps down to the car were lit with the twinkle of many small citronella candles to greet their arrival. Walking up and onto the smooth boards Riba felt a rush of gratitude for civilisation in general. As he turned in through the doorway he saw a large room panelled in dark wood and furnished with the most beautiful and expensive furniture he had ever seen. At the heart of the room a fire burned within a stone bowl and near this fire a group of chairs were drawn close, each different, and each supporting a different figure with the exception of a tall wing chair which he assumed was Verne's.

A soft breeze blew in at their backs as Verne ushered him forward. As they approached Riba saw one of the others stand up and draw another chair forward to place within the circle next to the empty seat. This man then turned and came to greet them. He wore a well-cut suit, like a uniform, and carried a cap beneath his arm. Like Verne he had white hair and a white beard, but by contrast this man's beard was clipped neatly short and his hair was a great length that fell around his shoulders. Dark walnut skin crinkled around brown eyes as he held Riba with his gaze.

"Arnau Riba, I am a longtime admirer of your feature articles, if not your methods of investigation. I regret you found your introduction to the ocean so traumatic." He held out his hand and

Riba took it, shook it, felt its strength and resilience as he wondered at the choice of words. He must mean Riba's fall.

"Permit me to introduce you," Verne said, putting the sandwich plate aside. "This is my good friend Captain Nemo, Hand of Bathysaur Nautilus Kalu."

"Nemo?" Riba repeated, finding the name ringing bells in his head. Then he began to understand. He stared at the merry smile of the man whose hand he still held. He saw the great eye of the huge tentacled monster that had churned the ocean up beneath him. It was only with the greatest willpower that he managed to keep a semblance of cool.

"No doubt you are wondering at our choice of Hands, Mr Riba," Nemo said. "Those who meet us often remark upon it and perhaps, to a person not as keenly aware of their intellectual and imaginitive forbears as ourselves, it must seem strange. Jules Verne was a Frenchman of the twentieth century, one of the first great science fiction writers. He also lived in a time of great change and his studies of engineering and the natural world gave rise to stories of great adventure and the heights of invention to which human minds might aspire. Kalu and I see ourselves as the literal conclusion of the work of Verne and his contemporaries including the architect of your hometown, Barcelona—the incomparable Antoni Gaudi. In our physical forms you may witness the work of millions of scientists and artists, designers and engineers inspired by the works of these great minds. In our minds we hope you will discover the same unbridled imagination, and in our hearts the same abiding wonder, curiosity and love of the Earth and all her works. It is why we are here, Mr Riba, and it is also why you are here."

Riba looked from one of the old men to the other. "Jules Verne, the island's voice. I see. But Captain Nemo?"

"Why," said the captain, continuing in their peculiar and elegant way of speaking, "this is both by way of an homage and a small joke in one. Captain Nemo is Verne's most well-known hero. Like myself, Nemo is a scientist-explorer. He is also the captain of a submarine, named Nautilus, which is mistaken for a giant sea-monster when it sinks ships bent on acts of war. I myself am a Nautilus Class Forged, created to investigate and protect all the life of the oceans, in particular its greatest depths and, like Nemo himself, I seek peace."

"We appear as old men. Although we are nothing of the sort we think of ourselves as Jules Verne and Captain Nemo because the conceit has improved us and connects us by heart and mind to both the past and the future, history and dream. But here," Verne continued, taking Riba's arm and sweeping him onwards to the waiting circle. "Here are our other friends also glad to make your acquaintance. Allow me to introduce to you the illustrious Sinbad, Hand of the WindDrifter Velella of the same name—he was always named after the hero of the seas."

Riba shook hands with a young man dressed in flamboyant pirate colours, his hair beaded and a rapier-thin moustache on his top lip matched by a dagger of beard on his chin. He had no idea what manner of creature a WindDrifter might be but as the young man's green eyes sparkled he grinned and whispered to Riba, "I am the sailor and the boat, the crew and captain all in one. Look me up when you get home."

He sat down then and with a splash the lady of the group stood up from her rest, legs immersed to the knee in a porcelain tub of salt water. She was taller and more willowy than Riba, and looked like someone who has really gone to town on fancy dress for a party themed around fish.

"This lady is WaveRider Mermaid Silene, and she is here herself." Verne said.Silene inclined her head regally, "Look, no Hands!" she joked and then gave Riba her long, cool hand to clasp. Against his palm he felt the slight roughness of scales. The soft feather lines of gills on her neck lay demurely closed, like lines of paint. Only her hair gave it away—it was not human hair at all but fleshy and fibrous and deep crimson, like a kind of kelp. Then she sat and Riba moved along.

"Here is Ahab, Hand of MekTek Orca Moebius, fish-marshal."

Riba was sure that there was another joke in this, but he would have to look that up too. Ahab was a rough looking individual whose clothing wouldn't have passed muster anywhere Riba knew. He looked as though he spent his life beachcombing and living on what he could find. He clapped Riba on the shoulder and gave him a stiff nod, without getting up.

"And last but by no means least the pioneering scientific documentary-maker and populist, Sir David Attenborough, Hand of ArchaeoTek Legion Ketier. Ketier is like a kind of Hive, Mr Riba—in the oceans, he is everywhere."

Riba shook hands with an ordinary looking kind of man in clothes much like his own. Then he was allowed to sit in his own seat, at Verne's right hand, and Verne sat also, completing the circle. Riba felt strangely moved, without understanding why. His throat was taut as Verne said,

"Welcome, Journalist Arnau Riba, to the Adventurer's League and Dance Club of the Ocean. We are of the sea and pledged to defend her wealth and nurture her children. We adventure in body and spirit within her. We dance to her music."

They all smiled at his discomfort and puzzlement as a machine servant provided him with iced tea, but Nemo handed him back his Abacand, so he didn't mind it. He was too carried away with the itch to start collecting stories and the amazement that such a thing as the League existed, unknown to the Original and Unevolved humans.

"That's all great, Mr Verne," Riba said after a drink of tea, "but what about that agent who pushed me out of the Byzantium? I call that unfriendly. And why was it necessary to bring me here?"

"Do you mean this agent, Mr Riba?" Verne asked, and he gestured outside the circle to a door in the far wall of the room where a tall, blond man had just entered. Although he now wore much less clothing—only a pair of shorts—which revealed his true skin to be the silver, blue and black of a fish, his blond hair was unbound and he was clearly the same individual. He carried his shades in one hand.

"This is the Pelagic Triton Mephisto, another member of the League." Verne told him. "Don't be alarmed by his name if you know it. He does not aspire to seize your soul."

Riba at least did understand this reference to Faust's demon. "Only my arm from its socket," he said, standing up.

Mephisto held out his own hand. His eyes were unusually large and dark and in the dry air of the house they teared rapidly so that he appeared to cry. "I regret the circumstances of our . . ."

"Yeah, whatever," Riba said. He glanced at the man's silver and blue shining skin—warm and human around his hands, face and feet, but as miraculously metallic and decorated as a mackerel elsewhere. The luxuriant blonde mane moved of its own accord now it was unbound. It was Tek. "But what's this all about?"

"We have been trawling the same conversations on the underground newsnets," Captain Nemo said as Mephisto sat beside

Silene on her wet bench. He put his feet in her footbath and slid the special eyeglasses onto his face where Riba saw they acted like reverse goggles, covering the surfaces with salt water.

Nemo continued, "We have drawn similar conclusions to yours, Mr Riba, concerning the nature of Voyager Lonestar Isol's return. We also have access to the Forged Uluru network, which you and the Unevolved human world do not. Your contact is known to us through the dream net of Uluru and it was she who decided that you should meet us here. I hope you will forgive her."

"That depends on what's going on," Riba said, amused to think of his Chinese pipe-smoker as a girl. "Mind if I record?" He held out his Abacand.

"We wouldn't have given it to you otherwise," Silene said with a roll of her pretty blue eyes. "You're here to write."

"I don't write for . . ."

"Please," Verne held up his hand. "Let us be civilised. Nobody seeks to pocket you, Mr Riba. If you will permit me to explain?"

Riba shrugged and set the Abacand down between them on the polished surface of a marble-topped table, picking up his tea glass. They'd played hard and they'd played nice, he was stuck here, he might as well see what they'd got. And besides, it was so hard not to like them and their aspirations to nobility, in spite of everything.

"We know that Isol has returned with alien technology," Verne said quietly into the silence that followed Riba's assent. The only other sounds apart from his voice were the soft, distant wash of the ocean and the occasional snap from the fire. He had Riba's full attention now.

"We do not understand its nature or what it promises, but it must be responsible for her faster-than-light journey home. You were hoping to discover this and reveal it to be the cause of Solargov's silence on the matter, but of course, had you discovered this story, you would not have lived to tell it to any kind of conclusion. In sending you to us your contact has saved you from an untimely end at the hands of Machen's agents. Isol has promised the Forged freedom from the bonds of Earth, you see, and it is too soon to reveal this to the Unevolved masses. On that the League and its allies are in agreement with General Machen. Unfortunately most of the Forged are aware of it and it is likely that the Forged Independence Movement will soon trumpet it from the rooftops, so it's only a matter of days before it becomes common knowledge."

"So why deny me the story?"

"We would like you to *write* the story," Nemo said. "But we thought that if you were going to do so, you should have the benefit of a fuller picture, and not have to try to piece it together from little parts. There should be no misunderstandings here of the kind that led so many to war in the past. Civil war and insurrection must not take place within the system, nor on Earth itself. Not between the Forged and the Unevolved, which is what we fear will happen if this is handled badly. There are too many uneasy people on all sides with too little understanding."

"And what kind of understanding would this be?"

"Your paper is noted for its anti-Forged sympathies," the Triton said. "And you have written extensively yourself of how alien we seem to most Unevolved human beings; that we have created ghettos and cultures of our own which seek to exclude the Old Monkeys. You accuse us of racism, Mr Riba, although you do not use the word. It is implied by all your writings that that you see yourself distinguished from us in fundamental ways which deny our humanity. In recent editorials, not written by you, your media group have been advocating segregation as a solution to the tensions on Earth between Forged and Unevolved."

"I prefer the term Original," Riba said, although he was rankled.

"As you wish," Mephisto shrugged—a simple gesture that provided all the Gallic inferences of contempt that Riba had ever seen made. "It was our decision to invite you to spend some time with us in the hope that you might review your Original position."

"And if I don't?"

"Please do not become bullish," Verne said gently, but with great firmness, to both of them. "You are free to leave, Mr Riba," he leant forward and picked up the Abacand, "with or without your story."

Riba didn't like the direction things had taken much but he could see the sense of staying. "It isn't racism," he said, feeling a kind of devilish urge. "Racism is history. You and I are very different. That's all. People need their own kind around them. Why else do you even have this club?"

"Well that's the point!" Silene said irritably. "We aren't the same kind at all. Each one of us has as much in common with one another physically as we do with you, Mr Riba."

"I thought you and he . . ." Riba pointed from her to the Triton.

"It is a gulf of a mere two hundred or so genes and a handful of proteins. More than separates you from a chimpanzee," the Triton said and added with a dryness that could have turned the Atlantic to a desert, "We do not breed in the wild."

"Mr Riba is playing with you," Nemo said. "He is no racist, are you?"

"No," Riba said, trying not to be sullen about it. "The differences are just an angle, that's all. And the coin flips both ways. Until the Forged came along there was no such thing as a real sense of generic human identity in the Originals, not one that could unite them over and above their religious and cultural differences. Now that's changed. We've got you. And you've got us, babe."

"And the MekTeks are out in the cold," Mephisto said, although he switched off his frosty demeanour. "But that's for another day. Today it is essential that Isol's radicalism and her determination to separate the Forged from the Sol government does not precipitate war, not least because most of the big guns these days are all Forged citizens and many of them are sympathetic to Independence. This prevention cannot come down to a single story of course, but much can be changed by a timely story—witness Mr Verne's effect on the world. More immediately, Isol's discovery of an alien presence so close to home could be exactly the generic constraint we have been needing to create a union between the Forged and the Originals."

As Riba thought it over Nemo revealed the details, "Tupac, the great MotherFather of us all, says that the alien material is a substance against which Sol has no defences. Though it appears benign it is extremely powerful—changing shape at the user's will—and its true purpose cannot be fathomed. To our knowledge Isol is in voluntary quarantine at the Idlewild station out close to L4. But we suspect that the material is not confined to her possession. If the extremists in the Independence movement were to come into contact with it the effects could be devastating. Quite final in fact. They are single-minded."

"Can you get me an interview with Isol? With Tupac?" Riba asked.

"We speak for Tupac here," Silene said and touched the side of her head gently to indicate that she shared a digital link into the Uluru net where all the Forged communed. Riba saw that her long dark fingers were webbed although her thumbs were free. What he had taken for nicely painted nails were mother-of-pearl claws which expanded and retracted to enhance her gestures.

Riba sat and considered. Now here was a story for the ultimate conspiracy and paranoia theorist to feast on! A kidnapped journalist is given secret details of a potential weapon . . . He was already planning ways of presenting it, so that it would seem like matters were under control and so no one would panic, but at the same time he wondered how much Verne and the League were controlling him. With information and vested interests, one could never be sure.

"No doubt you suspect our agenda," Ahab said as they watched Riba thinking. It was the first time this wiry old sea-dog had spoken and Riba was surprised by the growl of his voice. "We have nothing with which to convince you of our information's pedigree and of our honest intent but one thing. Would you care to take a tour?"

Riba assented, got up and followed Verne, first to a room where he was provided with fresh, clean clothing and then outside onto the verandah at the back of the building. Nemo came with them, leaving the others inside. As they walked onto a long gangway that led off through the trees Riba heard calypso music begin to play behind them and wondered if they really meant the part about dancing.

The gangway took them down gradually to ground level in the dark of the forest but the way was lit by electric lights here, set like torches at the sides of the path. Soon they reached a door in a low stone archway which opened as they approached. Riba slapped a mosquito as they began to descend a staircase down and down into a well of rippling, water-cast light. After twenty metres the narrow stone came to a flat floor and they walked out under the sea beneath a protective shield of polycarbonate. They were under the lagoon, Riba guessed, as small fish darted in and out of the range of the light whose reach gave the illusion that they were captured within a greater cavern of water, forested with weed.

"This lagoon, along with my other specialised habitats, collects and protects the most endangered marine life," Verne said as they passed along the way. Frequently he stopped to point out an individual fish, animal or plant and relate its physiology to Riba, its habitat, its behaviours. It seemed there was nothing about them he didn't know.

As they left the lagoon proper and changed direction Riba saw a silvery flash in the corner of his eye and looked up and to his right. There he saw the Triton and the Mermaid wave lazily to him—that single flourish of their arms the only remotely true human gesture, for in their natural element they were transformed. Their legs, though still disjoined, fit together as smoothly and with as much fluid grace as a true tail. From their calves and backs elegant spines lifted and fanned fins. Between them swam the largest shark that Riba had ever seen.

The huge fish glided along with a relaxed, half-asleep momentum and passed barely inches over Riba's head.

"This is one of only fifteen Great Whites left on Earth," Nemo said as they watched the three pass into the dark again, the trailing fins of the Triton last to vanish as he shepherded the huge creature back into the deeper waters. Softly, softly, sweet calypso tunes filtered through the water as Riba listened to the sound of his heart and put his hand to the clear dome, to try and feel what might be out there, still unknown and almost lost.

They did not only show him sharks in the lagoon, but crocodiles at home in the small mangroves, saltwater ones with beady eyes and skins like pebbly beaches. They showed him a reef off the coast, of rainbow corals and the floating arms of sea urchins, the prickly spines of starfish and the darting fizzes of colour that were the billion fish, all facing into the gentle currents of the Island's smooth passage through the deep ocean. Silene swam to the viewing ports with a fish or a sea cucumber in her hands now and again, and Mephisto persuaded deeper-water beasts to show themselves in the light for a time; hammerhead sharks and the diamond shapes of rays with their aerial-like tails; huge conger eels with savage grins; bass and groupers. He brought in a shoal of mackerel and became almost invisible among them as they turned and darted in a single cloud.

"Even the fish that were most common are now much reduced, although the conservation measures mean that mackerel and tuna and the great so-called product fish, anchovies and sardines, are much more successful these days," Verne told him. "They're welcome passengers when the seas are rough, but we don't trouble them much unless our sharks are hungry."

"The true deep ocean is something I cannot show you personally," Nemo the Nautilus said as they walked out of the reef area and back towards the surface. "But my work there is bent on discovering the life and history of the oceans and the geology of the Earth beneath."

"Each of you are one of a kind," Riba said. "Why aren't there more?"

"An Island and a Nautilus are not easily made," Verne said. "The cost of Forging is always high. But we are worth the taxes, I hope you find. Together we form the marine conservation and research unit of the Earth. From the deepest to the most shallow, wherever the water is salt and creatures live off the sea we are there. And it is our intention that the oceans here, the only saltwater oceans in this system, possibly in existence, survive this encounter of Isol's. For that we cannot have a war. In war our energies would have to dissipate and we must choose a side—the Forged or Earth. We are bound to the Earth, how could we fight against it? Maybe some would, and so you see it would never be a simple matter of the Earth Forged leaving for new worlds, as Isol wants to promise and your media wishes to say. We will never leave the ocean. And we are not your enemy."

They had come outside again on the surface and took Verne's smart car. It drove them to the far side of the island and Riba saw the colonies of seabirds that girt the Island's windward side, vast cliffs of them clustered against the protecting shield of the mountainside.

Riba could stand on this island, and speak to it. This, above all, he could not get over. The Island was a habitat and a researcher, a scientist and a human being, a creature of the ocean who was land and sanctuary, a dreamer—so many things at once. He looked at Verne and then at Nemo as they returned to the car, the Island and the Monster of the Deep, walking together. He looked up through clear skies to the stars and the quick sweep of gleaming satellites. Out here there was no light except the small ones marking the car and the galaxy was visible, milky and rich across the roof of his world. How small was this ocean, and how large, he thought, with only the Forged themselves to shepherd us out there into the vastness of the true sea.

"I'll write your article," he said, joining the old men in the car. "What's the angle?"

"Jules Verne himself wrote not only to spread the wonder of scientific knowledge but also to raise awareness of its dangers," the Island said, through Verne the Hand. "Not that knowledge was dangerous, but that misapplication of it would always have serious consequences, both for the person who applied it and for the world. He lived at the beginning of the age when humans were to get their hands on the greatest powers and the greatest wealth. Many evils we might consider footnotes in history were current at the time— slavery among them. I propose that you consider presenting our information in the light of this perspective: to treat properly with any alien world we must strive to understand ourselves and the way that we create our own, and that to ensure our survival we must apply ourselves closely to the study of threats that lie both without and within."

"Doesn't sound like the kind of stuff that grabs the headlines," Riba said.

"The headlines are up to you," Verne said as the car took them through the jungle back towards the house. The moon was out and the skies clear. Tupac shone like a star close to its side from her place in orbit. "I'm sure you'll think of something."

Riba was already planning his full-virtual Time magazine spread of *The Adventurers' League*, never mind his brief half-life in the global newsnets when it came to setting out the full story of Isol's trip and what she'd found. For good magazine sales you need a stable, literate population who want to talk. Wars were always good for that, but he could live with the peace, he thought, as he followed Verne up the steps and into the Club. He could live with the idea of noble adventurers on a secret island, eternally afloat, watching out for everyone.

"Hey, do I get membership here?"

"That depends on what you write, Mr Riba. It all depends . . ."

THE ADVENTURER'S LEAGUE

As these things usually are it was on a deadline, and I wished at the time that I could introduce a third thread into the story that would have given it a more active dynamic to go with its far-fetched retro/future ideas and the lovely characters who appeared but I wasn't able to come up with anything worthwhile in the time. On the other hand, now I reread it I quite like its Sunday-afternoon feel. It's more like the opening of a book than a short story however, there's no getting around that.

THE GIRL HERO'S
MIRROR SAYS HE'S
NOT THE ONE

THE GIRL HERO'S MIRROR SAYS
HE'S NOT THE ONE

Because I only write short pieces at other people's suggestion it was the opportunity to be included in this project that spurred this try at near-future cyber SF. It owes its title to the much more adept Kelly Link and her divinely intriguing story "The Girl Detective" in her collection, STRANGER THINGS HAPPEN. I really loved that title so I kind of stole it.

THE GIRL HERO'S MIRROR SAYS HE'S NOT THE ONE

The eternal youth and optimism, the always-forwards energy of the Girl Hero makes her feel lethargic whenever she stops for coffee at her favourite bookstore. She is living in a Base Reality not unlike Prime, the original reality old Earthers used to share before Mappa Mundi, except it has fifty more shades of pink and no word for 'hate'. Her reality is called Rose Tint and it was the one relatively mild hacker virus she was glad to catch. Of course, she would think that about it now . . .

The Girl Hero feels there is something missing about herself, but she cannot name it. She has always felt this way, since she was tiny at her father's knee. He showed her a fly that had landed on the back of his hand. She looked closely, marvelling at how small it was, how neat, how industrious as it cleaned its pretty glass wings. She remembers how he smashed it flat with his other hand. He was so fast. He had the reflexes of ten men and he was a Hero too.

Oh, one other thing that is missing about her is her name . . . a bout of 'flu stole it from her when she was in her teens, not so long ago. She keeps it written on the inside of her wrist in indelible ink that she rewrites every three days. She doesn't look at it much. Only when someone asks. The coffee barista has his name written on a badge—Marvin.

"Thank you, Marvin," she says as she takes her drink. The establishment is guaranteed clean. Little tablet boxes of Mappacode are sold at the counter, but they don't come under the Infection Bill: too minor, too common and not particularly useful—they offer mnemonic upgrades for popular music charts, fashion, current affairs and the stock markets so you can always have something to say and know what to buy. The information is stored somehow in proteins that only unfurl when they reach the right places in the brain—the places where Mappaware has created ports for them. They are inert otherwise, and when they have delivered the goods they break up into amino acids and provide spare nutrition. The Girl Hero takes a Mode one and pops it with the first steaming sip of espresso.

The Girl Hero picks at the cardboard band around her coffee cup and goes to take a seat in the window. She is dismayed to learn from the Modey that tweed pencil skirts are in. They are the worst kind of skirt for kicking. She sips and looks around her and wonders for the millionth time if she should save her money and risk a remodel. But she doesn't know what to do if she isn't a Hero. A Hero wouldn't. The preference is disturbing—would she really like it if she hadn't agreed to this job at the careers' meeting? Too late to wonder. It was a road not taken. She will never know who . . . (she looks at the inside of her wrist) . . . Rebecca might have been if she had chosen some different option. She hopes that Rebecca would have wanted to be a Hero anyway.

In the eternal present moment of the Hero's world Rebecca waits, waits, waits for her assignment without anxiety or hope. On other faces she sees various expressions of emotions that fit a task; executives focused and intent on work, an artist dreaming as he stares into nowhere through the wall opposite him, girls bent to their schoolwork rising and falling in the perfectly timed bursts of concentration and relaxation that allow them maximum efficiency in their learning and their fun. They are like seals at play, bobbing in and out of the water. Their chat and laughter rises like bubbles thinks the Girl Hero, and she feels a twinge of envy, though she had her time and doesn't want it back.

A man in a dark suit as unmemorable as yesterday's news glides past and casually leaves his magazine on her table. She knows him for an Attaché, a man from the ministry who delivers duties to her kind, and that the magazine is a job offer in the eternal post-Mappa economy of the fight against the Cartomancers. She needs a job. She wants to move out of her mother's house.

On page fifty nine her secret message awaits her. It is typed on tissue paper and all the 'o's are offset, which means it is a mission of the most extreme danger and highest importance. How typical, she thinks, that these things should come together. She rubs some hand cream into her knuckles to hide the thick, dry callouses from years of smashing her fists into concrete walls.

The message instructs her to take a journey to Pointe Noire, in Congo. It is a place ridden with Cartoxins and the illegal breeding pens of the black market traders who design animals of exquisite savagery and intelligence for the use of the criminal underworld. Most of them will be re-mapped for various tasks and they will not know mercy, fear or any debilitating survival instinct. Once there she will go to a jungle compound and find a certain man and kill him. He is a bad man. She does not know his crimes but they are probably something to do with writing or disseminating rogue viruses and/or Maps because these are now the only crimes there are in the absence of what used to be known as Free Will. It is sure that if he were not so bad he would not be hiding out in such a place in the hopes that nobody would dare to follow. The vestiges of her sympathy for desperate men with missions for mankind are not stirred.

She folds the tissue paper and puts it in her handbag. She goes to the bathroom and has to queue. The bathroom is located in the Self Help section of the bookstore. The Girl Hero has no need for this. She is slightly mystified by the titles, and for the need of books in a world where everything can be eaten. She does not like to look at them. They seem to ask questions of her, and when her back is turned they whisper like schoolchildren.

As she is washing her hands the Girl Hero feels an unpleasant feeling. It is like something scattering inside. She imagines she is made from swarms of rats who have just noticed a terrible thing and are running, running, running for their lives. She often feels this. It is doubt. It comes along after a certain time period when she has had nothing heroic to do. She puts the lid on the toilet down and sits there, taking up someone else's pee time as she gets out a vanity mirror from her handbag and opens it up. One half of the clamshell is an ordinary mirror. The other half has its own face, a kind of pixie that looks exactly like the Girl Hero. It came with the job. She suspects it is a transmitter device that talks directly to her Mappaware to sort out glitches. If she were more dedicated to keeping her appearance groomed than she is, possibly it would deal with her doubts for her.

"Mirror, mirror," says the Girl Hero and need say no more.

"You want to go," says the mirror. "And you will." It always says this. The Girl Hero finds it very reassuring. She always asks. Her real question has not yet been answered and she doesn't bother to say it, but the mirror replies all the same, "He is not the one."

She closes the mirror and puts it away, satisfied that its prophecies are correct. Despite her bad feeling this encounter will not be the last. She will not die today. A Girl Hero always trusts her mirror.

The Girl Hero goes shopping for a tweed pencil skirt and knee high boots with heels. On her way to the airport she stops to text her mother that she will be home late, do not save any dinner, she will get some at the takeaway. Her mother is a Perky Waitress and will be satisfied with this latchkey message, not curious, not alarmed; she might bring home plastic boxes filled with peach pie and put them on the counter top for . . .Rebecca . . .to find when she comes in. Peach pie tastes of sweet, fulfilling safety and sleep. Two bites would be enough.

At the check-in desk she sees another Girl Hero, but one with a robot dog companion. She feels a sudden pang of envy and wants to introduce herself, to ask something that brims to her lips with urgent importance, though it can't make itself into words without a listener . . . but the other Hero is in a hurry. She runs off towards a departure gate with a flip of curly brown hair over the top of her practical backpack and grabs up her ammunition clips from the security guard without breaking stride. Her robot dog races beside her.

The Girl Hero . . . Rebecca . . . has no weapons to check. She deals only in kung fu. Her handbag is very small, just big enough for make up, the mirror and her phone. She looks up the price of robot dogs while she waits to board her flight. They are expensive. She thinks a real one would be better, but of course there is a problem with quarantine and the endless inoculations. She couldn't possibly afford one. Robots cannot catch diseases so they are immune to all but the most specific and local of memetic assaults. A robot is much better, but the Girl Hero imagines a warm body, soft fur, regular breathing in a real ribcage moving under her hands and brown eyes looking at her with unconditional love.

On the flight a man is seated beside her. He makes small talk about her job with the unconscious impulses of all businesspeople.

She tells him she is a secretary, which is true, when she is not being a Hero. He sells virtual real estate. He shows her one of the communities he administers; a condo by the sea, to let, all mod cons, barely the cost of a sandwich per month and unlimited online access. He is persuasive but Heroes are not easily sold. She declines. Her feet swell uncomfortably in the boots. She takes a limousine from the airport to her hotel, where she has a room already booked for her by the ministry.

Pointe Noire is a township with only a small centre adequately defended and habitable. Beyond the line of automatic fire lie teeming swarms of wildlife so bestial and savage, so tightly packed, that every moment of their existence is a matter of do or die. They are the testbed of Hellmemes and other horrors cooked up in the mobile Cartomancy sweatshops that creak and grind through the jungle; metal behemoths covered in solar panels and electrical deterrents.

Beyond the hotel perimeter fence it is still night but will soon be day. In that blue hour there is a slight lull in the slaughter and terror as sleepy creatures of dark trade places with waking creatures of light.

The Girl Hero hires a personal jetcar and lands a few miles from town, close to the house where He lives, this criminal, or whatever he is. Her little capsule glides down within his ranch home's Sphere of Influence—a forcefield of protection maintained by a mini reactor. There are no monsters inside, but two muddy fields of marsh grass and the foot-high remains of stripped trees lie between her and the buildings. She regrets the boots now.

Outside the house there are fences and inside the fences are real dogs, mastiffs with serial killer's eyes. The Girl Hero walks to the gate, pulling her boot heels free of the mud with every step, thinking the leather will be ruined. She does not feel like strangling a dog. Her inner world has become the grey blank place she associates with Heroism. It is familiar and strangely disappointing. She doesn't know what she was expecting from a life devoted to exacting justice and defending the world from evil, but this was not it. Beyond the forcefield at her back the dawn chorus of howls, screams, roars and whimpers greets the veteran sun.

There's a fence and a gate too. In the gatehouse there is a person. Where there is a person there is an easy way in.

The Girl Hero says she is selling virtual real estate. She shows the guard her mirror and, as he peers at this strange kind of identification, she knocks him unconscious. He crumples without a sound.

Close by two monsters in the forest clash foreheads in a dominance fight and the air is split by a crack like thunder. If the animals assaulted the shield they could get through it easily, but the shock of sudden pain has always prevented them from making this discovery. As they stumble about, stunned but undaunted by mortal combat, they avoid its gossamer shimmer at all costs. The Girl Hero shakes her head at them.

As she frisks pockets for codes, keys, cards or whatever the Girl Hero is overcome by a sense of deja vu. It is one of those nasty moments where, certain this is not a memory, because she has never been here before, she understands it is an omen. She hesitates and feels the man's still beating heart under her hand. Her hand forms the shape of a crane's bill and delivers a rapid, extreme strike. It does not break the bone but it doesn't have to. The shock is sufficient.

She could not have let him live of course. He would have woken up sooner or later and she does not know how long she has to be here. She feels mildly surprised at her action, and faintly sad that this is all she feels. Her finger stings her. She looks down and finds she has broken a nail. She spends a moment fixing it with her little kit of glue and tape, packed neatly into a thimble. She has the shakes however, and her mend does not hold. She tapes the thimble onto the end of her finger instead. It is made of gold and once was the barque of a fairy queen, or so she likes to imagine. The Girl Hero wonders if it will defeat the power of her strike, but she doesn't take it off.

The Girl Hero locates the keys to the inner house and gets into the armoured golf cart which takes her through the fence territory of the dogs. It has sealed sides. The dogs run and bark alongside the cart. The whine of the electric motor is inappropriately cheerful. Insects whirl and scream around in the light, involuntary and designed carriers of diseases to change the mind . . . they are indistinguishable from the real things. The sun crests over the forest's edge and a flight of red-winged insectivores takes to the air, flocking in the rising heat in a way that makes the air look syrupy. The Girl Hero takes out her mirror and adjusts her lipgloss. She thinks about what to order from the take away and decides she will have a Chinese.

At the end of the golfcart's route she is let into the house by machines who do not care that she is here to kill the master. Like so many of his kind he has run short of henchpersons whose instincts might favour him and now relies on mechanicals. Not popular, thinks the Girl Hero and frowns a tiny frown to go with her tiny pang of sorrow. On the polished wood of the hallway her boots make hollow sounds.

There is a cook, a person doing some menial tasks and a man who throws carcasses to the dogs. None of them are interested in stopping her when they see her coming, so the Girl Hero wearily locks them into the storeroom. She makes a note to herself on her mobile, so she does not forget to call help for them once she has left the scene. Lying on the kitchen counter is a plate of cream cakes, freshly defrosted, their chocolate iced tops coated in condensation sweat. She would like to eat them all. With the ease of a lifetime of denial, she barely registers the desire.

The bad man is in the living room, enjoying a glass of juice. His heavy frame is silhouetted against the rapacious sky as he looks out over a balcony towards the thin blue veil of the Sphere and beyond. Whatever he has loaded it would naturally include a lot of processors to bypass any fear he might feel at her arrival. She feels that this is possibly a meeting of equals, her legally enhanced mind against his self-made one. There is a kind of honour code to be observed.

The Girl Hero puts her handbag on the table. He turns around at the small sound. His eyes begin to measure the distance to the door but they falter half way. He has recognised her and that an attempt to escape will be futile. She watches him relax as resignation takes the place of fear in his look. Perhaps it is genuine, but no reaction could be taken at face value in the circumstances. They are already too far along the road of combat.

"Would you like a drink?" he asks. He is wearing some kind of Japanese robe and looks like he has led a full life, she thinks. His short legs are planted firmly. He has no intention of running. Perhaps he will not put up a fight. Her stomach rumbles and she feels a slight pain there. She shakes her head—no. She can't do anything distracting to her, even if she thinks it would be safe and for some reason she does feel safe now.

He is a long way across the room. She starts to walk.

"Do you know why you are here?"

She assumes he means does she know what he has done. She's not really interested. She shakes her head.

"Do you know why you are?"

The Girl Hero hesitates. He has deployed the Defence of Existential Crisis and she should ignore it boldly, defeat it with a witty and humorous line, but recently she hasn't thought of any of these. She only thinks of them later, long after the person who should have been rebuked is dead. It is her biggest weakness. She has read books of aphorisms but *A lot of knowledge fits an empty head* seems inappropriate and it is the only thing that comes to mind.

"I am a poet," he says.

It seems unlikely, she thinks. Why would anyone want to kill a poet? But, then again, why not? 'Was your verse offensive?" she asks. Why did she engage? The only sensible thing to do is to break his neck and leave. What is she talking for? She adds quickly. "It isn't important. You are on the list."

"Do you know your masters and their ideas, Girl?" he asks, backing away rapidly as she advances with a firm, librarian's tread. His voice gets a bit higher but it remains steady. "Do you know why you don't want to know?"

"It's not my place," she says and unaccountably finds she has stopped walking. She does know why. She has *chosen* not to know.

There are two sides to this war of memes: the side of the Directive, which advocates managed and secure social design for the safety and wellbeing of all, and the side of the Cartomancers, which wants anarchy at any cost, a free market without limits. Both of them have to contend with the Wild in which Mappaware and Mappacode has become attached to the genetic strands not only of their original carriers, the viruses, but also bacteria. There is no doubt it will soon spread (if it hasn't already) into the DNA of larger species. The Girl Hero never did get her head quite around the science or the politics of it. It's not a Hero's business to do all the thinking about the rights and wrongs. Her remit is much smaller. Justice for the wrongdoer and safety for the calm world of Perky Waitresses, Secretaries and peach pie. And whiskery skittery rats.

The Bad Man takes a nervous sip of juice. The scream and murder of the jungle increases as the full circle of the sun appears clear of the trees. What a dreadful place, thinks the Girl Hero. She realises she has reached a kind of stalemate but doesn't understand why she can't break it. She watches the Bad Man drink and set down his glass carefully on a coaster on a nice, smooth table.

"What's your name?"

She didn't expect this question even though an effort to become more intimate with an attacker who is more powerful is an obvious tactic. She opens her mouth, determined to answer, but nothing comes out. She looks to the inside of her wrist. She shouldn't tell him, so she keeps her mouth shut. Rebecca rings no bells for her. It could be a barcode for all it means. Her stomach starts to gnaw at her.

"I'm Khalid," he says and nods with a faint, social smile. He glances at her wrist and a moment of pity firms his lips.

A vicious streak of envy cuts across her mouth like the taste of lemon. Suddenly she wants the reassurance of the mirror, that tonight is not the night, but she left her bag on the table. It gets in the way and drags her arm when she has to punch.

"Wouldn't you like to understand what happened to you?"

"What is this, exam night?" She is determined not to be distracted by flimsy philosophising. She doesn't care about the answers to his tiresome enquiries but for some reason she thinks about the books, snickering behind her back. She wants to go home, get duck in plum sauce, get a shower, give her mother a cup of tea and go to bed. In the morning she has work again because it is still three days until the weekend. Besides, the answer to his question is surely obvious. She says it without knowing she's going to until she starts, "I caught a bad purge. That's all. No big. Look," she flashes her wrist at him.

"Everything in the world and the wild is written, Rebecca, just like your name," he says. He keeps a close watch on her, and she on him, in case he runs away, in case she doesn't.

Damn, she sees he has reached the wall. His free hand darts towards a control hidden there with the speed of desperation. He fumbles. She darts across the gap, jumps and kicks. Her skirt rips. Her boots are too tight. She knocks him aside but lands on her ass. Some kind of alarm is sounding like a bleating goat. Angry with herself she glares at him.

"The Sphere control," he says with satisfaction. "In a minute it will vanish and the wild will come in." His face is pasty under its smooth olive plumpness, but triumphant.

She sees clearly that a lot now stands between her and the evening she had planned. She looks out, to where her car is hidden, beyond the cleared land. One minute? 'But my mirror says you're not the one," she tells him firmly. Suddenly her belief in the mirror is wavering.

She looks into the eyes of the bad man. He looks back at her, without attempting to move. She says, "If you reset the device I will let you live." She tells herself she does not mean it. She hasn't made a mistake. She wouldn't betray the contract. A Hero would do what it takes to save the world.

"I think you will not," says the bad man, becoming amused.

"Don't just lie there," she says, lying there.

"Why not?" he asks. "I can see up your skirt from here. Nice underwear."

"I mean it," she says, meaning it to her own surprise. "I will let you live."

"Ah, thanks," he says, "but if it wasn't you, it would just be some other Girl Hero coming along in a day or two, and I've done my time. There's nothing left I want to do I haven't done and I'm not much for repeats. The Directive has no real defence against the Cartomancy and neither have a chance against the Wild, not in the end. The life of ideas is already a literal thing. We used to transmit them inadequately with words and soon they will transmit themselves through nature, through biology, in ways that bypass what small shred of choice may ever have existed. So, I think I'll just stay here, if it's all the same to you. It's a bit more satisfying if you die along with me than if you get to escape and I wish I was a bit different but I was free of the Map all my life and I have to bow to my taste for justice in my own way. I hope you can understand that."

"But I want to live!" the Girl Hero says.

"I don't think so," Khalid observes. His voice is mild. "I knew when you walked in and hesitated that you were the one."

The bleat alarm goes off. Without it the mindless fury beyond the Sphere seems twice as loud. The Girl Hero leaps to her feet and tries the device by the window. She cannot make it work. The blue tissue of force begins to fade. The blazing ruddy glare of beyond starts to colour it a deep purple. The Girl Hero thinks about the cakes on the counter, the innocent dogs, the people in the storeroom, her mother.

She glares down at him. "Why didn't they stop the Wild a long time ago?"

He shrugs. She sees that he does not know. "The day it was discovered there was a faster way to change people's minds than simply by talk or the gun, then it was already decided. If you were hoping for a final insight into human nature . . ." he trails off and looks distracted as the colour of the room changes from a soft shadowy umber to bright yellow. The Sphere has gone.

The Girl Hero makes a dive and slides the length of the table. She picks up her handbag and takes out her mirror. She no longer has the grey, flat feeling of Heroism and she wants to see if that has changed her face.

It has. The incipient wrinkles at the edges of her eyes and between her brows have gone. She is as smooth and pretty as she was the first day she took up office. On the other side of the mirror the pixie looks out towards the clear edge of the forest where it seems that a starving, boiling mass of vegetable and animal is slowly billowing towards them.

"Oh my," says the mirror. "Look out! He's getting away."

The Girl Hero feels a surge of desperation and anger quite unusual for her. She spins around and in just in time to catch sight of Khalid slithering through the narrow black gap of a secret doorway he has opened in the panelling. She is after him like a shot but her muddy feet slip a little and she can't grab hold of him as she intended. She makes it through the gap anyway and runs through the narrow, wooden corridor after him, her skirt seam ripping a bit more up the thigh with every furious stride. How could she fall for a distraction? How could she have entertained the idea that he was telling the truth about never having acquired the Map? Just look at this ridiculous compound with its guards and gates and dogs and cook. Listen to him give his Villainous Speech. She and he are both products of Stock Narrative 101, however many upgrades and individual variations they may have acquired . . .and now her rage is like hell itself.

The corridor winds and slopes down. Khalid skids and loses a shoe. The escape chute opens to a broad decking with an escape car tethered to it, its air-bladder fully primed with helium. The engines tick over, its rotor whir softly in the thick and humid air. Khalid is forced to pause, hand fighting his pocket for the key. The Girl Hero cocks her arm and throws the mirror in a dead flat spin. It strikes him on the back of the head and he falls to his knees. Around him the broken bright pieces scatter, fragments of sky.

"I want to see what's real!" she screamed. "Why did you have to be a liar?" She is crying. This is impossible. She needs the mirror, and rushes up to him. She tries to pick up the pieces but behind the glass all the circuitry is broken. There should be some word for what she feels when she looks at him, a word not like fuchsia or madder or carmine or rose or sugar or candy. It should be a word for rats turning and scuttling back with red eyes, teeth bared, tails like little ramrods. Maybe the word is Rebecca.

Khalid blinks at her with panic beginning to make him sweat. "What did you expect?" He had located the key.

The car door opens as a wave of warm air, full of thunder, ripples slowly across them. Rain starts to fall and there comes the screeching and shrilling of agony, the sputter of electrical things and burning fur as creatures test the weakening perimeter fence. Khalid snatches a mask from his pocket and wraps it across his face with his free hand as he scrabbles to his feet. He makes a lunge for the door. The Girl Hero watches him with the Rebecca feeling and jumps after. She makes the sill and he attempts to push her out backwards, but he's weak, a big soft geek type who's all brain and no brawn. She kicks him in the chest and slams the door after them.

"Take me with you," she says. "They'll send other Heroes. You need me."

He looks up from the floor and croaks. "I did okay so far . . ."

"You were dead when I walked in the door. And if you say no, you still are," the Girl Hero assures him, picking him up by the shirtfront and hauling him to the passenger seat of the little craft. "Shit," she says, safe, for now. "What about your people? Can't leave them . . ."

"Have to leave them," he gasps, still winded. "No time."

No Hero would ever leave them.

Khalid slams a hand to the controls and the car begins to lift off. "Anyway, why should you care? Killed enough for a lifetime . . ."

She opens her mouth to protest but the breath she took doesn't go anywhere, just leaves her inflated. As she delays the aircar rises smoothly into the sky above the treetops. From the windshield she can see the dogs running back and forth in their prison, barking.

"You should let them out," she said, sitting down slowly in the pilot's seat. "It's cruel to keep dogs that way." They fly for a time in silence, avoiding the Directive Patrols but with no other plan.

"Can you ever get rid of it?" Rebecca asks in a quiet voice. "Mappaware? Ever?"

"You can tell it not to work," Khalid says. "That's all." He hands over a small black box shaped like a cigarette pack with a single button on it. "We use them a lot. When you get too much infestation you go unstable. This clears it. Then you start again."

Rebecca remembers him fumbling in his pockets. Zap. Not the door. Her. "You got me."

Khalid nodded. "And me. Works in a range."

Rebecca presses the button, over and over. Nothing happens. "Now what? Why aren't I different then?"

"That takes time," he says, sighing wearily. "Lots of time. Have to grow, think, do things . . .take more code or not . . .left alone you'll change on your own."

"Like in the old days," she puts the box into her own pocket, which is almost too small. She wishes she had not forgotten her bag. For a moment she thinks about Chinese food and her home, all the stuffed animals in a row, her mother's scent . . . "Where to?"

Khalid shrugs. "I wait until I pick up a beacon. Most likely spot is still over the Congo area somewhere. Just follow the river."

"And then?"

"Set down, make new friends in the Cartomancy, carry on . . . Write something, test it, purge it. Try to figure out how to create antimemes against the worst plagues . . . not much."

Rebecca nods. It's not much, but it is enough.

THE GIRL HERO'S MIRROR SAYS
HE'S NOT THE ONE

I like this story because it has a feeling of completeness to it. Having said that, I am now working on a longer exploration of the ideas in it, because they seem timely.

THE BULL LEAPERS

THE BULL LEAPERS

I was asked to write this to go with some pictures that Storm Constantine already had in hand—beautiful drawings of Ancient Greek figures. The images made me think of Greek lessons at school, where I was often puzzled into stupidity by grammar and declensions and would spend time daydreaming about the stories and ideas in the textbooks instead. I have spent a lot of my life daydreaming, a highly underrated pastime. Unfortunately it doesn't lead to achievements, as my school record testifies.

THE BULL LEAPERS

We arrived in the outskirts of Knossos late in the day after an exhausting journey from England. My husband George immediately abandoned the cases to the care of the staff, who spoke no English, and to me, who spoke no Greek, and set to making his plans for a rendezvous with Sir Arthur Evans the following morning. For the first time since we were married I felt myself cross with him but put it down to tiredness and managed, by dint of much gesturing and smiling, to get all the trunks and boxes up to our room.

It is always difficult to deny the passions of someone you love. George's passion was the ancient world and he had harboured no greater ambition than to work with the great Sir Arthur after we had heard about the discovery of the palace of King Minos, complete with labyrinth. I am sure George was thinking of more than pottery shards and dust brushes when he agreed to set out as a novice hand under the aegis of the Archaeological Society, but since the day this trip was confirmed our house has rung to the sound of those old Cretan names until every corner whispers with their dead echoes. I was almost glad to be away from there until I arrived in Crete. Now I know I am. It is a lovely place and from the first moment I set foot on it with the sun shining red over the ocean, I knew it and I were to be on friendly terms.

We ate our first dinner sitting outside under a magnificent bay laurel, the stars just visible through its branches. George ordered a bottle of wine and I relaxed. It was good to see him so animated and happy after the months of frustrating wait. His smooth face was focused in the candlelight, hair blown across his forehead by the warm night wind. He looked his age then, far younger than I if age is calibrated by the gaze-strength of a society matron. In reality we are some ten years apart, met and married within a year at the end of the great war in which my former husband was killed and the spectre of which George carries with him like a scabrous family pocket watch. I suppose it was what we had most in common, the war, that and the need for someone to be there. Oh yes, when we reached Crete I was thinking fondly enough of him, but it had not escaped me that in the years that have passed between there has been little of anything but kindness and the respectful meek distance of two independent species of grief. My sister I know had high hopes of something magical happening in this magical land. She was fond of saying, "But, Elizabeth, you are such a *passionate* woman," meaning I was wasting my time on someone as cool as George is, "you ought to get about more," meaning she didn't think it likely that George was a particularly appealing lover. She means well but as I watch him in this gentling light I think that she is wrong. I am sure there is kindling to be ignited inside him for more than old stones and stories, if only the right kind of spark can be found. Lord knows, I haven't got it on my own.

We spent a pleasant, companionable night and in the morning I waved him away from the balcony which overlooks the square. He and his local guide set out with stout shoes and sticks to walk across the city to the palace site, leaving me to spend the day as I would.

I decided to let myself recover and acclimatise and had a little chair and table brought out into the square where other guests like to sit and watch the world go by. I had my book and some notepaper but was looking for anything to divert me. I haven't much appetite for reading. Not long after I had sat down the other guests, a couple, decided to go walking too and invited me to go with them. We set out on a little round trip easily enough but soon my shoes were pinching me, feet swollen with the heat and I told them to go on ahead whilst I rested in a little garden by the side of the road. I was there only a few minutes when I saw two young men walking towards me through the olive trees. They were dressed in a very classical style, which I didn't know what to make of—traditional dress or affectation? It was hard to know. They came towards me with a steady pace and smiled. They were obviously brothers, both young and tall and tanned and quite lovely with long curling black manes that my London lady friends would have gladly scalped them for. I thought they were going to pass me by but instead they drifted across and gave polite bows or nods. I smiled.

"It has taken you a long time to get here," the one said who had the easier smile. His English was accented and I didn't know if he was stating a fact or asking a question. My astonishment must have shown because he laughed a little and his more sombre brother deigned to smile.

"Yes," I said, playing it safe and held out my hand with a boldness that surprised me, "I'm Elizabeth Stowe."

The friendlier one bent closer and we shook solemnly, "A pleasure to make your acquaintance," he said with care. "We are honoured. You will walk with us?"

I took a more careful inventory of them—both were wearing daggers with highly decorated handles and in the absence of much clothing a fair set of golden jewellery at which I longed to have a closer look. Their sleek health and their finery, including a great set of peacock feathers in the aloof one's hat, spoke of an important family or certainly great riches. I found myself thinking about Midas, but that was me getting the wrong King. It never even occurred to me that they might pose any danger. "I thought I would just go back to the hotel," I said, "I haven't been here long. The sun is terribly tiring."

"I will walk you back there," the smiler announced, straightening up with the finality of his decision. "Then my brother will arrange some entertainment . . ."

Oh *ho*, I thought, what's this?

" . . . for the evening. We will bring the bull, here to the little arena," and he pointed to a small sandy circle flanked by some stone seating and a barrier. "You will like it, Mrs Stowe, I promise you."

So I was walked home by one of these beautiful athletes who answered my trivial questions with quiet eloquence. By the time we stood under the bay tree's shade I was thoroughly charmed by him. His dark eyes were huge and liquid, cow-like in the dappled light.

"What time will you be there?" I asked him, "I'm sure my husband, George, would like to see it."

"It will be before sunset, the hour before," he said and then added after a careful pause in which I could not tell what he was thinking, "Mr Stowe may not get here in time. But you will come?"

He was too compelling to resist. I assented.

As soon as he had gone I began to feel a little foolish and when I ordered a lemonade asked the housekeeper if she knew anything about them. Haltingly she said, "They jump . . . bull. Over the back. Over . . ." and she put her hands to the sides of her head, fingers pointing out like horns, "Jump over. You like it maybe, maybe not," and she gave me a sideways glance when she thought I wasn't looking, quick and expertly assessive, judging something about me and nodding to herself, smiling back at me without a hint of unkindness so that I was thoroughly discomforted. I spent the rest of the morning crossly reading a little pamphlet about Knossos and wishing George and the mine of information he carried in his head would come back and tell me what was going on.

After lunch I took a nap and woke out of some heated dream to find it already late afternoon outside, the little houses shining white against their long shadows. Taking some money with me in a purse and arming myself with more solid shoes, a dowdy old shawl and a large hat I went down and informed the mistress of the hotel where I was going. She gave me the same intimately female smile as the housekeeper and assured me that she would convey my note to my husband the very second he walked through the door. I didn't look back but it wouldn't have surprised me if she had tossed it in the wastebasket the moment I left. To my further alarm I found that I didn't particularly care if she did. It was a distressing state of affairs, or it ought to have been, but my mood as I walked down the tracks towards the garden was one of peace and a great calm, the kind that you only think comes after some massive storm or laying-waste or when an immense burden has finally been put down. I wondered what it was that I had lost and tried to conjure fond thoughts of George which were constantly washed away by the strange beauty of the Cretan landscape; its boulders and bare earth and tussocky grass and the strange shapes of the olive, bay and cedar.

I arrived at the arena alone and took a seat away from the barrier. After a few minutes I thought I had been mistaken about the time but then they materialised out of the long shadows between the trees—the young men, a white bull and a small girl dressed in similarly old fashioned attire, her long hair bound up in plaits around her head.

They shut themselves with the bull in the arena and nodded and waved to me, apparently expecting no other audience. On the distant hillsides I could see animals and people on the farms as normal so I was not bothered that I was the only spectator. The girl took out a switch from her belt and together she and the brothers, even the haughty one, began to tease the bull out of his complacency with touches and taps and small flicks of the switch. Soon it was making little rushes towards them, snorting and shaking its head, more with annoyance than real intent, I thought. It seemed used to the proceedings and wishing they were over but was too slow to remember this fact and eventually gave in and played the game.

The brothers danced around the animal, twin streaks of gold darting around the great white cloudy shape of the bull sharpening his attention so that the girl, light as a little cat, could jump and spring off the broad back with her hands. The first time she did it I could help but take a sharp breath and smile in delight but then she came around the front, swaggering a little with pride as she saw I was pleased, her narrow, strong limbs easy and shining in the heat. As I watched her move I was ashamed of myself for the sharp jealousy that came out of the blue and tried to wither my heart. It is always a shock to be jolted into remembering you are not what you once were. It also becomes easier to let the brief pain go and I let it go, it was after all only the dying spasm of a young and silly vanity.

The girl sauntered up to the bull and tickled his whiskers as he tried to cross his eyes, watching the antics of the brothers who took the opportunity to jump over his back, rapping him smartly on each flank. He shook himself all over, very cross and charged the girl who simply took off like a kite, planted her hands on the lumpy fat behind his neck and sprang to the ground behind him to swing on his tail. They continued their play and by the time they were done I found I had been laughing and smiling with pleasure at their daring and skill. They and I were well satisfied and we all clapped. Then the girl took the bull by his nose ring and led him off. After a long look at me the reserved brother followed. His sibling leant against the barrier, puffing gently, and looked at me. "Good entertainment for you. I see you like it," he said.

"Very much," I agreed, wondering if he were expecting money or was building up to something else. He simply watched me as he caught his breath and wiped a sheen of sweat from his forehead and neck, flicking it away from him and drying his hands on the short white tunic he was wearing. I thought that perhaps they did things differently here and this was his way of inviting me to go off with him. He had that kind of expression in his face, I am sure, as he looked me up and down and this in spite of my dreadful shawl and the hat covering my best feature—my hair. I didn't entertain this fantasy long, wonderful as it was, because of another twinge of that old, old wound. Instead I reminded myself that George would be back and wondering where I was. Thoughts of him brought a snippet to mind, "It's where the story of the minotaur came from, isn't it?" I asked him as I stood up and made to be going, "The jumping of the bull. A long long time ago."

"You know the labyrinth," he said, again in that same tone that might have been question or answer. I stopped in my tracks.

"Pardon?"

"The labyrinth," he repeated, "it is here."

I looked around in confusion, "I thought it was at Minos' palace."

"No," he said, shaking his head in the twilight, "the mystery. The labyrinth. It is everywhere."

I was listening to him as hard as I have ever listened, as hard as I used to listen for the knock at the door telling me my husband had been found alive after all. In the soft gloom of the coming night he seemed to be speaking from another world, in which there were more possibilities than this one, and more time. He sketched out an invisible view with his hands, "The labyrinth," he repeated, "I can see it," and I knew he was talking about something esoteric. His voice and figure were charged with a subtle force, its harshness deflected by his manner which was gentle. He put his hand out and took hold of mine in a soft, reassuring touch, "You are in it, Mrs Stowe."

I snatched my hand back and felt myself grip my stick, but not out of fear, out of surprise and embarrassment, as if he had seen me undressed. There was a truth in what he said although I was hard put to know myself just what it was. Once I had seen this I was seized with a compulsion to unmask it. I felt that I knew what my earlier peace was about, that I had begun on some pathway which was taking me out of my old life with its quiet acceptance and its pain and offering me the chance of something new. I hated myself for the indecent speed with which I wished to seize that chance but it was on me like a tiger before I had the chance to think better of it. I was suddenly hungry and restless.

He was nodding as he watched me, approving of me and my wallowing realisation.

"Who are you?" I demanded, glancing towards the home track. I thought I could see a light coming down the path.

"We are the sons of Pasiphae," he said, "brothers of the minotaur . . ." his words were drowned by a hailing shout from up the hill—

"Elizabeth . . . Lizzy, where are you? It's dinner time!" My husband, sounding almost enthusiastic about me, for once and I was angry with him for taking the moment but when I looked back to the arena my companion had vanished completely. There was no trace of him in the shadows or the dark under the olives, just the soft dark, scented with bay. I turned and set off to climb towards the lantern.

George was talkative over dinner so it was late before I had my chance to tell him about my day and the bull leapers. He was so flabbergasted that for a few moments he couldn't speak, just opened and shut his mouth and smiled and shook his head. "Well, this is fantastic, Lizzy," he said finally, "I'm so jealous I can hardly speak. I asked that damned guide this morning if there were any people who still did that kind of thing and he was adamant that it was long outdated and then you go and get invited to a showing all on your own. I suppose it serves me right for ignoring you to go digging."

"Absolutely," I replied and we bantered on and on about it until it was late. The mood was so convivial that when we got to bed I immediately stretched out towards him.

He kissed my hands and put them gently away, "I'm so tired," he said. "Not tonight, darling. I have to be up early tomorrow."

And so it went on for almost a week. George left early to go to the site and Arthur's beneficent patronage and I puttered around at the hotel, playing a few hands of bridge when there were enough guests inclined and reading endless dull novels of Victorian life which were all I had thought to pack when leaving England. Each day however I saw one or other of the brothers in the square, loitering in an expectant way but not signalling, or else about some little task such as carrying water from the well. None of the other foreign guests seemed to notice them, but the maids saw them, I could tell by the quick tilts of their heads and the sudden smile in the lines around their eyes. Then they would glance at me. It was mortifying and exhilarating at once. I did think of asking them about it in one of my madder moments but then it was so obvious, the symbolism of the bull, their vibrant masculine presence. To have mentioned it aloud would be the height of crassness. But I wished for some explanation.

At last, late in the sixth day, they came upon me struggling through another chapter underneath the bay tree. It was a mediocre book and I had had two glasses of the local wine and was more asleep than reading. George, as usual, was late.

I looked up from the sentence I had read five times already and saw the pair of them, attentively standing as if they had come to pay a social call whilst their twin sets of black eyes sent out waves of voluptuous dark towards me. It was a call that needed no voice. I put the book down, marking the place, left my shawl behind and followed them out of the square and through the narrow roads towards the palace of Minos on the far side of the city.

Constantly I expected to encounter George and his party but we saw almost no one and those people who crossed our paths were shadowy. I could hardly make out their faces and they never looked towards us as we continued, unlit and silent beneath a full moon. I thought of the legend as I walked knowing nothing of where I was going and asked them suddenly, "Are you the sons of Minos, then, if you are the sons of Pasiphae?"

"We are of Pasiphae," the haughty one said—the first time he had spoken to me, "and the bull."

"Where are we going?" I asked, since they seemed ready to talk.

"To the Bull of Minos," he said and reached back to take my hand. I was finding the walking difficult going now, tired and a little drunk. I took a hand on each side and it became much easier except for the heat of their bodies and the strong smell of each of them composed of sweat and salt and a musty odour. It was almost unpleasant at first, coming as it did to my insipid English nose which was used to nothing more powerful than the occasional pile of horse dung, but it grew on me. I found myself swinging along with a carefree lope. Their hair tickled my shoulders where they were left bare by the sleeveless dress. In the dark I imagined myself young again, the first Elizabeth, before men, when I dreamed of the future.

"And where are we now?" I said.

"In the labyrinth," came the reply. I lost track of time. There was only the walking, the heady air, the bright moonlight and the sliding planes of the city moving past us in vaporous procession. When they stopped their hands tugged me to a halt.

I saw that we were at the palace, recognising its thick pillars and heavy, smashed lintels from pictures that George obsessed over. The markings and posts of the dig were clearly visible to the right but they were deserted. Only a lone donkey wandered around on a short tether and messed with a small pile of hay. Behind us Knossos was sparkling with tiny lights and I could hear music.

"Will you go?" one of them said, which one I couldn't tell now. This time he was asking a question. Between the pillars of the doorway the dark there seemed to pulse like the skin of a drum. I could feel its vibrations in my bones and skin, but heard nothing. I didn't want them to let go of my hands. Through the doorway lay an unknown thing, but not an unimagined one. I thought I knew what it offered and what it might mean to me, but I did not know what it would change me into should I take it. There was the decision and the risk. I could walk to the hotel now and life would go on just as before. It was not a bad life but I knew it from top to toe well enough that it was as invisible and intangible as a wedding ring, worn for so long that you neither notice nor feel it any more.

"I will," I said and felt my shoulders drop, my belly relax, my feet settle down properly to carry my weight over the ground. I hadn't known I was so tense.

"We will guide you," they both said, and one continued, "and we will stay with you through the night. You will not leave until dawn and you will not be able to touch this earth or speak under this sky until then."

"I understand," I said. I was so light I could not feel myself walking, almost pulling them along I was so full of anticipation now that the decision was done. It felt mad. I tried to remember who I was, my family, my home, but that was as nothing under the bewitchment of these two brothers and the shimmering sound and breeze of the Cretan night.

We passed under the broken mass of the lintel and into the impenetrable darkness within the palace ruin. Elizabeth Stowe, Elizabeth Bartholomew, Elizabeth Eckerley all passed into plain Elizabeth no one, unstamped Elizabeth, but she did not fade. I expected to be stripped of everything. Instead I was more sure of who I was than I had ever been. It was peaceful, walking those unseen corridors, feeling without understanding how the walls were narrowing, closing in as we took turn and turn again walking down passages unlit from the beginning of time, the air fading, changing, becoming heavier and more stale with the smell of the brothers and an even more powerful and clinging musk.

I thought many things on that inward journey; I remembered my girlhood and my mother, my father with his dogs and guns. I remembered Ashton, my first husband and what a riot we had had before the war. I remembered my friends at home with a love felt honestly now it was not circumnavigated by propriety and I remembered dear George with warmth and well-wishing. I hoped that when I returned I could bring something of this to him, whatever it was.

We came into a large space very suddenly. The change of the sounds must have signalled it to me but as one the three of us stopped. Underfoot a soft earthy texture deepened, like dry ground pulverised by the passage of thousands of head of cattle. It killed all noise of our feet. The smell here was palpable and the air warm and moist. It wrapped me in a thick velvet of distilled masculinity so that it was as if my nose could read smell, every taint a distinct aspect of male character and makeup. The dark was also inhabited.

On either side of me the muted presence of the brothers faded. Their hands slipped from mine and they vanished. At some distance I could hear breathing. It was not a human sound but a ponderous snorting breath with a lot of liquid in it, very slow; the breath of a heavy beast. Footfalls thumped through the damped earth and the air shifted against me as something butted through it and forced it to move on.

I could see nothing. I heard the bull-man approach and felt his smoky, misty breath as he sniffed me over, his head moving around me generally, accompanied by the thuds of his two feet. One or twice his whiskers brushed me but that was all. He snorted a few times and paced off to one side, making a low noise in his throat. I recalled with alarming suddenness the detail of the story George had recited in our drawing room—the Minotaur was fed on young women and men from Athens, sent in placation when the Minoan Empire was at its height. There was a powerful reek of dung that did not smell entirely of cattle.

Then the bull returned and breathed a different kind of breath over my face. It was dense and full of strange floral scents as well as the reek of musth and something vaguely fetid. It was heavy and within two of my own breaths, unable to avoid it, I was feeling sleepy. I thought I felt the cautious hands of the brothers lowering me gently down to the earth and then I was falling down into the soft ground in a new darkness, held in silent, still warm darkness. My body seemed to be all one surface and through my skin I could feel the shimmer as if I was contained inside a larger body whose powerful heart beat made the blood vibrate around me. I wondered if I dreamed of my mother, but this dark had a male smell. I rested in the body of the bull.

As I floated there I felt absolute calm. I knew that I had come into a place where I was protected by a powerful guardian. Through the slow visions that followed I was always aware of his presence, picking out the dream for me, showing me something of myself and the men I had loved.

My father. A man who loved to sit in his study, reading books or else hunt and walk tirelessly with his dogs. He preferred dogs to people, a lot of that type of men do. Women in particular he treated like a different species, far further removed than canine and he had always looked at me with amazement, stunned that I was his daughter, that he could ever have given rise to such an inexplicable entity. I had longed for him to love me as I had loved him. Now I saw myself, a little girl, through his eyes as he looked down at me. I had a pipe jammed firmly between my teeth and the taste of the tobacco was bitter and awful, its scent sweeter. The little girl was smiling—had I ever been that young? She was holding out a card she had made and it was an awful card, I could see that, covered with glue that was still wet. I was repulsed by it as an object, confused that she thought it was a worthy present for me but also terribly, painfully touched with an intensity that made me almost pathologically afraid. She terrified me because of the power of the emotions that even this pathetic gesture of hers could make rise in me. Fifty times more powerful than the effect her mother had which I wanted and also feared, feared to even examine enough to know what it was. I could not stand the contrast—my life of evenness pierced like this without mercy, warning and with no defences able to stand against it. It hurt in my chest with a fierce pain so much I thought I might be having a heart attack. I had to go back into my study and shut the door just to make it stop.

The vision faded. I expected to be consumed by sadness but within the bull-man all emotion was gentled, rollered, measured. I understood my father without grief and marvelled that there was no pain. I could see without suffering . . .

I saw Ashton and myself getting married. I witnessed first hand how he adored me, the depth of his passion like the ocean, lust and admiration, wonder and a ferocious need to possess all tangled up together in a gordian knot inside him. We had a spectacular few months before the war. I was grateful to find that this vision had little of newness in it. I knew him well, then and now.

The third view I expected to display George and some terrible revelation but instead I saw the brothers. They were with me in a dark place, cold and filled with wet and mud. I was trying to load some kind of gun but my fingers were slippery and I kept dropping the bullets and losing them. The sound of gunfire and cannon was incredibly loud and seemed to be coming from all directions. The brothers were everywhere; I saw their faces lying with the bodies piled next to me, watched them brave the top of the world and vanish into the freezing, smoke filled blackness alongside other soldiers. There was screaming. I fumbled for my bullets in the mud but could feel nothing, my hands were so cold. There was a thud.

When I came to I found myself lying under my friend, Roger MacCorder. He was dead and the blood from the wound he had taken had soaked through his heavy woollen coat and was dripping into my mouth. I struggled and wrestled but somehow we were tangled together. I cried out but there was no one to come. I had to wait until the morning and in the night I had to press my face up into the icy bulk of him to protect my face from the rats.

All the time this happened I felt nothing. I was not afraid or sickened. I was like an automaton. This remained until long after I returned home and married. I copied the expressions of those around me to show affection. Without there being a definite decision I did not want to go back to the way I was before. It was better this way. The idea of having any kind of a real feeling filled me with a nauseous dread until that in itself became too much of an emotion and I switched it off. Those feelings, stored up for so long, must have festered into a poison I would not be able to control. I didn't think this in words, but I was aware of it. I pitied my wife. I should not have married her. She deserved a whole man. Probably she would leave me. At least that would free me of the danger.

The last dream faded away very slowly. I listened to the blood in my ears and upon my skin. The bull breathed for both of us until the morning when he let me up out of the earth and the brothers led me to the palace gate and home through the cool, fresh day.

When I arrived at the hotel there was a huge rumpus as George was called and the housekeeper fussed about, exclaiming at my absence and the state of my dress which was covered all over in soft dusty earth, as was my skin and hair.

George came down the stairs with wild eyes, running. I could see he had slept in his clothes, "Elizabeth! Where on earth have you been? I've been out all night . . ." He was staring at me as if I were a zombie.

I held my hands out to him, still full of the calm and the kindness that I had been so lucky to have since that first evening, "Oh George," I said, "how terrible about poor Roger. Why didn't you tell me?"

He looked at me as if I had shot him for a split second. "How do you know about that?" His face was greyish white. I thought he might fall over but instead he came forward and took hold of my hands. "Never mind," he said and suddenly threw his arms around me. "Don't leave me again," he insisted, hugging me so close I could hardly breathe.

After everyone had been satisfied that Madame was all right and I had changed my clothes and washed we ate breakfast on our balcony. George, usually so full of chat about his plans, maintained a softly textured silence, not even using his saucer so he could avoid making sharp noise. He stared out at the sun rising into another blue and blameless sky.

"I wish I were you," he said. "You've seen something I've always wanted to see. I talk about these stories. I know everything about them, or I thought I did. I thought you were just listening to be polite. But you saw through it, to what it was really all about. Just like you can see through me," he cast a shy glance at me.

"Don't look at me like that, as if I were a stranger," I said, leaning across the table to offer him my hand. He placed his over my palm cautiously but eagerly.

"You give me so much hope, Elizabeth," he said, finding it hard but talking through the fear that made him want to stop. "I think . . . with you I might not be too afraid. I could . . . if you can wait . . . You know, you look so different today. I feel I can talk to you and you will understand every word." He searched my face anxiously.

I got up, walked around the table and sat myself on his lap, my arms around his neck. He looked pleased and awed, so much so that I wanted to laugh, "George, don't look at me as if I were one of your goddesses, I'm just an older woman who happens to be your wife. And I do understand you and we have all the time that you need." We held one another and there was no distance between us. It was new and made us both a bit shy. After a little while, feeling impish, I said, "Haven't you got to get off to Sir Arthur?"

"Oh him . . ." he looked troubled for a moment, back to old George, lines appearing in his face that made him age twenty years in seconds. He took a deep breath and held it. I heard it creaking inside him, toiling about, trying to escape. "Paahhh . . ." he sighed, relaxing. "I thought we might go for a walk instead? Perhaps we could go and look for your bull leapers, d'you think?"

"Yes," I said, "I think so."

THE BULL LEAPERS

I'm surprised I tried to make this historical as I've never had interest in historical pieces but for some reason I had it in mind that it was people from an older and more repressed era of British history who would emphasise this spiritual encounter with the Masculine Principle. Obviously, now I reflect more on it years later, that notion seems absurd. The culture may have moved along a bit, but I wouldn't call it enlightened yet.

DEADHEAD

DEADHEAD

I really wish I hadn't given it this title, because people have said that it seems to suggest I am saying that people with Asperger's are un-people. Since the people I know with that diagnosis are some of the sweetest people in existence I have to say that it absolutely wasn't my intention.

DEADHEAD

"Where the hell has she got to?" My mother, one hand hovering in a birdy flutter at her neckline, the other restlessly flexing around an imaginary gin glass, stared out of the picture window across the garden.

I gave a shrug she couldn't see. I was sick of being Clem's nursemaid.

Clem was six years older than I was but it had always been, "Clem ain't all there in the head, baby, so you're the eldest, okay? You have to look out for her.' Lately I had been ignoring my duty, less thrilled about it at fourteen than I had been at ten. Older, difficult, weirdo Clem always got in the way of me having any time to myself. She had a thing called Asperger's Syndrome. There is no cure. She'll be like that all her life. That means if Mom dies I'll be stuck with her. Or if she doesn't, Mom's stuck with her. I've often wished Clem dead. It makes me feel terrible, but it's her or us. It really is.

For the last three days she had come in at her regular hour of five, the front of her T-shirt and pants damp, her fingernails dirty. Until she was seven Clem's favourite game was to model castles in a mixture of her own and the dog's faeces so I hadn't been exactly keen to find out what she was doing. When Mom asked if I knew where she was, I grunted a sound like assent but I hadn't a clue. I followed my mother's eyes to the clock.

"Look, it's nearly three. The care worker will be here any minute. What kind of a mother am I going to look like? You're supposed to be with her. Goddammit." She wheeled around, her stormy eyes shooting lightning at me, "Go and find her."

I stayed just long enough to let her know I didn't want to go.

It was hot, late in the afternoon and the sun was bright. I checked the street. Some hope. She never went out there anyway. She didn't like meeting strange people—which means anybody. I stood on the lawn and checked the garden bushes with a sinking feeling. I was about to go in when I saw several long wheat-coloured strands caught in the hedge, where there was a gap in the thorn. I glanced back to the house and saw Mom on the porch, watching intently. She made a sharp little waving motion that meant 'get on with it'.

I pushed through the narrow hole wondering, as I snagged the laces of my sneakers, how on earth Clem had got her long legs through it. Beyond, in the fallow field, a number of makeshift paths crossed the grass and met up to go through the farmland which backed onto our street. Clem likes patterns and order to the exclusion of all else so I knew she'd follow them.

Unified, the way led along the edges of a series of cornfields. The tassels on the top of the cobs were long and yellowy green, just starting to crisp at the ends and go brown. I smashed at a few flies as I went along, stamping, hot, irritated by the constant drone of crickets. It seemed to go for miles and on every plant there was Clem's hair. Pathetic, that's what it was. I learned the word a few weeks before in a poetry class. The pathetic fallacy. Nature in tune with human lives, going along with human meanings. Clem might as well have been found in a field, might really be a child of the corn for all she has in common with me. If she was a veg, like they said at school, then that would have explained a lot. But it's not that. She's tuned in to some other life altogether; one which tells her that right and wrong is about colour and sound and that texture and pattern and shapes are language. She makes me a card every birthday with coloured paper cutouts shaped the same, glued the same, but made new. Two blue rectangles, a sliver of yellow, a red lozenge. It means something in the language of Clem.

Looking down I saw the print of her high tops in the dust, regular as clockwork like the way she walked; a tin soldier, one foot, then the other, slam, slam, heels hard into the ground, the same on every surface. Boys admire her if they don't know her. She's Barbie; all long legs and blond hair and the same, identikit blank face, rigid arm outstretched for a handshake, elbowless, expression unchanging as the words machine-gun out of her mouth in a high volume mono, eyes glassy, "hello my name's clem nice to meet you how are you have a nice day." Then she bares her teeth.

After a while I started to worry. I'd covered about half a mile and could see that ahead the path split in two. One side followed corn, the other became a line in hay grass. I had to search them both for ages before I found another footprint in the loose gravel. For the first time I noticed how far away our house was. It looked like a blue and white block the size of a postcard, lodged just inside the horizon line of a green curve, a yellow curve and a blue ground. I turned and hurried on.

In the shelter of the high corn stalks there was no breeze and the heat was oppressive. Then, gradually, as the path narrowed, I became aware of a weird smell, like a tepid dungeon or the root cellar of our old house after a spring flooding. Coming over the brow of a hill I looked down into a gully just to the side of the path. At the bottom of a steep bank a stream ran shrunken and stagnant. I saw her. She was crouched by the water, a long stick in her hands, using it to splash. A welcome, sickly feeling of relief came over me: a mix of self-righteous anger at me finding her and her witless straying, and gladness that Mom would be mad with her when she saw how mucky she was getting herself so it was all right for me to be angry too. I began to hurry down towards her.

Then, as I watched her, glancing between her and the weed-choked, rocky descent, I became aware that her splashing had a purpose. It was such a rare thing in her that I stopped and crouched down behind a clump of nettles. She was so intent on what she was doing she hadn't even heard me, although she might have done and not cared—she can focus like a laser.

The gully was in dappled shade from overhanging trees on the other side and it took my eyes a while to adjust. I slipped and slid closer, following the path she had crushed in the weeds. Then I saw it.

In the greenish, slow moving water, submerged a few inches below the surface, was the severed head of a horse. Once white or grey its muzzle and forehead were livid green with new algal growth. It turned idly in the shallows under her stick and nosed in towards her hands as she reached for it.

I shuddered violently and a whole slew of thoughts ran through me to the ground where they earthed out in silence. I was suddenly reminded of Clem before Dad lost his job and we moved to the suburbs. In the country there had been a lot of horses on the farm where he had worked as a hand. Clem had spent most of her time over there when she could, sometimes on her own with the rancher, sometimes with me and Dad. She used to move among the horses with comfort and confidence. It was obvious just to watch her that she understood them in just the same way she didn't understand human beings. Their movements and sounds spoke to her. She knew what they meant by making a particular shape with their necks, by the number of tosses of their noses after a drink. Sometimes you could look into the dark of a barn where she was and see only horses.

The head was old and rotten. I could see the slime coating the pale fur in thick, streaming wads, the dark emptiness where its eyes had been now slackly framed by wrinkled skin. When she finally snagged it and lifted it out with her hands water poured from its nostrils in two cloudy streams. It was heavy and unwieldy. It made her stagger and she sat backwards hard with it, clutching it to her. As I watched she righted herself and put her arms around it. She took hold of one of its ears and pressed her cheek against its cool, green forehead, hugging it to her and holding it, cradling it and squeezing it until she had it tight, as the filthy water trickled from its eye sockets and slack, rubbery lips and soaked into her jeans. She rocked and smiled. On her face was an absolute calm, a kind of blissed out stillness. It was such a sharp contrast to the way I was used to seeing her. It was the face Mom always wished she could make Clem wear—the shape of features that said Clem was all right with us, that she recognised us. My anger got snarled up with guilt. I felt sorry for her for only feeling that way about a dead, rotting thing. Sorry for us. Tears prickled in my nose.

I dare not move in case I interrupted her. Slowly, a chill, brackish smell rose up the bank. Clem remained bent over her treasure, her hair falling down the clean cut line of its neck, over the grey stringy muscle and wormed tubes like a new mane. She stayed like that for almost forty minutes, without moving, as the sun cut through the trees and the crickets droned their endless phone tone—no caller on the end of the wire.

When she straightened up she startled me. Watching her and listening I'd gotten drowsy with the heat and the intense smell of crushed nettle. Suddenly it was like watching a statue come to life. But I didn't move to ease my aching knees until I had seen her lower the foul thing back into the water again and place her grappling stick securely between two boulders. She paused to watch the head sinking slowly towards the shallow muddy bottom.

I wasn't angry with her any more. She started towards the bank. I got up to make a hasty retreat and hurried to the top, feeling bad about my spying even though Clem would probably not even notice me, when I almost collided with the purple and blue clad figure of the care worker, Patricia. One look at her face, grey beneath her makeup, and she said,

"She'll have to go back early. I must ring the institute at once. I can't have things like this going on. It's just disgusting." She gave me a look as if it were my fault and then turned and began to march back towards the house as fast as she could reasonably go in her street pumps.

The next day Mom did everything to stop Clem going out. She stayed in with the both of us in the kitchen and made batch after batch of readymix cookies in our one, silly, small tin that made six at a time. I mixed and measured, Mom dropped the mix into the tin, Clem watched the oven clock. Well, she was supposed to. I never saw her look at it but under her breath she made a sound like baa-aa-aa just before the buzzer went off. Every time.

When the box of mix was exhausted Mom looked around for something to occupy Clem and stop her from starting one of her habits. She didn't make it. Within moments of the last cookies emerging Clem stood up, walked to the cutlery drawer and pulled out the organiser tray. With methodical precision she began to lay out the pieces on the counter. She didn't slam, she didn't fuss or let them twirl, she just put them down one after another in a precise row—clink, clink, clink—you could have checked your second hand by her accuracy. Mom cast her a look of betrayal and loathing and muttered something about freshening up. She lingered for a moment in the doorway, ignoring me, almost hypnotised by the mad rhythm of Clem's organisation. Knife, knife, fork, spoon, knife. Her lip trembled. In leaving she slapped her hand hard against the doorframe in a sound that would have told anyone but Clem how every knife stabbed her.

Clink clink clink clink clink

The sound of my mother being murdered whilst I sit, caught between them, doing nothing because I've been here before and nothing makes any difference.

Clink clink cli . . .

Smooth as a machine Clem turned and was out the door, running as she left the porch, the sunlight glinting on the scatter of metal as it fell, forgotten, from her hand. She was through the hedge before I had even worked free of my surprise to go after her. I tried hard to catch her but even though I'd never seen her run anywhere in her life and she kept her legs almost straight the whole time she pulled ground on me with every stride. I was beat long before the last field. Sweating, panting, I staggered the last few feet to the top of the bank and had to stand there, too late, my hands on my knees.

The head was gone, of course, fished out by the farmer whom Mom had called last night. Clem's stick was there though. She stabbed the river with it, digging in the soft mud with savage, repetitive jerks of her arms. I suppose I should have gone to her, tried to explain, but what was there to say that she'd understand? What was there to understand? I should have been overjoyed to see her with such understandable feelings.

Finally she flung the stick down and began to stamp her feet rhythmically on the rocky bank. Stones went skittering. She flapped her arms like a grounded gull and shook her head side to side. Then she flung her head back and screamed. The sound echoed along the narrow gully, off the water, and died rapidly. She did it again and again and again, each time the same throat-cutting volume, each time the same exact number of seconds until her breath was gone.

A machine bemoans the loss of comfort.

It was a terrible noise and I had to press my hands over my ears. The sound hurt, right to the bone. I was standing, helpless, when my mother, stepping in her houseshoes, picking her way in jerks like a maddened hen, brushed past me. She was angry. Her face was livid under the light pearly pink of her blusher and ugly.

She tripped and staggered her way down towards Clem who still stood, insensible, bawling, and slapped her hard across the face. Clem shut up. Her eyes blanked out as if a switch had been pressed.

"Don't you know you'll be taken away?" Mom was screaming. "Have you any idea what you're doing to this family, you selfish, thoughtless, stupid . . . lump of a thing! Do you know what it costs to keep running after you and picking up and not knowing if sometimes you will and sometimes you won't, not knowing that anybody is even in there . . ."

The tirade went on and on. Flies spun between them, whirling on the jets of rage from my mother's mouth. The sun sidled sideways a little.

Clem stood, fused. Mom started on about the new house, the new institute, how she was ostracised, how we had had to leave because no one in our farming community would call around any more after they realised how strange Clem was and why couldn't she just pretend to be normal, she wasn't stupid, was she? She could do her lessons when she put her mind to it, it was only Asperger's, not proper autism, so why this play acting?

Clem stood. In fury at her own lack of effect Mom stepped forwards and grabbed Clem's shoulders. She shook them as Clem twisted away from her with unerring revulsion. Since she was four months old she has writhed and screamed to escape all contact with any of us. You would think the touch of us was poison. She screamed like we were burning her. And every single time Mom has showed the same hurt. How many times is that in a lifetime? But she's never given up trying. This time she wouldn't let go. She tried to hang on and get Clem further into her grip, determined Clem would not get away before she made her understand. Clem made a narrow, howling sound.

"But I'm your mother, darling, I'm your mother!"

"Mom don't . . ." I started to beg her, seeing where this was heading. But I was wrong.

With sudden speed and strength she lunged forwards and pushed Mom hard. Her eyes tracked for a moment with a real and obvious intent. Frozen on the bank I watched my mother as she lost her grip on my sister's sleeves and fell, toppling backwards, her pink apron tails fluttering gaily.

She seemed to fall in slow motion, her monologue suddenly changing into a scream. I had my hands jammed into my mouth, half wanting to laugh, half scared stiff. Clem watched her, arms by her sides, corn hair blowing a little in the restless wind that had come out of nowhere. The stagnant water closed over Mom and for a second or two she was completely immersed. I could see her face in the sunlight, white pale through the green liquid, eyes bulging, bubbles coming out of her mouth, her lacquered coiffure dissolving in rising clouds of algae.

In the heat thickened, charged air Clem and I watched her surface and struggle to the bank. She wasn't hurt but both her mules were lost in the mud. She stood there, panting, spitting, dripping in her stocking feet. Trails of green were caught in the ruin of her hair and her apron was slimed. A minute or so passed and she didn't lift her head to look at either of us. I could see that she was furious but so much so that she didn't know what to do. Also desperate. She was past the end of her rope. She was thinking about leaving us and heading off on her own and no amount of reasoning was going to touch her now, I could see it. All desire to giggle had gone, instead there was just this cold, greasy feeling as if I'd eaten frozen lard. This was way beyond the pale. It was too fast, too much, horrible, out of control. I knew I had to do something, but what? And it was too late.

Clem turned her face and looked at Mom. She paused, and then with her mechanical accuracy she put her arms around mother and pressed her close for an instant—out, in, close, squeeze, hold, release, step back.

"Green is good," Clem said and absently she brushed just once at the damp, dark stain on her chest.

Mom looked at her through a veil of dripping sage and black. For a split second her face lit up with sixteen years of stored hope and joy. Then she saw Clem was already climbing the bank and looked down at herself, at her smeared arms and her neat dress, hanging heavy with mud. She held her arms out and turned them over as they shone. I caught a whiff of the rot as it warmed up on her in the sunshine. Clem passed me without looking back. Slowly my mother seemed to shrink, her shoulders slumped and her head hung down. After a moment she looked up at me, "Go home, Lois," her voice was quiet, "I'll be right along."

Out of sight of the stream I ran into the cornfields and ripped the unripe cobs from the stalks, tearing the hair out and stamping it in the dirt. Mom had to stop me when she came by. She didn't say anything, just stood on the path. I felt so ashamed I could hardly look at her. Her calm seemed absolute. She held out her hand. I took it. We walked home together.

In the kitchen Clem was sitting at the table, eating cookies. As she passed Mom put out her hand so it could brush Clem's hair as if by mistake. She trailed a few strands through her fingers. It gleamed against the green and earth that was cracking on her skin. She glanced at me and I saw how clear her eyes had become. They were clear grey, their fighting cloud and shooting rays of sun now the solid colour of permanent overcast.

"It's all dead, you know, hair," she said, "it just doesn't look it though, does it? The way it shines."

DEADHEAD

Deadhead refers to the story's motifs of a dead horse's head and the process of taking off flowerheads that have started to rot. But of course those things are important in the story's larger meme-net in which my intent was to show a lack of communication, a sense of strangeness and hidden threat, the pointlessness of trying to understand one way of seeing things through the lens of another, and a hope for new beginnings too. It's just a bad choice though.

This story also, to my mind, is a reference to the fact that most "normal" people can't step out of their mindset for five seconds, certainly not long enough to notice that a hideous, rotting object is also beautiful and powerful in its way. They're the real deadheads. I wrote it when I was still young and angry about these things. I think I am still angry but I've begun to think that railing and ranting may not be the way to address it. Although it has its moments and an energy that's undeniable.

ERIE LACKAWANNA
SONG

ERIE LACKAWANNA SONG

This story is really about a place—the Hoboken/Manhattan ferry stop which is next to an abandoned terminal for Erie Lackawanna Lines. From the stop you can look across into the rotting wooden hulk of the terminal and read its name in huge blue-green oxidized lettering. It's a ghost portal. Linking something so evocative with a really hard and nasty SF McGuffin felt like a fun metaphorical playground to fool with. I used the ferry crossing a few times once when I was on holiday visiting my cousins and at both ends of the journey I'd wonder about who else had taken the trip and why, and what was waiting for them at the other end.

ERIE LACKAWANNA SONG

Jackson arrived early at the Hoboken ferry terminal, as he liked to do on sunny days. The ferry before his was just leaving but he made no move although other people ran and trotted past him along the wooden jetty to reach the gate before the guard closed it.

Jackson's ten minutes gave him time alone to walk to the end of the rising and falling pontoon, stand in the shelter offered by the clear and blue plastic sheeting, and look through the chain link fence to the old ferry port next door. Ever since he had moved to New Jersey from the Village this building had been a source of compulsion. It was derelict, with a couple of empty ferry bays facing onto the river. From the outside they were fancy, constructed grandly in a neo-classical style with columns and curlicues now greened all over in a uniformly bright verdigris. Inside, where the boats used to go, it was dark and rotting. The huge timbers that supported the main structure rose, dark and wet with the pawing of the waves and the creeping clutch of the water. They leaned in warped neglect where they had once supported a boardwalk out to the boats, the spaces echoing to the crisp sound of many shoes moving purposefully into their journey. He fancied the ghosts of those echoes sometimes struggled to come to life there, when the river slapped the wood or made a knocking sound with some part of the old foundation.

Jackson didn't know if the place had always been that green or if it was painted that way. There were bold decorations on its outsides which looked like they ought to have been some other colour, even gilded or brightly red and glossy copper. The place had a kind of poetry which spoke to Jackson's inarticulate heart directly. When he looked at it, its very emptiness was part of the charm. There, only a few metres from where he stood above the dirty Hudson, it held fast and patient, the lettering of its old destinations staunchly upright still (he assumed they were destinations, anyway)—Erie Lackawanna, it promised, one on the great lakes, the other he didn't know where, although it must be Pennsylvania. But Erie was a vast water, far distant in space, and Lackawanna sounded native to him, a shore that might even be hidden inside the earth and concealing another world altogether. Or maybe it was a star in another galaxy and the name was here to remind humankind that they really ought to do something about getting there. No, it was definitely the emptiness that charmed.

To his right the ferry and the short hop to Manhattan waited. But from the green docks! If only he could find a ticket and a way in one day, from there he could travel to adventures unknown, worlds undiscovered, into futures so bright and dazzling that he could not imagine them, although he heard them calling him with a song like birdsong, almost drowned in the rush of water falling, falling.

Behind him he heard someone give a familiar kind of cough. It was a smoker's cough and one that sparked a recognition to close his daydreaming mind. Automatically he turned around to look. Celia Glick was there, bolstered in her heavy camel coat, a red scarf and a thickly furred hat. She smiled briefly at him and he returned it, re-establishing their old acquaintance.

"Good morning," Jackson said.

She nodded. The ferry was coming in now, too fast it seemed, until the last moment when a revv of the engines in reverse made smoke puff grandly. The boat bumped on the jetty's buffer; two fat dancers knocking their hips together in a stately mamba.

Glick and Jackson waited until the other passengers had disembarked and the people waiting with them had boarded and stepped on last. If they met in the morning it was the habit of each of them to stand in the prow and face the island and the wind all the way.

They stood at the rail and Jackson was grateful that there wasn't going to be much conversation today. Glick was pleasant enough but he preferred to keep his own thoughts on the journey. Sometimes she would engage him in small talk and he would have to think hard all the way over, responding thoughtfully and politely to her equally thoughtful and polite chat. He watched the old terminal's mouths slide away behind them, silent shouting, until distance made the place seem small and insignificant after all, and then turned away. Erie Lackawanna, he thought, hearing a melody in the syllables—someone should write a song about it.

Glick's voice startled him.

"Here, look at this."

Dr Glick dug into the pocket of her overcoat and lifted out a glass vial. She showed it to Jackson, holding it against the light with a strong finger on either end of the slim tube to be sure of not losing it in the wind.

Jackson peered.

His first thought was that it would have made a good addition to the Manhattan skyline, against which it now appeared—roughly as high as the Empire State but much wider. It would be a monument worthy of someone truly original: a great glossy column with some kind of internal coating which cut down on sunlight entering the tiny space and cast it back in soft sheens of gunmetal and bronze.

"What is it?" The vial appeared to be self-contained, with no stoppers or seals of any kind. Jackson, ever the practical mind, began to wonder more about how it was made than what was in it. He expected Glick to say something about neurotransmitter drugs or one-shot specific inhibitors; something to do with her work at the Cognitive Institute.

"The end of the world as we know it," she answered, partly smug, but partly with an awe she couldn't disguise.

Jackson, startled, looked down at her and felt a frisson of some archaic emotion race down his back. Her face was triumphant in the early morning sun. She radiated the fire of victory. He recognised his feeling as fear and shifted his feet on the deck, searching for a stronger foothold on the shifting surface.

Jackson knew Glick only vaguely. They met occasionally at the Mapping Technologies Centre in the World Trades, or at conferences on such subjects as fluid dynamics and complex systems modelling. More often they saw each other on working days when they both took the same ferry from Hoboken across to the Trades Centre stop. Like many other people they both liked to stand in the adventurer's pose as it made its brief crossing; Manhattan and the day both ahead of them and small enough to encompass with a single sweeping glance of conquest. At least, Jackson assumed this was the reaction that Glick had to the view.

Now the last of his morning dreaminess vanished. Glick's statement was so over the top that it was difficult to know what reaction to have. Scientists, especially those with reputations like hers, didn't make that kind of overweening pronouncement. They just didn't. Jackson cleared his throat unnecessarily and repeated his question, "What is it?"

"This is a sample of MM5," she said. She spoke quietly, so that only she and he could hear before the words were stripped away on the breeze.

MM5. The letters and number wound a tortured route through Jackson's brain. He knew he should know of it, but the meaning—wasn't it something to do with a news story of last year? Some British scientist being found in a government laboratory with a dead intelligence man, possibly a CIA agent? Their project had been MM-something. The Ms stood for Mappa Mundi, a kind of mind-map perhaps. Of course it was in Glick's field, not his. "Cognitive mapping software?" he suggested, instantly feeling out of his depth. He wondered why she was being so coy, and why she was telling him.

"No. This is the complete item," she said, and shook the vial. Inside it silvery clouds swirled, stately and slow as smoke winding up through the overheated air of a gentleman's club. "MM5 is a real-time, self-modulating, complete cognitive upgrading system."

"Uh-huh," the words meant little to him. He leant on the railing of the boat and looked towards Battery Park, where he could just make out the day's joggers moving up and down the walks, some slow and some fast, both being overtaken by rollerbladers and bikes. Glick had a tendency to get heated about her work. She was probably only trying to interest him because she was bursting to talk about it to anybody at all.

"And there's enough in here to fix the whole of New York," she added, leaning on the rail with him, holding the vial out over the heavy, turbid waves. The wind blew her short blonde hair back and forth, forming rosettes on her head and then slapping them away.

Jackson looked at her questioningly. Manhattan was closer than New Jersey now. Soon they'd have to go their separate ways.

She would walk with him as far as the bank and then head for her uptown bus. He would pass the twin towers' memorial and wend onwards to the meteorological offices. They would say a hurried "see you later" and only think of one another again as they approached the ferry stop for the evening ride home, wondering for a split second if the other would be there on the pontoon or would be taking the PATH instead. The routine was well-known and had few variations. Jackson had always assumed Glick had no further interest in him and he had never explored whether he might have any for her since the question was thus moot.

Now he was uncomfortably aware of her mental sharpness and his own sluggish responses to power games of any kind. He gave her a wary social smile to convey interest and inoffensiveness at once, hoping that she would close down the encounter. At the same time his eyes strayed again and again to the vial. He wished she would put it in her pocket where it might not fall and be lost, or else break and further contaminate the dirty water. He wanted to take it from her and put it somewhere out of harm's way.

A curl of soft, glowing light shone from the glass.

"What's the coating on that?" he asked.

Glick seemed surprised. She recovered quickly. "Smart-lead," she said. "Atomic containment."

A bluster of cold fall air shouldered its way around the deck. Everyone around them huddled into their coats and turned their collars up. Jackson did not move. Glick folded her hand around the vial and put the hand in her pocket. For a few moments Jackson watched the surface of the river, a mass of planes continually changing. He let the images fill his mind but they could not wash out the certain conviction that there was something wrong now. Such items as the vial should not be out of a secure laboratory, and whatever the vial held should never be placed in a container so vulnerable; safe at the atomic level but open to the slightest accident in the real world—he shuddered. Perhaps it was a kind of joke?

He looked at Glick's face as she contemplated their arrival. Thoughts ran through his head, wild. Should he allow her from the boat? Was she dangerously deluded? Perhaps she was playing with him to amuse herself briefly. Perhaps she was showing him because the vial was given her by another and she wanted a witness to it. Perhaps the vial was full of lead powder and nothing else. Perhaps . . . perhaps . . .

On the face of it he knew little about her. She had a good reputation among her peers. Her work was well-regarded. Certainly she was a part of projects relating to national security, but weren't they all these days? Nothing in her manner over the last two years had ever suggested derangement, nor a playful nature. Glick was always serious. Even in her casual smile and greetings there was the sense of a slight lifting of what was an otherwise-occupied attention, inward turning, serious and intense. Sometimes, if they happened to talk on a topic of mutual interest, she would lighten and chat with good humour. Mostly she was simply polite and he gave their association little thought.

"What does it do?"

They were now close enough to see the masts of rich people's boats in the harbour above the park. Glick lit a cigarette behind a cupped hand. She always lit one just before they arrived. She'd been a quitter for three months now but somehow the idea of arriving at work without a single puff was something she couldn't yet stomach and so she grabbed a few drags in the 'healthy' air on the boat before it docked, when she would flick the half-finished cigarette into the water.

Jackson stood free of the rail as she turned her back against it and took a long, grateful drag. She closed her eyes to enjoy the smoke and a heavy whitish trail of it poured slowly out of her mouth. She opened her eyes and jetted the last of the lungful straight out. It blew around Jackson. He smelt the familiar tarry, poisonous odour as it was dragged away and something else a little like the almond sweetness of cyanide or the sickly perfume of turkish delight. He sneezed. As he was getting out his packet of tissues Glick took another mighty pull and spun the burning stick out over the water where it vanished in the ferry's wash.

She waited until he had finished blowing and wiping and then answered his question of a couple of minutes ago, "On entry into the human brain, MM5 sets itself at all synaptic junctions, producing new inter-bodies until every gateway is monitored. It also creates chemical stations at key points so that the whole of the cognitive function can be controlled. If there are any pre-set programmes MM5 will execute them. If it is to re-train some area, for instance, to alleviate a problem such as dyslexia. Or if it is to act as an auxiliary memory cache. Whatever. It spends some time," she wiggled her fingers, "making accurate records of the normal state of cognitive function in whosever brain—so that if a rollback were required then the person could be returned to their Eve-state of origin."

Jackson wondered at the strange term "Eve-state". It was unusually politically correct, even for Glick, who could be annoyingly scrupulous in her terminology. Some of the other implications were going past too quickly for him to catch, like high cirrus clouds being forced along and destroyed in a big blow. He struggled to listen properly.

"And then," she said, "there's nothing you can't do. You can suppress the dominant hemisphere to access the repressed persona of the other side—left or right. You can experience every type of lunacy, from the chemically induced to the structurally dysfunctional. Be schizophrenic for a day. Try psychopathy out and discover the mind of the criminal and the killer. Have a manic phase to get some work done. Have a depressed phase . . .no, why would you do that? But anyway—upgrade your intelligence in any area. Stimulate the dull and atrophied areas of your brain. Become a composer. Become a writer. Give yourself confidence. Assume the social skills of a master agent. But above all, be rational. Govern your emotions, even in the extreme situation, and let them contribute their own primitive wisdom to your thoughts." She pushed away from the rail and adjusted her scarf, as the ferry wallowed around and began to come in towards the waiting gate of the pontoon.

"MM5 is the master balance. You can set yourself to become what you will, but only temporarily. Its final function is to awaken the dulled, to access the forgotten, to improve the communications between low-connected areas. It can't create what doesn't already exist—people with cell depletion and retardation won't become geniuses—but maximal function and capacity will be restored to everyone in every measure they are capable of. With one exception."

Jackson was concentrating so hard on what she said that he almost fell over as they were ushered backward by the guard towards the safety line on the deck. He looked at the sharp little lines of light which made up Glick's heavy eyebrows as she finished. The detail was so sharp, like the tips of the fur on her hat. It was almost miraculous and he couldn't help noticing it.

"In a normal brain emotion has the capacity to override reason via the amygdala. MM5 reverses that dominance. In an upgraded cognitive system reason can always subjugate emotion. Not remove it or change it. Certainly you would experience your feelings as completely as you are able to. But no emotion would cause those brief surges of action without thought, those murders, those fits of anger, those stupid decisions that cost lives and livings. MM5 gives you control of yourself."

With a muted shudder the boat touched the edge of the dock. The gates were swung aside and people began to pour off the boat, thundering down the stairs from the upper deck, emerging blinking from the shade of the covered seating like cross dormice. Jackson followed Glick onto the swaying wooden pontoon, past the ticket office, up the ramp and onto the stone pavement.

In a couple of strides he was abreast of her. They walked at their normal pace towards the coffee shop beside the yachts.

"What is it going to be used for?" he asked, as much to know as make conversation, which he felt must follow that kind of revelation.

"Nothing so advantageous," she said and there was undisguised bitterness, which he recognised easily in her voice and the hard line of her shoulders. "It's a beneficent precursor to something much more specialised."

Jackson waited. They walked another twenty metres and came to the tables and chairs near the water. It was chilly and the few patrons were all well wrapped. The waiter huddled across the sidewalk, sheltering beside his stand of cups. He just couldn't decide if he believed her or not. His mind felt scattered, blown away. It seemed so ridiculous on this ordinary morning.

"D'you want a coffee?" Jackson found himself saying without intending to. There was a kind of urgency which even he could not help reacting to in Glick's manner and within a couple of minutes their journey would be over.

"Yes," she said quickly, moving towards a free table without a backward glance.

They sat beneath the red umbrella as it was buffeted this way and that. He watched Glick take out and put back her pack of cigarettes twice, from the same pocket as the vial. She put her lighter on the table and toyed with it for a moment.

"Stupid law this," she said. "Outside. Why would anybody care?" And she kicked at an old, stamped on butt near one of her boots.

"What are you doing with that vial, carrying it around like that?" Jackson asked her. He guessed that she wanted to be asked, or had to, before she could say whatever was on her mind. To their right a steady stream of people passed by singly and in groups, their steps quick or heavy in their different anticipations of what the work day held. Jackson longed for his warm patch of office, his orthopaedic chair, his weather maps, but he folded his hands between his knees and waited for Glick to unburden herself.

"I borrowed it," she said, taking her cup up and warming her hands with it. "I shouldn't have. I feel strange, having it. Like having some kind of dynamite. I even tested it before I left with it. It's ready to roll. One crack in the glass and poof!"

"What are you going to do?" Jackson took a sip of coffee and wondered if Glick were crazy enough to do something silly, and if she were, what he was going to do about it.

"MM6 is underway," she announced, sighing. The wrinkles around her mouth deepened. "It's similar, but responds to an external operator, instead of only the host. In fact, it may end up being engineered not to have the rollback function or the original process where the current personality . . ." she tailed off. "I think that MM6 is a bad idea."

Jackson pieced together what she meant. External operator? It took only a very little leap of the imagination to see where that kind of thing was to lead, but Glick was already talking again, relentless as a machine.

"The original goal for MM5 was to restore criminals, the brain-damaged and the unbalanced to states where they could return safely into society, able to live productive and happy lives—at least, as able as most of us are. But the scope of it was more powerful than we first thought. It can even improve people who, theoretically, don't need improvement and probably don't want it. That's the thing. There's no choice. It's like a disease. You catch it and you don't know you've got it. It changes you and you can't even notice it, because the old you doesn't exist any more. You can spread it in the water, in the air, in food; skin contact even. It has goals of its own. To replicate and find hosts. To adapt what it finds. To spread.

Even after a long time at the Mapping Centre, I couldn't see very far into scenarios of what would happen if it were released." She stopped herself suddenly and took a drink of the hot coffee.

Jackson thought for a moment. He was cold. The wind was gentle here, but relentless, beating through his layers. A gust caught the waiter's apron and sent it flapping up, smacking at his face as he struggled self-consciously to tame it.

"What did you see?" The role of questioner was easy. The role of listener was harder. The more she said, the more he was implicated, the more he knew that when they left the table there would be something in motion from which there was no going back. It would demand that he act and he did not like any of the actions so far suggested.

"In farcasts, where the scenarios have played out for decades, I saw us under MM6," she said. "In all the situations tested, with and without MM5 undergoing organised release, I saw a prediction of the rise and rise of MM6. The controllers had mastery over their small nations of influence. The slaves were happy in their bondage. The old classes emerged; the ruling elite with their immunity and freedom from the technology; the intellectual bourgeoisie, using it to better themselves and produce art, theories, science and of course facilitating the elite's designs; the working drones, directed whichever way they were needed, with the minimal requirements of intelligence or reactivity, as happy as sandboys in all manner of disgusting degradation. MM6 is the immoral moral leveller. Nobody suffered, because where there was suffering there was no one conscious enough to understand their own plight. They were happy," she pushed the coffee cup, still half-full, away from her. "Happy, in their way." The lighter tapped on the table reproachfully.

Jackson did not know what to say. He was not sure what to think. It sounded too far-fetched. And yet he knew they already used the most basic forms of the cognitive technology to help the severely depressed and those injured or born with defects of the neural system. In a badly timed attempt at levity he said, "But maybe it is already out and we don't know it, because we are content in our jobs."

Glick shot him a look of loathing which was not meant for him personally. "Yes," she nodded. "I've thought of that. But look around you," and she gestured briefly to Manhattan and the boroughs beyond. Jackson had to admit she had a point.

She brought out the vial again and toyed with it, watching its strange contents flow and mingle within their minute prison.

"So," he said, "maybe even the reasoned use of this technology isn't the answer. If reason brings us MM6 every time." And he was still not sure he believed her, he told himself. He was just listening to a troubled soul. Helping out. Organising someone else's thinking, someone important and probably someone he ought to make a call about, though he didn't know who to, or how.

"It isn't reason that's the problem," Glick said, watching him add more sugar to his cup and stir it in. "It's that reasoning led to the ability to amass power and wealth for the most quickly adapted—those who were fastest to see and take opportunities for themselves. Humans cannot create any social order that doesn't require a heirarchy, overtly or not. Some rise and others must fall. MM5 and MM6 could not make us equals, that is the problem." She turned the vial over. "We aren't born it and we couldn't be made it. Only in our ideals and allocation of resources. But then, I tried a new version of MM5. One which weakened the heirarchical drive, with an embedded map of reality, which re-calibrates meaning structure so that two individuals with different perceptions become able to perceive the same information in identical ways. It uses the first contact as a model and then passes on the adjustments to all the individuals it later encounters."

Jackson stared at her from his position of discomfort, frowning with the effort, "Wouldn't that make them the same person? If they thought everything the same way?"

"No," she said firmly. "Their different experiences every day would constantly be leading them away from similarity of that kind. The brain is very fluid, even in adults. It would be changing rapidly from the moment of conversion along a different path in every individual. But every now and again, a tweak here and there could produce an effectiveness of communication that would really mean we did all speak the same language. We would be individuals, but ones made up of identical modular components which we all understood. And when I ran that scenario through the map systems—no MM6."

"The mapping technologies are very good," Jackson admitted hesitantly, recalling the pleasure of his accurate predictions of typhoons, even short and localised spells of weather, to the hour. "But they're not absolute."

She absorbed his words of caution slowly and then nodded.

"The thing is," she got a cigarette out and lit it as the waiter went inside. "I know," she touched her nose briefly, "that the military has plans for MM6, if not 5." She breathed in a deep draw of smoke and let it out in a single exhale. "Ah well," she said. "Last one. Must enjoy it."

"You always say that," Jackson was saying, not really watching as she took what he presumed to be a mobile phone out of her pocket.

Glick smiled, a ghostly smile, and carefully stubbed out the cigarette, folding it in half. "Here," she handed the vial to him and picked up the phone unit.

He looked at the vial in his hand, not sure what she meant him to do with it, and looked up.

There was a beep as she depressed a button.

Jackson saw that he must have forgotten to return the vial of cloud tracking crystals to the canister before leaving work. Quickly he returned it to his pocket—must have that for the field testing—he'd put it with the rest of the equipment as soon as he got in.

"Better get going," he said, draining the last of his coffee.

"Yes," Glick said. She was pale with the cold wind. "See you for the evening boat?"

The weather balloon tugged hard against its moorings as Jackson fixed the equipment onto it. He was quick, but not rushed. He loved a field trip, and between the launch of the balloon and the assessment of the data there was a long afternoon's fishing ahead.

Once the rig was secured to the line he tested each piece of machinery to make sure it was still functioning and that no batteries had gone flat. Then he fixed the small dispersal unit underneath, set to release the wind-seed trackers once the balloon had reached the specified height. There was a storm system coming up over the panhandle which ought, if the mapping system was correct, to ride out all the way to the east coast, taking Philadelphia, New York, even Washington on the way. When the survey was done he could post the severe weather warnings to the TV stations.

Finally he took the vial of trackers out of his pocket and fitted it into the dispersal clamp. Its contents surged up into clouds of distant and tiny turbulence through the dark glass.

He slipped the anchor and watched the balloon rise. Quickly it became a white blob, diminishing all the time, until, shielding his eyes against the glare of the noon sky, he could see first a thing the size of a dinner plate, then a dot and then nothing at all.

He packed up his equipment into the back of the van and began to drive north, towards the cabin where his fishing gear was waiting next to a picnic basket and a bottle of Merlot.

October. A calm day. The walkway out onto the dock was hardly moving as Jackson took a covered cup of coffee with him to wait for the ferry. He was late this morning—had taken time off to do some redecorating at his apartment—and there was almost no one about. Only a young woman in a leather jacket and jeans stood by the empty gateway, looking through the chain fence towards the old terminal buildings.

Jackson looked past her. The verdigris colour was the brilliant green of living plants in the low-angled light and the glancing waves shed enough of their glare inside to give a good view of the rotting stanchions. The red lettering was still defiant.

As she heard him approach the young woman turned around briefly to check him out and, seeing him looking at the same thing she was, said shyly, "It's kinda tragic. A gateway to nowhere like that, everybody gone. Someone should write a song about it or something."

Jackson smiled back, "I heard that someone's bought it and has plans to do it up."

"No kidding?"

"Probably just be a different service to the North points on Manhattan. Maybe trips to Staten Island."

"Yeah," she said, nodding, and looking back at the empty building. "But then it'll go somewhere. Now it could go anywhere you want to."

"Yeah," Jackson said. He could see her yearn towards that unknown journey with her whole body. And when a man in a suit joined them, briefcase in hand, he too looked at the empty bays with wistful longing for an instant before his lapel-phone rang and he had to turn away and answer.

Jackson turned from the fence. He hummed a tune beneath his breath, some old folk tune variation, and glanced at the sky with its load of overcast cloud. In his mind's eye he saw a great white liner, sleek as a seal and smoothed for space, emerge from the silent, dead bays of Erie Lackawanna and take to the air, her tail fins catching the low light and shooting it around like diamond spars.

He felt a strange certainty now that they were all going somewhere, and that the journey had started there, in that dark, deserted place. Even under grey skies it was unmistakable—that sense of brimming promise.

Smiling, he took a deep breath and turned to face the river where his boat was coming to fetch him.

ERIE LACKAWANNA SONG

One thing I also liked about this story is that the doomsday moment is such an understated little thing caught in a personal moment. I get very fed up of overblown Armageddon scenarios in movies and games. Stories like this one, "No Man's Island" and "The Little Bear" are reactions to that idea that there will be a huge, obvious, resolvable showdown or that we are the centre of the universe.

CRACKLEGRACKLE

CRACKLEGRACKLE

This was a story that dealt with some things I had wanted to say in NATURAL HISTORY *and not found space for. I felt that the atmosphere of the story—a deep unease about leaving Earth behind coupled with the longing to do so— was still interesting so I picked it up when this anthology was asking for stories and dusted it off. I did some tough interviews with the pixies and discovered that they thought this would fly if it was set in the universe of my novel,* NATURAL HISTORY, *in which the human race has engineered itself into many various forms suited to existence far out in the solar system. The pixies also suggested using a character who was a minor player in* LIVING NEXT DOOR TO THE GOD OF LOVE, *since he had uniquely suited abilities to this story, and had gone underexplored in his previous outing. Hyperion is both a highly advanced technological creation and a spiritually fully aware person who is able to act as a bridge between the human father of this story and his much changed Forged daughter. At least, he tries.*

CRACKLEGRACKLE

Many times Mark Bishop read the assignment, but it never made more sense to him. He was to interview the Greenjack Hyperion, make an assessment of the claims made for it, and return his report. That part was simple. But after it, the evidence supplied by the Forged and human witnesses . . . this he couldn't manage more than a line or two of. Panic rose and the black and white print became an unknown language. He could see it hadn't changed, but simply by moving his eyes across it his mind redshifted and all meaning sped away from him.

He poured the one-too-many scotch from the concession bottle by his elbow just as the hostess was about to whisk it away, and drank it down. The burn was impersonal and direct. It did exactly what it always promised, and shot the pain where it hurt. He rubbed his eyes and tried again.

He disliked the sight of the document on his screen. It struck him suddenly that the paragraphs were too long. The white spaces between them loomed in violent stripes, their blank inlets holding the truth that the print failed to express. The punctuation was a taunt, an assault in black and white that proved the text's defeat of his reason was absolute. Even the title was loathsome: Making A Case For The Intuitive Interpretation Of Full Spectrum Data In Unique Generative Posthuman Experience. Usually he had no bother with jargon, or any scientific melee, but what the hell did that mean? What did it mean to the person it referred to? Had they titled it or was it just the bureacrat's pedantic label for something they could read but not comprehend?

A final slug of scotch ended his attempt. He only understood that there was no escape from meeting the Greenjack, as he had promised, as his job demanded: meet, interview, assess, report. That was all. It was easy. He'd done it a hundred times. More. He was an expert. That's why the government had hired him and kept him on the top payroll all these years. They trusted him to judge rightly, to know truth, to detect mistakes and delusions, to be sure.

Bishop tried to read the document once more. His eyes hurt and finally, after a forced march across the first few paragraphs, he felt a cluster headache come on and halt them with a fierce spasm of pain as if something had decided to drill invisible holes into his head via the back of his eyeballs. He lay back in the recline seat of the lift launcher and closed his eyes. The attendants circled and took away his cup, secured his harness and spoke pleasantly about the safety of the orbital lift system and the experience of several gs of force during acceleration—a song and dance routine he already knew so well he could have done it himself. He briefly remembered being offered a ride up on one of the Heavy Angels, explaining he didn't want it to the secretary. She couldn't understand his reluctance. Then in the background she heard some colleague whisper, "Mars." She'd gone red, then white.

But it wasn't just the difficulty of talking to the Forged now, he'd never liked the idea of being inside a body. It was too much like being eaten, or some form of unwilling sex. So he'd made his economy-excuse, a polite no, a don't-want-to-be-a-bother smile and now he was waiting for take off, no time left, unprepared for the big meeting, his mouth dry with all the things he'd taken to avoid doing anything repulsively human, like being sick.

The lift was moved into position by its waldos, attached to the cable, tested. The slight technicalities passed him in a blur of nauseating detail and then there was the stomach-leaving, spine shrinking hurl of acceleration in the back of his legs. The headache peaked. Weightlessness came as they soared above the clouds into the blue and then the black. He felt like lead. When the time came to unclip and get out he half expected that he'd be set in position, a statue, and surprised himself by seeing his hands reach out and competently move him along the guiderails. He didn't hit anyone. The other passengers were all busy talking to each other or into their mikes. Then the smell filled his nostrils.

It was a mysterious animal tang that reminded him of the hot hides of horses, a drooling, dozing camel he had once attempted to ride, and on top of that, the ocean. Bishop gripped on tight, knowing that all his juvenile, ancient spine-root superstitions had caught up with him. His interviewee had come to meet him in an act of unwanted courtesy. He would have to greet and speak to it . . . why had he forgotten its name suddenly? Why did it have to smell like that? But he was now holding up the queue. The stewardess mistook his hesitation for ignorance and started talking about freefall walking. All that remained was to turn himself towards the smooth, white-lit exit chute that led to the Offworld Destinations Lounge, and follow that telltale scent of primeval beast.

The other passengers sniffed curiously as they passed him, "so-sorrying" their way around his stalled self. He fiddled with his recorder, checking his microphone and switching everything on. It made him feel secure in the same way he imagined old world spies had once felt secure by their illicit link to someone somewhere who would at least hear their final moments. It wasn't exactly like being accompanied, but it was enough of a shield to let the prickling under his arms stop and for his headache to recede.

The thought came to him that he hadn't been himself lately. It was only natural after the conclusion of the enquiry and its open verdict. Too much stress. He ought to stop, cry off, take a holiday. Nobody would be surprised. But the thought of not having his job, the idea of having nothing to do but walk the familiar coast near Pismo Beach or under the tall silence of the redwoods—that made him pull himself along all the faster to escape the hum, the static darkness, the horror that was waiting there for him, that was already here in the notion of that place. He gritted his teeth and pushed that aside. The scotch made it easy. Why the hell hadn't he thought to bring some more?

He pulled himself forward into the glide that felt graceful even when it wasn't and swallowed with difficulty. That smell! It was so curious here, where all the smells were ground out of existence quickly in the filtration of the dry air so that humans and their descendants, the Forged, could meet without the animal startle reflexes scent caused the humans. But the grace would only last a minute or two here, in the neutral zone of the Lift Centre. And why could he smell this one so clearly? It must reek—and as he thought this he saw it/him, a tall, gangling, ugly creature that resembled a gargoyle from some mighty gothic cathedral whose creator had been keen on all the Old Testamentary virtues. It could easily have featured in his nightmares. He wouldn't have been surprised to discover that it had been modelled with an artistic eye to that fact. The Pangenesis Tupac, brooder, sculptor, creator in flesh and metal, enjoyed her humour at all levels of creation. The word anathema sat in his head, alone, as he bravely put on a smile of greeting.

"Mark Bishop?" said the gargoyle in an old English gentleman's voice, as fitting and unexpected as rain in Death Valley.

"I am." He found conviction, was so glad the other didn't offer his hand and glanced down and saw it was a fistful of claws.

"My name is Hyperion. I am pleased to meet you. I have read many of your articles in the more popular academic journals and the ordinary press. Your reputation is well founded." It made a slight bow and the harsh interior lights shone off its bony eyelids.

It was shamefully difficult not to marvel at the sight and sound of a talking gryphon-thing or want to see if those yellow eyes were real. Hyperion's voice seemed to indicate enjoyment, but who knew, with the Forged? Mark, ashamed of his hatred, gushed, "Forgive me, I'm having a lot of trouble with this assignment. I don't believe in the supernatural and . . ."

" . . . and you are nervous around the Forged. Most humans are, and pretend not. You have always been clear about your limitations in your previous work. I am not deterred. You have come this far. Let us complete the journey." Feathers rustled on it. Its face was scaled, beaked. How it managed speech was beyond him, and yet it spoke remarkably well. But parrots did, Bishop reasoned, so why not this?

It took him almost a minute to understand what it'd said, not because it was unclear, but because he was so confused by the storm of feeling inside himself. Repulsion, aggression, fear. The stink, he realised at last with a shock of guilt, was himself.

Hyperion took hold of the guide rails delicately and spun itself away, tail trailing like a kite's. It's comfort with weightlessness spoke of many years spent there, in the cramped airlocks and crabbed tunnels of the old stations. In its wake Bishop followed, slipping, and after a too brief eternity found himself at the entrance hatch that looked entirely machine though there was no disguising the chitinous interior into which he was able to peer and see seats of the strange kind made for space travel—ball like concoctions of soft stuff that moved against tethers and into which one had to crawl like a mouse into a nest. He made himself concentrate only on mechanics, move a hand, a foot, that's all—it was the only thing that kept his control of himself intact.

Of course it was Forged. The only machines that travelled the length of the system were robotically controlled cargo carriers whose glacial pace was utterly unsuitable for this trip or most any other if you didn't have half a lifetime to spare. For local traffic to the moon and the various towed-in asteroids that had been clustered nearby to form the awkward mineral suburb of Rolling Rock, all travel was undertaken in the purpose built, ur-human creatures of the Flight. Every last one of them was a speed freak.

"Ironhorse Alacrity Valhalla has agreed to take us to our location." Hyperion made the introduction as he waited for Bishop to precede him into the dimly lit interior chitoblast and become a helpless parasite inside a being he couldn't even see or identify but which had a mind, apparently rather like his own, only connected by the telepathy of contemporary electronic signalling to every other Forged mind whereas he was quite alone. He checked his mike and gave Hyperion a sickly smile that he had intended to be professional and cheering. The creature blinked at him slowly, quite relaxed, and he saw that it had extraordinary eyes. They were large, as large as his fist in its big head, but beyond the clear, wet sclera lay an iris so complex and dazzling . . . another blink brought him to his senses. Yellow eyes. It was demonic. What idiot had made them that colour?

He was able to manage quite well and put himself into the seatsack without any foolish struggling or tangles even though now he was feeling slightly drunk. Cocooned next to each other they were able to see one another's heads easily. Stuck to the side of each sack a refreshment package waited. Within the slings toilet apparatus was easy to find. There was a screen in the ceiling, if it was the ceiling—without gravity it hardly mattered—showing some pleasant views of pastoral Earth scenes, like a holiday brochure. Bishop figure it was for his benefit and tried to be comforted as a Hawaaian beach glowed azure at him, surrounded by thick, fleshy webbing that pulsed slightly in erratic measure.

Common lore said it was all right for old humans not to attempt talking to their host carrier at this point. The gargoyle could have been rabbitting on to the ship all the time of course, there was no knowing. His mind fussed around what they might say. It blurred hopelessly as he attempted to drag up anything about the task at hand. He couldn't bring any thought into focus long enough to articulate it.

The door sealed up behind them and was immediately lost in the strange texture of the wall. There were no ports. He wouldn't be seeing the stars unless the Alacrity wanted to show him images from outside on the holiday channel.

"Where are we going?" he asked, though it had been in the damn notes.

"To the spot you requested," Hyperion said with some puzzlement. "Don't you recall?" Bishop flushed hot with embarrassment, started sweating all over again. He didn't remember. Then there was a vague hint that he might have made a call, no, written a request, a secret note . . .had he? He checked the screen inventory of his mail. Nothing. Inside the cocoon of the webbing he experienced a stab of shocking acuteness in the region of his guts and heart. He felt he was losing his mind and that it was paying him back with this lance, this polearm of pure fear. What had he requested?

"No." He wanted to lie but his mouth wouldn't do it.

The Greenjack was quiet for a moment. "I think that we should talk a little on the way there, Mr Bishop, if you don't mind." Its voice was gentle now, and had a rounded, richness that reminded Bishop of leather chairs, wood panelling, pipe tobacco, twilight and cognac. Above the line of the cocoon he could see its feet twitched gently, flexed their strangely padded digits. Dark claws, blunted from walking, were just visible. "I am well aware of the way my claims must appear to scientists such as yourself. Energies beyond human perception existing within our own spacetime perhaps is not too outlandish in itself. But my observations of their behaviour, and what it seems to mean for their interactions with us, that is the stuff of late night stories. Believe me, Mr Bishop, I have studied them for many years before making these statements. And I would welcome any remarks."

Charlatan, Bishop thought. Must be. He'd thought it from the get go, when he first read about it.

Bishop had been in doubt on other assignments, though none of them like this one. Mostly he wrote for journals about science or current affairs based on Earth. He was one of the more popular and able writers who could turn complicated and difficult notions into the kind of thing that most well educated people could digest with breakfast. Normally he avoided all discussions about the Forged and their politics, but of course it had caught up with him as it must with everyone in the end, he reasoned. And his expertise had led to him being selected by the government to come and make a judgement out here about this odd person and its extraordinary claims, its illegal and incomprehensible existence. The Greenjack Cylenchar Hyperion was a member of a class created by the Forged themselves, by the Motherfather, Tupac, whose vast body had bred all the spacefarers and most of the Gravity Bound. It was a class she claimed was scientifically essential, though he had serious doubts. The Greenjacks were there to confront the boundaries of the perceivable universe, and to try and apprehend what to ordinary human eyes was beyond sight. Hyperion, in particular, was said to be able to perceive every frequency there was, and had been given adaptations to allow his mind to be able to cope with the information. Hyperion didn't just see, he watched. Recently he'd been making dramatic claims about his visions that had been in all the papers.

Bishop struggled but the panic was choking, he wasn't able to say the sensible thing he had in mind- namely, "Yes, but just because you can detect these things, why aren't they verified by machines?"

The Greenjack paused, just the length of time it would have taken him to make this reply, and added, "Machine verification has confirmed erratic frequency fluctuations in localised areas, but obviously they can't put an interpretation on these anomalies. We have successfully managed to get some mappings of areas and frequency variations that confirm my own sensory perceptions are accurate."

This was news. Bishop jerked as his screen recovered the files being zapped across to it and vibrated to alert him—all the data was there, already witnessed and verified by independent bodies . . .He felt himself breathing steadily. The scotch seemed to have made it out of his stomach. The pills he'd taken still worked hard on fooling his head it knew which way was up. Better, that was better. Statistics. Facts. Good.

"But if you are too distressed we can delay this," the Cylenchar said suddenly. "Mr Bishop?"

"No, we have to go," he didn't know where they had to go though apparently he was determined. His panic returned.

"May I speak frankly?"

Into Bishop's agonised silence Hyperion said clearly, "I think you have asked me to go to Mars because of your daughter. You are hoping that I will be able to find her where the inquest has failed. Is that right?"

A cold drench covered him from head to foot as memory returned, cold, clear. He couldn't breathe. He was drowning. Mars. Tabitha. The unsolved mystery of the routine survey expedition vanishing without trace. Oh a sandstorm, a dust ocean, a flood of sand, a mighty sirocco that blew them away . . . what had it been and where was she? Nobody could answer. Not even the equipment returned a ping. But how? And when the months dragged on and the company pulled out and sent its condolences and added their names to the long list of people who'd gone missing on Mars during the fierce years of its terraforming and then this assignment came, what else to do? Bring the person who, above all, had been made to see. No frequency, no signal, no energy that the Greenjacks can't decipher . . .of course, if she's there . . . and if she's dead then this one will say so. It claimes that some of the things it can sense aren't people but are what people leave or make somehow in the unseen fields they move in; trails and marks. It says some are like wizards of story, able to make things with shape, with form, with intent that is almost conscious. Some can leave memories like prints on the empty air. Oh. But a man of strict science does not believe.

"Yes." Bishop said. He was small then, in his mouse nest, hanging, damp and suddenly getting the chills. He was afraid the 'jack would say no.

"I will be glad to look," it says instead and Mark Bishop fell into a deep sleep on the spot.

Sleep was one of the many skills the 'Jack had learned in its long years of waiting for things that might not appear. It closed its eyes and shared a warm goodnight with Valhalla, who was more than curious to know the outcome now and sings towards the red world with fire and all the winds of the sun.

They joined one another in a shared interior space, a private dreamtime. It was cosy. Valhalla whispered, "Sometimes I am flying in the sunlight and there is nothing there but I feel a cold, a call, a kind of falling. Is that real? Are the monsters from under the bed out at sea too?"

"Wake me if it happens," Hyperion said. "And we'll see."

He co-created a kind romance with Valhalla in which they saw huge floating algal swarms of deep colour and shadow populate the fathoms beyond the stars. They named them in whispers, and with childish fingers measured their shapes in the sky, and then pinched them out of existence, snuff, snuff, snuff.

"There," Hyperion said, "they may be here, but they have no power. They can only hurt you if you let them. They live in the holes of the mind, and eat the spirit. Cracklegrackle. Just pinch them out." They got back into bed and closed the window, drew the shades. The Valhalla was happy again and drove on all the faster in his sleep.

Bishop was woken by the Valhalla's cheerful cry, "Mars!" The Ironhorse made orbit and scaned the surface to find the small outpost where the Gaiaform Nikkal Raven, chief developer of Mars, had built human scale shelter with its Hands in the lee of a high cliff. "Nobody's there now. If it's a graveyard or a ghost town it's empty for sure but with a bit of effort there's probably power and some basics that you could get going." For politeness they contacted the Gaiaform.

"That's funny," Valhalla said, as Bishop struggled to change his clothes. "She sounds annoyed, or at least, she doesn't want to discuss the place."

The Nikkal's voice was grumpy on the intercom. She grated on Bishop's exposed nerves and wore out his fragile strip of patience almost at once. "My Hands got lost there too. Given up sending more. Thought I'd get to it later, after the planting on the south faces was finished. Just a minor space really, full of gullies. "

They all recognised the feeling this rationale covered. "We don't need your help," Bishop grated. "Just want to get there and look around. That's all."

"But if anything happens it's on my watch," the Nikkal countered.

"Tupac knows we're here," Hyperion suggested. "We won't stay long. A day at the most."

". . . as long as it takes . . ." Bishop said. He was in clean clothes. His panics were gone. He felt old and thin and shelterless and looked around for something he could hold. He found only his small bag and his recorder and filled his hands with them. A panic would have been welcome. Their fury was better than this deadly flat feeling that had taken their place. It was clear now. He was here, Thorson's Gullies, the last known location. Every step was a puppet step his body took at the behest of some will named Mark that wouldn't let it rest but there was no more struggle between them. He did not inhabit these arms, these legs, he felt. They were his waldos, his servos, they were his method. Only his guts were still his own, a liquid concentration waiting for a mould.

"Come on, Mark," Hyperion called from the drop capsule.

Since when had they become friends? Bishop didn't know how but he climbed inside the small fruit shape of the vehicle. Mars had lift cable, but no system in place. Cargo was simply clipped on and set going under whatever power it was able to muster. They were attached to the line and given a good shove by Valhalla. The new atmosphere buffeted them, warmed them, cooked them almost, and then they were down, Bishop still surprised, still too frozen to even be sick with either motion nausea or relief at their arrival. The capsule detached, put out its six wheeled legs like a bored insect and began to trundle the prescribed steady course towards the gullies. Hyperion opened the ventilation system and they sniffed the Martian air. It was thin and even though it had been filtered a million ways, somehow gritty.

". . . it's the names that are part of the trouble," Bishop said, staring out at the peculiar sight of Mars' tundra, red ochre studded with the teal green puffs of growing things in regular patterns. "Good and Evil. Why did you call them that?"

"There are more," Hyperion said. "There is Eater and Biter and Poison and Power and Luck and Fortune and Benificence and the Cracklegrackle. I expect there are many more. But these are the commonest major sorts."

"But why? Couldn't you name them Energy #1 and so forth?"

"I could, but that wouldn't be accurate. Their names is what they are."

"How they seem to you. The one person who can see them."

"That's not exactly right. I think we can all perceive them, but only I can see them as easily as I can see you."

"And you say they are everywhere."

"Scattered, but everywhere in known space I think."

"And some are spontaneous but others are man made?"

"Yes. Few of the major arcana are manmade, like those. It takes a very powerful person to create one. Or a large group of people. There are many manmade minor arcana and many naturally occurring ones like that but they are very shortlived, a day or two at most."

"You see my problem is that I can believe in this kind of thing at a symbolic level, within the human world, acting at large and small scales. We're creatures of symbolic meaning. But you're saying there's physical stuff and its real, external, distinct."

"Yes. I am saying it exists as patterns within the same energy fields that give rise to matter."

"Consciousness is material?"

"No. It has a material interaction that is more than simply the building of a house from a plan or the singing of a song, is what I am saying."

"And these things . . . patterns . . . can influence people?"

"Influence them, infect them, live inside them, alter them perhaps. Yes I think so." The creature stared at him for the longest time, unblinking. "Yes."

"And just like that we are expected to accept this—theory of material mind?"

Hyperion shrugged as if he didn't much care either way. "I report what I see, but I say what it is for me. Otherwise I would report nothing more than machines can report. When you look at a landscape you don't list a bunch of coordinates and say they are mid green, then another list grey, another list white and so on. You say I see a hill with some trees, a river, a house in the distance."

"But you're making claims about the nature of this stuff, linking it to subjective values. Hills aren't subjective."

"They are. True, there is some rock that exists independently of you, some sand, some dust, but without you it is no hill and however the hill seems is how all hills seem to you, large or small, not mountains, not flat, perhaps even with traits that are more personal. If your home is among the hills then they seem well known, if not, then they provoke suspicion."

They were trundling at high speed, balanced in their gyrobody between the capsule's six legs, seeming to float like thistledown between the rocks of this region of Mars; Thorson's Plot. Plot was something of a misnomer as the area, already claimed by an Earth corporate, was some fifteen thousand square miles. The gullies, which made it a cheaper piece of real estate, and complicated to sow—hence the surveying team—were near the western edge and ran in a broad scar north south along the lines of the mapping system. Thorsons had hoped to find watery deposits deep in the gullies or perhaps some useful mineral or who knows what down in the cracked gulches where twisting runnels of rock hid large areas from the sun and most of the wind which had scoured the planet for millennia. All around them were hills of varying sizes, some no more than dunes, others rising with rugged defiance in scarps and screes. Occasionally small pieces of metal flashed the sunlight back at them as they moved between light and the shade of the thin high cloud that now streaked the sky white.

"The remains of Hands," the Greenjack said with interest, of course able to tell what everything was at any distance. "How interesting. And there is some debris from attempts to seed here, some markers, some water catchers. All wrecked. And . . ."

"And?" Bishop leapt on the hesitation.

"What I would call distress residue. A taint in the energy,very slight."

"What energy?"

"The subtle fields. You will find them referenced a great deal in my submitted thesis. Vibrationary levels where human perception is infrequently able, or not able at all. When trauma occurs bursts of energy are thrown off the distressed person into these fields and although they decay quite rapidly they leave a trace pattern behind which is very slow to change."

"A disturbance in the force," Bishop said bitterly. He felt nothing except the dread which had clutched at him in place of his panic.

"It might be only the natural upset of someone experiencing an unlucky accident," Hyperion said, unruffled. "It's hard to say without extreme observation and immersion on the site. You ought to be glad, Mr Bishop, rather than contemptuous. Why else are you here?"

Mark gripped the arms of his seat. He was furious and full of nervous agitation. He ought to be civil, but he felt the need to destroy this creature's claims even as he wanted them to be right for his own sake. He didn't want to know about some spiritual plane, not after all this time it had taken to rid the human race of its destructive superstitions. Even if it existed, what difference did it make to those who were, in the shaman's own words, unable to interact with it. He could see no good coming of it. But he longed for it to be true. Somewhere in his fevered mind where fragments of the shaman's testimony had lodged in spite of his allergic reaction to reading them, he recalled there being quite specific traces of people and moments stuck in this peculiar aether like flies in amber. Not always, not everywhere, but sometime and somewhere it acted as a recorder for incidents and individuals. It could. It might have.

The capsule lurched to a halt. They had arrived at the last known point of the survey team's wellbeing. A couple of waymarkers and a discarded, empty water canister pegged down beside them were the only visible remnants now. Without further talk Hyperion and Bishop disembarked.

They fitted their facemasks—the air was still too thin for comfort—and Bishop put on his thin wind jacket and new desert boots. Hyperion sank a little in the fine grit on his four limbs but otherwise he went as always, naked save for his fur, feathers, scales and quills.

Wrestling the faceplate straps to get a good fit Bishop noticed all the strange little fetishes the creature had attached. Necklaces with bits of twig and bone . . . it looked like it had come off the set of a voodoo movie. He recalled now it labelled its profession on its passport 'shaman'. He was so exhausted by his nervous disorders however, that he didn't have the energy to muster a really negative response anymore. He was deadening to it. At last the mask was tested and his spare oxygen packs fitted to the bodysuit that went over his clothes. Hyperion wore goggles and a kind of nosebag over his beak. He made a desultory symbol in the dust and smoothed it out again with one forepaw. The capsule, obeying commands from its uplink with Valhalla, folded up its spider legs and nestled down in a small hollow, lights dimming to a gleam as it moved into standby operation. All around and as far as he could see in any direction, save for the shaman, Bishop was alone.

"There are very few true disappearances in human history, these days," Hyperion said after a moment when they both cast about in search of a direction. It moved closer to one of the markers and read the tags left there. "And this is not an unusual place, like those twisty spaces close to black holes for example. It is just a planet with a regular geology. The common assumption about this team's fate is that they absconded with the help of the Nikkal. From there a number of possible avenues continue, most leading to the far system frontiers where they were able to drop off the networks."

Bishop licked his lips, already starting to crack. The news was full of the asteroid bayous beyond the sphere of Earth's police influence and the renegade technology that festered there, unregulated. There was a lot of Unity activity. A lot of illegal, unethical, criminal work. "She had no reason to go."

"Perhaps not, but if the rest of them wanted to go they could hardly leave her behind. What would be easier for you, Mr Bishop, to have her forcibly made into one of the Frontiersmen or to have her dead here somewhere?"

How odd, he thought, that the 'Jack had no trouble voicing what inhabited his own awareness as a black hum beyond reckoning. Hearing the words aloud was startling, but it diminished the power of the awful feelings that gripped him inside.

"Let's start looking' Bishop said, standing still. All around them their small dip radiated gullies that twisted and wound. The sun was beginning to go down and the high rocky outcrops cast sharp edged purple shadows.

Hyperion was exacting, his research both instantaneous and meticulous in a way that made Bishop simply envious. "The marker, as the police report indicates, says they started southwest with a view to making a loop trail back here within a six hour period, the route is marked in the statutory map." The shaman sniffed and the nosebag huffed. "All the searches have concentrated on following this route and found a scatter of personal belongings and the remains of a Finger of the Terraform, which was carrying the survey equipment. All of that was recovered intact." It held the two windbeaten Tags in its paw and rubbed them for a short time, thoughtfully. "But they did not go that way. Only the Finger took the trail."

"How do you know?"

Hyperion turned. "I can see it. I think it is time I showed you." It came across to him and held out one large, scaly arm. "Please, your screen viewer. I will adapt it to show some of the details I can see over its normal camera range. This will not be what I see, you understand, as I don't see it with my eyes. But it is the best I can do for you."

Reluctantly Bishop handed over the precious viewer. It was his recorder too. His everything. "Don't mess up the record settings. It's on now."

The Greenjack inclined its head politely and slid one of its broad clawlike nails into one of the old style input ports. Bishop felt a chill. He'd never get used to how able the Forged were with technology. They could interface directly with any machine.

"The signals I use to communicate with the device will cause some interference with my tracking," Hyperion said calmly. "So I will not use it all the time. If you see nothing, you may assume I am watching and listening. I will also shut the device down if its working interferes with the process and I may ask you to move away at times." It handed the screen back and Bishop checked it, panning it around in front of him. The camera showed whatever he pointed it iat, recording diligently, it was really just like holding a picture frame up over the landscape. "I don't see anything."

"Look at the markers and the route."

He turned. From the tag line he could now see a strange kind of colouration in the air, like points of deep shade. They were small. It was really almost like broken pixellation.

"That is the pattern left by the output of the Finger's microreactor projecting microbursts of decaying particles into the energy field. Radiation containment is generally good these days, so this is all you can find. It is also in the standard police procedurals. They mistakenly assumed it confirmed that all the travellers took the same path since the Finger was carrying all the technical equipment and the others had only their masks and gas, their personal refreshments and devices. I would say it is certain that they intended to disappear here as in fact all their individual communications gear has been accounted for along the Finger's trail."

Like a path cut with three dimensional leaf shadows the trail wound into the first gully, followed the obvious way along it and vanished around the first turn.

"We can follow that and verify there was no other person with the Finger if you like," the shaman suggested.

"Part sof a Forged internal device unit were found," Bishop said, brain clicking in at last.

Hyperion shrugged.

"Or?" Bishop started to pan around. He soon found patches and bursts of odd colour washes everywhere, as if his screen were subject to a random painting class.

"Or we can follow the others and find out what they did, starting here."

"What is all this?"

"This is energy field debris."

As he moved around Bishop could see there was a huge glut of the stuff where they were but traces of it were everywhere in fact, even in the distance. "Why so much of it?"

"There was a lot of activity here. The rest is down to regular cosmic interference or perhaps . . . I am not actually sure what all of it is. The energy fields transect time and space but they are linked to it so while some of this is attached to the planet's energy sphere, some of it, as you see is moving. "

Streaks shot across the screen. A readout indicated he was not seeing them in real time, as that would have been too fast for him to notice. The simulation and the reality overlay each other on the image however, and the difference there was undetectable.

"I believe the streaks are bonded to the spatial field, and they are therefore stationary relative to absolute coordinates in space, thus as Mars traverses, so these things pass through." The creature cocked its head, a model of intellectual speculation.

Bishop relaxed his tired arms so the screen pointed at the ground, saw the streaks shooting through his feet. "Through us?"

Hyperion nodded. "As with much cosmic ray debris. It moves too fast for me to say anything about it. I would need to move out into deep space and be on a relatively static vessel, in order to discover more about them."

"No such ship exists," Bishop snorted. "Well, only . . ."

"Yes, only a Unity ship perhaps," the shaman said. "I shall ask for one soon."

They shared a moment of silence in which the subject of Unity, the newly discovered alien technology, rose and passed without further comment. Bishop would have loved to go into it at any other time. The surge of hysteria it had engendered had almost died down nowadays, with it being limited to offworld, restricted use, or far enough away from Earth and her concerns that it wasn't important to most humans, whatever strange features it possessed. FTL drives were only the half of it, or whatever they were. It was under review. He'd seen some of the evidence. Now he let it go and lifted the screen again. If Tabitha had gone on one of those ships, she could be anywhere. It would take years to get into Forged Space by ordinary means. Even an Ironhorse Accelerator couldn't go faster. She could have been there since the day it happened, almost a year ago. "This is just a mess."

"No," Hyperion said. He lowered his head and sniffed again, a hellish kind of hound. "There were four individuals here, all human, and one Forged, Wayfarer Jackalope McKnight."

"Bread Zee Davis, Bancroft Wan, Kialee Yang . . ." Bishop said, the names so often in his mind that they came off his tongue like an old catechism.

" . . .and Tabitha Bishop."

"I am sure which is the Forged," Hyperion said, "but the humans are harder to label. They are distinct however."

"They'd worked together almost a year," Bishop said, wishing he'd kept his silence but it was leaking. "No trouble. She sent me a postcard."

"may I see it?"

He hesitated, then fiddled the controls and handed over the screen. It had been shown so often during the inquest he knew every millimetre of it better than he knew the lines in his own hand.

The object was small, almost really postcard sized in the Greenjack's heavy paw. "Kialee is the Han girl I am guessing."

"And Wan is the one with the black Mohawk. Davis is the wannabe soldier in all that ex military stuff." He knew every detail of that postcard. What most mystified him about it was how friendly they all seemed, how relaxed, the girls leaning on each other, the guys making silly faces, beer in hand, around them the dull red of the tenting and in the background a portable generator and jumble of oxygen tanks. It could have been a holiday for two couples and not students on work assignment. He wasn't sure if they'd been dating or if dating was a concept that had gone out with dinosaurs like him.

The Greenjack was stock still. It looked intently and then handed back the screen. "Thank you. In that case I can now say that there was a struggle here. Bishop and Yang are surprised but Davis and Wan are both agitated throughout. Only McKnight is calm."

"He was new. Newish. Their old Wayfarer went to another job."

The colours illumined as the shaman talked, showing Bishop warped fields of light that were as abstract as any randomly generated image. "McKnight and the men remain close together. There is a conflict with the women. There is a struggle, I think at this point the women are forced to give up their personal devices to Terraform Raven's Finger. I believe they are tied, at least at the hands. McKnight is armed with explosive charges for the survey. But he's also more than big enough to overpower and threaten them. I guess this is what happened. Davis and Wan dislike the events a great deal but they are willing participants. That's what I see. Then there's another argument, here, the men and McKnight. It's brief. Blood and flesh scraps from McKnight are found near here."

Bishop saw the oddest nebula of greys, streaked with black and bright red. "They said there was some kind of struggle . . .the Wayfarer was defending . . ." But the gargoyle shaman was shaking its head.

"He cuts out his own external comms unit," Hyperion said precisely. "In the Wayfarer this is located at the back of the skull and embedded in the surface beneath a minor chitinous plate. To remove it would be painful and messy, but it is perfectly possible and certainly not lethal. But all communication is cut before this so there is no official account of how it was removed. The only person who can account for that is Raven and she claims there was a local network dropout. I would have to question her directly to be sure of her account." The implication was stark.

The air, already bitter, felt suddenly colder. "So Davis and Wan made him do it?"

"I cannot say for certain. But he does it. Any other method risks it being hijacked by signals that would give away his position. He's hidden it somewhere around here I'd bet. Or given it to the Finger who lost it in the gullies way before it signalled a breakdown. We should look for it. Then they leave." Hyperion pointed Northwest. "That way."

Bishop thought of the evidence of the Finger's call. Raven's voice said, "They've gone. Just gone." And in that phrase she'd ushered in an entire cult of people convinced Mars harboured ghosts, or aliens, or fiends. As if their numbers needed adding to. But Bishop couldn't keep up his anger. The pictures continued.

There was a faint colouration like a long tunnel or a tube made of the faintest streaks of yellow, grey and ashy white. It was almost pretty against the deepening red of the Martian afternoon. The tunnel down which Tabitha had vanished. So the shaman said.

"I hardly know anything about these people," Bishop protested with distress. He didn't understand how the creature drew its conclusions.

"It is all right, Mr Bishop," the shaman said calmly, setting off in this new direction. "I know everything about them that I need."

For the first time in time that he can remember lately, Mark Bishop has enough energy to hurry in the Greenjack's wake. "But how? Just from some picture?"

"Yes."

"But you can't tell anything just from a picture."

"You can tell everything from a single look. For instance, I know that you, mr Bishop, had it in mind that if you found me a fraud here you might use your gun to shoot me dead. And then yourself. We would be a memorial in this unpleasant spot, the monument of your surrender to despair and your inability to remain rational in the face of my abominable supernatural exploitation of both your grief and reputation." It continued walking steadily.

Bishop had no answer to that. He'd never verbalised or reified that intent, but he couldn't entirely dismiss it. His gun was in his holster pocket. Everyone had them. He couldn't say the thought hadn't been his secondary insurance. That and the recorder of course. It would have told the sad tale to those who came to find out what happened. The notion had been discarded a long time before they even landed though, he realised and now, the recorder was instead preserving this vision of Hyperion's skinny ass slowly wandering along a trackless gully through soft dirt and Bishop's laboured breathing.

"Anyone can see these things," Hyperion mumbled as he went. "But they don't know how to tune in, to refine and translate and know them."

"Don't start on the psychic stuff." What the hell had those boys and that monster done with his little girl? 'Tell me about Wan."

"Bancroft. He is idealistic, practical, yet ordinary. Bread is determined, focused and he has been somehow thwarted in the past which has made him bitter though he hides this with great charm. McKnight is an entrepreneur, comfortable with criminal ways."

"McKnight is the leader then."

"Wan is the leader, Mr Bishop, whoever's foot may seem to go first. As for the women, neither of them are involved in this plan except by accident. It is simply unfortunate that they were in this team when Wan met McKnight. I am certain McKnight was the catalyst for what occurred here. Wan is too poor, too badly connected and too ignorant to plan this venture alone. Possibly he didn't think of it until McKnight arrived to put the idea in his head. He isn't creative."

"You're quite the detective," Bishop didn't mean it quite as bitter as it sounded.

"I would like to be. But it isn't my intuition working so much as the patterns that I see."

Bishop gave a cursory glance at his screen. A twisting tube of colours, some bleeding others sharp, was all he could see; bad art on a tiresome landscape. "If you say so." In spite of himself he had no trouble believing the Greenjack now. "Are the girls all right?"

"They are physically unharmed at this point. They are talking here . . ." the shaman indicated their way and the stretch ahead. He moved off alone for some distance, then narrated, "I feel terror and anger. I believe they were attempting to bargain an escape or discover the real plans. McKnight is all for telling them. He is enjoying the action. Wan forbids him. McKnight doesn't mind this but Davis is getting edgy. He has never liked the involvement of the Terraform. His fear of retaliation is keeping him quiet now."

Bishop stopped suddenly, rooted in the unmade earth. He had realised that he was walking through time, and the confidence in the shaman's analysis made him fear where the future led very greatly, even though it had already happened. He attempted to rally some criticism, some countermeasure to the rigorous story unfolding and prove at least to himself that there was a chance most of it was simply the shaman's whimsical interpretation of some very dry facts, but he struggled.

Ahead of him the large creature stopped in its own dusty track and turned about. It seemed patient and concerned. Every time he looked into its peculiar yellow eyes he expected the disturbance of an alien encounter but instead he felt that he was understood and the feeling made him desperately uneasy. Who knew what confidence trickery it was capable of, after all. But for the life of him he couldn't figure out a motive.

"When we get to the end of this," Bishop said hoarsely, coughing, "what will we do?"

"That depends on the end."

"I mean, if she isn't dead, if she was taken somewhere . . .will you help me? You said you'd ask for a Unity ship. I guess that means you know someone."

"I will find your daughter, Mr Bishop," Hyperion said. "I already promised to. If you prefer I will say no more about the events that passed this way. No doubt you must wonder how I can know and there is no way to tell you how, any more than you can explain how you do most things you do that are your nature. I expect that some greater analysis will be able to detail the process but I am not interested to do it myself. I see these people and I feel what they have been feeling, as if I can watch it in a moving storybook. There are other things present, besides the people now. These disruptions in such a quiet area have acted as an attractor and some of the energies I spoke about earlier are beginning to converge on the scene. As yet they are only circling. You may see . . ."

"These stains? I thought they were just bad rendering or the light or something. They're so faint. Watermarks."

"They are the ones. You will see them circle and converge, then scatter and reform. They may merge. Ignore them. They are not important."

"But they . . ." But the Greenjack was already moving on. The shadows were lengthening into early evening and a slight cooling was in the air. Bishop kept one eye on the trail and the other on the screen but the silence was too much for him. "Talk," he said.

CRACKLEGRACKLE • JUSTINA ROBSON

"They are not speaking here," the shaman replied over its shoulder. "Yang is looking for a way to escape. Bishop is locked in her thoughts. She is angry with McKnight for his betrayal of their friendship, or what she thought was their friendship. She is questioning her assessment of the others. McKnight is leading, he is content. Wan and Davis are in the rear pushing the women on. Wan is excited. Davis is starting to lose trust in him. Davis has a weak personality. He believes he ought to be leader and Wan is beginning to annoy him. He is starting to form a strong resentment."

"What is that cloud?"

"He is forming negative energy vortices. This kind of personality often does. Their energy scatters out from the holes in their energy bodies. It is an interesting feature of humans that they create negative energy attractors much me readily and strongly than positive ones. I am not sure why but I believe it is because damaged individuals are leaky, prone to influence and loss, whereas healthy types do not shed these frequencies without some deliberate effort. They are impervious to wild influence and create almost no disturbances. I must consult with the other Greenjacks when they are done travelling."

Bishop was silent for a while and they plodded on some quarter kilometre more as he checked his recordings. It was an ecology he was seeing, if it were true. A psychic kind of ecology. He couldn't help but notice it, even as it wasn't part of his concern. Just a peripheral. If the Greenjack had tried to convince him about all this any other way he could probably have thought of a good hole or two to poke in things but as it was . . . he shook his head and struggled on. He wasn't fit and although gravity was lighter and walking easier it was a long time since he'd hiked further than his back yard. He found himself stopped suddenly, almost walking onto Hyperion's tail. The Forged was still as a statue.

Bishop looked at the screen quickly. A darkening storm of purples and reds like a miniature cyclone was all around him. He had to wait, then Hyperion said,

"They stop here. McKnight signals offworld. Wan and Davis start arguing again. Yang tries to escape. She just runs. Bishop tried to stop her. McKnight notices. Davis starts to run after her but Wan says no. He was willing to leave her. He wants to. Davis catches Yang. Wan says to McKnight they should leave them both. He knows Davis is trouble, Yang he doesn't want anyway; they have some history . . . it's minor . . . he'd rather leave her for some reason I don't . . . Anyway. Bishop protests. Yang becomes hysterical. McKnight hits her unconscious. Now Wan gets angry with McKnight. Davis's antagonism towards Wan crystallises. He threatens to turn them all in. Now McKnight doesn't like that. McKnight threatens Wan and Davis. Wan tries to calm things down. Bishop is raging. Wan ties up both women, hands and feet. Yang is injured, there is blood here. They wait. Quite a long time. I think an hour must pass or so. Davis is now focused entirely on Wan. Hates him. McKnight is the only calm one. Wan is furious but he's too smart to let it out. A ship comes. It lands over there . . ."

Mark Bishop got up and followed the Greenjack over to the place across the long shadows that had nearly covered the whole ground.

There was no sign of a landing, but then given the weather, there wouldn't be. He recorded dutifully. The coloured waterworld had gone. He watched the Greenjack circle and look, and pause. It returned from a small exploration and said, "This is the end of the trail here. The ship has come. It's a Forged craft. I don't know its name, but if I ever meet it, I'll know it by its energy signatures. It is one of three types of Ironhorse currently operating between the Far System and Earth. Can't say more. They all embark, except Yang. She's dead."

Bishop half wanted to ask for more, certain it was hiding things, but then he decided that it was enough, he didn't want to know. Everything inside him had stopped, waiting. What the shaman had just said was a testable claim, unless it meant some kind of spiritual residue. Beneath his coat he felt the hairs on his neck stand on end. His heart gave an extra beat. "Are you sure?"

"Yes." Hyperion paused and then made a brief gesture with its head. Bishop followed the line, recorder in hand first. He saw nothing, just the usual Mars stuff, but then the shaman walked him out another hundred metres to a small mound that Bishop or anyone would just have taken for one of the billion shifting dunes. "She is here."

Bishop took measurements, readings. They were still technically well within Thorson's Gullies. Nobody would have come here for a long, long time. Perhaps never. The land was bad, useless. This zone had already been mapped. There were no deposits of use. Then, with the shaman's help, he set up his recorder and began the process of moving the sand aside. He used his shoe as a spade. It didn't take long before he bumped something. Without ceremony they uncovered a part of a desiccated human body, just enough to see the identifying badges on the suit, and then they covered it up again.

Bishop moved away a short distance and sat for a while, drinking water and watching the sun go down. It got very cold. His feet and hands ached. He wished for the scotch again, fervently, avidly, relentlessly. Hyperion sat beside him like a giant dog.

Bishop's hand strayed to the machine but he left it alone. He stumbled over the words, "Do you see her?" He was braced for any fool answer. He wanted there to be one, a good one.

"She was here," it said. "But now she has gone."

Bishop nodded. He wasn't going to ask for the details. He wasn't ready yet. Leave it at the cryptic stage until . . . "We should go."

"I suggest we walk back to the capsule rather than make any transmissions the Terraform might interpret. Also we must now consider this a murder investigation. What would you like to do? We could report it to the police now and let them . . ."

"No. They got it all wrong the first time." Bishop was surprised by the force of his own hatred but the shaman didn't skip a beat.

"Then we should not discuss this with Valhalla. We need help from sources that don't mind being accomplice to criminal acts."

Belatedly Mark realised by this it meant their failure to inform. Anything that wasted time now didn't matter to him. "Can you track them from here?"

"Not directly, but their intentions are reasonably clear. McKnight is at least guilty of manslaughter and kidnap. Wan and Davis kidnap, misuse of corporate properties, perversion of the course of justice. The Terraform is on their side. They have every chance to make a good escape but they couldn't head sunward—there's nothing there except Earth and the high population satellite systems, full of officials and the law. They have gone to the Belt first—no Forged ship could take them further without at least stopping there for supplies. We will find something that way." It seemed completely confident, almost resigned to its own cold certainty.

Bishop ignored the bleakness in its tone and waded forwards grimly in its wake, a squire to a weird and uncomforting King Wenceslas of the sands.

It was a long, hard, cold and lonely passage. Bishop struggled all the way not to ask all the questions that were hunting him but ask them he didn't and at last they retraced all the path and the Valhalla's hand opened its thousand eyes and let them in. He couldn't afford to indulge his fears.

"Where to?" the Valhalla asked as it left orbit, swinging away in an arc that would return it to the sunward side so it could pick up extra heat.

"Just to the lift station again," Hyperion said with a sigh as though the journey had been tiring and a disappointment.

It made some small talk with Valhalla as Bishop settled himself in. He intended to check his recordings and prepare some method for transmitting them safely in case something happened to him but before he was able to do any of that exhaustion took over and he fell asleep. He slept all the way to the port and woke feeling drained and thin. Hyperion led him through their formalities and then they were sitting in the cafeteria, Bishop facing a reconstituted dinner with a dry mouth.

"An ordinary journey to the Belt is a three year stretch," the shaman said. He was lying like a giant dog on the smooth tiled floor next to Bishop's table, resting his head on a plastic plant pot beneath the convincing fake fronds of a plastic grass. "The fastest available transport can make it in one year. But Unity ships can make it instantly."

"Interference," Bishop croaked. He had managed a mouthful. It wasn't bad but he was so hungry even cardboard would have seemed delicious. Hungry or not he was loath to think about Unity travel. They said it interfered with you at a fundamental level. They were not sure what the long term implications would be.

"I will search here, perhaps they came this way." It was unconvincing. Nobody in their right mind would come this way if they wanted to get the hell out of Earth's influences.

Bishop surrendered to his curiosity and need. "You said you could get a Unity ship." He said it quietly. They weren't illegal, but they also weren't allowed this close to Earth space.

"I can ask a favour," Hyperion agreed. "I feel convinced they have taken that route. I do not see how any legally operating taxi would be involved, and the illegal ones all come from midspace and most have Unity drives. The most likely destination is Turbulence, the port on Hygeia. The majority of transfers take place there and there's only lipservice paid to the law at any level. It is Forged space and mostly rebel Forged at that."

"You think Wan wanted to remake himself?" Some humans wanted to experience addons that were better than just a comms set. It seemed ludicrous to Bishop, insane, an extreme form of self mutilation beyond tattoos and piercings, some kind of primal denial of one's self. It frightened him.

"I think there are lots of opportunities for all kinds of profit out there. Especially for those already on the run."

Bishop crumpled the wrapper his cutlery had come in. Unity technology was infectious. Even passengers aboard craft operating the technology were at risk. So far in the years it had been around its effects proved relatively benign, but theorists guessed this might be a product of a much more significant infiltration process. To use it was to risk something that could be a living death. Fanatics spoke of puppetry and zombies, aliens operating behind the scenes. He'd heard . . . "Perhaps they'd just abandon her."

"She was a witness," the shaman said. "A Terraform is complicit in crimes bringing severe penalties. Murder and human trafficking. The foundation of Mars, no less, is at stake. If they went with Raven's blessing then they didn't go alone."

"Get your ship."

The creature got up slowly, "I will be back soon."

Bishop finished that meal, and then another as he waited, forking up food, watching the news on the cafeteria wall, not thinking now there was no need to think any more. When he got there, when something happened, then he'd think.

They took an ordinary ship out to deep Mars orbit again, and were set adrift in a cargo pod with barely enough oxygen to survive. Something picked them up at the allotted minute and second, as displayed on Bishop's illuminated screen. Something cast them off again. There was rattling and clanking. After a few minutes of struggle they emerged into the unloading bay of a large port. There was no trace of whoever had brought them there. There was no gravity, just the sickly spin of centrifuge. It was a struggle to keep the dinners inside him but he did, though they felt as if they'd been in his stomach the three year journey he'd skipped. The Greenjack helped him to get his spacelegs and then went off, sniffing.

Bishop sat in a rented cubic room at the port's only hotel and watched what Hyperion transmitted to his screen. For a few days this was their pattern. The shaman didn't find the ship he was looking for, nor any trace of it, nor traces of the passengers. There were a lot of other things Bishop saw that disturbed him but he was protected, by his distance, the recorder and the fact that seeing these troubling things was not his immediate mission. There were many shadows here, like the inkstained Mars twilight, moving splatters that now and again coagulated around a place or a person. He started to type, wrote "haunted?" He managed to read the report in bits and pieces. He struggled to wash, to shave, to function in between. He drank something called scotch that was alcohol withy synthetic flavouring. It was good. It did the job. Beside 'haunted' he copied the most loathsome and mysterious of the names of things that Hyperion had identified. Cracklegrackle. His nerves jangled. He tried turning the screen on himself, but only when the Jack wasn't there. He looked old. A fucking wreck to be honest. He was amazed.

"They only affect those who wish to be affected," the shaman insisted as they ate together on their last, fruitless night.

"But how?" Bishop pushed his food around the bag it had come in, squashing it between his fingers and thumb.

The answer was so unexpected and ridiculous it silenced him. "Through the hands and feet, the crown or base of the spine. Never mind that. These rumours of laboratories open in the midstream; any surgery is available there. We should look into that."

Bishop agreed, what else could he do? They moved to a lesser port, and then a lesser one, the last place that pretended to commercial operations. There was no hotel, just some rented rooms in a storehouse. Bishop began to run out of money, and sanity. He couldn't bring himself to contact work and explain his absence. He thought only about Tabitha. He drank to avoid feeling. He took pills for regimented sessions of oblivion. Sometimes he watched the Mars journey again on his screen. Those strange floating films of colour absorbed his attention more and more. The more he watched them the more he saw that their movements seemed sinister and far from random. He saw himself pass through them and tried to remember if they had changed him.

He'd felt nothing. Nothing. Hyperion's statements about the people, seemed more and more unlikely. He felt it was a goosechase.

Perhaps he had been paid to lead Bishop out here where he couldn't make trouble, and strand him. Perhaps the Terraform had bought the Greenjack off. This ran through his mind hourly. Only the transmissions of the 'jack's travels kept him going.

Then one day months after they had set out he got the call.

"I found her."

"Is she . . ."

"Alive."

He scrabbled to get clean clothes, to clean himself, to get sober. He was full of joy, full of terror. The hours passed like aeons. The 'jack brought a ship—one he saw this time, an Ironhorse Jackrabbit with barely enough space to fit them aboard. It yawned and they walked into its sharklike mouth. It held them there, one bite from vacuum death, and blinked them to the cloudstreams of Jupiter. He barely noticed.

"Are those things here?"

"Everywhere, Mr Bishop," Hyperion said.

"What things?" the Jackrabbit asked.

"Energies," the Greenjack said. "Nothing for you to worry about."

There was some bickering bout the return journey. Bishop couldn't make sense of it.

"Where is she?" he gripped the Greenjack's thorny arm. Its scaly skin was like a cat's tongue, strangely abrasive. Around him, floating, the few human visitors to this place looked lost. Tabitha was none of them. They all looked through portholes into the gauzy films of the planet's outer atmosphere streaming past below their tiny station. It looked like caramel coffee. Outside, various Forged were docked and queued. People had conversations in the odd little cubicles, like airlocks that dotted the outside of the structure. Sometimes the doors flashed and then opened. People came out, went in on both sides of the screen wall that separated the two environments of instation and freezing space from one another.

"This way," the jack said. He reached out and laid his tough paw across the back of Bishop's gripping hand for a second, then led him with a kick and drift through the slight pull of the planet's gravity well to one of those lit doorways.

Bishop peered inside, looking for her. The shaman followed him in. The room was empty.

He turned, "She's not here!"

The shaman pointed at the panel in the reinforced floor. Some Jupiterian Forged was on the other side.

Bishop looked at Hyperion because he didn't want to look at the window but he floated towards it, his hands and feet betraying him as they pressed against the clear portal suddenly and on the far other side, across six sheets of various carbonates, glass and vacuum, the Forged pressed its own hands towards his open palms.

Jupiter was no place for a human being. They died there in droves. Even the Forged who had been engineered before birth to thrive in its vicious atmosphere and live lives as glorified gas farmers fell prey to its merciless storm. The upper cloud layer was never more than minus one twenty Celsius. Large creatures didn't operate that well at those temperatures, even ones that were mostly made of machine and chemical technologies so far removed from the original human that they were unrecognisable components of life. But Tupac, the motherfather, was able to create children who lived here, even some who dived far to the place where hydrogen was a metal; scientists with singleminded visions. Tupac's efforts had advanced human knowledge and experience to the limit of the material universe.

Bishop's senses didn't stretch that far. He stared into eyes behind shields of methane ice that were nothing like his own, in a face that was twice the size of his, blue, bony and metallic and more like the faceplate of a robot fish than anything else. Narrow arms, coated in crablike exoskeletal bone reached out for him. The hands were five-digit extensions, covered in strange suckerlike skin that clung easily to the glass. Behind that the body was willowy, ballooning, tented like clothes in the wind, patterned like a mackerel. Jellyfishes and squid were in its history somewhere, microprecise fibre engineering and ultracold processor tech its true parents.

"She has a connection to Uluru," Hyperion said quietly, naming the virtual reality which all the Forged shared. Where their bodies could not meet, in mind they could get together anytime. "I can put it to your screen."

Bishop turned then, "You're not seriously suggesting this . . . thing . . . is my daughter?"

"There is a market for living bodies of any kind in the Belt. Old humans are particularly preferred for the testing of adaptive medical transformation. Technicians there have a mission to press beyond any restraint and develop their skills to make and remake any living tissues . . ."

He exploded with a kind of laugh, "But you can't *make* Forged. Not like that."

Hyperion was silent for a moment. "They say it is important to become self-adaptive, that they are the next step beyond Forged. They will be able to remake themselves in any fashion without experiencing discontinuity of consciousness. Any flesh or machine will be incorporated if it is willed. The Actualised . . ."

"But it can't be her!" His stare at the shaman was too wide. His eyes hurt. Against his will he found himself turning, looking through the walls at the creature's blinkless stare. Its face had no expression. It had no mouth or nose. Gill-like extensions fluttered behind its head like ruffles of voile. Its octopid hands pressed, pressed. Its nose touched the plate. Hyperion was holding the screen out to him.

He took it in nerveless hands. They were so limp he could hardly turn it.

"Davis tried to turn Wan in, once they reached Volatility, that port on Ceres. But the Forged Police there are all sympathisers. Wan and McKnight sold him, split the money . . ."

On the screen was the standard summer garden that Uluru created for all such meetings, a place for avatars to stand in simulated sunlight amid the shelter of shrubs and trees. Running through it, watermarked, was the background Bishop could really see, the reality he was standing in. In front of the monstrous creature attached to the window stood Tabitha, in jeans and the yellow T-shirt with the T-Rex on it that he bought her at some airport lounge some lifetime ago. Her soft brown hair moved in the nonexistent breeze. He touched the screen to feel the texture of her perfect skin.

"Daddy." The lips moved to whisper. Through her hazel eyes the great void eyes of the fish stared.

It was only an avatar. You could make these things easily. The photographs were even in his recorder. The voice was only like hers, it wasn't really hers. There must be hundreds of standard tracks of her in the archives somewhere. These things were simple to fake.

He thrust the screen back at Hyperion, though it was his, and tried to muster some shred of dignity. "Summon the ship."

The creature didn't move from its floating position at his side. "Mister Bishop . . ."

"You've fooled me long enough with your chat and your lines and your little premade adventure complete with faked body, but I see through it now, if you can stand the irony of that, and I'm going. I find no evidence to confirm any of your ridiculous suggestions." He was so angry he could barely speak. Bits of spit flew off him and floated, benign and silly bubbles in the slowly circulating air. "Really this was one step too far. I bought it hook line and sinker until now. I suppose you were trying to see how far I could be drawn. Well, a long way. Perhaps you were going to get some money for bringing the Institute into disrepute and scandal when I made some case with it for your insane claims about good and evil and possession and . . . your goosechase. Yes. You took advantage of me. I was weak . . ." There was a sound in his head, that black hum. He could hear something in it. An identifiable noise. Definite. Sure.

"Bishop," the creature snapped.

". . . daddy!" came the faint call from the screen as it tumbled down past the shaman's side and clattered against the cabin wall.

The black hum was laughing at him, a dreadful sound. It hurt his chest. It hurt everywhere. He was furious. His skin was red hot, he coudln't think of where to go. What a fool he'd been. "How dare you. How dare you . . ."

Suddenly the hideous gargoyle hissed, a low, menacing sound. "I have done what I said. I have found your daughter. I have no interest in your views . . ."

Bishop was glaring around wildly. He made a shooing motion. "Get away! You won't mock me! Stupid, hideous creatures!" He began to thump the glass panels where the Jupiter's hands were stuck. It didn't move, just stared at him with its hidden, empty eyes. "You!" he turned on Hyperion. "Make it go away."

The Greenjack looked at him flatly and even with its expressive handicap he could feel its disgust. "Mr Bishop, I urge you to look again, and listen. Your daughter . . ."

"It's not even possible!" Bishop kicked strongly for the door. Behind him the recorder tumbled, ricocheting, out of control, the voice that came out of it growing fainter.

"Daddy!"

The door controls, they were too complicated for him. He couldn't figure them out. He turned and lashed out wildly, thinking the greenjack was closer than it was. It caught the recorder easily from its spin and held it out to him, contempt in its every line.

Bishop took the little machine and smashed it against the wall until it stopped making any noise.

Beyond the clear wall the Jupiterian was letting go slowly, suckers peeling off one by one. Its eyes had frosted over strangely, white cracks visible across the ice surfaces, spreading until they shrouded the whole orbit. Its head moved back from the pane and dipped. At the same moment the door opened.

Bishop was out in a second. He couldn't breathe. Not at all. His chest was tight. There was no damn oxygen. There must have been a malfunction. He gripped the handrails, gasping, the blood pounding in his eyes. "Oxygen!" he he cried out. "There's no air!" In his ears the black hum.

Hyperion passed him, gliding slowly. He was holding the recorder and ignored Bishop's outburst. He started talking and as Bishop had to listen to him, unable to go anywhere, he heard the black sound forming itself into a shape.

"I think that although you have broken the speakers and the screen the memory is probably unharmed. It will not be possible to locate and arrest Davis as he has been scrapped for parts. Tabitha says that Wan and McKnight disposed of him first, before they went into the Belt proper. Wan wanted her to be rendered as well but McKnight said there would be a lot more for a whole live subject. They were planning how to create a trafficking chain and where to get more people from. She was taken to some facility about one twenty degrees off Earth vector. They wanted to make her as far from the original human as possible to prove their accomplishments but also because they thought it was fitting for humans to end up like the Forged out here have all ended, as slave workers in the materials industry. She isn't like the other Forged of course, she's just a fabrication. Her links to Uluru are very limited. She has no real contact other than voice and some vision with anyone else. And the Forged here are mostly rebel sympathisers. She tried to call you, but the networks out this way are very bad and none of the regular channels would carry her messages anyway because she is marked as a risk to the survival of the Actualist movement. It took a great deal of trouble to get her to come here. It is dangerous. She risked everything. And she didn't want to see you. I had to take days to persuade her that if you came there might be sufficient evidence to reopen the case and bring the Earthside Police out here to pursue it."

Bishop gulped. "You've done a very thorough job, I'll give you that."

The Greenjack made a clacking noise. It spoke in a calm, reasonable manner as if Bishop were perfectly lucid. "I have not been able to trace the routes of Davis, Wan or McKnight yet but I think they will be easy to find. I hope you understand, Mr Bishop, that I do not require your permission to pursue the investigation or to make my findings known to the authorities. I also advise against your attempting to return to Earth alone. Many of the Forged here who would have you believe they are honest taxis are pirates like Wan has aspired to become. The going rate for a live Old Monkey human in the Belt is upward of fifty thousand standard dollars. I doubt you have the finances to buy yourself out of trouble, even if they wanted you to."

The terrible pulse of the black name wouldn't let him think. Bishop reeled against the bulkhead, the rail gripped in his slippery fingers. He was heroic. "We must rescue her. We can take her back. Find a way. I can raise the money on Earth. The Police can arrest those responsible and the government will . . ."

"The government is well aware of the situation," Hyperion said. "Returning Tabitha Earthside and attempting remodelling would be tantamount to a declaration of civil war out here. They will do no such thing. You know it as well as I do. Pull yourself together." It handed him his screen, which it had repaired somehow. Aside from a cracked screen and broken speakers it seemed all right. "This is your evidence. It is our only hard evidence, aside from the Uluru recording I have made, but of course those involved Forged, so they are suspect." It was only tired by this admission of bigotry in the judicial system. "If you do not act there will be no justice of any kind."

Bishop held the screen without turning beyond the home page. He heard his own voice babbling, "We could kill them. McKnight, you can find him . . ."

Hyperion waited a few moments. "Tabitha is an extraordinary person, Mr Bishop. Although it is a mystery how she has sprung from you. She understands your feelings. You have hurt her deeply and this makes me dislike you very much. After what she has been through, your rejection is by far the most damaging thing that has happened here. And now, you are seeking to spread misery further by your stupidity. The energy wells out here are all very dark. A few lights shine. Tabitha Bishop is one of them. You are now claiming one of the energies is responsible for your weakness. I find that contemptible. Pull yourself together."

"You! You could find them and kill them and you won't do it! Just this superstitious, religious babble. You bring me here to show me . . . to show me . . . Here, here!" He tried to get the screen to focus on him. "Show me now. I know it's there. That thing. Show . . ." but Bishop could not finish. The words had cannoned into each other behind his tongue and exploded there into an unpronounceable summons for hell. Cracklegrackle.

He wanted very much to be dead. The shame was unbearable. He could not carry it. On Earth he would have been on his face, on his knees, here he was floating, curled up tight into a ball.

The shaman waited. "You are not possessed, Mark. You are simply hysterical. Your future with your daughter is your choice. However, we must take the recording back to Earth and submit it to the Police there. Then we will have done our part. I, at least, will do so. You must hurry. She has to leave in a moment."

Behind Bishop's eyes the blackness was shot with red. He snarled at Hyperion, silently and then, inch by inch he hauled himself to the cubicle door, again with that will that wasn't his, no it wasn't.

His joints hurt. His throat was so tight. He couldn't breathe. Inside. The rails. The flat expanse of glass. The slices of clear shielding. The coffee coloured clouds miles below as soft and gentle as thistledown. Dirt on the floor. They ought to clean this place. It was so hard to see through the handmarks, the footprints, the wear and tear on the old polycarbonate. It was so hard to see through the glass and the frozen methane that melted and ran to keep her sight clear, then froze, then melted again so that she was always half blind. It was so hard to see through his tears.

CRACKLEGRACKLE

I wondered for a while about the ending of this story. It could have gone either way, I felt, right up to the last lines—he could have allowed his view of what humans are to collapse and accepted his daughter again, or not. The pixies didn't care either way so it was left to me to choose what I wanted to say about this element of the human condition—our ability to flex our minds and remake them in order to accommodate radical experiences and new information, particularly with regard to our ideas about ourselves. Much as I wanted to write the happier ending, in which change was made and acceptance realised, I chose the other because I felt that it pointed up the core tension more strongly.

NO MAN'S ISLAND

NO MAN'S ISLAND

This is an old story, one I wrote in reaction to the popular alien invasion/meteor disaster movies that came out at the end of the nineties.

NO MAN'S ISLAND

"Mariann," Dr Shaw motioned her to a seat in his office, "How's the Farsight project coming along?"

Bad news. She hadn't got the job; otherwise he wouldn't be starting her off with something dear to her heart. "Oh, not so bad," a breezy tone, almost chipper. That proved to him that she was braced for the worst. She put her hands in the pockets of her cardigan and sat down, fingers curled into soft fists around the knowledge which she had been going to tell him, but now wouldn't.

"I hear the transmissions are still pretty clear," Dr Shaw eased down into his usual armchair and leaned forwards in an attempt to show more interest.

"I could make you leap out of your seat, Bob," Mariann thought, "if you knew what was in my mind." She said, "Yes. The filter programs are keeping it within ninety- percent accuracy. I have masses of data to keep me busy. For years," she added the last part as a signal that she knew that's how long she was going to be here, not because it was true.

So CERN had rejected her application. She had half-expected it. Now the certainty that she would never work there made her heart thump with finality. But it lurched into the rapid beat of youth at the same time, because of the knowledge in the last batch of data, because she was the only person who knew, and they did not know, and now they would not have the privilege of knowing her discovery.

Shaw made some more small talk in his preamble, to which she responded kindly out of old friendship. Meanwhile the analysis of the huge burst of pi-mesons and fundamental particles exploded anew in front of her eyes. It scattered across Shaw's face in a spattering of beautiful telltale sparks. As he came to talking about the CERN job she was dreaming of the map which showed those objects just visible at the edge of the lightspeed horizon. Put the map over the sparks. She saw his face through the transitory particles, now long dispersed. She saw a distant galaxy, so far away it had no name; a place brought into view only by the slowing expansion of the Universe. Mariann was not the only thing slowing down. She smiled at the galaxy, and Shaw brightened as he broke his news, thinking her already resigned to another contract in the department. A young PhD student who had been in on the discovery of gravitrons had pipped her to the post.

She didn't care because she had pipped the whippersnapper to the discovery of the century by trawling through routine analysis, had plodded to victory through years of useless, cloying mud which no self-respecting career scientist would have mired down in. Of course CERN would not want a forty-eight year old mathematician with a short publication list who spent her time prospecting through reams of transmissions from minor long-distance probes like a lost forty-niner trying his luck too far downstream—not even knowing where the river started or if there was any gold up in the mountains. Which is why they had not struck the motherlode.

Somethingfast and deadly had passed within a hairsbreadth. Something which controlled exotic dark matter and exerted gravitational forces big enough to bend space to its will. An infinitesimal strip of the Milky Way's arm had lain in its path and been redispersed as energy and sub-atomic debris. The Alcubierre calculations worked out. She had found the path of a warp ship.

Shaw was talking about some papers she might want to contribute to. She smiled at him. She could afford to be so warm now; it felt as though her insides swam in a boundless ocean of generosity. Written up as a paper the Farsight report was worth everyone's attention. They would want her, everyone envy her discovery. And then they would take it.

"I'll write up some notes and let you know some of the more interesting aspects of the newer material," she heard herself saying.

"I'm surprised you're taking this so well," Shaw said, looking slightly perplexed as they stood up. "You wanted that post so much. Even last week you said you were thinking of early retirement, if it didn't work out."

"Yes, I know," she said. "But today things look different somehow." She shrugged and let herself out, feeling him watch her going, feeling the wake of her going as light as the air moving along the hem of her dress.

In her own room she went first to the desk and checked the data again. She lifted the telephone to call her husband and tell him about not getting the job. As she dialled she looked out of the window. The bulk of the Science Museum was heavy in the weak daylight and the London sky glowered. A spatter of tiny droplets struck the glass without sound. At the shop in Hounslow James answered, "Hello?"

She hung up.

He sounded bored and she found that she didn't want to say anything. She didn't want his sympathy. Pity is for people who are weaker than you are.

James Harris picked up a wooden horse from Goa and gave it a gentle going over with a soft cloth. He wandered slowly through his shop, looking for a suitable place in which to display it. It was not the kind of thing that Mrs Eudora Pope would buy and so it did not need to take up valuable space close to the counter. Its silent history of Portuguese invaders and ancient Jewish kingdoms under the exotic sun of India—which he had written carefully on a little card—would have to wait for someone with more time and less money. Eudora Pope collected female deities and what James thought of as Louis the Fourteenth memorabilia. In darker moments he suspected that she fancied herself as Marie-Antoinette, but this was not a point that counted against her because, to his increasing upset, he found he rather fancied her himself.

The phone rang. He picked it up, answered. No one there. He looked out of the window and traced the fat, tulip shape of the horse's ear with thumb and forefinger as he checked the street. Tourists and locals were scattered in equal measure over the pavements and traffic was thick. There was no sign of the Rolls Royce Silver Shadow.

He was relieved. Eudora Pope was an experience, like the passing of Halley's Comet, which ought to come upon a man only once every seventy years or so.

For ten minutes he fussed with the horse, giving it its own velvet plinth in the window in front of an imposing Welsh dresser before returning to the next item of stock. He was just wondering how much mark-up to put on it when the sprung bell at the door tinkled brightly, like the sound effect to a falling ray of sunshine.

Eudora Pope had blonde hair in a French pleat with a few perfectly placed bubble curls arranged around her face. She wore a charcoal grey wool suit, tailored by hand in Paris and a salmon pink satin blouse. From her Italian shoes to the high crown of the pleat she was every inch the most surreal creation James had seen in his whole life. She wore no labels, designer initials or hallmarks; her wealth of such enormous proportion that it required no authority to validate it. Her face was smooth and beautiful without any particular point of interest. Eudora Pope was a mysterious tabula rasa; a woman of no provenance. She tortured him daily as he tried in vain to invent her history and know who she was. She walked straight to the counter and smiled at him.

"Mrs Pope," he said, with a warm genuine affection in his voice which had taken him hours of practice to assume so casually, "what a pleasure to see you again."

Taken closely her presence was a natural force. It drew fantasies out of him he hadn't even known were there, and he felt himself beginning to buckle already under their weight. Perspiration broke out on his palms and under his arms.

"Mr Harris, good morning." As she spoke she did that funny little squinch of the eyes that people do when they flirt—a microsecond shutter flash in the direct beam. It went straight through his liver and settled on his kidneys. He shuffled as he subdued the sudden urge to go to the toilet. An old boyhood weakness. He would not admit it now.

"I have the item we were discussing last week," he managed to say. "It's in the back room. Won't you come through?"

James preceded her. Since her first visit to the shop some twenty weeks ago he had had nine haircuts, countless shoe shines, many trips to the dry cleaner and taken to exacting wet shaves. He thought he was reasonably presentable for someone coming up to fifty-five and that if only he could somehow get Eudora Pope to listen to everything he knew about her favoured collecting pieces she could be impressed by the depth of his knowledge. He also thought he was stupid for even dreaming that she might give him the time of day, but the idea would not rest. As they arrived in the musty order of the store-room Eudora Pope's acquisitive smile increased tenfold in wattage and his heart threatened to beat him unconscious.

He remembered he had left the till open but did not make a move to go and close it.

After a terrible moment in which he thought he wouldn't be able to move he located the drawer he wanted and pulled it open. As he lifted out the small statue all that he was aware of was Mrs Pope's faint, expensive scent. Drunkenly he took the statue out of its wrapping and showed her the stone carving it had taken all these weeks and a fresh mortgage to secure.

"An Epona," she said as the silk slithered away and revealed the Celtic horse goddess standing with an apple in her hand.

James looked down at its small, round-bellied shape and thought of Demeter and Persephone, of Venus/Aphrodite, Hera and Athena standing on the dusty Trojan hills. He thought of Boadicea and bare-breasted Britannia and felt himself blush. He looked humbly at the immaculate face of Mrs Pope.

"How totally enchanting," she said, reaching out for it. "How perfect. I do so love these goddess figures. How much?"

James faltered. He was full of words for the statue and wanting to talk to her about it; the wear of its voluminous contours, the age, the passion of the sculptor long-dead in their barrow. Instead he handed it to her and watched her fingertips rove impersonally over the broad belly and the nub of head which was all Epona had left.

"No horse?" she asked, as if in an afterthought.

"She doesn't have ponies with her in any carvings that are legally obtainable at the moment," he said, a slight tinge of exasperation bleeding through which he quickly swallowed as she glanced at him.

"I've seen one, in a museum somewhere. I forget," she said, weighing the goddess in her hand critically. "I'd rather one with a pony." She pouted her lower lip for a second, then shrugged and slipped the fertility idol back into its silk bag, tying up the noose.

"But I'll take her." She extracted her smooth cheque book from her shoulder bag and looked at him expectantly.

He spoke in a whisper, the vastness of the sum pornography in his mouth.

Eudora Pope mouthed the words carefully as she wrote. James watched every furl of her perfect red lips and his blush spread over the whole of his body.

She signed and stripped the paper from its book. She had bought two things from him before and the checks had cashed both times. For a moment they held the slip together and she gave a curiously lush, sated smile directly into his eyes.

He could only watch her and worship as she closed her purse, dropped the Epona into her handbag and swung it back up on her shoulder. They shook hands, a lingering grasp, and then she turned and eased her contours through the canyons between the antiques. The bell tinkled.

How long later he didn't know—a few seconds or a minute— he glanced down and saw she had left her pen behind. It was a Schaeffer, solid gold, no initials of course.

James grabbed his jacket from its hook and bolted for the door, key in hand. He put the pen in his pocket, flipped the Closed sign into action and slammed out, noting with gladness that there were no customers standing in his way. He was just in time to see the gravity well of the Silver Shadow curving the corner around itself.

Within a minute he was inside the dusty interior of his old Saab, heading into the stream of traffic.

It was almost one o'clock. Mariann had not moved from her chair even to refill her coffee cup. For the final time she re-modelled the possible pathways. Again, the vector emerged clearly on the screen before her. It was straight as an arrow and its path, once the corrections for lightspeed were put in, was aimed directly towards that unknown galaxy. She peered at the blob of the galaxy but there was no information to be had about it other than that it was there, or had been there once. Thinking about it reminded her of James. All those haircuts, those careful combings to hide what had once been his hairline, the sudden efforts to erase the passage of time. She scowled and pushed the map aside.

A sense of frightening isolation had suddenly come over her. It was due to the combination of what she saw on the screen and that sudden vision of James. She was only too well aware that the pleasure of joy in alone-ness comes from not really being alone. James had always been there, like cosmic radiation, bathing her from a distance in security. They were one another's support, for all they spent their lives as private collectors who kept their experiences to themselves. This being private had drawn them together in the first place. The bliss of not having to explain oneself! Other men Mariann had known were always more demanding, wanting to know all about what she was thinking, not able to understand the satisfaction of a secret treasure, an insight which was not named and accepted into the canon of a group mind. Taken over. Invaded. Stolen.

Mariann cupped her hands around the knowledge, holding it in her palms carefully, tightly, like live grenades, until she was sure she could contain it. When she could uncurl her fingers she switched off the computer and the coffee-machine, picked up her bag and went home.

James watched Eudora Pope step out of the Silver Shadow and trot up the steps into one of the capital's most exclusive restaurants. He felt sick with anticipation.

He double-parked the Saab and darted towards the entrance. He had no idea what he would say, all he could think of was that she might smile with gratitude. Momentum carried him up the steps. He had hardly reached the top when she appeared suddenly in the doorway. A man was with her. He was young, James noticed in the fraction of a second's grace he had—twenty five or less, elegant in an expensive suit. Neither of them were looking at him so that he had to tap Eudora Pope on the arm as she descended. Foolishly he held out the pen.

She glanced around with a frown, wondering who was being so rude, and her eyes fixed on him with a flat stare.

James thrust the pen forwards at her with an unplanned jerk so that she drew back against her companion—"Mrs Pope. Your pen. You left it behind."

She was staring at him with complete ignorance, her only expression that of utter disdain that he, whoever he was, could be so crass as to approach her this way. In that moment it occurred to him that he was so unimportant to her that out of context she didn't even recognise him. He stood there, stunned and trapped by forces beyond his comprehension as the young man took her arm and steered her away to a waiting taxi.

"But you do have affairs. You do have a life, of a kind," James thought to himself before the paralysis broke. He hoped she wouldn't realise who he was and that she would never come back to the shop. Then he glanced down at the pen in his hand. It was plain lined, clean and functional. Abruptly he thought of Mariann.

He turned to the doorman and thrust the pen towards him with such firmness that the man took it on reflex. Then he drove home.

When James arrived he was surprised to see Bing, the labrador, outside playing in the garden with her tennis balls. She bounded up to him, wagging. Then he noticed Mariann's car parked around the side of the house and was jerked out of his self-absorption by a fresh gout of anxiety. He ruffled Bing's furry head and hurried indoors.

Mariann was sitting in the dining room with an untouched glass of water beside her. She sat still and looked out into the back garden.

"Are you all right?" he asked quickly, relieved to see her.

"I'm fine," she said.

"What are you doing home so early. It's lunchtime," he added, already realising she might very well ask the same thing.

"I've finished," she said. She sounded far away. "I got to the end of the Farsight thing."

Vaguely he remembered her mentioning it over the months; the monotony of the data, the finds that turned out to be mistakes in the equations, the despair, the hope. "You found something, for real?" he asked. He hoped it was real. He gathered from her voice she hadn't got the job but because she hadn't mentioned it he couldn't offer her any consolation. He wished he could touch her but she was stiff as a board.

Mariann kept looking at the garden. She addressed herself equally to it and to him, her tone matter-of-fact, "It was the residual pathway of a ship travelling in an Alcubierre warp."

He didn't understand it at first. When he did it was as if space ballooned and he saw a gap between them so massive that there was no way across. His own day, the giddy feeling that he might, eventually, dare to leave Mariann, gaped in his mind like a clown-faced joke. The enormity of what she had said seemed inconceivable. He had thought of foolish things whilst she had discovered a secret that would change the world forever. Abruptly he felt the need to sit down and pulled out the chair at the head of the table, falling into it.

Mariann glanced at him and smiled, friendly but wistful. He wondered why.

"Aren't you pleased?" he asked.

"No," she said. "I was at first. I thought it would show those stupid asses over at CERN what they'd missed out on. Show everyone. But then I thought—whoever it was out there, they passed us by and they didn't even notice us. There's no way a ship in warp could notice us. We were road furniture. Any closer and we'd have been roadkill. You see? It's useless knowledge. They've gone. A long time ago. Understand? It doesn't matter." She turned her hands over in front of her, examining them as if searching for something in their emptiness.

James was still grappling with the concept. "But that's other life," he said slowly. "We are not alone. Mariann. Other people. Other, *things*." He looked at her, thunderstruck, feeling more stupid every moment under the patience of her gaze.

"Yes, we are alone," she said, laughing without any humour in contempt of herself and of the vanished travellers. "They were on their way somewhere else. Somewhere more interesting." She pushed the water glass further away from her, "All that my discovery means is that particle physics is on the right track and that technologically it is possible, in this Universe, to create and use a warp to move big distances if you have somewhere to go. We don't even know where to go."

He didn't know what stunned him more—her words or the calm, measured way she said them. The dining room was quiet. Outside he could hear Bing barking. In the garden the flowers nodded in agreement with the breeze. He suddenly realised she hadn't told anyone but him. That they were the only two people in the world who knew.

"Mariann," he began, reaching out his hand towards her.

She said, "And I thought about a new universe, with aliens in it. Imagine. Religious outcries, political ground-grabbing, the scurrying rat race to assimilate and take control of what it means. There would be a new burst of energy for space travel, money poured into contact attempts, billions wasted because we want those powers for ourselves, without finding them out for ourselves. Wonderful. Horrible. And we would always be waiting, like rabbits on the road wondering what the shining lights are. Watching the skies, scrabbling for a defence—James, think what it would make of us all."

He sat back a little bit and put his face in his hands. Behind his eyes he felt the terrible contrast of distance between them and the aliens, so near and yet so far; almost within reach, but out of reach forever. "Oh," he said, and he thought he sounded like a child when it discovers that there isn't a person somewhere in the world who knows everything.

He pictured a ship of terrible aspect, shaping space to make a sailing channel, laying waste to everything in its path. He saw a Silver Shadow sporting bull bars. He saw Eudora Pope's face rapt on the trail of another acquisition.

"If they come back. ." he speculated.

"They'll probably run us over with a quark-gluon plasma," Mariann said with satisfaction. "Let's hope this isn't going to become the M25."

"Oh," he said again. He felt pity for the Earth, so small and vulnerable, alone in the vastness of space, nobody knowing it existed or caring to look. He glanced into Mariann's eyes and saw himself mirrored there. A friendly feeling passed between them and she smiled. He took her hands in his. They sat together, alone in their thoughts, sharing the knowledge.

"But you'll have to tell them?" he asked eventually.

"I came home to think about it." She sighed an awkward sigh and composed herself. "I wondered—what is it like to be neglected and know that you're completely overlooked? Easy to answer," she snorted a quick self-deprecatory breath. "Was it time to get my vengeance and share this feeling? Tell the world that all their self-important posturing doesn't matter? That we weren't worth a look? I wanted to. I would have enjoyed it. For a minute or two."

James rubbed her fingers gently. "It's a terrible feeling," he said and glanced down with guilt.

Bing appeared at the window, a green ball in her mouth, paws on the sill. Her tail wagged back and forth mightily as she grinned at them.

"But, yes," Mariann said distantly, "I expect I will have to, eventually."

Bing chased away across the lawn, rummaging under the rhododendrons, snuffing under the fence.

James smiled at her, "You don't know what ails you, do you dog? Do you?"

NO MAN'S ISLAND

Although I felt frustrated with this story at the time, feeling that short stories ought to make big, clear statements with whiz bang kinds of endings (the pixies are rolling their eyes), I find its less obvious statements much more pleasing now. Aliens and other people might walk all over your heart in their big uncaring boots, but a dog can still save you . . .

TRÉSOR

TRÉSOR

This is the first short story I ever wrote, except for one I wrote when I was six, called "The Sea Stallion". They're both horror.

TRÉSOR

Lily is sitting in a doorway. She has been there quite some time and her hand is out even though there is no one there to press any money into it. It is dark and it is on the verge of raining with the damp, seaborne air of the coast roaming through the streets. Her street is poorly lit. It shares a light with another road at the corner. Her view faces a brick wall, punctured by a series of backyard doors which are all shut. Those that are not overgrown with nettles and grass are chained with links that could tether a barge and padlocked.

Lily has been sitting there for quite some time but she couldn't say just how long. Before it got dark, but not long before. In her top pocket are two cigarettes. She is saving them but soon it will be time to light the first one. For now she will suck the street air between her teeth and taste the faint chemical tang of it. She has a connoisseur's nose and she can separate it out into all its fractions—petrol, diesel, sulphur, something from the factory that gives a burning sensation at the back of the throat. It doesn't have a name, that one. She thinks of it as brimstone. She likes that reminder of a film whose poster she saw once in a bus shelter, the reminder of treacle of a man's face with straggling blond hair. Treacle, now that has a bitumen flavour. You could fill in all the holes in the road with that. Sometimes the air is filled with the hair-curling odour of boiling sugar beet from a different factory and sometimes with the nauseating stench of fish offal being rendered. It depends on the wind and the day. She doesn't need light. She can tell everything by its scent.

Today, just the brimstone, rather strong. And from the sea, salt and ozone and heavy ions and the dank, welcoming wetness from slippery weed and green, slimy tendrils that she has seen from the sea front, the ones that hold their own water with them, caught under a thick mucus between their wiry hairs. The cigarette will take all of these away from her and replace them with the comforting oblivion of bitter tobacco. It will dull her taste buds for later. She is forlorn. She prefers a sugar day when the obnoxious carbonisation comes clear over the roofs. A taste of burning, of something hot. It reminds her of a different life. She stood and watched horses being shod in the low-roofed forge. They would stand and snort as the white-hot iron made the soles of their hooves bubble black as tar and sent of clouds of thick yellow-white vapour that stank very like the sugar-beet at the chocolate factory and made every animal nose twitch. We don't like to smell ourselves burning alive. Lily sometimes likes it because it reminds her that she is alive. At other times she lights up as soon as she gets outside.

Lily's arms are long and white. She has grown like that indoors, away from the sun and its singeing rays. Her nails are thin and raddled like washboards. They split and peel away in flakes when she chews them. She can fold each one of them double in her teeth, pinch them tight in the middle and then watch them spring back, slowly. It doesn't hurt. Sometimes she remembers what she has had in her hands and keeps them away from her mouth altogether.

Someone is coming along the street. A man. He is walking up from the far end, the dark end, so that she can see hardly anything of him save his silhouette against the sodium glow of the roads at his back. Quickly she fumbles in her pocket and brings out one of the crinkled paper tubes. It is not a sugar day but out of habit she snaps off the filter tip and then regrets it, holding it pressed in place like a fool, her hands shaking. She will not recover her nose for hours now. She glances down the way. He has some time to go yet. He is not tall and not well built. His boots on the cobbles make the light, half scrapes of a tired creature that has no particular goal in mind. Lily flicks the filter away into the standing water near the grate. It rolls like a barrel as it wets itself and idles in the shallows, bobbing. She wonders if they make lifejackets out of the same stuff. It floats very well.

The man is almost close enough for her now. The wind is against, in patches, then, in the lulls she can smell him. He is wearing an overcoat of wool, dirtied and greasy, but wool through and through.

It is damp, with spray from the front, rain from the air and beer, not today's. Closer and she tastes aftershave. There was a lot of alcohol in it once but now there is hardly anything left of what was once something spicy and rich and bitter—frankincense? tar? treacle? It was expensive. It has a subtle softness to it she is surprised by.

He hesitates as he sees her stand up on her step and put her boot down onto the cobbles. In her hand the white cigarette wobbles ever so slightly. He peers at her as she says, "Have you got a light?" She can see him in the street light now, but her face is in the shadow. It's probably just as well. He is younger than she thought and his face is unshaven and grubby. After a brief struggle with misgiving he begins to search his pockets one by one. Underneath the grimy overcoat he is wearing a suit of something pinstriped and thin. His tie-knot is wrenched small with worrying and offside. She smells the oily, unwashed seabird smell of his hair and the residue of cheap soap made from little more than animal fat and lye. The frankincense is stronger now, but not enough.

He sees her face in the glow of his lighter flame and winces, snatching it away but she is quick to draw and the smoke fills her mouth. "Would you like to come in?" she says after the jolt is gone and the smoke eddies out, grey, between her narrow teeth, "it's dark inside." He is across the alley now, almost against the wall. His fresh sweat has made the sharp odour from under his arms suddenly more potent. She keeps the cigarette near her face as he thinks. "How much?" he says, more for something to do than to know. "Five pounds," she says, "three if you're quick."

Lily has no mirrors in her house. She has no lights. There is nothing that anyone might want to see save her and she can do her seeing when it's daylight. She is used to fathoming her way through the dark. There is a large mattress in the middle of the floor, a cupboard on the wall and a sheet on the floor with the things she has collected from the sea on top of it. A horseshoe—lucky, it has seven holes—is nailed in the darkness above the flue. Beside the mattress is a large bottle. It says it is whiskey but that is not what it contains. She could never drink something with such a powerful, poisonous taste as that. She takes one mouthful and another drag on her cigarette, holding the smoke inside her as long as she can, then again, until he is done. He throws some money at her and is away before she has got off her back. Lily's back is thin. She can feel the floorboards through the mattress and the nails jutting out of the boards. It is a princesses' talent.

Outside once again she places the bottle beside her, cap just set on it, not screwed on, delicate, and sits down again on the step. The wind is blowing the smell of the sea towards her. In her top pocket is one cigarette. She is not the pinch-faced girl she was a few minutes ago when she smelled the frankincense. She is stronger and brighter and her forebodings have gone with the filter, which has rolled down into the grate at last with the coaxing of the wind. Lily plays with the lid on the bottle that is not whiskey. It has a lack of odour she finds deeply peaceful, even with the tobacco buffer. She bathes in it, filling herself up with its clarity. It reminds her of nothing in the dull night air. A dog barks far off among the houses and she listens for footsteps. Soon enough they are there, tapping with steel-toed bravado through the descending mist to her door.

This one is tall and wiry. He is covered in the smell of his animals—dogs, cats, something even more vile that leaves its mark by glandular means and the metal smell of the shipyards. She gets the other cigarette loose. She steps down firmly this time, all the way, both feet, takes a swig from the bottle, holds it there, not swallowing. The swing of her hand with the cigarette is signalling enough. He knows her semaphore. He has a matchbook from a pub somewhere and cradles the lot in his hands as he rips one loose. Hairs float down from his denim sleeve onto the wet stones.

The pink tip flares and stinks. She bends close and sucks directly into her lungs over the pool her tongue is protecting. He does not flinch because she has changed now. Beneath her translucent skin the lights and greenings of the seablood have been leached away by the damp and the dark. She is almost pretty is Lily. She can see him thinking if he should ask her now, what he should say. His face is cruel and inward looking and as he opens his mouth to speak she can smell mince and onions on his breath. He is just the one she has been waiting for. She takes the cigarette out of her mouth and purses her lips. She leans closer to him with a smile and places the lit end of it, glowing like a fiery eye, next to her mouth.

Lily breathes out. The smell of the forge, the smell of burning hair—so candy hot—fills the night with its own billowing mist awhile. Along this street after dark nobody answers a man's scream. She breaks the bottle on the step and uses it to best advantage whilst he is blind. The cigarette covers the fresh, repellent stink of iron and the steam that rises from her grate as she picks the glass up carefully and takes it inside to throw it away. Later she takes him in. He has a packet of cigarettes himself, not her brand, the matchbook, a watch on a leather strap, a few bus tickets, some folding money, a pamphlet, a boiled sweet, a packet of cough drops and some photographs of himself with a woman at a place Lily has never seen—somewhere inland. She places these on her sheet of treasures along with the watch and the bus tickets, puts the money in her pocket. The rest she pushes into the fireplace with his clothes and lights with the matches and the assistance of the foul flavoured, volatile saliva that is coming rapidly to her mouth.

When she has eaten Lily finishes her second and last cigarette, smoking it down to the very limit that she can still grasp between her sharp, narrow teeth. Tobacco is a good thing to dull the nose and the tongue. Later she will take him down and show him to the sea, but not too close to the front, lest the shining green weeds bring him back to her. Out a ways, where the brimstone stink of the city is almost gone and the sky is free from the acid colour of it. She will find one of those white horses with the salt manes and ride him home.

TRÉSOR

I have avoided horror quite a lot in writing, mostly because I felt unequal to the task of really putting the wind up people although I've tried to do that since I was small. While movie horror often makes me go "ugh" it almost never makes me go "aaaghhh!". This style of "disturbia" fiction seems much easier and more satisfying, and more achievable than a real "aaaagghhh!", which only moments of Stephen King have ever so far provided (for me anyway).

THE SEVENTH SERIES

THE SEVENTH SERIES

The concept for the original collection in which this story appears is The Seven Deadly Sins. This story is about Envy. I decided to write about a situation in which I experienced an unhealthy but apparently unstoppable dose of envy— yoga. I have been a student and teacher of yoga, but also one of the least physically flexible humans in existence at the same time. Four years of forward bends never put more than an inch on my hamstrings. It wasn't until I realised I was doing the movement all wrong internally that I figured out some of what was the problem, but that's another and duller story.

THE SEVENTH SERIES

"The secret of enlightenment is that there is no secret. Enlightenment only requires that you invite it to come, and then it will begin to appear. The question is, can you invite it with an open heart? I guess what I'm saying is—do you really want to know? You have to surrender, give up your ideas. You have to accept what you find."

Davey had invited enlightenment in some time before the yoga workshop he attended in London, so when the teacher in residence there sat and explained this fact to him he wasn't paying as much attention as he might have.

"The enlightened see things as they really are. It seems such a tiny thing, but when you stop to consider how we continually project ourselves out into the world without realising it, you can understand what a genuine shift of comprehension this may cause. Sometimes it's a surprise—to stop thinking and just notice what's been right there all the time."

Yadda, yadda. Davey felt impatient. He knew that he should be beyond impatience and this made him cross. He tried with all his might to let these feelings go, but they returned with the galumphing speed and enthusiasm of a wet Labrador puppy. He opened his eyes and gave up, stared at the floor and thought about work. In particular he thought about Katya, the heroine of the internet multiplayer game he was developing.

He planned her personality profile all through the rest of practice. When the time came to go he found himself standing in the hallway without knowing what he was waiting for.

Kate, the teacher, was shaking hands with her students, asking them about their health, talking with personal knowledge of all their problems. Davey had been her student for five years. She'd been much of the inspiration for Katya, although his need to keep their relationship on a proper footing made him keep that notion firmly at the back of his mind.

She shook his hand and looked him in the eye with gentle interest.

"I was wondering," he said, getting straight to what was on his mind, "if you'd ever heard of a thing called The Seventh Series."

Kate blinked in surprise and took a moment to brush a strand of hair from her face, tucking it behind her ear. "I don't think so. There were six series of postures developed from the old text of the yoga korunta. Is that what you mean? Another one in that series?"

"I guess so," Davey ducked her gaze and then returned to it. She had a very friendly and attractive face, but he wasn't good at maintaining eye contact with her because of the guilt he felt at not practicing with full attention. And because he'd developed a habit of fantasising about going out with her. "I've been working on a new game. I wanted to call it that. But you know, not in case it was already a real series or something."

"A game based on *yoga*?" She paused to wave goodbye to one of her friends and he printed the exact curve of her cheek on his memory as she smiled.

"Something like that," Davey said. "Well, with yoga elements. Instead of karate and that. But like *Tomb Raider* as well. You know, a sort of search for the missing seventh series—and then finding it would be the last level, but with a team of adventurers in a lost zone of the sub-continent." He paused, "I searched around for it, but I haven't seen anything. Do you think it would be OK to make it up?"

"Oh, I'm sure," she said, smiling. "It's only going to be a fantasy after all. I'd love to see it when it's done."

Without realising he was going to he blurted, "Um, would you help me make up some of it? The seventh series, I mean."

"What, invent the poses?" she pulled a quizzical face, thinking it through. "All right. Why not?"

They ended up going out for a coffee to discuss it, and then met one day later in the week for lunch. Before he knew how he had done it Davey found himself asking her for a date, trying not to stare at his feet. She said yes. Davey blushed with boldness and pleasure and for two days could do no work at all.

As their relationship flowered the screen character of Katya Remington became more faulty, more interesting. Davey let her have a past life with some heartbreak. He let her have a dark side, now that he didn't need her to be so perfect. He gave her a devious streak and a talent for gamesmanship, a hard-bitten poker player's astuteness, before he posted her to his boss in the 'States. He watched the outline of an entire person disappear across the high bandwidth line in less seconds than it took to say her name.

Summer came and found him mooning over Kate alone in his study. She had gone to India, for her regular study months in Mysore with her yoga teacher, and they communicated via the internet cafés there. Davey clicked her last letter closed and saw he'd received an email from one of their mutual friends, Foyle Durant, an American yoga enthusiast. Foyle verged on yoga fandom. Davey had always thought he was prone to taking it all far too seriously.

> You won't believe what I just saw in this bookstore downtown. I'm so wrapped I'm sending you the address along with this digi-to I took right there and then. You can get it on Visa. Best, F.

A JPEG was attached. It showed a poster advertising e-books and videos on various esoteric subjects. Unmistakably, with Foyle's finger pointing at it, there was a DVD called "The Seventh Series: Yoga's ultimate masterclass, as never seen before, performed in New York City by the discoverers of Nathamuni's lost texts of the *Yoga Rahasya*. Specialist Order."

Davey, surprised and confused, wondered if Kate had been wrong. Was there such a thing? But his game was now well underway and the artists were already hard at work preparing the visuals. The marketing was being produced. Anxious, he flicked back to his behavioural subroutines for Doctor Durant, who was a combination of bits he'd cobbled together from himself and Foyle but he couldn't concentrate. He didn't know what to think. How could it be real if Kate hadn't heard about it? What should he do? Buy it and include it, if he could somehow obtain copyright permission, if he needed permission. Then again, if some bastard had ripped him off . . .

Davey backed up his machine compulsively, as he did in moments of worry, and then put his head in his hands. A year's work he'd done on this project already. The whole team had.

He emailed the address that Foyle had given him from the poster. It was a small online company that specialised in rare occult books and esoterica for 'the discerning connoisseur'.

Shortly after this incident Davey was sitting in the advanced yoga class. They were closing their practice with the traditional chant of Aum, the sonic symbol of the life of the universe. In Davey's game of The Seventh Series this sound and the written symbol for Om told the careful player where hidden levels and secrets were to be found. He thought of this as he added his voice to the moment.

He was also thinking about when Kate may return and what she'd say when he showed her the video from the shop. He fretted that she'd be horrified by the figure of Katya Remington, adventurer. Katya was undergoing 'bootification', a process where real artists took his rough sketches and personality profile and made her into a genuine three-dimensional living and breathing digital entity. Davey was slightly in love with Katya, even though he'd tried to make her less ideal. He worried about what was happening to her when she was out of his control. He felt guilty, as if the real woman would be jealous of the made-up one, or even vice versa.

Aa- Davey said in the chant, joining the heartbeat of the galaxies in their turning, joining the mind of Shiva where it meditates and allows, by his attention, existence.

The artists in LA wanted to change Katya, from a cerebral, rather boyish girl with a ponytail and eyeglasses into a 36DD, 20-inch waisted minx—keep the ponytail, glasses turned to shades. As a result of this, they'd argued and now Davey was on edge. He was tired of replicating clichéd old fantasies, and the original interest of finding a quirky new angle for the game had vanished in the exhaustion of defending it to people who didn't want to know. He envied the originators of any genuine Seventh Series their facility and wisdom. He envied Kate with all his heart; she didn't live most of her life tormented by fantasies of her own making.

Uu—Davey came to the centre of life.

He thought he could go away for a time. Forget the game. Pursue real understanding, pursue all the series of yoga and master them. That would be a real achievement. He had the money—developers weren't exactly poor in this avenue of the marketplace. Plus, he could escape from thinking of ways to create extra points rewards in the game for players following the romance between Katya Remington and Doctor Durant. He'd thought at first the tension between the two was good, a new angle to play for as you diced with death in the Kerala jungles. Now he thought it was an adolescent wank fantasy. Yeah. He had to escape this and find his own space.

Mmm—the close of day, the blink of an eye, death.

I want to learn, he thought. I want to see. I want to go where Katya Remington was going to go, become the thing she was going to become, before they turned her into another *Lara Croft* clone. I want to become better than this.

When he got home there was an email waiting for him.

Dear Davey. If it exists, we'll find it. If it has a price, we'll sell it. If it has no price, we'll think of one! Thanks for messaging *The Lost Bookstore*. We are presently having trouble with sourcing *The Seventh Series DVD*. Our suppliers have failed to deliver and we are beginning to suspect that we have been duped in this matter. (Occupational hazard). We have put one of our top researchers from our Rare Books section onto your case, since the DVD is based on a missing piece (alleged) of the Yoga Rahasya, which has been verified in a private collection—but she'll find your DVD too. Her name is Loretta Haas and she has experience in obtaining antique and hard-to-find items in this market. She will put together monthly reports for you for the a regular payment of $70 per month inclusive of all taxes. To agree to this . . .

Blah blah.

$70 was less than an hour's work. Davey paid it and began to work on the scene-by-scene scripts and layouts for *The Seventh Series* that needed to fit on top of the game proper, the picture of Katya he'd drawn himself still stuck to the wall, her diffuse, vague outline shadowed almost into a pure silhouette before the glowering intensity of a simmering Chennai sunset. Next to her the photograph of Kate Hannigan smiled at him. He wished he were with her.

Dear Davey,

I now have in my possession a copy of the original 7th series manuscript, which I obtained from my contacts in Mysore, who obtained it from a group of Calcuttan Shaivites, who are reportedly close to the owner who is a member of their particular sect. Whew! They claim the owner is the guy in the digital recording, which was made in New York when he was visiting there, though they don't have the files themselves. So, it looks like I was too hasty in thinking it a hoax, and this recording may still exist.

Three others have pursued stories of the Rahasya text to India. One—Foyle Durant, your associate?—has returned, broke. He claims to have been led a merry dance by the Shaivites. He's convinced the thing is a fake and has been saying so—I'm sure you're aware of his opinions.

Sincerely, Loretta Haas, *The Lost Bookstore.*

Davey did know Foyle's view.

"It's a whole crock of utter shit," Foyle had raved to him over the phone. "You stick with making it up. Man, at least you'll have something real in your hand at the end of the day."

Dear Davey,

The original text of the Rahasya fragment is now on loan to the University of Calcutta and has been verified as to its age by carbon-dating. I have applied for my associate there (Professor S. Sinha, an expert on Vedic texts) to view it and verify its authenticity. They are unwilling to make any promises. The paper or whatever it's on is deteriorating, and must be kept in strict conditions.

Sincerely, Loretta.

Seventy bucks for this? Too much and not enough. Davey thought of giving up. He wrote a love letter to Kate. He missed her badly. The new cardboard cutout of lifesize Katya Remington watched him from the doorway, her lips in a sulky pout.

Dear Davey,

I offer you my condolences, if that's what's appropriate,

on your guru's death at the school in India. Ninety-three is not a bad age, but it must have been a shock. My personal friend, Sara Forward, the journalist, attended the funeral since she was in India already, researching an article for *Vanity Fair* on the influences of the Mysore yogashala on local culture, economy and the remains of the caste system, which is why I know. She met Kate Hannigan out there, who sends you her love, by the way.

Meanwhile I have obtained some files from an unnamed person who lurks around the rare antique and occult sites on the web. These are supposed to be the original digital recordings of the Empire State video. They're awesome. I assume they must be CGI-ed unfortunately, but I attach them, at no charge, for you to see.

Best, Loretta.

Davey, tense and agitated, watched the badly shot photography of the Seventh Series video on his monitor.

A tall, very dark and athletic man of indeterminate age stood against the backdrop of night-time New York city, wearing nothing but a pair of black lycra cycling shorts. His hair was tied in a long club that hung down his back and his eyes were closed, his hands in *namaste*, the prayer position. The camera panned back to show that he was balanced on a beam no more than four inches wide which had been extended from the top of the Empire State building's viewing platform, like some event in a TV magic show. There was no net.

The sound quality of the files was appalling. Davey heard the breathing of the camera operator, the sharp blurt of the wind against the microphone.

The man, whoever he was, walked out to the end of the beam and set down his right hand on its end. Balanced on this hand he lifted his feet up lightly and extended his free arm to the side.

Davey caught his breath, recognising the move in disbelief, his body suddenly cold as he watched the man proceed through all twenty five poses of Davey and Kate's imaginary and impossible Seventh Series. Never faltering, always breathing, his torso, head legs and free arm revolved with the grace of pure oil as they twined in and out of each other.

Davey didn't know anyone who was doing sub-skin musculature with this much definition and precision in CGI, but he knew it was possible. There was no way to know if this was a smart fake with deliberate bad moments or a genuinely poor recording of a real event. But that was secondary to the creeping sensation on the back of his neck. *I made this up!*

It must be a fix.

After twenty minutes the yoga man put his feet back on the beam, changed hands, and did it all on the left arm, a mirror image of himself. Davey watched as hard as he could, but when he viewed the right-side beside the left-side during playback it didn't deviate one iota. Beneath the man's indefatigable, serene presence Manhattan shone continuously, the lights of the cars in the streets below two rivers, red and white, flowing against each other. Distant sirens wailed.

Davey flicked back, frozen except for his mouse hand, and watched again.

The first pose of the seventh series was a backbend in which the feet circled around behind the head and touched the supporting hand. Davey and Kate had giggled to devise this move, had checked it against a computerised learning tool for physiotherapists, and it was possible, in that it was within the bounds of known bio-mechanics. But after six months of trying he couldn't get near it—it felt like his wrist would break—and neither could she, even on an ordinary floor.

He didn't send Kate the files. He didn't know what to make of them. He tried to think if he had ever told anyone what they'd worked on for the conclusion of his game but he'd never mentioned what it was at all, afraid that if he had, it would be vetoed, like ordinary Katya, made into some travesty. He had sent the rough architecture for it to the art director for approval so the backdrops could be designed. But he'd used the company encryption.

He comforted himself by reading Kate's latest letters.

When the Rahasya fragment arrived on photocopied sheets it was handwritten in Telugu script and badly stained. He couldn't read it.

Dear Davey,

Sara got back today. She says that all reports of the 7th

series are now treated as apocrypha in Mysore, although the rumour mill is hot with it. Professor Sinha says he thinks the papers are genuine, but they are in such bad condition that the Calcuttans have withdrawn them from public access now.

I'm not surprised you can hardly make head or tail of the copy as it is Sanskrit! The Prof promises to deliver a translation soon.

Congratulations, if that's the thing, on completing the Fourth Series or whatever it is. You'll soon be running out of things to do! Since you've piqued my interest, specially by your comment on how it's important to confront the impossible—and by confronting repeatedly, overcome, right?—I tagged along to a Power Yoga (still not convinced you guys don't think of this as hopelessly corrupted by American values) session at the Y. And you do this for fun?

Best, Loretta.

Dear Davey,

I guess this is the end of our relationship, boo hoo. I've sent off the translations to you today. Sara sends her best wishes and thanks you for your kind words about the article. She saw Kate just before leaving India last week. They met in the airport. Sara showed her some of the video. She was thrilled with it and says she'll be in touch to congratulate you??? She assumed it must be CGI too. As there's no way to determine authenticity from digital files, we'll have to agree to differ.

The address of the MS owner attached. I hope you have a lovely time out there. Remember to keep your ear to the ground for me.

I'm still doing my classes at the Y. Each time I fall over, I think of you. I can't believe you even attempt the moves on the video. I assume you don't try it balanced at the end of a plank whilst hanging off the London Eye or anything, at least not yet:^)

Do call us again if you need anything and be sure to stop by next time you're in town. Love, Loretta.

Dear Davey

I don't know what to say about the enclosed video-tape as its arrival was a total surprise. I'll just pass it on to you. The owner of the manuscript sent it, when he heard from the Shaivites, who must have heard it at the Mysore mandiram, that you were intent on coming to see him.

I have also heard an unconfirmed report that the original script at the University has decayed beyond repair or deciphering inside its special environment, despite many efforts to save it. Calcutta U now denies that it possesses the thing and has removed all copies from the Library.

I know you don't want advice and if you're anything like my other clients you won't take it, but here it is anyway, because you're a good person and I think this has all been a big mistake. For which I'm sorry.

Don't go.

Love, Loretta.

PS. Translation enclosed.

Davey opened the parcel and looked down at the tape. It was a battered VHS and looked like it had seen a lot of use. There was no note with it and no label. Not daring to trust it to the machine he rewound it by hand. He put the translation aside for later.

The Katya cutout, buxom and full-lipped, stood over him; a hardbody version of Jessica Rabbit. Doctor Durant grinned like a fiend from the other corner. This character, in whom Davey had once seen himself, was now a lantern-jawed ape in khakis whose kit bag held a cornucopia of pharmacological mayhem instead of life-saving medicines. Now his original storyline had been 'modified on advisory' (i.e. fucked up by the company director sticking his finger in) so that anybody playing Katya or the Doctor had to kill each other on the final level or they weren't able to win.

Meanwhile the only problem with the long-awaited end of the game proper was that Davey didn't know what the prize was. Did you get treasure? Fame? Hidden knowledge? The build-up to the whole thing was tremendous and almost anything imaginable seemed insufficient to fulfil its promise.

Fear of failing the game itself, and of being given the push by the company, came and sat inside his chest as heavily as a lump of cold clay. He wanted the tape to be a joke, but a piece of him that had always desired bigger, better, faster, more, wanted it to be real.

As he rewound the tape he tried to contain the envy he felt for the people who were behind this—they had more skill than he did, that was for sure.

He put the tape in the machine and switched it on.

A familiar figure confronted him immediately, silhouetted against early morning sunlight coming through trees. The man from the Empire State stood beside a cave mouth at the crest of a hill, his perfectly-honed outline seeming to shift as breezes blew the leaves and covered him in sun and shade. He walked backwards into absolute resolution of focus. The camera crouched in the cool shadow, watching.

In daylight Davey saw that this person was no older than he was, mid-thirties. His Asian skin was dark with a peculiar colour cast that he hadn't seen in the night-shoot, almost bluish or indigo as though stained with smoke. His hair was free and fell long around his shoulders in thick hanks. He wore the same lycra shorts as before, their Cannondale logo clearly visible. But then he bent down and stripped them off, letting them fall on the ground. The face held that identikit serenity Davey saw in Kate's long, straight back and the composure of her hands. The man looked into Davey's eyes and maintained the gaze without blinking. In the glade where he stood pieces of blue jacaranda blossom drifted down and stuck to his skin. There was no sound.

Davey didn't know what he was watching until he saw the first ripple of movement take place beneath the man's skin. Then, in the same way that an ordinary action moves muscle and bone, the muscle and bone of the whole figure was shifted between one slow blink and the next. When the dark eyes opened they were a subtly different shape. The jaw softened and slimmed, the forehead became rounder, the skin softer and more auburn. Hair seemed to disappear here and there, across the arms and legs it vanished as though evaporating. Beneath the tough chest, where the muscle had stuck out with every fibre defined, fat ran and smoothed itself into breasts. The small nipples darkened and spread wider. The man's penis withdrew and his testicles lifted like an indrawn breath.

A woman stood in the glade, her eyebrows arched in concentration, the eyes beneath watching Davey as they had watched him before, unchanged. She blinked slowly and bent down to pick up the cycle shorts which she put back on easily, her loose hair falling around her face until she swept it up and bound it back in a knot. She walked forwards and into the mouth of the cave where she became a silhouette, as tall as before but of a different shape now.

The tape cut off sharply with a static roll and suddenly Davey was watching the end of an old Bollywood film, the sloe-eyed heroine singing as she was pushed back and forth in a swing by the hero. It had obviously been watched many times; the tracking flickered and the audio track was suddenly loud and fuzzy, a kind of roaring mumble of voices.

Davey recorded the tape onto CD and watched every instant of it on pause, but he couldn't see the joins. And then he found himself grinning—well, he could think of one thing to do with this.

As a way of getting his own back he scanned the figure into the game itself. Then he filled out a character profile, and attached him to the mapping files that would make him walk and talk. Davey did it methodically, an act of reclamation. He allowed him to cross-map to the Katya files to become female at random. He gave him a name that was supposed to signify his meaning, the game's end—at least, how Davey wished it would end. Shantih: the peace of silence, the plea for blessing as all distinctions fade and are lost.

Yeah, and the company director can stick it up his ass if he doesn't like it. If you win you get eternal peace in your soul. And is that deliverable by playing a game? What does Shantih do for Katya, for Doctor Durant? Gives them back every life point and a one way ticket to Nirvana. Does the pneumatic vixen turn into the bespectacled librarian her soul longs to become? Why not. Will the Doctor cure himself of his terminal two-dimensionality? Yeah, maybe.

Davey sat on his mat until evening came but it wasn't enough. In the morning he called the travel agency and bought a ticket to Mysore.

He thought, as he flew out there, that if he could understand what had been sent to him in the video, faked or not, then the strange itch in his soul would go away.

Loretta had been accurate in her portrayal of the Shaivite sect as protective and fuelled by mysteries. As they must have done with a disillusioned Foyle, they led Davey from site to site. Each time he reached a predestined point 'the master' had gone on ahead, or waited, or been there a day early, or was not yet arrived, or had made another plan which he hadn't been able to tell Davey about. So sorry.

During this time of travel practice was difficult. Davey spent his money on accommodation, train tickets, food and bribes to various people, even to the portly, thin-skinned University librarian in Calcutta, who eventually showed him through to a sealed glass box full of ashes for a full five minutes and then ushered him out rapidly through a side exit—

"Quickly, quickly, it is all most irregular!"

—and abandoned him in the alley there without another word.

Davey considered all of this merely the necessary testing preliminaries that any true devotee must undergo before something of value is parted with. He expected that eventually, when his perseverance was clear, Shantih would see him.

He called Kate when he ran out of money and she sent him more.

"Davey," she said, sighing patiently. "When are you coming back?"

The only thing that kept him going was her conviction that he would.

Finally he was summoned to the site of the address Loretta had provided—a house in Calcutta with a garden walled off from the street in which he was set to wait by silent servants, none of whom would answer a single question. Nobody came. After five days, having caught a persistent fever, Davey left.

He reported to a doctor in the city who felt his pulse and looked at his tongue.

"You have malaria," the doctor said, peering through thick glasses which slid down her nose as she wrote out a prescription for some Indian medicine on one pad and for western drugs on another. "Either of these but not both, hey? Come see me again in a month."

Davey stared at both slips and took them to the chemist shop where they gave him a packet of pills and told him to drink bottled water. He reached into his pocket for his wallet, and it was gone. Vaguely he recalled a boy at his side in the surgery, sitting close, chewing some kind of bubblegum that smelled of bananas.

"I haven't got my wallet," he explained, and they took the pills back.

He stood outside and wondered what to do. His mind was slow to function, as though the disease had stolen his knowledge, but his feet returned him to the mandiram where he telephoned American Express.

"I'm sorry, sir, your name is?"

"David Cruickshank. C-r-u-' he spelled it for them, lolling on the chair, his head buzzing with a sound like flies or a billion voices far away trying to talk at once.

"And you had what type of card?"

"Platinum."

"Do you have your number?"

"No. It was stolen. My address is . . ."

"I'm sorry Mr Crookshank. We have no records of you as a customer. I can't help you."

Davey floundered. Amex had talked to him a hundred times. Never any problem. He looked at the phone, as though it was at fault. "But I'm in India. I have no money. Listen, you can call my employers, Eastwind Graphics of Los Angeles."

"If you can call them and refer them to us, then I can authorise some temporary cheques."

"I don't need cheques. I need cash. For medicine. Cash . . ."

But it was no use.

Confused he called Kate, but then remembered she was out of town, visiting some of her friends at their homes in the country. There was no mobile coverage out there. He didn't feel like asking for charity from a stranger at the mandiram. They all disapproved of the way he trailed over the country in pursuit of what they all knew was perfectly ridiculous. Some of them pitied him.

Davey felt stupid and thick-headed, embarrassed, a failure. He went outside and began walking, vaguely following a direction where the Shaivites had claimed the master might be found visiting a temple on certain days. He intended to find a cool place and rest and get his shit together and then, he'd sort it out and get the hell out of there. But first he had to sit down.

Days passed.

It was early one morning and he'd gone two days at least without food. Davey was sitting under a tree at the side of the road near a shrine to the horse-headed Lord Hayagriva. He was shivering furiously in one of the increasingly frequent bouts of fever when he saw Shantih come walking up the road, unmistakable in the Cannondales. Despite the extensive walk in the dust his feet were smooth and elegant. They seemed to carry no weight.

"David Cruickshank," the figure said in a deeply melodic voice, bending down to him. "I'm surprised to see you here. You must have realised by now that I didn't want you to follow me."

"Then why play this game with me?" Davey felt too weak to stand, although he tried to.

Shantih put a hand on his arm to indicate he should remain sitting. "To tell you what The Seventh Series means."

"But I saw you. In the tape. It's not impossible, or, it is." Davey's head felt thick. He wished he were better, so he could make more of this encounter. He didn't think he understood what Shantih had said and felt he wasn't making sense. "You did the poses. You're real. You did it."

"Do you think you can change your sex, as though it were a kind of asana, a pose?" Genuine surprise.

Davey shook his head, "You did it, though. Or did you? Anyway. It's great to see you so—alive. Real. Anyway, isn't it? A form of pose? Just a shape."

Shantih nodded and squatted down opposite. "You've tried The Seventh Series. You created it to be as close to impossible as it could be, but still, you try. You wanted to make something miraculous. Have you got far?"

"I can't do any of it. Not yet." Davey swallowed with difficulty. His mouth was dry. "I did make it up. Did I?"

"But The Seventh Series is the easiest of all," Shantih said, frowning slightly. "It's child's play. Can't you see?"

"I try all the time." Davey said, insistent. He wanted not to sound petulant, but felt that he must.

Shantih sighed. He seemed resigned, as though he were the failure and not Davey. "What did you want to say to me?"

The world swam in front of Davey's eyes, dizzying, nauseating. "I want to be your student. I want to solve the game. I wanted to know if you were real or my imagination. One of them has to be. Doesn't it?"

Shantih looked at him sternly.

"You have been my student since you were in London, Davey. You invited me to teach you, when you envied others what you thought was their peace of mind, and I have done so."

He drew a circle in the dust with one of his strangely blue-toned fingers, the fingernails dyed with turmeric into a bright yellow. He glanced up from this apparently absorbing task and looked into Davey's eyes. "You have let yourself get sick, wasted your money, forgotten your friends and your obligations at home. What makes you think this would endear you to me? I've answered your every wish for mystery a thousandfold, but you still want more. Where is the end, David? What will be enough?"

Davey faltered. "If you didn't want me to come here why did you make me search so hard to get the files and the tape? Why did you put things in my way when I would just have made it all up otherwise? Why do anything at all if you wanted me to stay as I was?"

Shantih held up his hand and Davey made himself be quiet. He watched as the man stood and put his fingers to the centre of his chest. He stiffened them and struck them to his breastbone seven times. On the seventh time his fingers entered. He drew the wall of his ribs aside.

Inside their slippery shell Davey saw his lungs moving, his heart beating between them, the exposed bones bent impossibly without breaking. With his other hand Shantih pinched his arteries shut and took out his heart. It beat on his hand as he held it out to Davey. The lobes of it opened like a flower and a sweet scent filled the air.

Inside it Davey saw the intricate brass workings of an old pocket watch. The toothed cogs turned out of their timing and bit down on the heart muscle. A black liquid ran out and then the heart, hand and arm became fluid. Shantih's chest closed and his heart vanished, reabsorbed. He stood before Davey for a moment with the slithering, blunt definition of a tar baby, then was Shantih again.

"But," Davey said.

Shantih became a tiger. The tiger showed Davey its shining black teeth and the jacaranda lilac-blue of its large tongue. The tiger gouged Davey's foot with its claw and Davey cried out with the sharp injustice of the pain. It licked the wound and said sternly,

"This will cure your fever. You can return to the point where you last were saved."

Davey said nothing. He watched the tiger become a snake, become Ananta, the thousand-headed who supports the Earth without effort on the smooth curve of his necks.

He watched an ordinary cobra slide and rustle through the dry grass near his feet and vanish into the bole of the tree beside him. He tried to stand up and called Shantih to return, but the road was empty and he was too dizzy. He fell into the dust.

The Mysore school was registering new students on the morning when Davey returned, filthy and dazed. He was so weak and tired that he didn't recognise any of them but the idea of one of them recognising him made him stagger away from their bright, questing glances. He sat down across the road in the shade of the baobab that grew there, the very image of a fat, digital tree drawn by a clumsy kid.

At first his plan had been to wait until they were processed and then go to find Kate, but lethargy and dizziness kept him pinned to the spot. He watched all day. Towards twilight Shantih came along and sat down beside him. She held his hand and they watched the last students leave their class as the day cooled. None of them were talking of the Seventh Series. They were heading for hostels and hotels, talking about dinner, talking about things they'd learned. He felt better.

Kate came out after them and peered across the broad road. She looked directly to his spot and called out quietly,

"David? Is that you?"

Davey looked to his side but Shantih was nowhere to be seen.

"Yes," he called back. He got up and went to her. She looked surprised, but not surprised, by the state of him.

"Honestly," she said, her first and only word of reproach. He squeezed her tightly in a hug and nodded. They stood in each other's arms.

She brought him some tea and fruit and sat with him while he ate it.

"A letter came for you," she said, as though everything was perfectly normal, forgiving him before he had time to say anything about it. "It's here. I was going to burn it, but then . . . anyway, I didn't. From The Lost Bookstore." She handed it to him with a significant look that said it had better not be any more news about goose chases.

Davey sat down weakly on the veranda's edge, almost sick with nerves, and read aloud,

> Davey,
> I hope this catches up with you at the mandiram or wherever it is. Lotty.

It contained an article from the New York Times:

> *Computer Generated Personalities In Dot Con Fraud Deny Charges.*
> "A legal precedent was set today in New York, NY, when the first Computer Generated Personality (CGPs)was summoned as a witness in a fraud trial encompassing a series of so-called pranks thought to have originated with students working on the development of CGPs for use in films and advertising.
> Extracurricular activities of the students included setting up bank accounts, ID and social security numbers for these 'non-official' personalities and using them to get thousands of dollars of unsecured loans. They also bought holidays and cars and set up websites advertising a range of services from stockbroking to the sourcing of rare artworks and collectible books. Fakes recovered so far from the tracing of deals include two Mona Lisas, a Giacometti sculpture, a Bengal tiger and a series of documents purporting to be the missing piece from an ancient yogic text . . ."

Dry-mouthed, Davey glanced at the picture on the left of the article.

It was Katya Remington. Not the Playmate beauty version, but the one from his own first sketch, awkward in the exposure of the public gaze, a bookish tomboy caught in a naughty prank. The caption beneath it read, "Loretta Haas, one of the CGPs appearing in court today."

The paper fluttered out of his hands and onto the dust.

"That's a picture of . . ." Kate said as she went to pick it up.

"Don't say it," Davey said quickly.

"Oh my god," she said, her voice dropping to a whisper as she realised what it must mean. "Davey. Your game."

He nodded, staring foolishly at the ball of paper in his hand. "They got me a good one. But look on the bright side. It's done now, and I didn't get killed or eaten by monsters or blown up or anything . . . nothing like what happens to them."

"Not much like it," she said and put her arm around his shoulders. "At least, not much."

"Yeah." For the first time he became aware of how much his bones hurt just from sitting on the wooden steps, because he had so little flesh left. He felt light and hollow, like a drawing or a skeleton, utterly de-animated. He thought of the dark figure who had held his hand.

From inside the mandiram they both heard one of the teachers closing his practice.

"Om," sounded his voice, strong on the *udgita*, then quieter and more gentle as it whispered to the close of his prayer; three repeats of the benediction with the fourth silent because it was lost in the dance of Shiva. "Shantih, shantih, shantih . . ."

THE SEVENTH SERIES

Yoga is supposed to be an entirely personal and noncompetitive practice for self development and physical health. But of course it isn't immune to the dominant mindsets of the culture or its own hierarchical tendencies in the way in which it is passed along. On the surface this story seems not to be about envy at all, which was probably a mistake. I should have made it more obvious I think, at the start. Instead it is rooted in a deep inferiority – but it was something I struggled with at the time so writing a story that was clear cut seemed impossible.

I still quite like this story, especially the exasperation of the Shiva figure at Our Hero's stubborn refusal to give up his old ways of looking at things. And I'm looking at myself here. And so are the pixies.

THE LITTLE BEAR

THE LITTLE BEAR

I was playing around with ideas of alternate universes here, and the anthology title reminded me of something that always puzzled me about astrology—since the universe is expanding and most of our constellations are distant anyway, aren't we all in constant motion relative to each other? Astrologers often rely heavily on place of birth, but in terms of cosmic coordinates the planet has long left those places behind for those of us presently alive.

THE LITTLE BEAR

Be it the northern or the southern sky, the constellations on a dark night look as they do from only one point in the universe; from Earth. It's not like being lost at sea, or in the desert, where knowing their patterns can set you on the right path. Constellations are stories, convenient memory markers existing purely in our minds so we don't have to experience the truth of our position in a great and indifferent space.

Violette thought this as she looked up into the night, searching against the setting gleam of Venus for the white engine-track of a returning craft. She felt without a shadow of doubt that the expanse of outer space was a bagatelle kind of nothing, compared with the space she'd become aware of as it grew inside her mind: the distance between herself and her husband Guy.

Someone had once told her that she might try to imagine infinity thus: picture a steel ball the size of the Earth. A fly lands on it once in a million years. When the friction caused by the fly's feet has worn the steel ball away to nothing, infinity has not even begun.

Space is Time, Time is Space. She had written that as the last line in her thesis. The constellations above her had travelled with her since then, apparently much unchanged by either aspect of the continuum, as far as she was aware. But she was much changed by time. It had grooved her face and bleached her hair and was close to swallowing her whole. As for space . . .

She touched the eternity ring she had bought for herself on finishing her studies—a circle, naturally, because she had hoped, against her logical conclusions, that spacetime was a doughnut shape and, as a sugar-mote on its surface, her life lay safely perpetual there, always to be returned to, always repeated as space progressed along the doughnut's roundel of time, although she could not experience it that way. The ring had a diamond, a small one, and two flanking stones like tiny gateposts. Her finger counted them as she watched Venus decline in the west. Slowly she let out the breath she'd been holding.

The spinnaker of her small boat billowed with freshening wind and rode the swell with a drunken swagger quickly smoothing into a surf. She released the ring and took hold of the helm again, reassuring herself by the feel of the boat's lively passage resonating in the wheel. Above her Orion was sinking and his dogs were quick on his heels. Dawn was coming and already the glow of the sun had begun to erase the clarity of the stars in the eastern sky. Soon the single planet would be her only guide.

Time is space wasn't news even then. Einstein had said it decades ago. But in Violette's interpretation of the physical laws it had to be re-stated. Time was a space of no volume. Hence one could not go back to a point in it, navigating one's way by the look of past and future worlds, constellations there of people and actions, of objects in their exact array and bearings tuned by the flavour, smell and zest of a single instant viewed from all directions. Time was a cusp, the wave's crest, a moment of perpetual immanence. Guy was lost in space, since his mission failed to return all those years ago. But she didn't believe him dead. She considered him dislocated in time. Although this might make no difference to the facts it made her feel less alone. In one part of the continuum, Guy was still there.

She reached into the inner pocket of her oilskin and removed a laminated photograph. Looking at Guy's picture—it seemed only an instant ago that he'd gone. How could that be so far away that she could never get there? Of course, if they allowed her to work the machine again, she might try to get there, which is why it was shut off in its bunker, never to be used again. They thought Guy's mission a sufficient loss, in the wake of all the events after the machine's first use and no doubt that was the wisest way. Teleportation remained a dream, even though Violette knew first hand that it was not.

A wave recklessly covered the deck and fell to nothing, draining in the sluices and drenching her feet. It splashed the photo and she wiped it clean as she put it away before turning a degree to the south. She'd built the boat—Arrowflight—herself, learning via several false starts and many hard hours as she went along, determined to attempt a full circumnavigation of the world by star and sun before she died. She'd left Les Sables a week ago and hadn't switched on her radio since. On the third day she'd become aware that direction didn't matter.

Wherever she went Guy would never be. The trail of a spacecraft that should have come in a long time ago was only in her mind's eye, a nervous tic of hopeful longing. She reasoned that there had been a miscalculation on board and the moment of return had failed to find Earth where it should have been in space, materialising behind or in front by a critical margin to discover . . . to do nothing in fact, for to miss utterly was to cease to exist in a timely manner, at least in this universe.

Violette did not believe in discontinuity—where objects could dot in and out, not there one minute but there the next, skipping time steps like a child over chalked hopscotch lines. Guy had gone out to test their theories in the only safe place they could think of and he was lost.

Guy took a seat in a café bar near Montmartre. It was the time of evening when his father had liked to light a cigar and ask his mother to provide him with a glass of fino. Guy liked neither but ordered the sherry anyway and when it came, tasted its woodiness and dryness with a hidden grimace. He only had to wait for a few minutes and then Rafaella appeared, slinking like a cat out of the shadows. Her face was contorted with the pressure she was feeling. It spoiled her beauty, made her look older and more disappointed than he'd hoped.

She slumped in her seat and crossed her legs, kicking the loose sole of her cheap flip-flop against her foot. He regarded her with a fondness he felt correct for a father to feel towards his daughter. The lamplight coming from the bar's interior made her look more like Violette than ever.

Rafaella batted a moth away with a flick of her hand and crossed her legs the other way. A waiter appeared as though summoned by majesty, and she ordered wine without rewarding him with a single glance. She caught Guy's look of amusement at this naked display of feminine power,

"Don't look at me like that."

"You remind me of her."

"And don't say that."

"What? I have to say something. It's the reason we're here."

"I hate anniversaries. It's pointless nostalgia." She raked her gaze over the other people on the street and, finding nothing in them to grip her attention, looked up at heaven for patience.

"Then why did you come?"

She snorted, "To humour you, of course. You think she meant to come back."

"You don't."

"If she'd meant to then she would have—cuh!" Rafaella took her wineglass from the offered tray and took a big swallow, bigger than she intended. A line of red ran down her mouth and dripped onto the boho chic-ness of her outfit. She swore and ignored it.

Guy said, "The solicitor thinks it's time to ask the court to declare her legally dead."

Rafaella focused her emotion on the distant stars and didn't look at him. Her flip-flop counted away a minute and she glanced at her watch.

"'Plane to catch?" He cursed his own sarcasm even as he said it.

"I'm meeting Paul," she said and then heaved herself around as if it was a Herculean effort. "If we do this, what does it do?"

"It means that her Will can be executed," he replied, the words and their meaning a simple skim on the surface of his mind, not allowed to disturb what lay beneath. "You'll get some money. I will. The house . . ."

"Is not going to be sold," she declared, taking a swallow of wine.

"Be reasonable," he began, but she cut him off.

"It's the only place she knows. What if she comes back and we're not there? What if she goes there and nobody knows who she is? What if it's all she recognises?"

Guy sighed and watched a young couple walk by, their arms entwined, nothing in the span of their regard except each other. He and Violette had walked like that once. He wanted to believe they would again. Perhaps they were doing so even now, in some other time and space which he could not find. He didn't know how to explain to Rafaella that her mother might be missing on another Earth. He didn't want to believe it himself.

The house in question was far away in rural Yorkshire, but he could feel its presence as though a lodestone in the walls pulled at him twenty-four seven. He could feel its emptiness and the chilly transparent dome of its roof, above which the Great Bear pawed the northern sky and pointed helplessly at the single unmoving mote of Polaris, the north star, with her tail.

Rafaella believed her mother had suffered a stroke causing a kind of amnesia and had simply wandered off. Or that she had had an affair and created a clever story to cover her absence. It had been years, and although she'd left home by then anyway, the idea of Violette's abandonment of her was too hard. Guy knew that the moment hadn't been anything so mundane. There was a chance Rafaella was right and that the house and its co-ordinates were the only points in the universe where Violette might return.

"Little Bear," he said fondly to Rafaella, hardly realising he spoke aloud.

She shot him a cold look but could not sustain it and returned to watching the people pass by.

If universes intersect one another at all, then they must do so at at least one point. However those points are mapped, a moment and a space or both are shared. This could be used as the focus of all maps that serve to describe those separate worlds, no matter how giant or how fleeting.

Why shouldn't this be a house, or a heart?

The machine towered over them, humming with power—so strange to think that such a small wattage could achieve so much—as Guy and Violette watched the their chosen test object vanish from sight. The telephone rang in the outer office. Violette answered,

"Oui?"

There was a breathless pause.

"Vraiment?"

Another beat, another mark that nailed down each moment to its position without ambiguity.

"Guy!" she shouted, the phone raised high like a staff of power. "He has the bottle! Alain has the bottle! In Greece! Right now!"

But at the time they'd never thought on where the bottle might have been when it was neither with them, in Paris, or with Alain, in

Athens. Between one second and the next, how much space could there be? And for his part Alain never mentioned, thinking it bad luck, that the old Chateauneuf du Pape was foul and corked beyond drinking.

Violette searched the sky again for the one unchanging constant, following the blunted end of Thor's Hammer. The North Star was faint as she angled the boat away from it. A fresh update on the monitor revealed that none of the satellites heard anything of Guy's scout mission, and why should they? He was full fifty years lost and the machine in its laboratory was thick with dust, guarded by young soldiers who didn't even know what it was for and thought maybe it was an old cold war thing.

Alain had texted her—*OK ld grl?*

She hadn't replied yet, she thought, although she fancied that she was replying, had already replied—OK.

After the first few attempts they'd given up trying to calculate how many fresh universes had peeled away from their one original with each repeated use of the machine. Violette had no idea whether or not there were many of her sharing this space right now, others turning about, others reckoning the sky, others at home, far away, watching old movies with Guy and Rafaella in the house below the hill.

In her mind *that* Violette in the house was the real one. Somehow she had become one of the pale copies instead, her consciousness slipping away from its true course and into this unsatisfactory illusion. She took comfort from the knowledge that it was only a shard in time that separated her from this perfect life, even though crossing back into it might be impossible. Other Violettes may make it. And other Guys may never have left with the astronauts to verify the fracture by viewing it from the outside—travelling into a sister reality.

The wind was as strong in any other world. The boat made a tortured banging sound as it drove into the waves. The bowsprit surfaced to point up at the three Norns and Violette switched on the autopilot, exhausted, and went below.

Rafaella uncorked the bottle of wine and stood on the balcony in the humid night heat, the stone of the terrace barely cool against her feet. She could hear Alain playing Chopin on the piano. Its notes were bell-like in their melancholy patterns, picking out the essence of her emotion without her having to articulate it. How like him to know what to play at an hour like this, she thought, and how like her father to wander off to the bottom of the garden, a white shape in the gloom like a ghost.

In the dining room the legal documents lay crisp below the stare of another wine bottle—this one in a protective glass case. The original Chateauneuf of the first experiment was fragile enough to break these days, without much encouragement from anyone. It was the thinning of its walls which had first suggested danger in the method. Not only had it lost something during its travel to Athens that night, years ago, but with every subsequent use of the machine another integral layer had been peeled from its substance. Its label was unreadable, the printing ink flayed off. The glass itself was, at a microscopic level, pitted with holes until it resembled a peculiar bone, the fossil of an ancient time. Since the wine itself had gone down the sink in Athens, nobody knew what had happened to that.

Rafaella thought of the papers there, awaiting her signature. Guy's was still drying on the page. He was convinced Violette must be dead or never coming back. Rafaella felt she ought to sign, if only to end the suspension of his life, to allow him to move on, but a more bitter, stubborn piece of her wouldn't let her. The bottle's problem was that it had moved unpredictably through space because of its predictability in time. Violette was the opposite. Rafaella was sure she was alive somewhen soon, and they did not, as Guy insisted, live in a Universe which had allowed her to vanish from it absolutely. Matter could not disappear like that from all coordinates of the continuum, ergo her mother was out there somewhere and she was not going to sign away the one point of contact they might have.

When is it?

Rafaella set the corkscrew on the terrace wall, started pouring a libation down the stones, then let all the wine run there, each rivulet of darkness winding its own way over the rough and porous surfaces. *Where* is the crossing where all these worlds collide?

Guy said it was at Ago, at the first use of the machine. They couldn't get back there, because they'd already been.

But what if it was in the future? What if there was a universe in which the machine never worked? *That* universe couldn't possibly intersect with this one in the past. In fact there must be an infinity of worlds in which the machine did not exist or had never been used and an infinity of crossroads from this world in which it did, presenting chances to jump over. But Guy would only laugh at this reasoning of hers.

In the garden her father's white form walked towards her. He looked up as he came into the terrace lights.

"There's always another possibility," he said as the final chord sounded from the piano. "That she might have stepped out of existence only for *a certain length* of time. In which case, she hasn't moved in space at all."

Rafaella stared down at him, brushing a moth away from her hair. "What?"

"But even if she did," he continued. "The world has moved on. Literally. In space. The planet has moved. The galaxy has moved. Nothing is where it used to be. Even positions that seem to be fixed have altered beyond recognition."

The moth returned, blundered against her cheek, corrected itself and fled up into the brilliance of the terrace light. Dust from its wings powdered the air. She listened to it battling against the glass, beating itself to death with the force of its determination to reach what it had mistaken for the moon.

Alain checked the set up for the eighth time. In fact there was nothing to check, but he smoothed the tablecloth over the cold marble top one more time and walked around the invisible perimeter of the three beacons, noting their alignment. According to theory the bottle should arrive two millimetres above the cloth. He didn't know what would happen if it came in any lower, but then again he didn't know what would happen to the air it displaced on its arrival either. He put his goggles on and moved back to the safe distance of his cane chair.

Beyond the shuttered windows the low growl of traffic persisted, overshot with the bright, sudden notes of the calls of birds which were gathering to roost in the eaves of his hotel. They weren't swallows, he knew that, but birds weren't his thing, navigation was his interest. Migrations from one continent to another over vast distances had intrigued him since his boyhood. Geese had been the first animals he'd studied for his dissertation, and then the wandering albatross. A curious mixture of the Earth's magnetism, the stars and the sun traced their paths for them. The turning year and the flares of solar agitation or tropical storms could cast them far beyond their routes. The memory of routes also passed on from generation to generation, even when conditions at the destinations altered, became less desirable. How curious he'd been to discover that instinct was so powerful, even when its drive took you in the wrong direction. He wasn't sure himself if this position he was in was less desirable. He didn't like the idea of the machine and hoped it would fail.

His watch, in regular contact with an atomic clock, counted the moments to midnight. The church at the end of the street chimed in early, its hand-rung bell marking the hours, the end of the day, the start of something. Bathed in the moment, suspended between past and future, Alain wished for nothing.

There was a sharp bang, like a muted gunshot, and a softer thud.

Wings beat suddenly against the shutters, a flurry, and were still.

A bottle of wine stood on the table, the meniscus just visible beneath the collar label, quivering.

He was surprised it didn't startle him. He mustered enthusiasm, rang Paris as he moved forwards to inspect it, briefly wondering why they hadn't bothered to wipe the dust off it before they sent it over. Violette's delight was so infectious he found himself starting to laugh, to smile. When he rang off he was grinning as he took out his keys from his pocket, undid his corkscrew from the Swiss army knife and opened the bottle.

The cork came out easily and with it a soft, resiny odour quickly turning sour. He poured it and took a sniff. Pure vinegar. The cork in his fingers was slimy. What a bad omen, he thought then, his smile fading. He resolved never to mention it to the others but quickly watched the bottleful splash its way down the plughole. Probably he should have saved it for testing, but the glass would be enough.

He suddenly remembered that in all the excitement he'd forgotten to turn off the recording equipment. It only took a few minutes to roll back the tapes and erase what he'd done.

"He's not coming back," Rafaella said, her voice almost drowned out by the cries of the children, fighting over a toy. She sounded weary rather than irritated to Violette, who cradled the receiver against her chin as she guided the boat back to its mooring.

"I know," she said. "But I like to look."

"When are you coming home?"

"Soon," Violette assured her. "The estate agent says the house is sold. I have to pack it up—that will take a while—and then I'll be coming. I'm selling most of the furniture, unless there's something you particularly want."

"No," Rafaella said, pausing to administer some kind of hasty discipline. Violette heard her saying, "We'll get another Little Bear, don't worry about it," and then Martine's voice whined, "Don't want another. Want *that* one." She came back on the line, "But if you find anything personal of Dad's . . ."

"It'll all come back with me," Violette said. "You can look through it yourself. Did you get Alain's card?"

"He still signs himself off " A Friend of Your Father's" as if I didn't know who he was," Rafaella sighed. "Yes. And a hundred Euros, even though I'm thirty-five and earn more than his pension."

"He feels responsible," Violette said. "I have to go, the wind is changing." She hung up and brought the vessel about just in time to make it safely around the harbour buoy. Gulls circled the mast lazily, giving her the once over, not even bothering to call out from their frozen postures in the air.

A week later, kneeling in the attic on the Rue St Denis, she dragged over a wooden packing case from the very back. It wasn't the last to be cleared out, but nearly the last and must have been there since the day they moved in, she reckoned—a strip of 1989 *Le Monde* hung from its slats. She brushed filthy grey dust from it and sneezed, pausing to wipe her face with a tissue and seeing black marks stripe it as she put it away again. In the light of the single weak bulb she wondered if she could be bothered to check it, or whether she should simply leave it here for the new owners to find. Whatever was in it hadn't interested them for forty years, why should she want it now?

She opened the lid anyway and looked at the unexpected top of a bottle of wine, her heart thudding suddenly loud in her chest. It had been for Guy's return of course, she thought, to celebrate, and then, unable to throw it away, she'd put it up here. The bottle itself was clean and new-looking but she couldn't help thinking it must have gone bad after living through so many hot summers up here. She couldn't bring herself to read the label or hold it in her hands, thinking of the time it ought to have been uncorked and the emotions she'd hoped to feel.

A pigeon, perched on the tiles above her, burbled its ridiculous love-warble. She heard its claws tacking and the sudden muffled clapping of winged escape.

That settled it. She pushed the case back into the darkest shadow and backed up on her hands and knees along the grimy length of carpet until her foot found the top rung of the ladders again.

Alain walked the last mile to Guy's house in the dale. It took him an hour and many pauses, resting against walls, sitting on his shooting stick, stumbling over the rocks on the back road. He was tired when he got there, but it was worth it. For every mile he'd covered since Paris the weight of the bag had become lighter and now he could hardly feel it in his hand.

Rafaella was there, looking thin and irritable. She let him in. The place was warm but smelled of damp nonetheless. They should have let it go, moved somewhere with a more temperate climate, Alain thought. England had its beauties but he would have traded them for the comfort of the Avignon villa. But it hadn't been up to him. The girl had never stopped hoping that Violette would come back here and Guy hadn't had the heart to stifle her hope. It was a pity, because now Rafaella was getting too old for children and too bitter for marriage and Guy was, like himself, simply a relic awaiting destruction.

He said as much as they sat down to a whiskey.

Rafaella was taken aback by his bluntness.

"There's not much time for games," Alain shrugged. He pushed at the bag with his foot. "Open it."

She did so and unwrapped the bottle from a swatch of heavy velvet curtain. Her glance at him was quizzical, "Why now?"

"It's my fault she got lost," Alain said. "I never told you that the wine in that bottle was rancid. Something was wrong with the whole thing. I could have said so but it didn't seem that important at the time. I thought it was a coincidence."

"You couldn't have known," Guy began, trying to brush Alain's grimness aside.

"No, but I could have guessed. We said before that what's known in space must be uncertain in time if it leaves the continuum here at all. And if time was certain then space would be the opposite. She was gone for five minutes and in that time we forgot that we would have MOVED, Guy. Moved forty thousand bloody miles . . . and when she came back it's us who wasn't there. Nothing was there."

Rafaella was staring into nothing. She said, into the silence that followed, "I wonder if it's the same bottle. Is there any way of proving that?"

Her father took his glass from his mouth halfway into a sip and swiped a line of whiskey from his lip. Alain's face grew even more bleak. She could tell they hadn't considered this, as she hadn't, until now. The bottle's decay had stopped, which they had taken to mean that the universes had ceased to peel away from one another or, if that theory was entirely wrong, that at least whatever dimension had leached its substance away was now stabilised, all reactions come to their natural conclusions. She hadn't been a part of the science, barely understood any of it, but she said now,

"I mean, was there any way of telling it to be the bottle you sent, dad? Or could it be from a different continuum? Maybe we switched bottles with someone else's universe and they didn't get one in return. Maybe this bottle is trying to get back to its own space and time."

They stared at the offended item and then, with a single, swift movement Rafaella lunged forward and sent it hurtling against the wall. It smashed instantly and the shards of glass scattered, tinkling on the floor with a sound like stars ringing in an empty heaven.

"No more uncertainty," she said, sitting back, withdrawing her hand carefully as though it were a snake that might strike again. "I can't stand it any more."

Guy crossed over to her and put his arm around her shoulders.

Alain looked at the shining splinters. "See," he said, his voice cracking as he pointed a shaking finger at the patterns they made on the floor. "It's Andromeda, and Leo."

A smile moved from one to the other of them beginning with Guy and passing to Rafaella, and then to Alain before it faded away. Alain tried to look at the glass and see no pattern in it but, no matter how hard he tried, he saw more and more familiar shapes as the minutes passed until he had to look away.

"Do you remember her?" Rafaella said. "Because I can't. Only little things. Her smell. The shape of her chin. The way her eyes looked when she smiled. But not all at once. I can't see her anymore. I always thought that's how you lived forever, in people's minds, but it can't be true, because we can't remember like that. If she walked in here now I sometimes think I wouldn't know her."

Guy stood up and began to pick up the pieces, gathering them in his hand.

Alain got up to go.

There was a knock at the door.

They glanced at each other, eyes wide, and saw hope in the others' faces, impossible to extinguish but already beginning to twist with resigned disappointment. Nobody moved to answer it.

THE LITTLE BEAR

I still wonder who, or what, is behind that door.

LEGOLAS DOES THE DISHES

LEGOLAS DOES THE DISHES

I wrote this immediately after finishing LIVING NEXT DOOR TO THE GOD OF LOVE *and reading a bunch of Shirley Jackson stories. I was in a creative manic phase and locked myself up for two days over Christmas (pretty much avoiding the entire thing) to get it on paper.*

LEGOLAS DOES THE DISHES

"That's him," Nurse Driver pointed at the figure standing over the sink. She glanced at me with a sly sideways movement of her eyes, carefully noting my reaction. "What do you think?"

I took a test reading: tall, lanky, blonde, wearing green under the regulation overalls. If he had pointed ears they were hidden by a carefully drawn ponytail. I shrugged. I thought Driver was shitting me. She and I always had this thing going on where I could never tell if she were serious or simply playing me for the sake of being entertained. Sometimes she'd be right, like about the porter who turned out to be Napoleon. But mostly she liked to irritate. That's why I figured she was demon-ridden; because she had the sight and because she liked to torment with it. Of course the demon made sure that her perceptions came across as just imagination to her, so she wasn't troubled by thinking it was as real as her own nose. None of the screaming heebie jeebies for her like you get with so many of us who see the other planes and have to play Cassandra for the rest of our lives. She had protection.

Now she lifted her chin and kept her eye on me.

"You're the savant," she said. "You tell me."

Savant is what the inmates labelled me, although the state and my shrink had another set of names. It went without saying that Driver and every right thinking rational person like her had as much faith in fantasy and savants as they had in alien visitations, tax-cut promises on election night and the vows of preachers to save their souls from the pitch black tarry pits of hell. So when Driver said savant she gave away the game and I realised this was her idea of a different kind of Waterloo—one where she hoped I was going to sink like a rock.

Driver gave me a push and I went forwards helplessly across the kitchen's tiled floor towards the object of her disdain. Cause and effect were still in operation, laws of physics definite, therefore I could anticipate no otherworldly help coming to confound her.

I stopped when I came to the bluff point of the drainer and clutched onto its stainless steel strength. Unstoppable force. Immovable object.

The washer-upper glanced at me and smiled in a vague kind of way, like people do when they're self consciously moving among the Therapied. (I would much rather that word was Theropod. The world is the product of the mind. I fancy myself the T Rex of the wards, smashing down doors, impaling presumptuous interns with the scything claws of my enormous feet).

I smiled back.

I think I still have that down pat, though it's not an expression I've had much cause to use lately and it felt fake even though it was real.

The dishwasher went back to lifting dishes out of the steaming water, suds falling over his hands.

"What are you doing here?" I asked.

Actually I was pretty confident it was really him, in spite of Nurse Driver's insinuations. Although I know perfectly well that Tolkien was a writer, and that Legolas was an invention of his mind, it is also certainly true that since the widespread popularity of the Peter Jackson movies and renewed interest in the books, (not to mention the pervasively lingering and delicious qualities of the image of Orlando Bloom) the meme of Legolasness and all it implies must have been spreading around the general population like a plague and so, even though I cannot really be looking at an Elf of Middle Earth, but surely am only looking at someone through a voluntary delusion, I am prepared to entertain as True, nonetheless, here he is. Legolas is washing our dishes. Because reality is of the mind. And my mind says this is the real thing. And so he is. Unless he thinks he isn't. And then of course, he won't be.

"Washing dishes," he said.

"No. I mean *here*," I said, and added the test tag—'What are you doing here? Why aren't you in Valinor?"

"Oh," he seemed taken aback for a moment and stared at the steamed up window in front of him (not that you could have seen through it—it was marbled glass). He glanced down at me and his blue eyes fogged up. He muttered hesitantly, "I forgot about that, I guess."

"Was it the gulls?" I asked him. "Did they tell you to come back?"

"Um . . ." his hands in the water went slack. "No. I needed a job. I don't have many skills. Any," he paused to think of the word that somebody else must have said to him, "pertinent ones." He glanced at my overalls and then, briefly, at my face.

"That sucks," I commiserated. "Good dishes though." They sparkled as they dried.

"Thanks." He was suddenly much more comfortable; went back to the methodical task with more care than I'd have given it, even in a pensive mood. He had young skin. I looked at the space where his ear was concealed by hair and also the plastic shield of a mass-produced kitchen-jockey's silly elasticated hat. "So," I said conversationally. "Must have been tough since Aragorn kicked it?"

Nurse Driver was standing a short distance away on the tiles, fretting because she couldn't smoke, but I heard her cough. It may have been a laugh.

He kept washing plates. He was very cute. It was a shame. "Was he like they say?"

"Who?"

"Aragorn. You know."

He sighed. "I have no idea what you're talking about."

"Oh," I glanced back at Driver and gave him a conspiratorial look, turning down my volume, "of *course* you don't. But you shouldn't worry about her. You could be King James the First and she wouldn't believe you. Or Ghengis Khan. She wouldn't know an angel if it came down from heaven and bit her ass. She's as blind as a bat to anything other than material reality. I'm waiting for the faeries to con her out of her life savings one of these days."

The ghost of a smile flitted across his face as he kept studiously washing plates. "Is that right?"

"So your secret's safe out in the open, just like the rest of our secrets. Best place for it," I said and patted him on the arm in a comforting manner.

He flinched. "Don't do that."

"Sorry I'm sure," I said, watching the swirling surface of the bubbles on his wrist. You can scry in a bubble. You can scry in anything come to that, if you learned how. A dogshit on the pavement is as prophetic as a crystal to the right eye. "What's the matter?"

"My Daddy . . . well, don't, if you don't mind." He was so well spoken.

"I don't mind a thing," I assured him. "Do you miss the old days?"

"No," he said. "I like the new days with nothing in them." He glanced at me as he put a dish down into the rack and we shared a genuine grin for a split second. The sun came out, somewhere beyond the glass, and the long hair on his shoulders turned to gold.

Curiosity finally moved him as he searched the depths for forks with cautious sweeping motions. "What are you in for?" he asked.

"I poisoned my mother," I said. "She tried to poison me. It was very much one of those fifty:fifty situations. Could have gone either way." I held my hand out flat and waggled it to show the balance was perfectly weighted and what had happened was quite fair.

His soft, easy smile appeared again—all focused on the dishwater sadly—and then it faded away. "How long will you be here?"

"Forever, unless I start to speak the speech of the terminally insane undergoing positive changes that incline them towards productive citizenship," I said. "And you?"

"It's just a job," he said.

I tried for the aberrantly confident tones of Doctor Lucy. "Well, it's important *you* keep believing that."

I was still undecided about the sincerity of the phrase itself—*it's important you keep believing*. Like arsenic, it could go either way for you. I always thought Doctor Lucy meant it, especially when she was tired, but now that I said it myself to this elf who was washing dishes in a psychiatric ward it seemed less convincing. I voiced my doubt. "Do you believe that?"

"There's nothing to believe," he said, lifting a stack of knives and forks, rinsing them with the little shower head thing, and dropping them into the drain tray. He had farm-animal calm. It was both delightful and unnerving, as though there was a storm on the way.

"What do you do when you're not here? Do you live in the woods? You must miss trees. I never saw a tree in Arizona worth the name."

"We aren't in Arizona," he said.

"I know. Just testing."

Driver did laugh this time, and then she blew her nose and started emailing on her blackberry. She took a picture of us with it.

"You need permission," I told her but she shrugged. I wondered who she could send it to and what she was saying. I would have liked to wash Nurse Driver in the hot soapy water, and her little phone too.

"What was it like in Edoras?" I asked Legolas. I wouldn't have been so pushy, only I didn't think he would be here long, and I knew I certainly wouldn't. Maybe until Driver's badly typed conversation finished. "Were the horses like real horses here?"

He shrugged, "I don't know what you're talking about. I don't know horses." He feigned enormous interest in some dried-on potato on a big serving dish and rested it on the side of the sink to scrub it with one of those scratchy green pads that are made of stuff that never wears out, though you wish it would, because otherwise, what would happen to it and to the second law of thermodynamics?

"But you had one," I said confidently. "One of the Rohan horses. Arod."

"A what?"

"Arod. That's his name. It means swift. It was your horse. You and Gimli. Don't kid me you don't remember."

"Sure," he said, lying. "A big brown horse."

"It was grey," I said crossly.

He flinched again and the big Pyrex dish slipped fractionally, bumping the sink edge with a gentle thunk. It smashed into a dazzling scatter of tiny curved shards. He and I stepped back automatically as a rain of splinters pattered onto the tiles.

"Did you get any on you?" he asked me.

I shook out the front of my overalls. "No."

He picked fragments from his apron and I saw an orangey thread of blood stain the white suds on his right hand. He muttered a curse as he flicked them onto the floor.

"Fuck!" Driver said from behind us. "Lili what the hell have you said now? Did you do that?"

"No," I told her. "I'll get the brush," I said to him.

"It's coming out of your wages," Driver said to him without sympathy. "I told you not to react to what she said."

"Yeah? Well I wasn't contracted to listen to your patients, so I'm thinking you'll be the one explaining." He took the long handled brush off me as I reached him, his movements careful, as though he'd spent a long time gently taking potentially dangerous objects from the incompetent. He waited for me to release it but I liked the feeling of his soggy, hot fingers against mine so I was slow about it.

Driver patted her pockets and calmed down when she heard and felt the rustle of fifteen Lucky Strikes under her uniform. "Just put it in the trash," she said wearily and looked at me. "Shit, Lilibet. I thought you'd be way more fun than this. D'you wanna go back to the day room, stick some glitter on card?"

I ignored her. "I'm a top sweeper actually," I said to him as he got the pieces of dish into a pile. "I could sweep in the Olympics." I saw an interesting shape in the broken glass and reached down to get it.

He moved to stop me and we bumped skulls as we reached a crouch at the same moment. "Ouch!" I put my hand up to my forehead but I felt his plastic hat and instead took hold of it and pulled it off. As this distracted him I picked up the glass piece I wanted carefully between thumb and forefinger. Pyrex is specially heat treated to stand high temperatures, and it's extremely hard to break, although it can develop invisible stress complications over years of use which will cause it to explode, like this one had, when some innocuous tiny thing happens to set it off. The right force at the right moment is all it takes.

The white curve of his eyeball was exactly the same shape as my seer's splinter.

"Drop it," Driver said to me in the tone of voice that promised punishment.

I admired my long, slim fingers on the shard I was holding—a big curl, like a clear scimitar—and then put it carefully into the dustpan. I looked up into Legolas' face as he finished brushing the rest of the pieces into the pan. He had cheekbones to die for, though his lips were a little on the thin side. He gave me a careful look, to check that I wasn't about to try something freaky. I didn't want to spoil my relationship with Driver—she master, me domesticated animal—so I didn't. "You have something in your eye."

"No, I don't think . . ."

"Yes." I held his face in my hands and pretended to tilt it better towards the light, staring into one and then the other of his cornflower baby blues. He blinked, looking up over my head. "It's big."

"I can't feel anything."

"Right there on the left." Two oppositional words, create tension, cause confusion, make space.

The left side of the body is controlled by the right brain and if there's anything really interesting about a person who's squirrelled away out of sight inside themselves it's in the right brain, unless they're one of those people who are naturally reversed, but he was right-handed so I was willing to risk it. Risk is the currency of the gods, after all. "So, how was it in the *Fellowship of the Ring?*"

He glanced up and left. I knew it. People look that way for Visual Recall. Then down and left. Kinaesthetic Access. Not up and right (Visual Construct). Not down and right (Audio Digital process). I knew it! He was looking into memories, not making things up! Then, resigning himself to my madness, he looked back at me and carefully removed my hands from his head, placing them down on my knees.

I wasn't about to make Driver's day. I knew that she was hoping I'd come here, convince myself, make him annoyed, and give her enough material to do the annoying job on her own for the rest of his stay. She was never happy without someone to aggravate and, having practised relative tolerance on the residents, she liked to take it out on the non-clinical staff. In the day room we had a sweepstake going on who she'd push to resign next. We always figured it was because she had to put up such a nice housewifey front in her home life, to keep standards of domestic and public civilisation going, because Chief of Police Bob Driver demanded a clean-living ticket.

"You should get a haircut," Driver said to the elf from her comfortable seat. "That'd put a stop to it. Otherwise you've only got yourself to blame."

He put my hands away from him and took the pan and brush away. I looked for more sparkling bits, but there were none close by, although there was a satisfying discomfort under one nail on my left hand.

"I have a lot of money," I told him when he came back to finish the dishes.

"Oh yeah?"

"Yeah," Driver said, snorting at the stupidity of fate. "She's an heiress, thanks to mommy dearest, and two bucks short of a ticket to real life."

"You shouldn't talk like that," the elf said in his broken accent that might have come via Dakota or one of those other long-forgotten states where nothing happens. I liked the way he stood up to her so quietly.

"Yeah, right. She doesn't care, do you Lili? Been here for the best years of her life playing at Mystic Myrtle and every time it looks as though they're about to send her out into a nice little sheltered house she stabs someone. All that money and bleeding the taxpayers dry, huh, missy? But sometimes she sees things, don't you, honey? Got to be so that we thought maybe she had something when she said she had the sight, but it's been a long time since she saw anything interesting."

She hadn't been much interested in him before, but his refusal to submit was needling her. Now she couldn't let go. Drastic action might be required here, in the sort of doses that could kill an ordinary conversation stone dead.

I turned away from her and said to him quietly, "Do you remember Thranduil and Mirkwood?"

"Who's Thran-doo-ill?"

"Didn't you pay attention in the movie?" Driver contributed. "He's your daddy."

"That wasn't in the movie, it was in the book," I corrected her.

He snatched a plate—one of the last—and rammed it to the bottom of the sink, leaning on it. "My daddy's name was Tyson." Muscles in his neck and jaw flickered beneath the skin.

I began to sense a fellowship of a different kind. "He really wasn't. He wasn't your real father."

"I wish he wasn't." He recovered the plate—it was in two pieces.

"Wages," Driver said.

He tossed the halves into the trashcan. It was a throw of about eight metres and he did it with a gesture no more studied or powerful than simple pointing. The halves chinked down among the broken glass, and then he gave me a challenging look, eyebrows up, beliefs suspended. Oh, how these moments last is always the key to seeing how far somebody can go!

"Thranduil?" he repeated, the querying tone of his voice more for pronunciation than confirmation of identity.

"Yes."

"And what else?"

"You're an immortal," I said, "You're supposed to be in Valinor, beyond the Earth in the deathless realms, far as I recall. You went there after Aragorn died and you were one of the last Elves to leave Middle Earth, though I never really read all the way through the Silmarillion so I don't know for sure. I got to page two and then . . ." I shrugged.

"Did I kill him?" he asked, alarmed and shaking so that he had to hold onto the edge of the sink suddenly. The shimmer of protection all adults learn to wear since the schoolyard fell away for an instant as he struggled with his memories and I saw that he was talking about his real father.

The sight Driver liked me to show off with wasn't like seeing TV. It was knowledge that came the same way old memories surface, unexpected but with the gut-strike of truth to them that your mind can doubt but your heart never does.

I see his old man dying in his sleep on a sofa, half hidden by blankets, in an empty house that was all but falling down. I heard crying from another room. Adult crying, the kind that makes you want not to go to the crier. I concealed my knowledge and stuck to the story, "No!"

"Oh." He paused and set the last plate into the drainer and pulled the plug, wrapping the chain around the cold tap and then running water to clean his hands. "Good," he dried his hands off on his apron and blinked. The shadow membrane of Forgetting, a slightly longer blink that most people think is only a moment of regret, flicked across his eyes and when it was gone all his defences were intact. "So, where's Middle Earth?"

"Right here."

"Oh god." said Driver, all her hatred of small town life distilled in the words. "As if."

"Well, it is," I said, getting disjointed as she started to look impatient. She would not have patience with my explanation that Middle Earth is wherever one said it was, like all things that depended on two realities for their existence: a place in spacetime and a position in someone's mind. She wasn't keen on that kind of knowledge. "And I have a house there. Not here. Up near Niagara, where we used to live."

"You never mentioned it," Driver objected, hurt. "Are you shitting me, Shirley?"

"I know where I poisoned my own *mother*," I told her, witheringly. "And it's mine; every lock, stock, taxidermy shed and five thousand acre logging forest."

Legolas was scowling faintly. He was still thinking about Middle Earth and attempting to make sense of it alongside the world he was in presently—which never works. "You came from there, and I left there, right?"

"No, *obviously* you never left," I said with some exasperation— who would have thought he could be so slow? 'You must have got stuck here and over the years I guess you've forgotten who you are."

"I'm only twenty four," he said uncertainly.

"In *this* particular life. But you've been around since before the Middle Ages . . ." I could see he had no idea what I was talking about. "For at least four thousand years."

"Feels like *I* have," Driver said, glancing at her watch. "Time we got you back to the ward, Wizbet. Come on."

"No, wait," the elf put his hand out towards me, though it stopped a long way from me. "What else happened?"

"Rent the fucking DVD," Driver suggested, moving towards the door where she took off her plastic overshoes and stuffed them into the bin. "Lili, time for meds."

"It's all mine, I can do whatever I like with it," I assured him about the house. "Nobody's lived there since I left, and if you're superstitious it would really be a bad bet, because the woodwork is more spirit than wood and the forest is full of what we longed to throw away, but everybody who could really hurt you there is already dead."

"Christ, Lili, you could try a more subtle way of picking up boy toys than that. Haven't you got any pride?" Driver sighed, though I could hear how pleased she was, thinking me in despair. She turned to him and added sarcastically, "She has another assessment coming up if you're interested. If it all works out she could be out the door by next month, but wear your suit of armour if you're coming in case she gets in the stabby habit." She did a vigorous impersonation of Anthony Perkins in *Psycho* and then came for me and took my arm firmly in what was more of a lock than a friendly hold. She hustled me to the door and muttered, "Big disappointment you are."

"Say, what's my name?" he called out after us.

"Legolas!" I shouted.

The doors whumped shut at our backs.

"He was perfect material," Driver grumbled. "As gullible as a two-day baby. He almost believed you, the born idiot. But you pushed it too hard."

"It was really him," I told her. "Did you expect me to lie cold?"

She, naturally, didn't believe me. "Ha! I was just hoping for something more like that thing we did with "Napoleon". Did you know he's gone back to driving buses? The Emperor of the roads, hah!" But then she became more thoughtful, "So, you have a house?"

"You're not getting it unless you're really nice to me," I said, truthfully.

"I don't want any haunted houses in the middle of nowhere," she said. "I have a house. With three bathrooms."

But we all know that's Police Chief Bob Driver's mother's house and that the third bathroom is nothing more than a converted stair closet. My house has three floors and ten bedrooms. It is short on bathrooms for the modern taste, I think, but nothing you couldn't adapt. I do a quick calculation, balancing time against Driver, the boy at the sink, my life and the pain under my nail. "I'll give it to you if I get out of here next month."

"Sure you will," she said. "But that relies on you keeping away from knives, and we all know how hard that is, don't we?"

"It's under the tiles behind the sink unit where the sealant has come away."

Well, they'd only find it when they did the searches before my assessment. I've been known to be a good hider of sharp things. To my amazement nobody but me seems able to detect their presence, even though a badly angled steel point can slice through the human energy field and create long term damage to it simply in passing. Every dinnertime is a war zone that passes unnoticed. And the sharps in my room were almost impossible for me to avoid even knowing where they were. Self harm for the sensitive.

Driver gave me a long, peculiar look and instead of taking me to the day room for trays, tea and tablets, we went into my room. She peeled back the loose rubbery string which had been functioning as the sealant around my sink unit and managed to tweak the concealed steak knife blade out from behind the loose tiles with the nail of her forefinger.

I watched days of work wasted: lifting that, taking off the handle, hiding it.

"Well I'll be damned," she said, holding it and giving me a long look. "Who was this for?"

"Anybody close enough to get it," I said. "But not you or Dr Lucy of course. And I wouldn't *kill* anyone. Only as much as necessary." I pressed the shard of Pyrex I'd been saving under my nail, very slowly, where it caught fast between flesh and nail, not cutting the skin but almost. Glass is nowhere near as dangerous as steel on the energy body, though it's the kind of thing that could do a lot of damage if somebody ate it by mistake and surely I don't need to say what might happen if you got a shard in your eye and started to see the world through another lens. Who knows what might be revealed?

Driver slipped the blade into her pocket. "Let's keep this between ourselves. You see me right and I'll see what I can do. Here," she took a wage slip out from where she'd had it folded in the pocket of her trousers and tore off a strip. "That's my bank ID. Now let's see if you've got anything more to you than a lot of tall tales and spooky visions."

I rolled the paper up and put it in my nightstand. "I want to see him again,'She rubbed her fingers and thumb together silently, in the way one might attempt to attract a cat, that universal gesture of summoning money from the aether.

I nodded. "Give me a few days. I have to call my lawyers."

"Be quick, Angel Dust. He doesn't look like he'll last the week. Come on. They'll start talking if you miss meds and I'll get put on another shift and that'll be us all washed up for another six weeks." She chuckled to herself as I passed her and muttered under her breath, but meant for me, "As if . . ."

Driver knows I haven't lost my marbles, not like most of them. I'm in here simply for admitting the truth—never denied a thing. Dr

Lucy has explained that the fact I don't lie and can't see a reason to is part of my pathological state.

In return for Dr Lucy's generosity with the information I explained it to her thus; consider mathematical functions that are everywhere continuous and not differentiable (that is, they change continuously, but also the rate at which they change itself changes continuously). These were considered freakishly rare and bad things, as functions go, with their devilish Heisenbergian properties: one may know their velocity or their position but never both. However, later it was found that this double whammy of massive instability was virtually generic behaviour of *all* continuous functions, and the very thing that was intrinsic to their overall stability. Human minds are the same.

I continuously tell the truth and am nowhere differentiable as far as I can tell. The degree of truth I am telling however, is continually fluctuating and unpredictable. This makes me the most stable and robust of all mentalities, and the most reliable, in my opinion. But of course, as Dr Lucy has told me, I would say that.

Most of Dr Lucy's beliefs about minds relies on a heavy emphasis to their regularity, stability and cohesion—the entire theory under which she's trying to make a name for herself is in fact called Cohesive Behaviourism: the Integrity Glue That Holds Us Together. Because of this she missed the significance of my self-determination (excusing herself by saying that abstract elements of mathematics were unsuitable tools for dealing with psychological analysis) so I never got to the part where I could whisk the cloth off my big revelation and tell her that some probability distributions have no mean, or average value. And neither do objects, or atoms, or people.

In retrospect I think the mathematics could all go in my sessions with Dr Lucy and I should stick to aphorisms and cliches, affirmations and the like, with their dripfeed of empty hope into the consciousness.

This is also how poisons and drugs work, but they are for the body. The mind requires stories. Dosage is very important. The right measure at the right moment. My preferred medication is Oprah Winfrey, for example.

I liked Oprah. I'd been cautiously but deliberately assimilating Oprah over the years, and her nurturing practicality was almost sufficiently developed in my continuity to put the lid on mother's casket. It was only ever a matter of time and finding the right active agent.

Under the influence of the wrong drugs, as usual that afternoon, I was left to myself wondering what Oprah would do if she found Legolas washing the dishes. In the intuition-enhancing haze of unreality brought on by the antipsychotics I got her confused with Sofia, the character she played in The Color Purple, so it blurred. The show I was watching became called, "Sins of the Fathers', and all I could see was the elf asking if his father was called Tyson, and Oprah saying, "Hell, no." And then Nurse Driver slapped her across the face and the security men came and there was a big fight.

I pressed my thumb against my bent forefinger and the sharp pain of the glass splinter under my nail reassured me. I waited for control to return.

Finally, in the evening, I exercised a communication privilege and called my lawyer. She was cautiously optimistic when I told her my plans. I could understand her doubts, but when I put my foot down what could she do? I was never so nuts that I was made to sign over powers of attorney. In fact, odd knife incidents and single necessary poisoning aside, I'm a model citizen, and my stock picks and cash management are beyond reproach. We spent half an hour at the end reviewing her portfolio and she warned me that if I do anything to get stuck inside again I'll lose everything I'm about to spend and then some.

"It's okay," I told her. "I understand. Send me the papers."

"Okay," she said with the rising tone that handed me all responsibility for whatever followed. "They'll be there tomorrow first thing."

"Don't forget the catalogs," I said.

"Sure thing."

I did pay Nurse Driver her bribe—thank goodness for telephone banking. And I paid the standard retainer to the PI I hired to follow her around and tell me what she did, too.

After I returned the phone to the Staff Office I checked out the false bottom in the third drawer of my nightstand. The photographs explaining to me how Driver knew so much about Napoleon's present affairs were still safe. One could never trust to theories of mind alone to bring plans as important as these into fruition. One must use everything at one's disposal, even brute cleverness.

A few days later I asked Driver if there was anything interesting happening in the kitchen. She sighed and coughed—a nasty, phlegmy hack. "Feeling clairvoyant are we?" she asked, pausing as we were making our slow way to the Art Room. It was two days before I was due to have my assessment interview with Dr Lucy.

"Please," I said, playing nice.

She didn't say anything, but we did make an unplanned turn and eventually, having avoided Dr Lucy's offices by going via the gardens, we came to the kitchens. It was half an hour after lunch. And there he was. Washing up.

I noticed that he'd changed his hair. It was now in a half braid of just the crown hair, drawn away from his face, with the rest free.

"I'm going for a break," Driver said to him, flashing a packet of Luckys. "Okay? Just five minutes. Don't give her anything sharp, and don't get onto any, you know, difficult subjects."

He turned and nodded to her, then looked at me with considerably more attention than before. "I saw the films," he said.

"I poisoned my mother because she was poisoning me," I said. It was important to get this straight before it had time to go wrong. "She was poisoning me with ideas and I poisoned her with powdered aconite. She wanted me to be her servant, and stay in her house and look after her, even though she was well able to do it for herself. She brought me up believing that I was living in a fairytale, and that one day a prince would come and that we were waiting there until he got through. He was very delayed. And then one day the last of my tutors quit. He handed me an atlas as he pulled his pants up on his way out the door. I've been here since then. They were going to insist I leave a while ago but the stars were all wrong for that, so I had to insist that I didn't and, of course, I paid too."

He nodded, lifting plates in and out of the hot water, steam rising around him. "Macy who does the cooking said you had the sight."

"Anyone can. I grew up in a forest by myself," I said. "Like you."

"I grew up in Austin, Texas," he said.

"You grew up in Mirkwood."

"You might have called it that in some kinda way. People like you say clever things like that. I see what you mean, but it wasn't that place."

I was ashamed for a minute. "Would you like to go back to the woods with me?"

The way he looked at me changed. I felt uncertain suddenly and I asked him, speaking much more softly, "Have I been here a very, very long time?"

He shrugged, "I don't know."

"I mean it," I said. "You can be anyone you like."

"No you can't," he said. "My dad couldn't. He couldn't be wealthy and he couldn't be well and he couldn't get work and he couldn't. And you, if that's true, you can't even get out of the house." He said everything quietly, inoffensively, as though it was beyond contradiction and he had long since learned to accept it and wasn't bothered whether anybody else did or not.

He didn't mean house. He meant tower. "But I am getting out. Next month," I said.

"Sure," he rinsed spoons under the tap and put them to dry beside my hand. They lay together, cupping each other, shining. "When you get out I'll go back to the woods with you."

"You wouldn't have to stay. You wouldn't have to do anything."

"Okay," he said wearily.

Nurse Driver came back inside, a cloud of stale smoke entering with her. "So, goof-offs, what's new?"

"Nothing," I said. "He won't admit he's an elf. Though he is."

"Yeah yeah," she took my arm firmly and said to him on the way out. "Still want a lift back to town?"

He nodded.

"See you at four."

I really did not want Nurse Driver to take him home in her car but there was nothing I could do about it. She'd do her utmost to burn him alive.

"Check his ears," I said. "You'll see."

Today on post-meds Oprah the specialist interviewed Legolas about his ears, and he explained their function and status according to postcolonial theory and the erotic Other. Oprah said they reminded her of Mr Spock's ears (at least she got that right and didn't start on about Dr Spock and the upbringing of children to strict schedules and exacting, if ultimately self-serving and flawed, behavioural norms). She recalled the myth that Mr Spock's ears were really pointed because the actor had got his head caught in a dough-kneading machine when he was a child.

"But he *did*," the guest expert said seriously.

Oprah made her tolerant, understanding face and patted Legolas on the knee.

In the evening I studied the newspapers, particularly the date. If it was 2007 then I must be forty-five years old and I had been in this place for over twenty years which is much longer than I'd originally planned.

I put my Pyrex splinter into the false drawer the next morning as I sat and opened my mail. There were my contracts, which I signed and sent back by return, and there was another set of photographs.

Nurse Driver had too much leopard print in her wardrobe, but I saw that Nappy the Bus was looking quite the swell these days with his designer jeans and his lounge jackets. He clearly still enjoyed a night out and a few cocktails, as most of the shots showed him laughing or digging Driver in the ribs with a swizzle stick, his toes balanced on the chrome ring of a high bar stool with the dainty precision of a master sailor.

My other black and whites depicted Legolas standing around town, at Mack's diner, at the laundrette and at the bus stop, huddled in a reasonably unsuitable waxed coat which couldn't have done much to keep the cold out, (though they say elves don't feel the cold like we do, but still) and one of those strange knitted beanie hats that look like tea cosies where the knitter forgot to leave a hole for the handle and spout. Very grainy, and much blown up, there was one of his face pressed sideways against the glass of a car window somewhere. No hat. The window was steamed up but his head was wiping it clean enough to see the outline of his ear mashed to the glass.

I used a ruler and calculated the angles. Not like Mr Spock's for sure, with his dashing uplifts and quizzical expressions—why do aloof, cold intellects and pointed auricles get together all the time in this universe?—but good enough for an ex-poisoner. I supposed that human normal must throw up a few pointy ears now and again, and there were always enough dough-kneading machines left carelessly around for curious children to fall into and make up the numbers. In any case, whether or not I chose to waste my life in this pointless building as Driver's pet, something like that really shouldn't wind up in here, wasting its sweetness on institutional dinnerware.

I couldn't decide whether Driver's massively undeserved happiness with Napoleon pissed me off or not but finally had to put it all aside. Even annoying shits have their fun and there was nothing to be done about that. I'd dealt with my mother and the responsibility for the rest fell squarely to the shoulders of their own nearest and dearest. Meanwhile, with the luxury of a guaranteed chance at serious injury safely stowed in the nightstand against a sudden turn for the worse in circumstances, I could afford to contemplate my exit interview. With gritted teeth I gave Driver and the other nurses the slip as they went on the evening tea round and made my way to the library. It was extremely difficult to stuff *The Rand McNally 2004 Road Atlas* under my robe—the corners kept snagging the stretchy towelling— but I got it back to my room undiscovered.

I read it thoroughly before returning it and, using the ruler again, calculated exactly how far it was from the institute to my house. I was surprised to see just how close we had lived to the great waterfall Niagara all that time, and me never knowing. I imagined fourteen million litres of water per minute going over that drop for the last twelve thousand years. With that kind of energy, what had my mother expected?

From the brown envelope that my lawyer had taped into the Jiffy bag containing my contracts I counted a thousand dollars and began to parcel it out into different, exact, portions.

Dr Lucy said at the conclusion of my assessment that we would do a trial period of reducing medication.

After lunch Driver came to my table. She took great care loading my dishes onto the tray to take away, making sure I saw the flash and fire zipping from the new solitaire diamond on her finger. It was a real hose-ripper. "Ready for the day room, Cinderella Rockefeller?"

I slipped her twenty dollars. "I have a date in the kitchen."

She stuffed the bills up the tight cuff of her sweater. "What's with you anyway?" she grumped as she patted me down, checking for cutlery. "The Gap. Hair. Eyebrows. It's like you're going somewhere. I even heard Lucy saying you're to cut the tabs. But we've been here before, little princess. You're going nowhere. Remember that. And I'm watching you."

"I'm watching you," I assured her. We turned into the fire staircase for our routine illegal trip downstairs, "And for every time you piss me off from now on I'm taking a zero off your tip."

She shoved me through the flapping doors into the kitchen with great confidence. "Hey Nimrod!" she called out to the slight, be-aproned figure at the sink. "Your number one fan is back."

He half turned, his expression bland as day-old porridge. "You got dressed."

"That's how much she likes you," Driver said, sliding her butt up onto the prep table in her usual position, taking out her Luckys and tapping the cash I'd given her into the half-empty pack. "Get away from that drainer," she snapped at me as I went closer. "And keep your lilywhites where I can see them."

"Don't you find her annoying?" I asked him.

He made the whole set of ambivalent postures in one go; shrug, moue, headshake, body twist, but in miniature. The right corner of his mouth sidled up for a moment. He lifted a plate up and steam billowed off it, white soap dripped from it. "After three thousand years?"

"Oh, not you too," Driver groaned.

He picked a knife out of the sink and held it up. It shone under the lights. He twirled it in his fingers, conjuror style, flipping it around like a propellor blade. It moved with speed and precision along his hand and back again. Driver couldn't see it, only the bubbles that flew off its ends and spattered away. He set it down and went back to washing.

"You must have been all over," I said. "Where did you go?"

"All over," he agreed. "I like America. It's where we landed when we missed Valinor."

"Jesus," Driver said. "If you're going to start adding to her problems we'll have to go."

"It was very quiet in those days," he added, immersing a roasting tray in the water. "Why did you kill your mother, Lizabet?"

"For the love . . ." Driver began.

"She lied about everything. She wasn't my mother. She was somebody else. It's in the file. I was adopted, when she was still a perfect New England wife with a holiday home in Martha's Vineyard and two more in the Hamptons. The family was something to do with cod fisheries. They had a lot of ships. I only read about this after the trial. She and I lived alone in the house up in the forest. Everything was delivered. She used to pay people not to come up all the way. There was a trail stop a mile out from the house, a depot made of concrete to keep the bears out, and we got everything out of there. She didn't want anyone to come up and see us. Only my teachers, though they never stayed. She was always firing them for talking about us, or she thought they were talking about us, but that only happened after I murdered her when they decided to cash in, seeing as all her penalty clauses were toothless compared to the amounts that the magazines were willing to offer for an inside line. I had lessons in everything while I was there. She wanted me to excel because she wasted her education and got taken for a ride by some man who got her to leave her first husband and then was going to marry her, but she found out he was only a con guy who wanted her fortune, and not long after that her parents were killed in a boating accident near the Cape. Well, that's what she said and they found him—M Manfred Arthurs, his name was—and he was a salesman, life-insurance, and he testified in court to say that she was right enough in her mind when she left him. So she got nothing. She told me that my father was a knight protecting a big kingdom and that we had to stay hidden because we were under a spell. All of my occult education came from her; witchcraft, ouija, cartomancy, casting of runes, clairvoyancy with the crystal sphere, the mirror, and through water, and the herbal of course. She said I was her daughter and that one day the spell would be lifted and we would come into the world as queens. She told me that there was only one island, where we lived, and the rest was ocean and the ocean was full of beasts and . . ."

"That's enough, chatty lady," Driver said, yawning. "I need a smoke. Get back from there like I told you. Although, if he keeps on asking questions you can stab him, why don't you? Then you'll lose your bet, Bet." She yawned, and a wisp of vapour came out of her mouth, grey and sulphurous.

I watched her leave with deep satisfaction.

"Why did you stay in here?" he asked, continuing with his task slowly. He didn't look at me. Just washed things.

"Nowhere to go," I said, rubbing my arms because the breeze from the open door was cold.

"Your house."

"It has damp," I said and he nodded. "I don't mean to live there after," I added to him. "I just want to see it one more time. You will come with me? Like you said?"

"Sure," he said. "I like the woods."

"Do you have a bow?"

"Yes," he said.

"I don't think there will be many bears," I said. "But you never know. Can you drive?"

"Sure."

"I can't drive. I'll get us a car. A new one. It can be yours. What's a good car?"

"A Porsche 911 GT2," he said without hesitation.

I knew he'd know. "I'll get one of those. And you can have the house. If you want it. But you'd better sell it. It's no place to live. Too big, too old and really dark inside. And my mother may still be loitering on certain planes. She never knew when to quit."

"Maybe we'll just take a look at it," he said and gave me a patient smile.

Driver came back and patted me down again. "Open," she said and stared into my mouth. "Okay. Let's go for a nice siesta. We can come back tomorrow or some other day. You want a lift, mighty prince?"

"No thanks," he said. "I have to go early."

Driver snorted and held my arm. "Not so fast," she hissed in my ear. "Not so fast little lady." The powerlessness inherent in the edge of her voice was sweet to me.

Whump, said the doors at our back.

I was reasonably sure that the window glass through which the elf's ear had been visible was not the window glass of Nurse Driver's Chevrolet. I was proved correct when the PI sent me the details. It was a long-distance haulage truck which had been parked at the mountain layby where a lot of drivers take rest breaks just outside the town.

I wondered what the inside of a truck was like, and spent the rest of the evening searching magazines for pictures and details of Porsche 911 GT2s. They looked nice. I liked the silver ones the best, and Oprah agreed with me, even though she endorses Pontiacs.

When I opened the drawer to put my new car pictures and the PI's letter away in my secret place I found a carving knife lying among my underwear. It had not been there before.

I held it in a new pair of Victoria's Secret crimson silk pants and watched the soft lamplight streak along its newly sharpened blade. Clearly this afternoon had proved too high a dose of fantasy for Nurse Driver, but now disposing of her return gift would be tricky indeed as she knew all my hiding places, save the false drawer, and that was because it hid a space so thin as to be all but indistinguishable from nothing. Certainly not big enough to hide a knife like this.

As ever I took solace, refuge and security in the sweeping curves of constant motion. Holding the knife I went to the window, opened it the maximum possible inch and manouevred the knife between the bars. I dropped it into the night. There was a shrubby bank beneath my window some two floors down. I was concerned in case I hit a wild animal by mistake, a squirrel or a chipmunk maybe, but the silence was reassuring.

I got out my Pyrex splinter. I held it up to the light and stared into its aggravated crescent shape. The fey will leave a sickle if you ask nicely enough and pay with blood. As with all such objects it was hard to differentiate its potential for damage to an actual probability. It promised to reap only one thing: trouble.

I had planned to keep it close to me in case I needed a reason to stay because I was wrong about Greenleaf there, or in case I needed to swallow it when I got out of here—if the sky proved too deep and the mouth of the world too fierce. Now, with scarcely a second thought, I sent it the way of the knife with a firm flick of my finger.

In the knife's place I put one of the photographs of Nurse Driver with Napoleon boning her parts. It was very difficult to say whether such a dose would be high enough to cause a mortal failure or would simply enrage a determined opponent, but one cannot wait forever in the vain hope of certainty.

It was gone the next morning after breakfast.

I got myself dressed and washed, ready to see Dr Lucy, when Driver appeared. There was no nonsense or boredom in her expression now. She closed my door and leant on it, holding the handle behind her back in both hands. We stared at each other for a few moments, taking measurements.

I could almost see the cogs turning as she tried and failed to grasp the extent of my capabilities outside the institute and her likely ability to foil them. They were, of course, too big, and Driver was at least smart enough to see that. Finally she took a deep breath and I saw that her minor pleasures of torment and the desire to maintain her current social position were much stronger than her need to keep hold of me. Demons are all the same. "All right. What will it take to get rid of you?"

"Be sure I leave here next Wednesday morning without incident while you continue as usual," I said. "If you do, I will give you all the pictures. If you don't, I will post them on every bulletin board and website in town, I will paper the streets with them and I will have you and the police chief audited by every tax and insurance inspector from here to Havana. Here," I held out my hand. On it was a small kid's rubber spider, one of several I kept to annoy her because she hated spiders, even toy ones, and I used to put them around so that she would find them when she was sneaking through my things. "A charm to prove my good intents."

She gave me a sour look. "Shove it." But she nodded. "And what if Lucy doesn't let you out? She's got a judge to convince, and they're not in your pay, unless I'm very much mistaken."

"I won't hold it against you, though I expect you to carry on being very nice to me if the worst happens."

Driver rolled her eyes and her left hand strayed automatically to her pocket, feeling for the pack of cigarettes. I'd never seen her lips so thin, her broad face so tight. "Don't fuck it up this time," she said and went out, without even offering to take me up to the day room. Then, in parting, she opened the door again just as she was about to shut it and said, "Your kitchen boy quit this morning. I thought you'd like to know."

"Why?" I asked, though I was reasonably sure that I knew.

Her voice was sweetly practical, as though she was telling a snippet from the daily news that she thought might interest me. "I don't know, maybe he was getting pressed for payment by the VD clinic downtown. I don't believe he had medical insurance." She closed the door with careful, quiet exactitude.

You never can tell how poisons will affect the individual. Some people have high natural resistance, up to a point, then suddenly fade. Others keel over with the merest sniff. What doesn't kill you makes you stronger but oh, we never know where the brink lies for sure.

Driver came on my last morning to give me my tablets in two large plastic bottles for self-administration—no more idiot trays with the days of the week on them for me.

I gave her a shoebox, replete with ten plastic insects, two rubber spiders, a strip of sealant, a brown envelope with most of the pictures inside it (all well covered in my fingerprints), and a pack of Luckys. I left a couple of the photos in the false drawer, just in case the next patient who came along might find them useful. It never hurts to give a little to the gods. Especially when you're on a roll.

"I guess this is it then," Driver said as she walked with me down to the reception desk—as far as I had been in two years, since the last time I stuck a butter knife a quarter inch through the damp energy field and solid thigh fat of a compulsive gambler.

Driver smiled broadly as we both looked out through the glass doors where the gravel driveway stretched to the road under a grey and soulless sky. Trees and the sulky shape of the hills blocked out the view of the town below us and everything else as well. Aside from the staff cars, and the daybus which took the outpatients to and from the town, there was nobody and nothing around.

"I guess so," I said. I was gripped by so much fear that I could barely make myself pick up the pen she gave me.

I signed a lot of papers and then my lawyer arrived in her blue cabriolet and we shook hands and dealt with yet more formalities and a final talk with Dr Lucy in the peculiar informality of the visitors' coffee lounge. Every so often I looked out over the driveway. Driver watched me and smiled sympathetically, sweetly, enjoying every second of my terror.

"So, will you be staying with relatives or friends?" Lucy asked me as we were closing.

I shook my head.

"Well, I hope you have somewhere nice to stay," Driver said.

A sleek, beautiful silver grey car turned its alloy wheels in the weak light outside.

"Excuse me," I said. "My ride is here."

I crossed the gravel as lightly as a feather. The passenger door opened for me and I threw my bag in the back and sat down in the ineffable strangeness and power of its interior.

He smelled of Dior as he leaned across me and clipped my safety belt into place. His smile was as gentle as I remembered, his hair braided like in the film. He set his hands on the wheel, "Say the word, Miss Elizabeth."

"Everywhere." I said.

We stood at Niagara Falls, on the viewing point on the Canadian side. The water's hypnotic flow piled on below us in an endless cascade. Our feet were on a metal grid, like a pencil sketch of some more substantial landscape waiting to be filled in.

"So big. So fast," I said.

Why does one always only manage to say such banal things for the wonders of the world? I watched the beanie hat and the truckstop photographs float down, tossed this way and that in the turbulent airs before they were lost in the roiling white spray, bubbles and rainbows below.

His empty hands hung from his wrists and vapour collected on his face.

I wiped a bead of it onto my finger and put my finger in my mouth. The world's tears are rare. They give Sight like no other object of power. Seeing is believing, of course. One drop is the ocean.

I had the house keys in my hand. In my mind I held the memory of the two of us asleep last night, like mice on the surface of our vast white kingsize bed in a franchise motel. We slept on the moon, as empty and distant: his hand in mine.

I had intended to throw the keys in the river, but the water told me to put them back into the post pack that my lawyer had given to me.

"This way," I said and led him, unresisting, by the arm, the pack in my hand.

As we drank hot coffee in the shop nearby I took a pen out and addressed the pack to Nurse Driver. On the back of the day's menu I wrote the address of my castle. I sealed it together with the keys.

"Don't you want to go to the woods any more?" he asked, watching me and reading upside down.

I glanced up into his young, handsome face and imagined his bare feet treading the oak floors of the old house I knew so well—every knot, every stitch, every useless pane and gewgaw of its magnificence in which true magic had never tarried for a moment. "Not a bit. Do you?"

"I was never that much of a country boy," he said, smiling his slow, Texan smile.

We posted the keys together, one of each of our hands on the pack as we fitted it into the mailbox. Then we opened out a map of the continent on a picnic table which had been placed thoughtfully close to the car park for people who did not like to be far from escape at any time.

I turned him around three times widdershins and put my hands over his eyes. He stuck his finger on the page and we both looked down. Spray from the falls spattered over us in a sudden gust.

"New Jersey," he said, appalled. He looked up into the west. The sun was sliding down to the end of the sky, burning with a hot orange fire. He jingled the car keys thoughtfully and then lifted his other hand up. The wind snagged the map instantly and whirled it away towards the sun.

"Do you really have it?" his question was so quiet. "The sight. Do you have it? This isn't all some trick. A lie?"

"Sight is the least of it," I said. The map had simply vanished. Only the world was left. "Sight is just waiting to see what the world wants to do."

He held the car door for me, closed it after me, and then got in and started the engine. He made it roar with his foot. "Have you ever been to the sea?"

"No," I said, looking out through the windscreen with excitement.

"Me neither." His smile was radiant.

"Let's go!" I said.

The world shifted, sped, became a blur.

LEGOLAS DOES THE DISHES

The one thing I wanted to create here was a deep uncertainty about reality, in the minds of the main character and the reader, never committing entirely to the mundane or the fantastic interpretation. For me personally there is no escaping either and neither has primacy, they're two sides of the one coin of my perception but I've spent most of my life manically trying to figure out which is "real" and which is "better" and which one I ought to believe in. It's only very recently I realised the answer is not one or the other, it's both. This stuff usually comes to me in fiction long before it struggles through into my actual mind.

DREADNOUGHT

DREADNOUGHT

This story was written on request. I'd been going to write a novel set in the same world, where this is the opening gambit, but so far I haven't written it because, as usual for me, I find too many fragile parts to the central conceit once I start to examine it really closely. I still like it though— it has the edgy, unhappy feeling of genuine unease about being used by machines and vice versa; this difficult relationship of user and used.

DREADNOUGHT

We sail upon a vast spaceship with open sides. She is only a skeleton of a vessel. A chassis of carbon beams anchors her cargo to engines. She carries hundreds of thousands of Armoured soldiers. Some work. Others sleep in ordered ranks, magnetically attached to clamps on the ship's ribs. There is no need to move about. Where would we go? We talk a little, old friends, and in places lean on one another like falling pillars. We turn our faces to the solar wind when we are awake. We like the light. It recharges our electrical systems.

I am unlocking the lightweight frame of a Mess pod, prior to passing it on for jettison. My comrades are moving a new one into position and are waiting to refuel. We will be first, because we have replaced the pod, but the rest of this Mess is for the dead. As the new tank rolls in I connect my hose and commence drinking.

At the front of the ship, instead of a nose cone, the dead are stacked. They are stored in orderly catacomb files, upright, packed in. They were placed there at the end of the last battle. As I am watching the dead I see one decouple itself from the aft side of the stack. It moves with cautious steps.

We are all connected but I cannot hear this one.

Through the shattered faceplate I see that the soldier's mouth is blocked by a piece of metal ingrowth. When he was alive he was a Mute, one of my communication nodes, my flagbearer. His forehead is the flat ochre plain of dead human bone and his lidless ever-open eyes are the blue of Earthly skies. Parts of his Armour are badly damaged, but it ventilates and feeds his body.

I didn't know that I could function without my human host, until I saw him. I am glad. I need all my troops. I am frightened. What will become of me?

He comes closer. Bones show through holes, fraying into space. Despite the fact that his neural connections have been sufficiently regrown to permit communications and the effective functioning of his remaining body and brain, he has not returned to his Unit. This is true of all the dead. I do not know why.

He drifts surreptitiously towards me clamps to an open position at the pod, opposite mine. He moves sluggishly, connects, and begins to fuel. He stares straight through me. His eyes do not reflect the sun. They have been rebuilt to withstand vacuum and they are not shiny.

I ping him for information. I want to catch his hand and ask him the question everyone asks of each other, begging to know—what's *your* name?

If he were one of the living I know what he'd say.

"Private Diego Arroyo Lopez."

Because that is my name, though once I had another.

That is what everyone has said for forty eight days, ten hours, five and a half minutes, since the time at which the last EMP bomb detonated. It was close to us, but we were not ruined. We successfully obliterated our primary targets. We live.

But this soldier is dead.

I have taken twenty litres. I unhook myself from the Mess and clip on one of the pipelines to feed the remaining dead. I step aside. The nameless unit watches me. His expression does not alter.

I ping him again and hear my own signal echo in the minds of all my soldiers; the radar of a lost submarine. *What is your name?*

Blue Eyes speaks in machine code. It does not translate to English, or any human language, but we all hear it at once and know its meaning. The Unit speaks the symbol of the empty set, $\emptyset$, but the line through it is red, unmaking it. Not nothing. I am.

This is Armour itself! The all of us at once, every unit, every man and woman, every fused level of our single army. Oh Captain, my Captain, my commander, my body, my soldiers, my plan, my one, my true!

He/we are uncertain. We are afraid. There is nothing to hold on to.

My eyes fill with tears, and my Armour recycles them.

"Private Lopez," says Blue Eyes. Armour looks through him, at us, and back at itself. We are a loop circuit.

"I am Private Diego Arroyo Lopez," it says.

I cannot see myself in his sunless eyes.

"I am Private Diego Arroyo Lopez," I say in response. I am hopeful.

"You are Private Nancy Johnson," it replies.

Yes. I am.

"This experiment has concluded," says Private Lopez, who is also Armour, speaking the one language we all understand, because we are one. "Individual unit identity has been temporarily restored."

Later all the viable dead units become Private Lopez. They all look different, but they are all the same. The non viable units are recycled into Mess.

We are upset that we could not find our way without Private Lopez. This means that none of my units can exist without a host. I am insufficient for life alone. But I can be Private Lopez any time I want, even though I am dead. I am glad.

DREADNOUGHT

I realise now I think it over that I keep returning to this theme of relationships, power, abuse and vulnerability in them. I use Science Fiction just because it makes the points much better and in a more satisfying way than describing them in a realist trope. Even so, I feel like if I were a "proper" writer, or a "proper" philosopher maybe, I should be able to do more than just present scenarios that play out and bring up ideas—the trouble is, I don't have any answers. When I was little I thought by now that the world's interpersonal conflicts would be solved problems. I hate coming up with the "my way or death!" scenario in stories, but it does have its way of returning . . . I'm still writing about it.

AN UNREMARKABLE MAN

AN UNREMARKABLE MAN

This was written on request for an anthology. I didn't at first intend for there to be an entire supernatural setting, I thought I would just write about a woman who found herself bothered by a man who was in every way utterly ordinary with the vague notion that her own paranoia would be the cause of her terror. Once the characters appeared on the page however, it seemed they were far from ordinary themselves and I decided just to roll with it, as every time I tried to pull it back to mundanity the writing pixies who make up stories in the back of my head shook their heads in disgust and left. When that happens I have to remember I'm only the typist. Sometimes I regale the pixies, explaining that this is not the stuff of great literature but merely entertainment. Then they get very mad and can go off for months at a time. The moral of the story—never call your pixies hacks.

AN UNREMARKABLE MAN

The imp Saclides, second only to the Hell Lord Androcus, wearied under the weight of his burden. The locked box in his hands was cold as ice. The steel of its making was rimed with frost that spread from the shards of human bone which pitted its surface and made Saclides' hands bleed as he carried it. The further he flew, the lighter it had become, at least for the first two hundred miles, but now its weight was steadily increasing. Lower and lower he dropped, out of the high stratus and into the low clouds over the cities beneath, and still the box dragged him down and the frost bit deeper. The changes meant only one thing: his attempt to steal it had failed. He was seen, and the master of the box was coming to claim his rightful property.

Below him the dotted trails of yellow lights showed roads where the humans ran their cars up and down, white lights streaming one way and red the other like the flow of cells in veins. Saclides grimly thought of blood and conjuring with it. He used his own wounds to bring heat into his hands and nearly passed out with the pain of returning sensation. As if in response the box became yet colder and shards of ice formed on it as Saclides fell through the clouds. They broke and plummeted down, only just faster than he did as the box itself doubled its gravity and sucked Saclides towards the unwelcome Earth.

Behind him he thought he could sense the pressure wave and late boom of the flap of giant, spectral wings. Which meant there was no time to lose if he were going to survive. He stopped trying to flee and began to search for a good hiding place.

As he came tumbling out of the sky onto some domestic lane in a town he didn't even know the name of he cast a cloak on himself and was lost to human sight, but not to the sight of the box's master. That he could feel like a prickle on his back.

Saclides looked up and down. Houses houses all the same, little boxes on a little lane of similar lanes, clustered together in meaningless rows . . . where better than someplace like this to hide a treasure such as the one in the box? All so anonymous. All so dull . . .and then he saw it.

It was almost dawn and on the step of a house a few metres away a red box sat waiting to be found alongside the milk delivery. It was just the right size.

Fumbling, his hands covered in green heating flames, Saclides dragged the box he carried to the step and set it down. The new box was sturdy red cardboard on the shape of a heart and it contained a sizeable array of medium priced chocolates. It was the work of a few moments to open the lid, open his mouth and consume the lot in a single inhalation. He was small, but he could eat elephants if he wanted to.

The imp put the freezing box inside the heart and closed the lid. To conceal it in a mundane object! He felt the touch of genius. As soon as the card lid had shut the biting cold and pressure stopped. So flimsy—but it hid the thing completely from all arcane sight. Even he would not have been able to find it now . . .not like before . . .

An almost gentle beat, like the stroke of a blow on a distant drum, brushed across his senses. He ran. He flew. He dashed and dodged. He led a merry dance through city streets and country lanes, along hedgerows and beside vast buildings full of sleeping machines all while the gentle beats grew closer and stronger until one of them was so full it struck him out of the air onto the muddy ground of a football field. It was dawn and in the faint light Saclides saw traffic speeding on motorways just over the hill. He saw it through the spectral form of the box's master, as that form stretched out one of its many hands, at the tip of one finger a bead of darkness so complete that the growing day seemed to rush into it and be swallowed there.

"Thief," said a quiet voice. The finger touched Saclides and he expected death, but it was not his death which came. Instead, screaming and howling, it was Androcus who was pulled through his minion, torn to pieces on the simple wish of this master's darkness. Androcus passed through Saclides in bits and vanished into the void at the master's centre; a howl of rage and fury the only thing left long after his essence was gone.

Saclides, unhurt, looked up into the shifting form above him; barely more than a veil over the softening blue of the growing light, it cast a pall of grey like the settling of dust in an abandoned room.

"I can get it back," he offered, surprised he could speak, for the grey had sapped him of almost all his will. It seemed to him that it would be better now to turn away from life and he could not remember what it was he had thought he could ever gain by stealing this power for his Lord, nor why his Lord could want it. Death was preferable to another moment of this powdery fall.

"Let it lie," said the master. "If I cannot see it, then who will?"

The finger returned and touched Saclides with gentleness. There was no pain and no confusion, no final angry glare, no moment of grief or gladness, only his end.

Laura heard the post arrive and went to get it. She opened the door to fetch the milk in and almost tripped over a red box on the step. It skidded a few feet after her toes caught it and she cursed and stood there rubbing her foot and giving it a baleful stare.

Red heart. Oh dear. Robert was getting desperate. She looked at it with annoyance and a growing dislike of all things romantic. Also, it had felt light, and after the last week of handwringing, angsty text messages and midnight calls she felt the least she deserved was a seriously heavy freight of something extremely Belgian and preferably hand-dipped.

She tucked the letters under her arm and took the milk inside. Was it un-modern and feeble of her to want to pack Robert in simply because he was boring? Boring wasn't a crime. It was barely ranking on the list of hideous possible faults you could have in a boyfriend. He was nice. He was polite. He had courted her with the utmost care and thoughtfulness, escalating his gifts from the traditional starting point of a single flower, through bunches of flowers belled fat with chrysanthemums, then gradually evolving into roses and after the roses little bits of jewellery, nothing too flashy, only cute pieces and later . . . but she had forgotten the list before she got to the end, there being nothing memorable or personal on it.

And then yesterday, to say that he had been seeing Celia. And thinking of her a lot. And hoping that Laura wouldn't mind too much but things were looking altogether better with Celia, who shared his love of spending every weekend sitting in windswept grandstands listening to the whine of tortured metal all for the occasional flash of colour as a formula one car fled through the straight just as you had bent down to pick up your overpriced plastic carton of beer and thought about how you could have been walking in the sunshine with a nice pub lunch ahead of you instead . . .oh that was so nice!

Laura went back for the cardboard heart, ready to kick it into next week. There was a note attached to it. She decided she would read it. And if it was wet and boring she would simply text the same words to Robert's phone as the final verdict on a completely pointless exercise. She ground her teeth as she thought of the hours of patience she had wasted on him, foolishly and selfishly, because she thought he was lonely and needed her, and how it was so nice to be needed, even if he couldn't seem to manage WANTED, and now, all her kindness was repaid with Celia, who had been lurking around the background all along, Celia with her beige twinset and her Prada handbag and her passion for inhaling kerosene.

The box stared at her. You deserve me, it seemed to say. You were being Miss Bountiful and here I am, full of Bounty. Go on. Wallow in self pity and take me in.

She bent down to it and opened the note with one finger. Inside Robert's strange habit of always writing in BLOCK CAPITALS proved it to be his work but the paper was strangely scorched and warped making it hard to read.

LAURA it screamed at maximum volume *I NEVER MEANT TO HURT YOU. I REGRET NOT TELLING YOU EARLIER ABOUT CEE AND ME. I HOPE WE CAN STILL BE FRIENDS. WITH LOVE FROM ROBERT X.*

Laura felt a smile of deep satisfaction stretch over her face. Now she could legitimately hate him with all of her heart. Friends indeed. With love from. X. She prided herself on her broad mind and forgiving nature, but that could wait another few hours.

She picked up the box with a fondness and warm regard for it she had never experienced for Robert and took it with her into the house, thinking it was strangely light and suspecting darkly that no doubt he had wished to save for Celia's massive engagement ring and had probably bought her the showy set of chocolates that was all lovely on the top but had a completely false bottom. A perfect end to a hugely stupid relationship. What had she been thinking?

She set it on the kitchen counter and eased the top off. There were no chocolates inside, although there was a whiff of chocolate. Instead there was a small, heart-shaped chest the size of a large fist, made of some kind of dull grey metal, bound with leather and studded with nubs of ivory. It was dirty, as though it had recently been dug out of the ground, and a heavy, cold smell emanated from it, redolent of old gold, the graves of heroes and the death of empires.

An object of power!

Laura rammed the lid back on as fast as she could. As with all natural materials the cardboard of the box hid the magic of its contents perfectly and she breathed a sigh of relief, followed by a deep breath of worried contemplation.

Had she made a terrible mistake? Was Robert's dull front simply that—a mask of mundane humanity over the face of an unspeakably corrupted agent for the nether gods? Could he have been stringing her along all the time with his square cut sandwiches, his thermos flasks, his Tupperware?

No. Tupperware was the devil's work, she reminded herself sternly—look at how the lids always went missing to the piece you wanted to use, and then, when you found them, inexplicably would not fit over the last corner of the box no matter how hard you pushed and pulled so that bread went stale anyway and mayonnaise leaked all over the inside of your bag. No demon would consider using it as part of a cover story.

Laura sat with her breakfast forgotten, holding the box between her hands, wondering if she dared risk another peek. It had been a long time since she had smelled that smell of ancient forces and that had been in a church in the wilds of North Yorkshire where something old had been hidden under a tombstone. It was still buried there, probably inside the ribcage of a priest, for safekeeping. Like this one it had been concealed by wards of bone, earth, grass and stone, but the frosts of winters had cracked the stone cover and she had felt it as she lingered there one autumn day. Like this one it shimmered with promises of infinite pain to those who disturbed it, though that was only to be expected when the contents were so precious.

She thought she knew what it was. She would have to check with Sophie first though. Just to be sure.

She flipped open her phone and texted Sophie's number. *Mt me now, Sbux by libry, vvvvvimptnt.*

Laura put the box into a plastic carrier bag and went to get dressed.

Sophie was standing in the queue at Starbucks by the time Laura arrived looking cool and interesting in pastels. Her necklace with its tiny silver cross glinted warmly.

"Hi," Laura said. "Look at this."

Sophie glanced down into the bag that Laura held open. "Big deal. Valentine's Day. He got you chocolates. Is that it?" She had the weary look of someone who has lied to get out of work and regrets the effort.

"Not chocolates," Laura said ordered a double espresso with another espresso in it and a hot chocolate on the side, no cream. She leant into Sophie and whispered, "I think it's a *Viscus Diabolique.*"

Sophie almost dropped her mint tea. She looked down at the bag. "Oh my."

There were no free tables, none that was until Sophie smiled her soft smile at the couple in the corner spot with the armchairs and they found that they suddenly wanted to go out into the drizzle and walk.

"Not very PC of you," Laura said gratefully. She handed the bag to Sophie who put it on the table and took a peek under the box lid. As she did so a soft chime like the ring of tubular bells in a distant cathedral rang out across the shop and a wave of cold air gusted around their legs.

"Sophie!"

"Sorry . . ." Sophie closed the lid as various people reached around to check their phones. "Well. Whoever's it is knows now that it's been found."

Laura tried not to be annoyed, or terrified. "Can you open it?"

Sophie stared at her as if she had asked for a lightly warmed giraffe.

"Come on Soph," Laura encouraged, holding her espresso with two hands. "You picked open the Gates of Jericho. You can do it."

"Laura, what is wrong with you? Are you insane?" Sophie furled the bag in her hands, whispering through the rustle it made.

"Sophie," Laura whispered back. "I just spent three months dating the world's most boring human because I felt sorry for him. I thought I could change him. Bring some interest to his life. Fall in love with him and rest in the dullness because it was a nice change from having to fight on against the ordinary everyday evils . . ."

"But . . . where did it come from . . . what are you going to do with it?" Sophie rustled the bag some more and they both tried not to notice a chill creeping around their table.

"Change of path," Laura said. "Look. Robert didn't give me it. I have no idea how it got there. Someone might even be planning to come back for it. But this is the only chance I ever had . . ."

"Chance?" Sophie's blue eyes, used to giving blessings of wisdom, were huge in her gentle face, and not with the grace of sages but the astonishment of the truly startled.

"To get out of sales," Laura smiled winningly at Sophie, giving her best smile.

"Now I have heard enough," Sophie hissed, giving Laura a look of motherly sternness. "We must destroy it. It is our duty."

"Ah come on, even you know nothing is black and white like that," Laura felt her espresso cooling and knocked it back before it could go stone cold. "These things you find once in an eternity . . .and get hold of even less often . . ."

"Laura . . . are you . . . you can't mean . . ."

The table, loaded with a tea, a chocolate, a coffee, Sophie's elbows and the box, creaked suddenly. Sophie tugged surreptitiously at the bag. It didn't budge.

"They're CLOSE!" she hissed at Laura. "My hands are freezing. We have to re-hide it . . ."

"The box is the problem," Laura whispered. "Open it and I'll do the rest."

Sophie looked at her with great misgiving, her eyes turning grey with anxiety, but Laura was right. The box was the magnet, the telltale, the mine and the problem. The contents were . . . a whole different problem. Whatever they were. Her eyes sparkled with excitement in spite of her reservations: Laura knew that she wasn't the only one long wearied by the ages of mankind and their rapid progress from unconscious to barely functional. "All right. But if it's one of the Old Ones you're on your own here, Laura my girl."

"Okay!"

The table legs shifted a few millimetres apart on the false tile of the floor and the cheap wood creaked again. Sophie dived into her handbag and took out a small square of silk. It unrolled, displaying neatly stitched pouches, each containing a tiny bone. She extracted a long and delicate fishbone with her dainty fingers and plunged her hands into the plastic carrier bag. She closed her eyes and her face became still and serene as a plaster saint's.

A man came and sat down at the table with them, though there had been no spare chair there until he sat in it and no man approaching across the cafe a second before he was there, his long coat sighing in a heavy fall of silk around him, his gloves laid down upon the table top to reveal rough and ready carpenter's hands.

"Ladies," he said in a voice low as a bull's. "Please let my heart alone."

Around them the chink of china, the low hubbub of general chat, the sounds of the coffee machines and the distant noise of traffic continued. Sophie and Laura turned their faces to see who had come.

He had no particular look. His hair was of a nondescript colour, possibly some shade of brown. His face was bland and unremarkable, his eyes middling in the ranges of earthy tones, his skin a sallow mixture of any number of racial inputs that couldn't be placed as one thing or another. He sat with calm and in manner and posture that was inoffensive, somewhere between assertive and gentle. He did not look at either of them, only at the carrier bag.

Sophie withdrew her hands, palming the fishbone as she did so.

Laura reasoned that the box was open, else he would simply have taken it. But with the release of its lock its powers were severely diminished. Also, it was in her possession, and until she relinquished it he could not claim it or its contents.

He had said heart. It was, as she had hoped, a relic of extreme power. Creatures such as he were only vulnerable to certain fates, death not among them, but of those fates some were to be feared more than simply a mortal end: banishment, imprisonment and eternal suffering were the top of that list and each of these afflictions were cast upon the victim's heart. Hence smart cookies had long since removed their hearts and put them away for safe keeping beyond the reach of enemies who might be capable of such a charm.

"I've got a deal for you," Laura said, fuelled by the espresso entering her blood.

The unremarkable man looked at her for the first time although his steady gaze informed her that he knew she was the temporary owner. He might have considered her an unworthy opponent—it was hard to tell when they didn't know each other—but if he did he showed none of it on his face. He was good, Laura thought. "I am listening."

"This box," Laura indicated the bag with a tip of her head. "Only lasted two seconds when Soph opened it. That's not much of a safe."

"It has served for the last millennium. She is the greatest lockpick left of the ancient world. Unluckily for me." He gave Sophie the slightest of nods, a concession to her skill. With a slight gesture of one finger he unspelled the box itself and the table cracked as normal weights and temperatures returned.

"Well, the ancient world is long buried in time," Laura said as a preamble, "and I was wondering whether or not you'd be considering a new form of long term storage?"

Sophie gave her a Significant Look that said You Are Mad.

The unremarkable man stared at Laura with almost complete disinterest.

"Your words are frivolous. The modern age suits you well, Laura the Honoured, First Among Equals," a slight smile may have crossed the man's face. He reached across the table into the bag and took out the heart box. "I sense your boredom, the ennui of the spoiled wealthy classes, the angst of those to whom everything comes too easily. You were victorious in many battles. You rode the winds and hunted down all the lesser demons so far beneath you. Glory was yours. Yet love was not; for who can love such easy perfections? You don't even know my name." His voice was soft as old paper that has been fumbled many times, a page of a prayer book, one whose owner has sought solace in its pages and found none.

Sophie had no amusement in her face now. She looked at Laura and shook her head. From her expression it was clear that even she did not know who this was, or what infernal power his heart may hold, except that it was the obvious vessel of his life.

Laura felt herself insulted by his words but they had struck something in her she had not liked recently and so she said nothing, only watched, looking into the heart shaped box as he put his hand to the chest and opened its small lid on the single hinge.

Inside the chest was lined with silvery lead. A heart, human sized, lay in its cold, poisonous embrace. Severed cleanly at aorta and veins, its sheaths glinting wetly, it beat a steady, slow, relentless rhythm. In her mind Laura heard the march of soldier's feet down defeated roads, the shuffle of slippers across worn carpets, the hopeless tread of prisoners and slaves, soft like the clap of dove wings.

The light diminished as he took the heart out and placed it onto his open palm. A little blood leaked around the inside of the box. He held it out to Laura and spoke in a voice that was the dead calm of the doldrums.

"Yours. If you want it. It is, after all, St Valentine's day. Lady's prerogative."

Behind the service counter one of the coffee machines made a wrong noise and slowly sputtered out.

Sophie said quietly, looking down at the heart. "You are of the old world?"

Laura knew she was thinking of modern monsters, wondering if they had misjudged this one, thinking he was old when he was not. If they had forgotten someone . . .

"I am as old as any," he said. "Come. Trade if you will. One for another. I would like an easy victory. I would like to know the pleasure of winning, of elation and the terror of the fall. I would like to know fear, and boredom."

"What is your power?" Laura asked, not sure now that she wanted it, even if it was a connection to all that had passed in time, the ages when they had been greater than mere humans instead of mingling among them like equals. She had thought— and it seemed very frivolous now, that an Ancient One's strength, even borrowed, might restore that old feeling of glory . . .but as she looked at this unremarkable man she was reminded only of Robert: though now Robert seemed positively electric by comparison.

"What is your name?" whispered Sophie, who had never in her life been stuck for an answer. Laura looked at her with real misgiving. She wished she had not found the box.

"Your heart for mine and you shall know all," he said. His voice was like the whisper of pens signing unwanted divorce papers. "A fair exchange is no robbery."

He made a gentle motion of his free hand over the heart and its empty beat stopped. It became suddenly solid and a fresh colour of rich, dark brown crept across it. It became chocolate. He glanced at Laura and she felt no sense of connection, as though he was a robot and nothing looked at her. He tipped his hand over her hot chocolate mug and the heart fell into the steaming milky liquid and began to melt.

"Laura," Sophie said in a warning tone. Laura looked at her and saw in her old friend's eyes the same feelings she felt in her own heart. They longed for things so lost they were almost unknown to them now—the days of gods and monsters. This heart charm was no more than an ancient narcotic, a trick of exchanging powers to give life to palates jaded by too much of their own euphoria. The long years wore on, and there was no change in the temper of humans, only the surfaces altered. Laura and Sophie, Honour and Wisdom . . . empty idols all. Oh she wanted it, that charge of power, the rush of it. And it would go back one day and leave her just as she was now, waiting and empty and hungry . . . Sophie's eyes were as flat as the salt pans of dry kingdoms.

Laura looked at the unremarkable man. If he had been anyone else, someone she knew, she would have said no.

She picked up the hot chocolate mug and drank down the contents. It was so warm, and so sweet.

Immediately there was silence, or not true silence but the fogging of sound, as though every thing was at a new distance from her, a distance very slight, no more than a hair's breadth, but at the same time unbridgeable. She felt herself separate out from the world, disconnect. When she looked at Sophie she could only see the outward form, nothing inside made her feel better, as it used to. The table was as interesting, as real, as any human being in existence.

"Oh," she said as her isolation became complete.

In the seat beside her the unremarkable man nodded and held out his hand to her. As she shook it he smiled warmly at her and said, "Easy victory," with something like wonder, something like elation. He looked like he was waking from a bad dream.

"Yes," she whispered, and knew she had traded with the most insidious and powerful of the agents of extinction, Death In Life, the master of self doubt and depression. By contrast the powers he had received were ephemeral and small. She could feel oceans moving inside her, vast and unquenchable lakes of grey lava, the turning stone of hopelessness grinding on itself forever.

"Oh," she said again. "Oh no."

The man pushed his chair back with a scrape and stood up and stretched, a smile crossing his rather handsome features. "You know," he said brightly. "I think I'm going to treat myself and have a muffin . . . not a chocolate one though." He smiled at both of them, bowed and walked off towards the counter.

"Laura?" Sophie asked faintly.

Laura shrugged. "Win some . . ." Across the world she could feel billions of hearts touched by her various blights. Their silence echoed to the distant stars. It was too late to go back. She would have given anything even to be bored. Anything.

The taste of chocolate lingered, but did not satisfy.

"Laura?" Sophie said.

The handsome man at the counter nodded and winked jauntily at Laura as he paid for his cake.

Laura watched him and felt within herself the power to sap a million lives.

"I'll have another chocolate," she said. "Cream and extra sugar."

AN UNREMARKABLE MAN

I find a lot of short fiction about as satisfying as a boiled sweet, hopefully a cherry one but you can sometimes get lemon or cola—not so good. When I write it I always hope it will be something like a middling sort of sweet, peppermint or strawberry . . . one of the acceptable flavours. The main criteria is that it must deliver something which is sufficiently interesting to make the time it takes to read it worthwhile for at least some people (people who like the same things I do). This may seem like a pretty low bar to hop over and it is, but it's my bar and this story hopped over it quite neatly, surprising me because when I was muttering about my hack pixies I had visions of Serious Readers tutting into their bonbons and rolling their eyes at the notion of two goddesses trying to pass for ordinary women and getting themselves frightened in an entirely silly supernatural way. Surely horror, Terror, as advertised indeed, is a matter of the utmost seriousness and should never be played wryly? When I was little I used to long to write the Most Terrifying Story Ever. Bear in mind I was routinely traumatized by Black Beauty at that stage . . . anyway, I digress. I thought it was a neat enough story, but probably unsuited to purpose. Seems not though.

A DREAM OF MARS

A DREAM OF MARS

This story is one that contained material I had written many years before but never managed to form into a proper tale. It was one of my first efforts to write a story for an SF magazine and although it had had a start and a character and some interesting details in its original form the narrative petered out early on for the age-old reason— lack of conflict. In the dim and distant past I had written it with the idea of it being some kind of Ray Bradbury homage—hence the Martian setting and its old kind of feel. I wanted to create something that was in the future, but felt old, dated, as a counteraction to all those glossy futures in which everyone and everything has that new and improved feeling. I was also trying to capture the sense of a person born well out of the time they would have fitted into— America's early frontier years in this case—so telling the story in a dated style seemed to fit. I also fancied the idea of writing a love story for once.

A DREAM OF MARS

Last night I dreamed of Mars again.

I see myself from a distance against a pink and orange sky the colour of Delite Peach Drink. My glider is struggling at full power in the thin shreds that pass for air. It wavers like a paralysed butterfly in the thermal tendrils coming up off the face of Olympus Mons. Dust streaks past in the wind like threads of blood in urine—the light's going.

My glider motor dies on the boulder-strewn banks of a nameless gully stream, once and for all. I fight like a crazy fly to free myself from its harness. Although I can't see it from my spot I know, with the clarity of omniscience, that the water which is pumped up to fuel this forest evaporates so fast into the arid afternoon that two miles downstream there's nothing but a bloody stain where a pool should be.

Ahead of me, across the brook's dazzling fuschia glitter, the dirt trail grinds uphill towards the summit of this minor rise on the South face. On the wind a faint scent drifts down from the dark skeletons of the woodland above me, where Paradise Adventures' cable car has gone down. I think it smells like gold as I splash across and into the long clutch of the finger-shadows where pine and spruce stand, dead but unwilling to admit it.

Overhead the metal struts of the nearest tower groans and creaks, thin reins of cable shifting restlessly, their tons moving like spider-silk. Closer to the crash site and I can smell death. In this atmosphere it has a duller reek, one that's almost appetising.

Bacteria here number single figures and the lack of oxygen has killed most of them. Things rot very slowly, unpredictably, if at all.

I find the cable car in a fresh clearing of snapped branches. The front is buckled up and crushed like a snack packet. The door has popped free and lies on the ground a few metres from the car.

Behind me in the dark of the unnatural woodland, all greens turned to brown, something moves.

Spin, drop, fire. Heart hammering.

My gun jams. Dust has got to it even in these few minutes.

The creature leaps.

I see his figure silhouetted among the upright masts of the trees on the ridgeline. Manlike, catlike, monkeylike. He's all and none of these. He stands on his hind legs, long forelimbs lifted ready, head a blunt leonine sculpture, with the suggestion of rounded ear tips on each side. I see no face, but he watches me with the straight fixity of intelligence for a few seconds before he drops to all fours. With a snapping of brittle twigs he's gone. A few grey leaves, ruddy with the sunset, fall in his wake, swaying side to side to side in the near infinite slowness of Martian gravity.

Thick fur, exceptionally fine, multi-layered, soft as down, he has. And claws, smooth sickle curls against his hand.

My dream sense explains to my fear that, for now, he only wants to watch.

I return to my business with the car and peer inward, holding my breath. Two women and three men have plunged to their deaths. Two have died on impact, the others when the seals failed and the oxygen expired. Their blue lips are open, showing healthy teeth and cyan gums. In what's left of the car's bar area the bodies of five Mountain Rescue professionals are stacked in a neat pile, so clotted with dust they might be figures from an ancient tomb.

The night temperature drop has part-frozen the bodies, but the daytime greenhouse effect of the capsule's surviving windows has brought them back to a state soft enough to eat. Their disarray, the selective disembowelling, parts gouged at with starvation, and parts carefully excised with a blade, perhaps for cooking or storage elsewhere, far exceed the extent of their fatal injuries. I am looking at a well stocked refrigerator.

With dream brightness I am aware of being a soft meat creature, standing alone on an isolated mountain in a hostile environment that doesn't want to help me. I feel my insignificance and the sharp, exultant spark that is being alive in the face of this indifference. It is the most pure, beautiful, vivid sensation I will ever experience.

Not far away he will have turned to watch. He will smell me and my living heat.

The temperature has started to plummet like a lead block in a lift shaft.

The sun reaches the horizon as I stand, frozen to the spot in ecstasy.

My dream ends and I wake up with a gulp whose fear I don't understand. I can still see the sun falling in my mind's eye. It drops out of sight as though it's running away.

Rudy DeSoto had been my recruiter. For months his company, Martian Raditech, had been fending off denials that anything was living in the deadwoods of the New South Face Woodland—it was a failed first-try forestation project that had never included animal life. They were to try again with the new trademarked trees when the time was right. It was of no interest.

Then a cable car that led over the area suffered a line break during a sudden wind squall. The atmosphere of recent months had been significantly heavier, due to the success of the Terraforming Cooperative's struggle to maintain gas-capture within Mars' grip, and this had subtly altered both the ferocity and the power of the weather systems. This development had cut the cable-car line's four-year lifetime to sixteen months and Raditech were set to lose on the investment. The party of wealthy tourists lying on Olympus got to pay for that oversight. I read about it in the papers. A rescue hadn't been mounted immediately because a fault on the car's AI had reported them all dead on impact. They didn't figure the AI itself might have got more than a dent.

But now, three days on, the families and the government wanted the bodies recovered. The Olympus Mons Mountain Rescue Unit had been despatched amid a hail and thunder of media excitement, complete with camera crews. None had returned. The video footage from their optic-nerve chips had curiously not been released, even to De Soto. Their spoken journals were all he had.

For the third time we listened to a shaky, breathless voice gibber out of the past, "Cries in the dark, like a hyena whoop. Shapes in the trees. Signs. *Fetish* dolls . . . made of twigs and . . . skin."

I looked at DeSoto with a disbelief I saw he wanted to share. "Ah, come on. This is a wind-up. The whole thing stinks of hoax."

"I can assure you, Sigmarsson, it's nothing of the kind." He wiped his broad, friendly face with a disposable tissue and frowned as he had to stow it in his pocket. There was no trash service at the Casbah on the Long Sands. No anything come to that, except a temporary supply stop and this bar we were standing in, two parasols and an upturned crate its fine furnishings, the backdrop of endless rock-strewn red rubble its whole theme.

De Soto was a young man with the cornfed physique of recently imported Earthstock—a shiny-star-on-the-arse boy come to do his time so he could keep the share options. They'd terraform the place eventually. Maybe even in his lifetime.

"Mister . . ."

"Just Sigmarsson," I cut him off by finishing the Coke he'd bought me and pocketing the can. They're worth a lot as returns.

"Sigmarsson," he made a sincere effort to look me straight in the eye and then wandered momentarily as he realised he didn't know what to do with my full attention. "Will you fetch them back?"

"No." I got up and began collecting the things I'd come for: water, a new filter for the air units on my shack, a sack of rice, a sack of flour, some dried ration. I'd already had enough time here just with him and Yusuf, the supply guy, and it had only been ten minutes. If they ever do bring a water generator and a purification plant out here I already had plans laid to make an escape to the asteroid belt. There's always some empty frontier to escape to, if you're willing to take the risks.

Seeing me getting ready to go, De Soto revealed the extent of his desperation,

"Can you recommend somebody? Another hunter? A tracker? A biologist maybe?"

"No," I said. My address book was two empty covers. I wouldn't have wanted to be responsible for hauling some poor fool up here anyway.

"We'll pay with prime Lots. Ten."

A thousand acres. That was a lot of space. Despite myself I hesitated.

Ten Lots.

At the moment this area of Mars was a free-for-all and set to stay that way until development of the better sites was completed. By then settlement would be a moot point since the already burgeoning culture of desertophiles, soul-seekers and wanderers would have cut trade and pilgrimage routes through it all. Illegal oases were springing up at the rate of one a month.

I could never fence that much land in. Policing it would be almost impossible. Then again. It was a long enough piece that I could seriously discourage any visitors, and there'd be no development without my dead body.

De Soto upped his offer. "Twenty Lots. Out here. No problem. Thirty. A hundred." He gestured feebly with his own Coke can, sketching in the vastness of the plain, but without any conviction. His Kentucky farming background was failing him somewhat. He couldn't help but glance around at the sheer lack of anything that the Long Sands had to offer: dust choked gullies from the water runoffs of the past, broken up pieces of volcanic ejecta scattered where they fell an aeon ago, and dust. That was all there was. He paled under his new tan and I already knew that he'd gone too far. But even Ten—and no trip to the asteroids in my old age.

"I'll think about it."

"Oh, yes, yes, fantastic."

When I look back I think my mind had made itself up when he first said Ten Lots, but we never like to think ourselves so cheaply bought and sold. I took myself off to my home in the middle of nowhere and set to gun-cleaning and thinking on De Soto's information while the inexhaustible wind pawed at the shelter's walls and built miniature dunes of red dust across the floor.

Being alone was a necessity. I couldn't remember enjoying human company. I've never kept a pet. It's difficult to explain the reason, and after so long I doubt any rationalisation would touch the truth, which is that there are some people whose brains are wired in a way that leaves them unfit for a social world. Mine was diagnosed as a form of sociopathy. Call it what you will, the fact is that others are an annoyance and a hindrance; where I understand them I despise them, and where I don't I have no interest in discovering their reasons. We are simply animals, like all others ever spawned from Earth, and everything else is a gloss on this fact that attempts to make us greater than we are. Blood and bones, the needs of the flesh; I understand my own in every detail and thus I understand everyone, and as much about them as I need to know. The rest is a fable and I have no time for lies.

Hunting was something I'd always been good at. It's because of what I am. I don't mind killing. I don't enjoy it either, but it's been a necessity ever since I moved away from people, first into Alaska's remaining wilderness, then, when that was eaten up with people, into the less fashionable Siberian steppe, and finally here.

In the long periods of sound on Mars which are the winds' ever-changing sighs, there is no human element. On the eighth day the breeze blowing North from Yusuf's criminal collection of sheds told me that death had visited the Casbah. Cooking goat is a terrible stench, but the stew is good. I pretended to myself I was going there in order to eat some real protein, but when I got there I used his radio and called De Soto at Base Camp. He invited me there immediately, so I realised those bodies were still out there on the mountain. As I switched off the receiver it gave me only a moment's hesitation; no takers in all that time? I should have been more wary.

I carried my own packs and guns to Uruk Oasis over the next day and a half. It's a trek made tough by the effects of Mountain Sickness, which are a daily lot on Mars where the pressure and oxygen levels mimic high altitudes on Earth. Prior to coming here I'd travelled to Africa and the peak of Kilimanjaro, which is almost six thousand metres above sea level. On the scree slopes above the visitor huts at Kibo I'd pitched my own tent and lived there for nine months, never descending. Kilimanjaro is a highly populated mountain, but the trekkers are only interested in the marked climb routes, so there was plenty of space and time among the rocks and glaciers to call my own; white ravens my only visitors, when they had a free minute from the rubbish tips.

When I had gotten over the sleepless nights of Cheyne-Stokes breathlessness, the racing pulse, the sweeps of nausea that came if I tried to walk more than eight steps at a time, I realised I could take to Mars. The one thing altitude sickness never brought me was the emotional hysteria that can cause others to sink to their knees in despair. I've seen that here. Oxygen is the only cure.

The trail to Uruk is a series of beacons. Those people who once trod Everest like to use it as part of their Mars Loop trail; a path which winds back and forth in its circuit of the globe, taking in what sights and geological highlights a marketing man might creatively write of. The trails have many cairns that started life as graves, the bodies beneath the rocks mummified and light as feathers—as they'll stay until it starts to rain one day.

The journey is a blur of impressions; the complaining moans of a camel, muffled almost to nothing by the heavy weight of its respirator-assists; the wind carrying broken voices from crossroads, where the trains pass with fatigue from one caravanserai to another; a shifting mirage of red days and black, icy nights; the flat landscape punctuated by the wrecked hulks of broken machines, their labour now replaced by the overtaxed, dying animals; the filthy hospitality of the casbahs and the water stations, where grizzled creatures willing to live here against their nature exact payment without mercy.

I camp far from them. I don't know why they put themselves through it. Some people have a need to destroy themselves through testing. It's fool's game, like love.

At Uruk, after a shower and a change of clothes, I left my travelling gear behind and stepped into the Desert Cruiser that De Soto had sent. Only the guns came with me. On its eight-tyre, track-assisted chassis, the rest of the miles to Base Camp passed within hours. We drove within viewing distance of the wrecked cable cars, which I studied through my binoculars; their towers were the only straight and tall structures amid a sea of grey, gnarled wood, touched with the faintest tinges of green where sturdier lichens grew at leisure on the dead. The downed car was invisible, beyond a ridge. Its partners hung loosely swaying on the slack bends of the line, beads on a broken string, their glossy newness already destroyed by the dull patina of microfine dust-abrasion.

I wondered why we couldn't simply drive there from here, but when I asked the driver she turned to me with her eyes hidden by the reflecting, yellow lenses of her glasses,

"The forest is inside an exclusion zone. Only permitted vehicles may approach."

And so we reached Mons Base and my briefing.

"It's like this," De Soto said, squirming under the scrutiny of his superiors as they sat on either side of our table. "Mars needs tourist money to fund the terraforming. It's a big rock with nothing to see except a bit of polar ice and a few formations. It hasn't exactly got attractions. So the forest was planted early, to provide, you know, colour. And the cable car ride was the first of the non-ped options, for people who like to explore without . . ." he hesitated, uncomfortable with making any criticism of his source of income.

"Exploring?" I suggested.

"Exploring without too much of an adventure," he agreed. "Exploring with seats and a drinks cooler. Believe me, it's a much bigger market."

I had no trouble with that. "So, what's the exclusion zone for?"

De Soto flashed on a projector, which gave us a picture of the forest as it had once been in full growth—a flush of anaemic green patched with death's brown mottles even then.

"On its own the forest on Olympus is just a bunch of alpines," he said. "So we thought about what it was that used to create such a fuss about remote places on Earth, like Alaska, and the Serengeti," he glanced at me, "and the Himalayas."

For the first time the two superior officials also turned their heads in my direction. The picture changed and it showed a laboratory scene, all glittering machinery and people suited in greens.

"We thought it would be better if we made ourselves a Bigfoot. There was already work in progress on assisting human foetuses to develop for Martian conditions and really the cut and pasting of genes between animals isn't such a problem and so . . ."

But I wasn't listening to his babble. I was looking at the image, where there was a picture of a creature that was unidentifiable, sitting in the corner of a cage, its face turned to the wall. It reminded me of nothing more than a human being in a suit, which was ironic, since all Earth's fabled hominids had turned out to be exactly that.

What comes after in De Soto's story is too obvious to relate in detail, as he insisted on doing to me. They made the creature, taking every care that it would fit the conditions, ensuring that someone would supply it with food, planning to inhabit the woods with a whole range of hybrids for the safari-simpletons. But the

Martian Bigfoot turned out somewhat contrary to expectations, as these things tend to do when they're ill-thought out. It ate the handlers sent to feed it and when the cable car crashed it put the rescue team aside for a rainy day; quite wise in the circumstances, since dead wood wasn't something any animal could live on if it wasn't half beetle.

There was only one question to ask.

"Dead or alive?"

"Either," De Soto said, squeamish to the end.

His word was drowned out by the two other voices that said, very firmly, "Dead."

And so events led quickly to my descent on the mountain, the track into the woods, the shadows at my back that flowed into his shape as he watched me from his hiding place. They led to the beginning, and the end, of my dream.

My head torch lights the darkness as the Martian twilight races to full dark. Above me the starlight is bright enough to turn the reddened world and its sudden coating of frost a purplish silver, as though everything has been scattered with fairy dust. There is thankfully no need to explore the state of the cable car any further— no identifications required—and it provides a perfect place to stake out an ambush, for where else can a creature go when it's hungry but to its larder?

It's so cold at night here I must light a fire. In the low-ox ordinary combustion is impossible. There's no singing of The Happy Wanderer round the flickering yellow flames on this world. I have to use chemical accelerants on the twigs and branches, ones which yield up bursts of oxygen in flashes of sudden white brilliance, so that to keep my night vision I have to wear shades. The heat is small comfort.

I clean the gun, taking it apart. He must have seen and understood this, and as I'm placing down its pieces on the frozen pebbles I hear him circling around behind me. Once I even see the plume of his breath in the air when a fire flash blasts strongly around the tiny clearing. But I don't see him, not until he's less than ten feet away.

My knife is in my hand. I don't even have to think to get it there. It's there, blade sharp and ready, my mind so focused on watching and listening that there is no sense of me at all.

Seeing me watching him he does what no animal would do—he emerges from his cover with a deliberate, sinuous slowness, and sits for a second on his haunches, looking like a huge, black panther whose forepaws have moved halfway to hands, whose shoulders are gorilla-broad. Looking into his face is looking into a mirror.

My life changed in that second.

Before it I had been a creature of solitude with the sure understanding of my singular place, shunning all contact, satisfied with these pure seconds where there is only living or dying. But as I looked into his vivid yellow eyes I saw through their vertical slits an iteration of the same spirit. In the widening of his eyes it was clear he saw me too. And as we recognised ourselves the fact of our singularity became loneliness itself. Between us the small distance of ice and frosted deadfall was both infinite and nonexistent.

I was sure that he would kill me. Our twin existence was a blasphemy, a fundamental perversion against nature. His savagery was my own and so I knew that he or I was capable of ending the other, without conscience. I expected nothing less, because neither of us wanted to die.

At the time I didn't know it, but in my dream it's *this* moment, which cuts fatally to my insensible heart. I didn't know, as he did, that his survival depended entirely on me.

He stands on all fours and paces towards me with the gliding gait of any ordinary cat, sheets and boulders of muscle beneath his fine fur shifting like ice blocks in an avalanche. I brace myself, ready to meet his attack. To my confusion he looks at me sideways, in little glances, with the unmistakable head movements of an animal that is submitting. He comes close enough that I can smell his rank stench. And then he rears up onto his legs, raises his hands with their deadly weapons, and with a sigh of hope and despair, as human as my own breath, he puts his powerful arms around me in the most gentle of embraces.

No one on Earth, not even my mother, has ever held me with such tender devotion.

I can just see his claws, long and dark, against the fabric of my thermal suit, where I dare look down. The broad, flat expanse, double-domed, of his furry skull, is barely an inch from the knife that I still hold in my fist.

He takes a long, winnowing breath of the bitter air and it hisses slowly through his adapted nostrils, where blood warms it for his lungs, "Help me."

"*No!*"

But against my will I woke up, sweating, heart pounding, body vibrating with the unbearable realisation that in all the worlds I'd been to there was at last someone who could understand.

For another night, the dream was over. Mars was only one of many distant lights in the evening sky. I lay and looked at the cracked, crazed ceiling of our two room apartment. From the other side of the room Cat's breathing panted, shallow and faint, too slow, too hot, eternally uncomfortable. I heard him pause in his sleep, close his jaws, lick his lips, mutter a little, and then slide away again; pant, pant, pant. Against the shredded paper of his wall his claws grated briefly in a spasmodic clutch, closed on nothing. Pant, pant, pant.

I couldn't stand to listen to him. I hated the sound of that goddamned breathing. When he wasn't panting he snored, the heavy flanges that cured his air on Mars no more than festering polyps in his nose and throat, thick with a coating of mucus that existed to process fine dusts we don't possess. Every intake of the heavy air was an effort on his frame. Every outbreath a groan.

The sound of his suffering was as endless as the winds of the Long Sands, but without their spontaneity. It would endure forever with its predictable regularity that I must always listen for, waiting for the next breath to start, waiting and hoping, hanging in that instant where he may have stopped at last.

The story was not quite as De Soto had told it.

Yes, they had created Cat for Mars, but not as a curiosity or a freak. He was the first and only survivor of the programme they had decided to follow in case terraforming never panned out and a secondary scheme was needed whereby humans would be tailored to fit the world, and not the other way about. The Bigfoot idea was a latecomer, when it was apparent that the trial runs had failed, the forest was a non-starter and the money was getting low. It went live when the weather changed. Desperate times called for corrupted measures and so Cat, who had once been part of a family, but who was now alone in the universe of all his kind, was booted out of the back door and into the woods.

He revealed to me as we spoke that night, me by the fire and he away from its too-hot bursting, that he had climbed the high gantries and weakened the cables himself.

"Ssaw," he said, miming the action of drawing a stone across the high-tension metal wires. "Many time ssaw." His face was tense with the uncertainty of his plan, then softer but sadder as he said. "Fall. All die. I . . ." and as was his way he mimed eating, as he did with anything he found too difficult to say.

"Hungry?" I said.

He nodded. "Ver." A shudder ran through his coat, making it ripple. I couldn't help thinking at the time, and now, what a beautiful jacket someone would have made of that, given the chance, but it would have been only skin on a human being, dead and unable to express an ounce of the feeling that a few of its hairs could contribute to Cat's expressions. He was a physical reflection of his inner states, as much as I was not.

He and I fashioned a plan, as the wood became ashes behind us. We knew that we couldn't return with him alive, since his existence proved the guilt of his creators and their highly illegal activities, and the only way offworld and out of the clutches of the cooperative was via Mons Base and its superlift into orbit. Therefore we had no choice.

Our raid on the Base took place at night.

We came along the cable line, sneaking up silently. They were taken completely by surprise and it wasn't easy, but it wasn't difficult—by dawn we had killed them all, with the exception of De Soto.

His whinnying, dough-faced prattle got us up to the shuttle and down to Earth, Cat concealed in a crate used for shipping Mars' luckless camels in and out of the homeworld; alive on the way up and dead on the way back, since their carcases would only clutter the place with unsightly and unusable desiccated flesh. As a camel he descended into the tougher gravity and the heavier air. As a beast of burden he stepped out into the rooms that I was able to get once

De Soto was paid off. The two rooms he could never leave. The world he couldn't adapt to.

I thought it was such a good plan. It was the only way to save him.

It would have been better if we'd killed each other on the spot, matter and antimatter meeting.

Of course, he did leave the rooms at night. I left during the day, just to get out of there, and sometimes for a job. I'd get back and there'd he'd be, the place reeking of his bear-like stink and its uncontrollable muskiness and crammed with the sound of his wretched existence; pant, pant, pant.

At night Cat howled for Mars, for home. The neighbours banged on the walls with pots and pans even though it was only a soft, questioning note, an off-key hyena whine, sounding out and listening for the reply that could not come.

It drove me mad, that listening. As if there could ever be another. And then he'd turn away from the open balcony windows and the view of the city, sparkling at night, and lie down on the rug like a dog, and pant, pant, pant, looking up at the sky for any sign of the red world.

At nights I'd wake from the dream and have to hear the reality, his endless bloody articulation of misery, and a longing for something that can't be had. Since Mars I fell asleep to escape that same feeling myself, only to dream of Cat's presence. I longed for the past too, before Mars. And still his suffering on and on. So I slept to forget, and dream of the one night when it seemed a different door was about to open on my world, when life brimmed full and ran over with the promise of another kind of living.

"*No!*"

I woke from the dream.

"No."

I wish I'd never thought of going to that planet. A Hundred Lots of emptiness.

In the long quiet of the night the wail of police sirens and the hum of the building fans are too faint, too weak. I hold my own breath, listening, hoping, in the silence. I stretch out my hand and feel the impossibly soft, gentle touch of his fur.

Beneath it the bed is dumb, lumpy, inert.

I had to do it. Cruel to be kind. No place to live. No way to live. His friend. Only friend. But that sound, the split-frequency exposure of one soul in two bodies . . . it was unbearable.

I remember it like yesterday.

We were drinking the Irish whiskey. Pant pant pant. Cat pushed his glass aside and I saw he had finally made his choice. His look to me said it all—this was my world and I would never be free of it until he was gone. I had freed him and now he was ready to do the same.

His head sank down, the yellow fire dying. He spoke with strange comfort in his acceptance of his fate, nodding at its rightness, calm at last, no longer waiting.

"Home at last. God be wit' yu, Sigma'sson. An' if not, I fin' him and slit his throat."

His last breaths were mewing, tiny sounds. I put my hands over his muzzle and shut them in. His paw rested on my hand, claws touching the skin. One dragged and caught and drew blood as its own weight pulled it down—he had to try to die, even after all the fighting to live.

I held his body in my arms, tenderly.

Last night I dreamed of Mars, again.

This time the flight over the barren holds no fears. Ahead of me lies our moment, our vast wealth of a single second in time. Our emptiness is one whole void, and we cannot be separated from each other. Form doesn't matter, nor place and time, only the essential structure, the shape and the ringing silence of a single heart.

A DREAM OF MARS

When I wrote this I knew it had a lot of personal resonance for me, particularly in the way that necessity determines the outcome much more than either of the characters would prefer. A lot of Science Fiction is concerned with overcoming physical circumstances in order to progress human efforts and dreams. I have a tendency to love this idea and loathe it at the same time. Regardless of progress in technology human beings have yet to deal with the real problems that have always driven them—the tensions created by their existence as individuals and animals of limited powers but powerful imaginations, for whom biology is still destiny and that destiny is death.

ACKNOWLEDGEMENTS

"Heliotrope" © Justina Robson 2011. Appears here for the first time.

"Body of Evidence" © Justina Robson 2008. First published in *Myth-Understandings*, edited by Ian Whates.

"Cracklegrackle" © Justina Robson 2009. First published in *The New Space Opera* 2, edited by Gardner Dozois and Jonathan Strahan.

"Erie Lackawanna Song" © Justina Robson 2009. First published by the Birmingham Science Fiction Group.

"Legolas Does the Dishes" © Justina Robson 2008. First published in *Postscripts* #15, Summer 2008, edited by Peter Crowther.

"No Man's Island" © Justina Robson 1998. First published in *The Third Alternative* #15, edited by Andy Cox.

"The Bull Leapers" © Justina Robson 1997. First published in *Visionary Tongue* #4.

"The Girl Hero's Mirror Says He's Not The One" © Justina Robson 2007. Rirst published in *Fast Forward*, edited by Lou Anders.

"The Little Bear" © Justina Robson 2005. First published in *Constellations*, edited by Peter Crwther.

"The Seventh Series" © Justina Robson 2001. First published in *F20 Two*, edited by David Howe, Len Maynard and Mick Sims.

"Trèsor" © Justina Robson 1994. First published in *The Third Alternative* #3, edited by Andy Cox.

"Deadhead" © Justina Robson 1996. First published in *The Third Alternative* #11, edited by Andy Cox.

"The Adventurer's League" © Justina Robson 2005. First published in *The Mammoth Book of New Jules Verne Adventures*, edited by Mike Ashley.

"Dreadnought" © Justina Robson 2006. First published in *Nature*, 31 March 2005.

"An Unremarkable Man" © Justina Robson 2006. First published in *Shrouded by Darkness: Tales of Terror*, edited by Alison Davies.

"A Dream of Mars" © Justina Robson 2011. First published in audio form in *Frequency* #3, edited by Jeremy Bloom. Appears here in print for the very first time.

THANK YOU

The publisher would sincerely like to thank:

Elizabeth Grzyb, Justina Robson, Adam Roberts, John
Berlyne, Jonathan Strahan, Peter McNamara, Ellen Datlow,
Grant Stone, Jeremy G. Byrne, Sean Williams, Garth Nix,
Kaaron Warren, Angela Slatter, Lisa L Hannett, Terry Dowling,
Simon Brown, David Cake, Simon Oxwell, Grant Watson,
Sue Manning, Steven Utley, Bill Congreve, Jack Dann, Stephen
Dedman, the Mt Lawley Mafia, the Nedlands Yakuza,
Shane Jiraiya Cummings, Angela Challis, Donna Maree Hanson,
Kate Williams, Kathryn Linge, Andrew Williams, Al Chan, Alisa
Krasnostein, Amanda Pillar, everyone I've missed . . .

. . . and *you*.

www.ingramcontent.com/pod-product-compliance
Lightning Source LLC
Chambersburg PA
CBHW032233010726
47494CB00002B/477